OFFSIDES

TAM DERUDDER JACKSON

Also by Tam DeRudder Jackson

THE TALISMAN SERIES
(Celtic paranormal/fantasy romance)

Tracker (prequel novella)
Talisman
Warrior
Prophetess (novella)
Bard
Druid
Rogue

THE BALEFIRE SERIES
(Contemporary Rockstar Romance)

Play For Me
Sing For Me
Wild For Me
Hot For Me
Stay For Me

THE GAME TIME SERIES
(Contemporary Football Romance)

Finding the End Zone
Out of Bounds

Find me at *https://www.tamderudderjackson.com*
and subscribe to my newsletter.

NO AI TRAINING: Without in any way limiting the author's [and publisher's] exclusive rights under copyright, any use of this publication to "train" generative artificial intelligence (AI) technologies to generate text is expressly prohibited. The author reserves all rights to license uses of this work for generative AI training and development of machine learning language models.

This is a work completely created and generated by a human person. No part of this work was created with the help of artificial intelligence.

Offsides

Copyright 2024 Tam DeRudder Jackson

All rights reserved

This publication in its entirety nor any part of this book thereof can be reproduced, stored in, or introduced into a retrieval system or transmitted in any form, electronic, physical, or mechanical, or by any means. This includes recording, photocopying, or storage in any informational system without the prior written permission of the copyrights holder, except for the use of brief excerpts in a book review.

This is a work of fiction. References to events, places, people, brands, media, and incidents are a product of the author's imagination and are used fictitiously. Any resemblance to events, places, brands, media, incidents, or people living or dead is purely coincidental.

Editor: Bryony Leah

Cover Design: Steamy Designs

Formatting: Damonza.Com

Print ISBN: 9798989224937

eBook ISBN: 9798989224920

This story is for everyone who never gives up trying to do their best.

OFFSIDES

Chapter One

Chessly

THE FIRST SEMESTER of my junior year at Mountain State College settled nicely into its regular rhythms.

Then I met Finn McCabe.

Usually, I attended the Homecoming bonfire with Piper Maxwell and Saylor Davis—friends I'd made during freshman year when we all lived on the same floor in Hanover Hall. We did our best to coax our fourth partner in crime, Jamaica Winslow, to join us, but she'd made it as clear as glass she had zero interest in sports or any of the trappings that went with it. She never attended football games and couldn't be dragged from her books for such a waste of time as a Homecoming bonfire.

But Jamaica had recently started hanging out with Callahan O'Reilly, starting tight end for the Wildcats, and he'd bribed her other best friend, Axel Benson, to make sure she made it to the bonfire. Axel had commandeered me as his second in case she tried to bolt before Callahan could finish up with the football team's bit and join us.

That was how I ended up catching a ride back to the dorms with Finn after the team tossed the effigy of the Tigers onto the bonfire and all the fireworks had faded into the night sky.

"You sure you don't want to ride with us?" Jamaica asked for the third or fourth time since Axel and his boyfriend Drake had "abandoned" her, "forcing" her to catch a ride home with Callahan. Sometimes my friend could be a bit of a drama queen.

"I'm sure I want to avoid being up close and personal with the PDA I saw in front of the dorms last Sunday morning." I didn't even try to hold back my grin at my friend's wide-eyed response. Everyone in the lobby of Hanover had seen the lip-lock Callahan had laid on Jamaica before she let herself out of his truck the previous weekend. They'd practically steamed up the entire courtyard in front of the lobby.

"You'll be a gentleman with my friend—right, Finn?" Jamaica narrowed her eyes at the man in question. Clearly, his size—he was a defensive end—didn't intimidate her in the least.

Then again, she'd made her demand from the safety of the circle of Callahan's arm.

"Aren't I always a gentleman?" Finn sounded utterly perplexed, but I didn't miss the twinkle in his whiskey-colored eyes.

I kind of hoped he had his fingers crossed behind his back. After all, we'd spent the better part of the evening covertly eye-fucking each other at every chance we'd got. The way he looked at me left tingles on my skin that had nothing to do with the late-October chill in the air.

"I'm counting on it. Chessly is good people, not some jersey chaser with a dubious agenda." My friend's tone held all kinds of warnings.

Finn shifted uncomfortably from foot to foot, and I wondered at what Jamaica wasn't saying.

"She'll be fine. Promise." Finn saluted her with two fingers in what I supposed was his version of Scout's honor or something.

To me he said, "My truck is over here." He shoved his hands in the front pockets of his jeans and nodded in the direction of some vehicles parked in the next row of the parking lot behind the stadium.

The autumn breeze coming off the mountains carried a definite shiver of winter with it. Even dressed in my jeans and my favorite fleece-lined hoodie, I was missing the heat the bonfire threw off when we were standing near it. I didn't know how Finn couldn't feel the cold while wearing only his game jersey and jeans.

Stepping over next to him, I said, "Thanks. "As we started walking toward his ride, I called over my shoulder, "Don't keep Callahan out too late. He has a big game tomorrow."

Snickering at the not-so-discreet bird Jamaica flipped me, I double-timed my stride to keep up with Finn's long-legged amble. When we came up alongside an old blue Chevy that had weathered some hard times, he kind of ducked his head and opened the passenger door for me.

"Your chariot, milady." Under his breath he added, "Such as it is."

His deceptively ambling gait around the front of his pickup threw me because a second later he joined me in the cab, sliding in gracefully behind the wheel. For such a big man—he stood north of six foot six and must've tipped the scales above 250—he moved with the grace of a panther.

Clearing my throat to cover for ogling the guy as he slid his key into the ignition, I pulled the seat belt across my chest and buckled it. "You have wheels. That's a big step up from having none." I glanced around the inside of his truck. Though Spartan in terms of state-of-the-art bells and whistles, the interior was clean—a plus I also appreciated.

"You don't have a car?" he asked as he carefully pulled out of his parking space and headed toward the front of the lot.

"Nope. Haven't managed that yet."

As we waited in a line of vehicles to exit the stadium parking lot, he drummed his fingers on the steering wheel and slid side-eyes my way. I couldn't help the tiny smile that quirked the corner of my mouth. From the way he was acting, he was casting around for something to say. It kind of tickled me that this great big man who had his way with opposing offenses every Saturday afternoon was nervous sitting in the cab of his truck with me. I could have rescued him, but I wanted to hear what he came up with.

When we reached the stop sign, he had a decision to make. Clearing his throat, he said, "Where am I taking you?"

"To Hanover. You know where that is?"

"The all-women's dorm?" A wisp of a chuckle escaped him. "Yeah, I know where that is."

I crossed my arms over my chest. "Are you a player off the field too?"

Though I'd been eyeing him all evening, maybe I needed to rethink my interest.

He hunched his shoulders, and his mouth flattened into a line. "No. I just meant that's where Callahan's girl lives." The car in front of us inched into traffic, and he slowly pulled the truck forward for his turn. "Do you live on Jamaica's floor?"

"No. I'm the RA on the floor above hers."

That tidbit seemed to relax him. His shoulders dropped as he eased us out onto the main road. "What year are you?"

"Junior."

With a nod, he added, "Physics major."

My brow shot up. The kind of mesmerized stare he'd given me when Jamaica had introduced us had made me think he hadn't heard that part.

"And you're bio-chem."

Simultaneously we said, "Science nerds."

The awkward tension that had filled the cab of his truck from the minute we climbed into it evanesced with the grins we exchanged.

We rolled along at about five miles per hour below the speed limit. Apparently, Finn wanted to spend some time with me. The idea warmed me far better than the seemingly nonexistent heater in his truck. When I glanced at the dials, I noted he didn't have it turned on. Coupled with the fact he was wearing only his gameday jersey and no hoodie, jacket, or even an undershirt, I figured this guy's motor never stopped. I clamped my thighs together as thoughts of what that meant sizzled my brain.

As though he'd read my mind, he reached over and flipped a dial. The scent of dust filled the cab. "Sorry. I don't use the heater in this much." His sheepish tone pulled my eyes to his face, the dash lights revealing a dull red hue high on his cheeks.

"Guess you run hot."

Finn chuckled as I clamped my hand over my mouth.

"Sorry. That didn't come out right."

We pulled up to a red light and stopped. "From what I've heard tonight, I get the idea you always say what you mean."

The atmosphere inside the cab kept shifting, and I was struggling to keep up. My cheeks, already heating beneath my hand, flamed to red-hot as I recalled how rude I was when Jamaica introduced us earlier this evening in the bar at Stromboli's. I'd heard from my friend that Finn entertained jersey chasers—specifically Tory Miller and her posse of mean girls—on the regular, so my comments were admittedly harsh. Then I'd met him in person, and the only excuse I could make was self-defense in the face of how freaking hot he was. Until this evening, I'd never come up close and personal with Finn McCabe, so I had no business stereotyping him like that.

"Look, I'm sorry for what I said at Stromboli's about your taste in women and who you hang out with. I was way out of line."

He smiled over at me. "No offense taken."

His genuine smile momentarily stunned me. Did I mention how gorgeous the guy was?

We rode a couple of blocks in silence, the awkwardness different now as if each of us was aware of the other. He broke first.

"Why physics?"

"It's a good premed major for sports medicine."

A sly smirk tipped up the corner of his mouth. "You maybe want to work with football players?"

I shrugged. "Possibly." Before he could chase that thought, I asked, "Why bio-chem?"

It was his turn to shrug. "I want to help cure childhood cancer."

"Any particular reason?" I slapped my hand over my mouth again. "Sorry. Sorry. That was super-personal."

His warm chuckle filled the cab of the truck. "Relax. My major isn't because of some childhood tragedy." He sobered. "I saw those commercials on TV of those little kids hooked up to machines with tubes stuck in their arms, and it bothered me that they couldn't play with other kids their age." He turned down a side street, taking the long way to my dorm.

Hiding a smile at his not-so-subtle extension of our conversation, I said, "So that's the truth about Finn McCabe. You're a big ol' softy."

The terrified expression on his face as he pretended to look for eavesdroppers cracked me up. "Shh! Don't say that out loud. Everyone knows I'm a badass defensive lineman."

I pretended to zip my lips shut and toss away the key. "I wouldn't dream of revealing your secret. . .Softy."

"And you absolutely cannot call a 280-pound lineman 'Softy,' especially not in front of his roommates. Do you have any idea what that kind of nickname could do to a man?" He shuddered.

Tapping a finger to my lips, I added, "You're also more sensitive than I imagined. I mean, the way you blow through the line when you blitz would cause a person to think you have no feelings at all, and yet here you are, all Mr. Soft and Sensitive."

Pulling into the horseshoe drive in front of my dorm, he put the truck in park and turned in his seat, a wicked twinkle in his gorgeous whiskey-brown eyes. "I can show you soft and sensitive, if you're interested."

Now it was my turn for a full-body shiver. "Um." I bit my lip. "We only met tonight."

His eyes strayed to my mouth, and involuntarily, my tongue slipped out and soothed the indentation my teeth left behind.

With a subtle move, he unclicked his seat belt but otherwise stayed where he was. "And we're getting to know each other, yeah?" The low rumble of his voice rippled through me.

"I think so."

Wait. Since when was I ever anything but assertive? How had the tables turned? How had he gone from Mr. Bashful with pink cheeks to Super Hottie coming on to me with that heated stare?

How was it possible Finn could initiate that relentless pulsing between my legs with only his eyes and his voice?

Someone pounded on the window beside me. The only reason I didn't jump through the ceiling of the truck was that I was still buckled in.

"Finn! Hey, Finn!"

Even above the rumble of the truck's engine, I recognized that evil, high-pitched voice. Slowly turning my head, I came face-to-face with the biggest nightmare of my life.

"Finn! What do you think you're doing?" she demanded loud enough for the entire dorm to hear, even the rooms upstairs in the back.

Giving my attention back to my ride, I caught a guilty expression crossing his face for a split second before he shook his head and leaned forward to see around me. He gave her a one-finger wave.

Knotting my hands in my lap, I asked, "How do you know Tory Miller?"

"She and her friends like to hang with the team." His eyes darted to mine when he clocked the disdain in my voice. "Callahan keeps telling me not to let her hang out with us, but she's harmless."

Narrowing my eyes, I said, "Harmless, huh? You should listen to your friend."

Tory had made her way around the front of Finn's truck and was now banging on the driver's window. "Finn McCabe! You can't be serious."

"Sounds like you have something else to do." I unbuckled my seat belt. "Thanks for the ride."

When I grabbed the door handle, Finn stayed me exiting his truck with his hand on my arm. That one touch sent sparks cascading through my blood, but I ignored them.

"Wait. Can I get your number?"

"You said you weren't a player, but that out there"—I nodded to the cacophony still going on outside his driver's window—"tells a different story. I don't have time for players. Or for guys who hang out with girls like Tory Miller."

Pushing the passenger door open, I stepped out into the chilly October breeze, and I didn't look back as I marched into the dorm. I thought I was wrong about him—had given him the benefit of the doubt—but Jamaica was right: I needed to stay away from Finn McCabe.

Chapter Two

Finn

"**W**HO CRAPPED IN your Wheaties?" Bax asked when I stumbled into the kitchen after dropping Chessly at her dorm.

Making a beeline for the fridge, I grabbed a beer and downed it in one go. It wasn't enough. I tossed the can at the recycle box and grabbed another.

Bax's eyes rounded to dinner plates. "That bad, huh?" Crossing his arms over his latest slogan T-shirt which read "Life is an inherently dangerous sport," he waited for me to finish my second beer.

Pointing at his shirt with my third beer, I said, "That should read 'Dating is an inherently dangerous sport.'"

He snorted. "Dating? Since when do either of us do that?"

I drank down about half the can and leaned against the table, facing him. "Well, I thought I had a shot at it tonight."

Giving me the universal gesture for "go

on," he said, "You didn't have a date when I showed up at Stromboli's." He stilled. "Wait. Did you go after that cute little doll who showed up with Jamaica? Dude."

When he put up his fist for me to bump, I left him hanging. Grinning, he sipped from his beer.

"She shot you down, huh?"

"Everything was going well. I offered to drive her home so she wouldn't have to deal with Callahan and Jamaica's mush." I finished my third beer and went for a fourth. "She noticed I was taking the circuitous route to her place—"

"I was going to say something about slowing down on the beer," Bax interrupted, "but since you still have your vocabulary, carry on."

He laughed when I flipped him the bird.

"Anyway, we were having a nice getting-to-know-you conversation—one she was enjoying too, or she would have said something when she saw the route I chose to drive her home. But about twenty seconds after I parked in front of her dorm, Tory showed up and everything went to hell."

"Wait. Jamaica's hot friend lives in the dorms? She's jailbait too?"

The censure in Bax's voice irritated my nerves, but I didn't rise to it. "Nah. She's a junior, the RA on the floor above Jamaica's." Slumping down into a chair, I tipped back more beer.

"So what's the problem?"

Shrugging, I said, "Beats me. Chessly got the wrong idea about Tory, I guess."

My friend stared hard at me. "Wonder how that could have happened."

Glaring balefully at him, I said, "I didn't encourage one damn thing with Tory. She showed up out of nowhere and started banging on the windows of my truck right when I was about to talk Chessly into giving me her number." I swigged back more beer as

Bax joined me at the table. "Chessly took one look at Tory and jumped out of my truck as if the seat had caught fire. So while Tory yapped outside my driver's window, I just had to watch her stomp into her building without giving me a backward glance."

Crumpling up my empty can, I threw it into the recycle box and sighed. "The whole time we were at the bonfire, we kept sneaking looks at each other. From how she smiled my way a couple of times, I could have sworn I had a shot with her. Then Tory showed up, and I lost my chance before I could even take it." I stared at the ceiling and wished like crazy for a different outcome to my evening.

Chessly was so damn pretty, and she smelled like sunshine and summer. The way she flipped back and forth between self-assured and careful simultaneously intrigued me and put me at ease. Plus, she liked science.

Damn, did I want to spend time with her.

"At the risk of piling on the shit, Callahan and I have been warning you about those jersey-chasers, Tory especially, since the semester started. That girl is going to make life hell for some poor schmuck, and you don't want him to be you." He tipped up his drink and finished it, tossing the empty into the box and staring between me and the cans on the floor that I'd tossed and missed.

Dragging myself to my feet, I stepped over to the recycle box and cleaned up. Sitting heavily back on my chair, I asked, "Is it so wrong to enjoy the attention of pretty girls?"

"Depends on the girls. Tory and her posse are bad news." Bax leaned his forearms on the table. "Don't forget what happened to Freeman when he got tangled up with Tory's sister."

With a snort, I crossed my arms over my chest. "Tory's not interested in me anyway. She keeps asking about Callahan." My roommate started to say something, but I put my hand up. "So I've kept my distance." Narrowing my eyes, I added, "And as I recall, you're the one who outed us to her when we all met at Stromboli's before the bonfire."

He looked away, a dull red tinge coloring his cheeks. "Fine. Sometimes I get suckered by a pretty face too. But it sure sounds like the girl cost you a shot at that blonde angel with the smart mouth."

"I'll figure something out."

It was my friend's turn to snort. "Like that's gonna happen for you with a girl."

"Fuck off, asshole." I sounded petulant even to my own ears, and Bax laughed because we both knew he wasn't wrong. I didn't have a clue how I was going to score another shot with Chessly Clarke.

Yet when a picture of her porcelain skin and Delft blue eyes flashed in my head, I knew I was going to do my damnedest to find a way to make a better impression.

I lived for game days. Nothing fired up my blood like the anticipation of stepping onto the field with the goal of wrecking another team's offensive plays for a few hours. Homecoming was especially sweet because every man in the locker room knew the other team desperately wanted to ruin our big day in front of a sold-out stadium of our fans and alums.

As I suited up to face the Tigers, a team who was on the rise in our conference, Bax sidled up to me.

"You gonna be on your game today?"

I scrunched my brow. "Why wouldn't I be?"

"Just making sure some hot blonde isn't taking up headspace you need for running plays out there." He nodded in the direction of the field as he adjusted the pads on the fronts of his thighs, his nonchalant movements at odds with the warning in his voice.

Right then Callahan joined us. "Heard Chessly's not too impressed with you. You were a gentleman like you promised last night, yeah?"

I didn't hold back on the sarcasm. "I kept my hands to myself, Dad." My eyes took a tour of my brain that I made sure my teammates didn't miss.

"She shot him down," Bax helpfully supplied. "Over Tory Miller."

With an expression of total disappointment, Callahan said, "Finnegan, Finnegan, you haven't been listening. Jailbait is toxic. Especially the Tory Miller brand of jailbait."

Putting my hands up, I said, "I'm getting that." Standing, I tugged my jersey over my pads, adjusting them beneath it to make sure nothing pinched. "Maybe you could ask your girlfriend what I can do to get back in Chessly's good graces."

Callahan shook his head, but he said, "Get a sack in this game and I'll see what I can do."

"Ladies, stop gossiping and get your asses over here," Coach Ainsworth interrupted.

Coach Ellis, the Wildcats' head coach, stood in front of the massive whiteboard at the end of the locker room, opposite the showers. Ainsworth, our defensive coordinator and assistant head coach, stood beside him. Once the whole team was standing in a semi-circle around them, Coach Ellis launched into his pre-game speech.

"The Tigers have been down for a few years, but they've shown some spark this season. They beat the Trojans on their home turf and gave the Golden Bears a game before they imploded in the fourth quarter. We are not going to give them one second of hope that they can beat us today. Understood?"

He stared hard at every player in the room before we broke into a booming chorus of "Understood, Coach!"

"We are going out onto that field as Wildcats. Wildcats win championships because we give no quarter. Understood?"

Another echoing chorus of "Understood, Coach!" answered him.

"No quarter," he repeated.

Again the team echoed him loud enough to be heard in the visitors' locker room.

The senior captains then led us in a rousing chant of "Wildcats! Wildcats! Go! 'Cats! Go!"

As one unit we tugged our helmets over our heads and headed to the tunnel leading out onto the field.

For the next forty minutes, my brain only entertained thoughts of football. But when I strip-sacked the quarterback on the Tigers' twenty and Bax recovered the fumble, I allowed myself a brief scan of the student section. Not that I truly expected to find Chessly cheering there. At the bonfire, she'd mentioned something about taking Jamaica's call and staying in the dorms today. Intellectually, I knew she wasn't at the game, but I hoped she was watching it on TV or online or something. The woman liked football, so maybe my play would impress her.

When I returned to the sidelines, Coach Ainsworth slapped my back with a rousing, "Fuckin' A, McCabe! Great work on that series." Turning his attention to my teammate, he added, "Excellent fumble recovery, Baxter. You boys make me look good."

As I made my way over to the bench, a trainer squeezed some Gatorade into my mouth. I swallowed the mouthful of energy and sat my ass on the cold metal seat. Bax joined me on one side while our nose tackle, Jeremiah Fitzgerald, a.k.a. Fitz, flanked me on the other side.

"It's good for us when you play angry, Finn." Fitz laughed.

"It's good for me when you open holes big enough to drive a truck through. Makes my job that much easier."

He laughed again. "I'm enjoying having my way with their center. That big ol' farm kid is too easy."

"He's a sophomore, you big bully," Bax said with a smirk. "You'd better have your way with him."

Fitz reached behind me to give Bax a good-natured shoulder

punch. I might have leaned forward to accommodate him. Bax rubbed his bicep and grinned.

A loud roar interrupted their antics when Mick Patterson, our quarterback, connected on a pass to Callahan. We were off the bench in a second, running out to the edge of the sideline to see our buddy shake off defenders as though his uniform were made of Teflon as he ran the ball into the end zone. He pointed the nose of the ball toward someone in the stands behind our bench—didn't take a rocket scientist to figure out who—then tossed the pigskin to the ref while the rest of the offense mobbed him.

When he returned to the sidelines, I fist-bumped him and said, "Thanks for taking advantage of that turnover."

"My pleasure. Thanks for giving me an easy chance to show off."

"Yeah, we caught that." Bax laughed.

Since ESPN was televising the game, following 'Han's sweet touchdown, we had a media time-out. Coach Ainsworth took advantage by calling the defense into a huddle. "It's still early, so they're not giving up on the running game. Fill the gaps. Leave that slippery little son-of-a-bitch of a running back absolutely zero daylight. New set of downs. New game. Get out there and fucking win it."

He stuck his hand in the middle of the huddle and every man in it covered it.

"On three. One. Two. Three."

"Wildcats!" we shouted, forcefully dropping our hands and stepping out of the huddle right as the special teams unit trotted onto the field for the kickoff.

Though he was only a freshman, Dalton Sneed had one hell of a leg. He boomed the kickoff into the back of the end zone, leaving the Tigers no chance for a return. We lined up on the Tigers' twenty-five, and I heard Fitzy start razzing the Tigers' center. To his credit, the center didn't move early and incur the five-yard penalty for doing so. But he couldn't hold Fitz either.

Bax shot through the hole Fitz opened up and leveled the running back behind the line. In no time, we'd left the Tigers no choice but to send their punting unit onto the field.

Though our fourth roommate, Danny Chambers, was a freshman walk-on at wide receiver, he was the same age as the rest of us in our house. While the other three of us had redshirted our freshman year and played the past three years, Danny had served a stint in the Air Force. At the halfway point of the season, his four years away from the field didn't show at all. He ran the best routes of anyone on the team and didn't drop Patty's passes. That meant on the next offensive series, Coach gave him a chance, and his heroics matched Callahan's.

By halftime we were up by ten points. By the end of the game, we'd made our point about deserving our ranking in the top ten teams in the nation and as the top seed in our conference. With the way the four of us had played, everyone on the team expected the after-party to be at our place.

For once I was determined not to fuck up when the girls arrived.

Chapter Three

Chessly

SETTLING MYSELF INTO the oversize recliner that took up most of Jamaica's dorm room, I left her no doubt that I planned to stay until she'd given me all the details leading up to the lip-lock she'd shared with the Wildcats' star tight end in front of Hanover.

"I honestly can't figure out what it is about Callahan O'Reilly that makes me forget all my personal rules and common sense." Jamaica sighed and dragged her sweater over her head, tossing it over the back of her desk chair. A second later her leggings joined it.

With her back to me, she perused the contents of her closet.

"Stop stalling. Put on your favorite hoodie and your rattiest pair of leggings and tell me everything."

We'd known each other since freshman year when we lived on the same floor. I was roommates with Piper Maxwell, and Jamaica had roomed with Saylor Davis. Why the university decided to put two scholarship girls with two

rich girls still mystified me, but as it turned out, the four of us had become best friends. Sophomore year, Piper and Saylor both moved off-campus while Jamaica and I joined forces to become two of the youngest resident assistants in the dorms.

Since my dad ran a hardware store and could help me with some of my expenses, I didn't need an extra job to supplement my scholarship, and room and board were offered by my RA position. Jamaica didn't have my same luxury. She'd be heading off soon for her Sunday shift at the Sweet Shop in the Union, which meant she needed to start talking. Now.

"Jamaica," I drawled.

She threw herself onto the bed and stared at me with consternation warping her features. "I truly did not expect to get tangled up with Callahan. But he's so dang charming." Sitting up and swinging her legs over the edge of the bed, she added, "And freaking smart. I'm a sucker for smart guys."

"Doesn't hurt that he's easy on the eyes."

Her cheeks echoed the bright pink hue of the flowers in her headband.

"So?" I circled my hand for her to continue.

"Nothing happened, Chess. I swear."

"Which totally explains you making the walk of shame into the dorm a few minutes ago," I said, laughing.

"I was over all the noise and ridiculousness of the party, but we couldn't find Axel to give me a ride, so Callahan had me wait in his room while he went looking for them. The next thing I knew, I was waking up this morning in Callahan's bed."

"Fully dressed, of course." The sarcasm lacing my voice added another layer of color to my friend's cheeks.

"We were in our underwear. Nothing happened." She squeezed the mattress on either side of her thighs. "He said he doesn't put out before the third date."

I cracked up. "And you weren't happy about it."

"Get your mind out of the gutter, Chessly Clarke." Her expression turned sly. "A certain other football player was asking about you."

Rolling my eyes, I said, "I can't imagine why."

She leaned forward, rocking a bit on the edge of her bed. "Funny how you didn't ask which one."

"Look, Finn McCabe is one stupidly good-looking guy. But he hangs out with *Tory Miller*." Her name dripped from my lips like acid. Crossing my arms over my chest, I dropped my chin. "And he doesn't see a problem with it."

"She-who-thinks-her-shit-don't-stink and her little posse of freshman wannabes like to hang out with him at the library. But he blew her off at the party last night." Jamaica gave me the big eyes. "Wait. Did something happen with Tory after the bonfire?"

"At first, Finn comes across as kind of shy," I began.

Jamaica stifled a giggle. "Or supremely awkward."

"Shy," I corrected. "But when he warms up a bit, he's super-cute. We were having a fun conversation. He even managed to drop a line on me when we were parked in the driveway in front of the lobby. And then out of nowhere, Tory started banging on the windows of his truck." Wrinkling my nose, I said, "Across the bonfire I caught a glimpse of her flirting with some guy in a frat jacket—couldn't tell which frat—right before we all left. She must have hopped on her broom to make it back to the dorms ahead of us."

"Did he ditch you for Tory?" She flexed her fists. "I don't care if he's Callahan's best friend—if he ditched you for Tory, I'm going to take him out."

The image of my best friend, all five foot six and 125 pounds, soaking-wet, taking on the mountain of a man known as Finn McCabe cracked me up. I could picture him with one massive palm pressed to her forehead, holding her at arm's length as she swung her small fists at him and connected with nothing but air.

"Thanks, babe. I love you for looking out for me. But I don't have a clue what happened after I let myself out of his truck." I stuck my nose in the air. "He couldn't ditch me for anyone because I didn't give him the chance."

"He's Callahan's friend, but I don't know either of them that well."

"Ri-ight." I dragged the word out a couple seconds.

Gifting me with one of her around-the-world eye rolls, she continued. "But from what I've seen, 'Han despairs of his friend's taste in women."

I shot her a glare.

"Present company excluded."

"Thanks." My tone was as dry as dust. Picking at my sweater, I said, "So much for the four of us ever double-dating. After last night, I don't care if I never see Finn McCabe again."

Jamaica smirked. "Better work on making that sound like you mean it."

Crossing my eyes, I stuck my tongue out at her, and she cracked up. With effort, I dragged myself out of her comfy chair and walked to the door. "I have a paper to finish for Modern Physics, that'll take me right up to our RA meeting. See you later."

I headed upstairs to my room, but I couldn't concentrate on physics with images of Finn McCabe swirling in my head. Replaying that slow, sexy once-over he gave me in his truck before Tory so rudely interrupted us left me hot and itchy. I stared at the closed drawer of my nightstand and willed myself not to go for my battery-operated boyfriend while pictures of Finn played in my head.

"Don't go there. Do not even think about going there," I growled to myself. With a huff at the reflection staring back at me from the mirror on my closet door, I grabbed my yoga mat and headed down to the workout room beside the Passion Pit in the basement of the dorm. One way or another, I'd put myself in a better headspace to focus on what truly mattered, which definitely meant school and not a certain hot defensive end.

Mountain State's sprawling campus took up most of the south side of town at the base of the mountains. With its reputation for landing NASA grants and churning out engineers in every discipline like a well-oiled machine, the college was one of the largest in the Northwest. That made it easy not to run into other students if you truly didn't want to. The other thing that made it easy to avoid particular students who happened to play on the championship-caliber Wildcats football team was the college's insistence on listing their schedules on the team's website.

For the two weeks following Homecoming, I'd managed to avoid any chance of accidentally seeing Finn McCabe anywhere. Knowing he hung out with my nemesis stung because I'd truly wanted to see where that spark of awareness between us might have led.

Jamaica, the pest, never missed an opportunity to tell me Finn asked about me on the regular, like every time she met up with Callahan at the library or went over to his place to "study." As if I needed that info. Cue the massive eye roll here. I guess since she had a thing for a football player, she thought each of her friends should have one too.

It didn't help that our other best friend, Piper Maxwell, had hooked up with Finn's roommate Wyatt Baxter—who everyone knew as "Bax"—recently in what she insisted was only a one-night stand. It seemed she'd impressed him or something because he'd dedicated a pick-six to her during the Wildcats' big win against the Tigers last weekend. Watching Piper try to turtle down inside her massive yeti-looking faux fur coat when he pointed the ball at her in the stands was highly entertaining. Finn catching my eye after that play? Not so much. At least with the focus on Piper, she and our other friend Saylor missed that little exchange.

What no one missed was the scene Tory Miller caused in Stromboli's the Thursday night following that game. If she hadn't stopped at our table to throw snark at me, I probably would have ignored her. But when it came to looking for ways to make my life hard, Tory couldn't seem to pass up an opportunity. Even with her dad's bottomless pockets, she wasn't able to force me from the university after I busted her for breaking dorm rules when she was on my floor last year. The terms of the settlement with the college stated she couldn't accost me in the dorm or on campus. A more prudent person might have taken those terms farther afield. Say, anywhere she might run into me.

Tory was petulant, privileged, and petty—pretty much the opposite of prudent.

As she stopped beside the booth I was sharing with Piper and Saylor, she'd planted one perfectly manicured hand on her hip. "Did you honestly think you were good enough to hang out with a Wildcats player? You and your truck-stop-trash friend Jamaica Winslow have so much to learn."

"You know, Tory"—Piper's casual tone harbored a dangerous edge—"you're bad for every rich girl's reputation. You running around pretending you deserve the princess treatment makes every girl whose dad is well off look bad." She mimicked the way Tory wound a lock of hair around her finger. "Name-calling is so middle school. If you're trying to pass yourself off as an adult, you should try acting like one."

"Speaking of passing yourself off as an adult, how did you get past the bouncer?" I asked. "Oh, wait. Steve's not at the door tonight. It's someone new."

An ugly sneer twisted Tory's mouth. "You were born a bitch, weren't you, Chessly?"

I sipped my beer and set the glass back on the table. "Takes one to know one."

Our server arrived with our pizza but couldn't penetrate the knot of Tory's entourage creating her backdrop in front of our booth. "Excuse me. Excuse me. Hot pie coming through."

His words seemed to bounce off the wall of Tory's girl group and into the ceiling of the bar. From the corner of the booth beside Piper, Saylor threw me a "what are you going to do?" look before addressing Tory and her friends. "I prefer my Stromboli's hot."

When the knot of girls still didn't move, I caught the server's eye over Tory's shoulder. "I think the only way we're going to have our pizza is if you grab the bouncer."

His eyes rounded, then he headed in the direction of the front door, taking our pie with him. Not catching on, Tory snorted.

"Our IDs passed the test."

A minute later a big man who looked like he might be a member of the Wildcats basketball team loomed over the crowd in front of our table. "Is there a problem here?"

"We'd like to enjoy our dinner in peace, but this bunch of freshmen don't seem to want to move on—like to a place where they're legal," I said, my voice even.

"We are not freshmen." Tory threw daggers at me with her eyes, and I had the impression she was about an inch from stomping her foot. Turning to the bouncer, she flipped a switch and piled on the charm. "You checked us when we walked in, remember?"

"It's kind of dark by the door, and I'm new." The megawatt smile on the guy's beautiful brown face didn't quite reach his eyes. "May I see your ID again, please?"

The furtive expressions Tory's little tribe passed from girl to girl should have alerted him that he'd been had, and maybe they did. But since she was the leader and still impeding the server from delivering our pie, the bouncer started with her. When her girls gave her space to hand over her driver's license, the server took advantage by slipping inside their half-circle and sliding our pizza into the middle of our table. "Can I get you anything else?"

"Another lemon drop for me, please," Piper said with a grin in my direction.

"You got it." The server smiled at Piper.

With a glance at our half-full pitcher of beer, Saylor added, "We're okay on beer for now."

The server disappeared at about the same time as the bouncer slid a penknife into the edge of Tory's ID. She screeched in outrage as he discovered her subterfuge, her anger aimed directly at me.

"You are such a freaking *bitch*!"

"I'm not the one with a fake ID and a nasty attitude." With a shooing gesture, I said, "Run along now and leave the bars to the grown-ups."

Tory made as if to lunge at me, but the bouncer stuck his massive arm out, shutting her progress down with ease. "Miss, you and your friends need to leave, please. I don't want to have to call campus police."

At the mention of police, Tory's entourage melted away toward the door. When she caught on that her wall was no longer surrounding her, she threw back her shoulders and glared at me. "You'll pay for humiliating me, Chessly Clarke."

I reached for a slice of pie and slid it onto my plate. "No, I won't."

She gasped.

"I won't pay for what you've done to yourself." Blinking up at her, I added, "I hope I don't see you around again anytime soon."

Piper started a slow clap that Saylor obligingly took up too.

When Tory tried again to step in my direction, the bouncer cut her off. A cross between a growl and a shriek escaped her throat before she finally stomped her foot and swung for the door. Pushing through her little group waiting near the front of the bar, she swanned out into the cool evening. A server with a to-go box followed her, shouting about her owing money for their pizza. She turned and stared at one of the girls following her.

With a sigh, the girl I recognized as Penelope something-or-other from our dorm stopped and paid for the pizza before following her leader out of the bar.

My friends and I exchanged a look before I said to the bouncer, "In case you hadn't noticed, that one's trouble."

"I'll be keeping an eye out for her. Thanks for the heads-up. I can't afford a seven-hundred-dollar fine for letting the under-twenty-ones in." He touched a finger to his ball cap and headed back to his stool right inside the front door.

Only after the commotion ended did I notice our audience when Piper's attention zeroed in on the back of the bar. When I turned to see what—or who—she was watching, I caught sight of Finn McCabe. For a second, I could have sworn I saw longing in his features as he stared back at me. Then Wyatt Baxter stood up from their booth and headed back in the direction of the restrooms.

A few minutes later, Piper excused herself to use the ladies' room. While she was gone, Finn wandered up to the bar across from our booth. Though I willed myself to keep my eyes on my food, and on Saylor seated across from me, I kept sliding glances his way out of the corner of my eye. From what I'd seen on Homecoming, Finn and Tory had something going on. Now that I thought about it, she was making a scene at the back of the bar before she started in on me. So why was Finn staring at me via the mirror behind the bartender and making no effort at all to hide it? And why did he look so unhappy?

Wait.

Was he pissed at me for outing Tory to the bouncer and getting her kicked out of the bar? I slugged back the half a glass of beer in front of me and refilled it to the brim.

"Was it something I said?" Saylor remarked with a smirk. Her side-eye in Finn's direction said she'd busted me. Mercifully, she left it at a look.

"Have you noticed how much bullshit the beautiful people get away with?" I asked around a bite of cheesy chicken and artichoke deliciousness.

"Calling Tory Miller beautiful is a bit of an exaggeration, don't you think?" She sipped daintily from her glass and wiped her napkin over her mouth.

"You know what I mean."

"Is that why you went after her so hard when she lived on your floor last year?" Saylor pushed her plate with its uneaten crusts toward the middle of the table.

"Nope. I didn't 'go after' her at all," I said with air quotes. "From the moment I met her, I picked up on her entitlement and decided not to engage. But in case that little scene just now didn't alert you"—I nodded toward the empty space where Tory and her girls had stood—"the girl enjoys attention. *All* the attention." I sipped the foam off the top of my now overfilled glass of beer before picking it up for a proper drink. "She pushed and pushed until she left me no choice but to do what I had to do."

Finn's gorgeous baritone voice interrupted our conversation. "Hi, Chessly. Um, everything okay?"

Why does the guy have to have such a pretty voice? I glanced up at him. *And those shoulders? And those eyes?* It wasn't fair, especially when he wanted to waste all that delicious manliness on a human wrecking ball like Tory Miller.

"We're great, Finn. But I guess I might have ruined your evening, huh?" I shrugged. "Sorry about that." My tone conveyed the lie in my words.

He shoved his hands into his pockets, drawing my attention to his perfectly proportioned body, all shoulders and chest tapering down to his hips—and his package. It was difficult to dismiss that with it right there, a touch below eye level. I coughed over the sigh that escaped me and snapped my eyes back to his face.

"Tory and her girls like to hang out with the team. I don't think they're as bad as Callahan says they are."

My brow shot up. Across the table Saylor let out a derisive snort.

"But I could be wrong about that." His face expressed a combination of consternation and worry.

"On Homecoming we established you definitely could be wrong about that," I said.

He let go of an uncomfortable chuckle. "Well, you probably saved another bouncer's job tonight. I doubt Stromboli's will let Tory back in before she's a senior."

"So I did ruin your evening." My lovely dark beer turned sour in my mouth.

A ghost of a smile tugged at the corner of his mouth. "Not even a little bit. Seeing you here made it all kinds more interesting."

Out of the corner of my eye, I caught Saylor's smirk, and I shot her a glare. She burst out laughing.

"This"—she waved her hand between Finn and me—"is certainly interesting." Shoving her outstretched hand at Finn, she said, "I'm Saylor Davis, one of Chess's bestest friends."

Under the table my toe connected with her shin. The wretched woman didn't even flinch. If anything the gleam in her eyes ratcheted up from naughty to wicked. I absolutely did not appreciate her glee at what she *thought* was going on between Finn and me.

With a smile, Finn shook her hand. "Finn McCabe."

"Oh, I know who you are. Starting defensive end for the Wildcats. Up close, you're pretty cute, nothing at all like the animal you are on the field."

A dull red spread over his high cheekbones even as he smiled that smile that revealed his one endearingly crooked incisor. "Thanks. I think."

Nothing was going on between Saylor and the too-hot-for-his-own-good football player standing beside our table. Nothing.

So why did the green-eyed monster punch my stomach when he smiled at my friend?

Chapter Four

Finn

FROM THE FIRST time I set eyes on her sitting in our players' booth at Stromboli's weeks ago, all I'd wanted to do was impress Chessly Clarke. Judging by Saylor's comments, I'd impressed her friend, but the scowl on Chessly's face said I'd missed the mark with her—again.

Guess my friends were right. I was a glutton for punishment. "Are you coming to the game this weekend?" I asked, and I couldn't stop the hope that rose in my voice.

"We're definitely going to the game—right, Chess?" Saylor answered.

"Can't pass up an opportunity to tease Piper about her sudden interest in a certain Wildcats player," Chessly deadpanned. "Speaking of Piper, I should probably go check on her, make sure she didn't fall in."

"Didn't fall in where?" The purple-haired hottie who'd turned out not to be a figment of Bax's imagination appeared beside me.

Our roommates and I had razzed the shit

out of Bax about making up a girl he supposedly hooked up with a while back. Then he'd dedicated a sweet pick-six to her a couple of games ago, and we all had to admit she was real. Up close, she dazzled in a punk-style way. But she didn't make my heart hammer in my chest the way her smart-mouthed friend did. Chessly looked the part of the gorgeous girl next door, but she had an edge to her, a way of focusing on a man that made me feel seen the night we met.

I'd hated it when she dropped that focus the minute Tory Miller showed up.

"Glad you could join us. We left you a couple of slices," Chess said as Piper stepped around me and slid into the booth beside Saylor.

At about that time Bax, Fitz, and Johnson sidled up beside me. "Time to go, Finn," Johnson said.

"Not so fast." Fitz's eyes were on Saylor, and I let a little air out. "Hello, ladies," he intoned in his best James Earl Jones voice. "You coming to the game on Saturday?"

"Absolutely," Saylor answered for all the women at the table.

"And the post-game celebration at our place afterward?" I directed my words to all of them, but my eyes were on Chessly.

"That sounds fun—doesn't it, girls?" Saylor replied.

"Sure." The lack of enthusiasm in Chessly's tone worried me.

"Give me your number, and I'll text you the address." Too late, I caught my mistake. Behind my left elbow, Johnson snickered. Bax gave a hopeless shake of his head, and Fitz stared at me as though I'd just whiffed a game-ending tackle.

Somehow from her seat in the booth, Chessly glared down her nose at me. "Everyone knows where you live, Finn. Big old Victorian on Jock Street, right?"

"Yeah. That's the one." I coughed into my fist. "So we'll see you there after the game, yeah?"

"Possibly," she said while her friend talked over her.

"Can't wait," Saylor said with a flirty grin for Fitz.

When I opened my mouth to say goodbye, Johnson nudged me toward the door. We followed Bax and Fitz out to the sidewalk in front of the bar.

"I never thought I'd say this because neither of you two have any moves, but I think Baxter might have scored a touchdown considering the puffy state of Purple-Hair's lips while you whiffed on every down, Finn." Fitz's laughter echoed off the side of the building.

"Seriously amateur move to ask for her number in front of a crowd." Johnson shoved my shoulder. "Hope you play better than that on Saturday." Teasing mischief danced in the depths of his dark brown eyes.

"Asshole," I muttered. "You're all assholes."

"Yeah, well, at least we know how to pick up women." Fitz laughed again. "Here's a tip: you don't ask for their numbers in front of their friends—or yours."

Throwing up my hands, I headed in the direction of my truck. When Bax didn't immediately fall into step beside me, I half-turned and said, "You comin'? Or is the rest of the peanut gallery giving you a ride home?"

Their laughter followed me all the way down the block to where I'd parked my pickup. When I opened the driver's door, Bax simultaneously opened the passenger door. Guess he was catching a ride with me.

Before he could keep the joke rolling, I preempted him. "At least I'm classy enough not to do her in the can at the most popular hangout spot on campus. You know, like some people." I glared at him in case he thought I was talking about someone else.

"Piper ambushed me in the hallway. All I did was kiss her back."

"Which explains why you were away from our booth for days."

"What-the-fuck-ever."

Yeah, it was childish, but both of us sulked all the way back to our place.

When we walked through the front door, we heard Jamaica's soft laughter coming from the kitchen followed by Callahan's groan. Right about then, Danny stepped out of the dining room with a load of clean laundry piled in his arms. He nodded toward the kitchen.

"Yeah, don't go in there unless you're up for today's special—mush with a side of more mush." Danny shook his head. "I detoured through the dining room to grab my clothes from the dryer, but you might want to go all the way around the outside of the house and in through the back door if you have any laundry to do."

Shouldering past us, he headed upstairs to his room. Without a word Bax and I followed him.

Game day dawned clear and cold, exactly the way I liked it. When I strolled back into my bedroom after my shower, my phone buzzed with a text.

Ma: Good luck today, Finnegan. We're cheering for you.

With a smile, I texted back.

Me: Thanks, Ma. Love you.

Ma: Love you more.

Since the first game I redshirted freshman year, the ritual had never wavered. Mom and I exchanged the same text message in the morning of each game day. Even though I'd had dinner with the folks the night before and she'd said pretty much the exact same thing, here she was with the texts.

Whistling a little tune, I dressed in dress slacks and a button-down. Didn't matter to Coach if we were playing at home or away—on game days we showed up to the locker room dressed for success. It drove Bax nuts that Coach wouldn't let him wear one of his signature T-shirts even under his button-down. Thinking about my roommate's angst over that tugged a grin from me as I closed my bedroom door and nearly ran into the guy in question.

"What are you so damn happy about?" he asked as we fell into step down the hall.

I gave him a once-over, noting his dark blue button-down and gray slacks. "Nothing. Just wondering what T-shirt you're trying to sneak past Coach today."

His shoulders hunched slightly before he straightened and pushed at me so he could go first down the stairs. "Who said I'm wearing anything under this shirt?"

"Your sleeves have enough trouble stretching over your biceps, that they can't hide the telltale line of your T-shirt sleeve beneath them." For emphasis, I gave his bicep a little love tap with my fist when we dropped to the bottom of the stairs. "What are you hiding under your dress shirt, Wyatt?"

"You never learn, do you Bax?" Callahan asked as we entered the kitchen. "If Finn noticed your T-shirt, you'd better believe you won't sneak it by Coach."

With a snarl, Bax jerked at the knot of his tie, loosening it enough to drag it over his head. The ruthless way he unbuttoned his dress shirt had me fearing for the integrity of its buttons. When he pulled it back to shrug out of it, he revealed the shirt underneath it. We read "Fuck it. My final thought before making most decisions" and cracked up.

"What's so funny?" Danny asked as he joined us in the kitchen.

"Bax." Callahan chuckled.

I snorted. "I don't know what's funnier—the truth of that statement or the irony of it being your exact thought when you got dressed today."

Danny shook his head as he pulled his travel mug from the cupboard and filled it with coffee. "Even though I've only been on the team for less than a season, even I know Coach is never going to let you wear one of your favorite shirts on game day." He read over Bax's T-shirt a second time. "Even if it is totally accurate." He hid his smirk behind a sip of morning brew.

"I don't see what the big deal is," Bax grumbled. "I wear a T-shirt every other day of the week and no one says anything."

"It's about respect," Callahan said in his best Coach Ellis voice. "It's about pride—in yourself and in the team."

Callahan, Danny, and I, exchanged a glance and added in unison, "Now take it off."

No doubt the basketball players living in the house next door wondered at the loud laughter coming from our kitchen at a time most normal college students would still be in bed on a Saturday morning.

"You three are fucking hilarious," Bax growled, but I caught the twitch of his lips before he dragged his T-shirt over his head and draped it over the back of a chair.

The timer on the oven signaled our hot breakfast burritos were done, so Callahan pulled the pan out and set it on top of the stove. While Bax redressed himself, I poured us each a mug of coffee. Danny laid napkins on the table, our portable hot pads for the foil-wrapped burritos, then helped himself to one.

"You riding with me, Finn?" he asked.

"Sure." I snagged my breakfast off the pan and followed Danny out the front door.

After we survived the first day of practice freshman year, Callahan and I had become best friends. But these days his fascination with his study buddy, who happened to be best friends with the girl currently blowing me off, made it uncomfortable to be around him sometimes. I was glad Danny wanted to drive today.

Until he started in on our way to the field.

"What's this about you trying to snag a girl's number in the middle of Stromboli's last night?"

Out of the corner of my eye, I caught his teasing grin. Asshole.

When I didn't respond, he filled the silence. "Amateur move, Finnegan."

Crossing my arms over my chest, I studied the passing scenery through the passenger window. "I'm aware." Under my breath, I added, "Fuckin' Bax."

"She must be hot for you to lose your cool that way."

Sliding farther down on the seat, I mumbled, "What-the-fuck-ever. I had no idea I lived in a house full of gossipy old ladies."

Danny's laughter filled the cab of his Mustang. I ground my teeth and focused on the road. It was one thing for the guys to razz me about the jersey chasers whose attention I loved—which apparently was a problem I couldn't bring myself to care about. Sue me. But those girls were nothing more than a distraction, someone pretty to hang out with rather than looking at my friends' ugly mugs all the time. Chessly was different. Special. Not someone I was okay with the guys giving me shit about.

"Don't get pissy, Finn." Danny smirked. "It's game day. You're the one who's always reminding us it's the best damn day of the week."

One side of my mouth lifted in a sneer, which didn't faze my roommate in the slightest. Guess all his military experience left him immune to sarcasm.

We arrived at the facility to find Coach Ainsworth waiting right inside the doors, clipboard in hand as he checked off players' arrivals. If anyone even thought about showing up late on game day, Coach would make an example out of him for the next week. None of us had ever made that rookie mistake, even when we were rookies, but we also knew he was checking to make sure we'd followed all the rules—including the dress code.

"Nice shirt, Bax. Not so sure about that tie, though." Ainsworth coughed into his hand.

Back at the house I'd been so focused on saving my friend from his T-shirt-wearing stupidity that I hadn't paid any attention to his tie. Guess that had been true of our other roommates too because we couldn't help our grins at the light pink tie with the red lips all over it.

"That's as close to a girl's mouth as Bax has been in weeks," Callahan said, laughing.

"Not true," I corrected.

Callahan's brow shot up. "Yeah? Do tell."

"Shut up, asshole," Bax said as he shouldered past all of us and headed down the hall to the locker room.

For once I was on the giving end of the razzing. No way could I pass up this opportunity. "Bax's unicorn is a real person. He says she started it at Stromboli's the other night, but no matter who came on to who, they both had swollen lips when they came back from the can."

Coach Ainsworth narrowed his eyes. "I hope you boys are being smart. We don't need anyone putting the team in a jam over some woman."

That sobered the rest of us up quick.

"Got it, Coach." Callahan spoke for all of us.

As we headed toward the locker room, we couldn't help but to exchange snickers and grins. Since I'd been on the receiving end of Danny's jokes about women, it was fun to be dishing them out for once. Coach's warning notwithstanding. A picture of a blonde-haired, blue-eyed babe flashed through my head, and I tensed.

As I folded my dress clothes and stacked them neatly on the bench in front of my locker, images of Chessly Clarke played on a loop through my thoughts. Her friend said they'd all be at today's game. Maybe if I impressed her with my play, she'd forget about my clumsy fuckup when I asked for her number.

Then again, I don't think that was my fuckup at all. Somehow, without me having a clue, I blew it on the night we met when I acknowledged Tory Miller outside the dorm when I'd dropped Chessly off. When it came to women, I might be a little slow on the uptake—all right, a lot slow—but I caught on quick that bad blood swirled between Chessly and Tory. Wish someone had given me a heads-up about that before I found out the hard way.

After I pulled my pungent pads from my locker, I tugged them over my head and wrinkled my nose at the stink of sweat assailing my sinuses. Too bad these pads couldn't be run through a washer when the team managers washed our uniforms. I jerked my jersey down over them and yanked on my pants. As I laced my cleats, Bax sat on the bench beside me.

"You ready to knock some heads out there today?"

My response was automatic. "Damn straight."

He slapped me on the back. "That's how we impress a certain pair of ladies."

"Speak for yourself." Standing, I grabbed my helmet from the shelf above the lockers. "I plan on messing Crawford up for the beat-down he gave us last year when he had that NFL-caliber O-line. From what I saw on film, their replacements are mostly rookies." Flexing my fist, I said, "I'm going to own them."

"That's what we love about you, Finnegan."

My brow shot up.

"How you flip the switch from sweetheart to beast mode the second you pull on your pads." He held out his fist, and without thinking, I bumped it, wondering if "sweetheart" was a compliment. The gleam in his eyes could have meant anything.

Coach Ellis called us together for our final pep talk before we ran out onto the field. In his usual understated fashion, he had the entire team wound up and ready to kick some Bulldogs' ass. For a time, I forgot all about a certain hot blonde and how much I wanted to impress her.

As we exited the tunnel to run behind the tumbling cheerleaders through the gauntlet of marching band members playing our fight song, the roar of twenty-five thousand screaming fans rumbled through my blood, amping me up for the dogfight we all knew would be our latest contest with our archrivals. When I reached the sidelines where my teammates and I back-slapped and high-fived and fist-bumped each other, all I wanted to do was race out onto the gridiron and go to work.

Then I glanced up into the stands. Like a heat-seeking missile, my focus zeroed in on a certain hot physics major and her friends. For a few seconds, our gazes locked and the whole stadium faded away.

From somewhere beside me, Coach Ainsworth's voice penetrated my attention. "Get out there and kick some ass, McCabe!"

Dragging my eyes away from Chessly Clarke, I nodded to Coach and ran out onto the field.

Time to impress a certain sexy science nerd.

Chapter Five

Chessly

"**I** CAN'T BELIEVE IT took until our junior year for Jamaica to attend a game. The atmosphere alone is worth the price of admission," Saylor gushed as she raised her cup of "hot chocolate" to Piper and me for a toast.

"Guess 'studying' with a certain sexy tight end convinced her to give it a try," Piper said with sly air quotes before she touched her cup to ours.

Together, we waved hard in the direction of the special VIP seats on the fifty-yard line. Callahan had given Jamaica and her friends Axel and Drake tickets to sit directly behind the Wildcats' bench. When we caught their attention, they waved back, lifting their cups for an air-toast.

"Speaking of hot football players, you still haven't given us a proper explanation about why you disappeared for an age at Stromboli's on Thursday night. Those kiss-swollen lips you brought back couldn't have had anything to do with a certain studly middle linebacker whose lips were

equally swollen, could they?" I teased over the rim of my cup of spiked chocolate.

Piper studiously ignored me in favor of focusing her attention on the players swarming onto the field. My eyes strayed to the field too, and much to my consternation, I sought out number ninety-one: Finn McCabe.

Being an avid football fan, I knew exactly who he was before he offered me a ride home after the Homecoming bonfire. On the field, he was an animal. His speed and aggression knocking down opposing offensive linemen in his single-minded mission to hit the quarterback or the running back—whoever had the ball—impressed any true fan.

In truth, he was breathtaking to watch. The laws of physics said his grace and athleticism shouldn't exist in a man of his immense size. Yet there he was Saturday after Saturday, bulldozing through O-lines, pirouetting around blockers, and leading the team in tackles for the second season in a row.

I liked stats so I kept track of the team's. Especially the defensive stats. Especially Finn McCabe's. So imagine my surprise when I discovered that in person, he was a bashful, sort of awkward man with twinkly, whiskey-colored eyes. Those twinkles drew me in purely because I wanted in on the joke. Turns out, the joke was on me when Tory Miller showed her vicious face and blew the play to smithereens.

As though he knew my mind was on him, Finn glanced up from where he'd been high-fiving and fist-bumping his teammates to home in on me. Desperately, I wanted to look away, to not give him the satisfaction of knowing I was watching him. But even from a distance, those warm eyes snagged mine and wouldn't let me go.

At last a coach swatted him on the ass, drawing his attention from me, and Finn sprinted out onto the field. Only then did I catch on that I'd completely missed the opening kickoff.

Saylor's voice was in my ear. "You okay?"

"Sure." I sipped from my peppermint schnapps and hot chocolate. "Why would you think I wasn't?"

"Because you slipped away into some kind of trance for a minute and didn't shout your usual 'Go! 'Cats! Go!' cheer during the kickoff." Her expression turned sly. "Could it have something to do with another football player? One who had no finesse in his attempt at getting your number?" She smirked.

"Not a chance," I said. "Apparently, he and Tory Miller have something going."

"Huh." She sipped her hot drink. "That's not the vibe I was picking up the other night."

Her innocent act as she shifted her focus to the field didn't fool me for a second. Saylor loved to stir the pot. With something going on between Piper and Jamaica and a certain pair of Wildcats players, I'd think she had enough to keep her gossipy little heart happy. Besides, it didn't matter that Finn McCabe was gorgeous and talented on the field: his response to Tory in front of the dorm after Homecoming proved the man had terrible taste in women. I might have been interested in him for a minute, but after that night, I was over it.

Right as I swigged back a healthy swallow of pepperminty hot-chocolate deliciousness, Finn blew past his blocker and into the backfield. With his deceptive speed, he was on top of the quarterback almost before the poor guy had secured the ball from the center. As Finn covered the quarterback and dragged him to the turf, he somehow managed to punch the ball from his hands and another Wildcat fell on top of it.

All of us in the crowd went bananas as the Wildcat who'd recovered the fumble held the ball aloft and the defense skipped and jumped their way back to the sidelines to make way for the offense to take the field.

I wanted so badly to ignore Finn McCabe, but then he went

and played like a freaking rock star and all I could do was cheer for him. And watch him with his teammates on the sideline as everyone on the defense made their way over to him to congratulate him on his stellar play. When he gazed up into the stands, he caught me staring, and he had the audacity to salute me with a wide smile on his handsome face. My dad raised me not to be rude, so I inclined my head in his direction, mainly because he'd already caught me staring at him. It wouldn't do to pretend I wasn't. That would only give him something to believe about me that wasn't true.

At. All.

I had zero interest in Finn McCabe.

Beside me, Saylor shouted, "That play was incredible, wasn't it?" Then she clocked where my eyes had strayed and added, "Yeah, I can see you have zero interest in a certain Wildcats player."

Shaking my head, I mumbled, "Whatever," into my hot chocolate and swigged the rest of it back. My empty cup gave me an excuse to disappear behind the student section for a minute while I disposed of it. The time away didn't provide the breather I hoped it would though, as Finn's broad smile played across my thoughts.

The raw power he displayed on the field already raced my heart enough when I watched him play. Then after his field heroics, he had to go and shoot me that boyish grin that threatened to set my panties on fire. The man was a padded-up ad for sin.

When I returned to my friends, the offense was on the move. Mick Patterson, our star quarterback, called, "Hike!" and dropped back three steps after the center hiked him the ball. He scanned the field and fired a laser of a pass to number eighty-two, a new player I didn't know. But from the way he ran his post route, shedding the corner and making himself an easy target for the pass, everyone was going to know who he was sooner rather than later. The thirty yards the team gained on that play took them into the red zone, the area on the field within twenty yards of the goal line, and the stadium started rocking in anticipation of a touchdown.

The student section went wild when Tarvarius Johnson, the team's best running back, gained ten yards and another first down on the next play. Everyone in the stands was on their feet, cheering at the tops of their voices—us included. Mick handed the ball off to Tarvarius a second time, which apparently was a mistake because the Bulldogs were ready and tackled him behind the line of scrimmage, costing us four yards. On the next play, Mick dropped back again, and this time he found Callahan O'Reilly with a pass into the end zone for a touchdown.

When Callahan pointed the nose of the ball at the stands where Jamaica was watching the game, Piper, Saylor, and I cheered even louder. All of us bounced up and down and laughed as our friend pulled her Wildcats scarf over her face right as a cameraman caught her on film and broadcast her reaction on the Jumbotron.

Involuntarily, my eyes strayed down the rows from where Jamaica, Axel, and Drake were seated to the Wildcats' bench. I caught Finn engaged in a complicated sort of ritualistic hand game with Callahan. After their congratulatory silliness, he stepped back to the bench, snagged his helmet, and joined the rest of the defense on the edge of the field to watch the kicking team kick off to the Bulldogs. Right before he tugged his helmet over his head, he gazed up into the stands, his eyes zeroed in on me, and the corner of his mouth tipped up.

Ugh! He'd caught me watching him again—and judging by his smile, he was enjoying it.

Jerk.

I needed to find some self-control, pronto. No way did I want him to think I was harboring any interest in him whatsoever. After all, he was involved with Tory Miller, which proved he wasn't my type at all.

"Anyone else need a hot chocolate refill?" I asked my friends.

"Ooh, I could use one," Saylor said.

"Count me in," Piper added.

Yes, the defense was back on the field—Finn was back on the field—but I needed a break from watching him. And from thinking about him and the way his smiles lit up my insides against my will.

As I headed to the concession stand, I promised myself under no circumstances would I ever get involved with Finnegan McCabe.

Ignoring every excuse I gave, Saylor insisted I attend the postgame party at the big Victorian on Jock Street where Finn and his roommates lived. The Wildcats' win today had moved us one step closer to the conference championship and the playoffs, so the party was likely to be wild and rowdy—not my scene at all. If only I'd had to be on call at the dorms . . .

After the game, we'd headed to our favorite pub for a mountain of loaded nachos and beer. I'd backed off on the chocolate and peppermint schnapps before the end of the first half. The cloying sweetness of Saylor's favorite game-day drink made my teeth hurt. At the halftime tailgate, I drank a couple of White Claws and switched to black coffee to stay warm during the second half. By the end of the game, I was still sober, which was most of the problem with going to a party with a bunch of jocks and the jersey chasers whose mission it was to bag one of them.

"At least pretend to have fun," Saylor admonished as we walked up the sidewalk to Finn's house. "Who knows? Maybe if you fake it, you'll make it." She elbowed me in the ribs and laughed uproariously at her bad joke as we stepped onto the front porch.

The house was teeming with people. A big guy who seemed

to have no neck sat on a folding chair in the foyer checking IDs. When I saw the party had a bouncer, I let myself relax. We shouldered our way through the throng dancing to thumping hip-hop in the living room and discovered Jamaica standing close to Callahan in the kitchen.

"Hey! Look who made it," she said as each of us hugged her.

"Football parties are way more fun than frat parties," Saylor said with a smirk. "We'd much rather be here than over at the ADRs." She laughed. "But if either of you ever out me to one of my brothers, I'll toss you under the bus so fast it'll leave tread marks on your bones."

I shot her a look. "Overdramatic much?"

Beside Jamaica, Callahan laughed. "Grab a beer and join the fun."

Right as he said that, Saylor glanced over and caught the eye of the gorgeous Black guy from the other night at Stromboli's— the one with the knowing smile who couldn't stop staring at her then either.

"Don't mind if I do. You want one, Chess?"

"Only if it's still cold when you hand it to me." I was sure she'd have no trouble deciphering what I meant from my sardonic tone.

"What was that all about?" my best friend asked as we watched our other friend sashay over to where the hot lineman was manning the keg.

"We met Jeremiah Fitzgerald the other night over pizza. Saylor put on the flirt, and he jumped right in. If not for the fact he and his buddies were on their way out the door at the time, she probably would have shown up at this shindig with him instead of me."

"You would have liked that too, wouldn't you?" Jamaica teased.

"Too bad you weren't on call this weekend. I could have covered for you again. No charge."

I didn't miss the way Callahan's face lit up when I made my offer. Nor did I miss the way his hand snaked around Jamaica's waist as he held her close to his side. *Interesting.*

Saylor handed me a red cup full of nasty keg beer, but at least it was cold. "For you, milady. Enjoy." She touched her own cup to mine and downed a healthy swig, her eyes twinkling over the rim. Without another word, she returned to where Jeremiah was filling cups for the line of people streaming in from the living room.

Addressing Callahan, I said, "Guess we know why your party is more fun than the frat party where Saylor is a little sister."

Speculation narrowed Jamaica's eyes. "Guess we do."

"I'm noticing a disturbing trend among my friends," I said as I took a sip from my beer—more as something to do than because I wanted to drink it.

"What's that?"

"You're all hanging out with Wildcats players. You"—when she opened her mouth to protest, I stared pointedly at where Callahan's hand rested on her hip—"Piper, and now Saylor."

"Why is it disturbing that your friends are hanging out with me and my friends?" Callahan asked with a smirk.

"Because some of your friends have questionable taste in women." I sipped more beer.

With a sage nod, he said, "Don't judge Finn. It's not taste he lacks but finesse. Jersey chasers are easy to impress." He tugged Jamaica a fraction closer to his side. "Women who are worth impressing are harder for him to affect. He gets all tongue-tied and says stupid things."

I shrugged. "I don't recall referring to your roommate."

Callahan barked out a laugh. "You didn't have to. We knew who you meant."

Wrinkling my nose, I said, "Whatever."

The voice of the man in question sounded behind me. "Hey, 'Han. Jamaica."

When I didn't bother to turn around, Callahan smirked.

"Chessly?" Finn asked from somewhere behind my back.

Letting go of a long-suffering sigh, I shrugged and half-turned to incline my head at him.

Callahan's low voice held a note of mirth. "Cold, Chessly. Cold."

Jamaica's narrowed eyes told me my best friend was in solidarity with me. Whether or not Callahan was right and Finn lacked finesse with women it didn't excuse whatever he had going on with that witch Tory Miller.

"I didn't think you'd show tonight."

With another shrug, I sipped my nasty beer. "What can I say? My friends, apparently, are sadists. They enjoy torturing me."

Saylor's snorty laughter drew our attention to where Jeremiah Fitzgerald was entertaining her as he filled cups like a pro.

"Or they think everyone should have a thing for a Wildcats player." That last part came out huffier than I intended, and Jamaica shot me the big eyes. "Don't worry. I was referring to Saylor." Under my breath I added, "Mostly."

"I thought you were a fan of the Wildcats." Consternation crossed Finn's face, and I stomped on the mental brakes when a smile tried to twitch its way over my lips at how cute his expression was.

"Football is fun to watch."

Both Callahan and Finn stood a bit straighter and preened.

"So, yes, I'm a Wildcats fan. But being a fan doesn't mean I want to date any of you." I shot a glance at Jamaica, who narrowed her eyes at me and then at Saylor, who apparently didn't hear me, judging by the way she was smiling at Jeremiah's beer-pouring antics.

The way Finn's' shoulders dropped gave me a pang, like I'd kicked a puppy or something. My remorse made no sense.

"We're nice guys. We do community service and everything,"

he said, his earnest tone nearly tugging that grin from me after all. But I squelched it.

"By community service, do you mean entertaining freshman and sophomore girls in the Union?"

As soon as those catty words had left my mouth, I wanted to kick myself. His furrowed brow at my question told me more than I wanted to know. I thought he'd noticed me the other day when I saw him at a table surrounded by Tory Miller and her band of mean girls. Guess he hadn't. And what did that say about my interest in him?

Because I most certainly was not interested in him.

Not even a little bit.

"Um, I volunteer in the pediatric ward in the hospital. 'Han here walks dogs at the animal shelter." He nodded in Jeremiah's direction. "Fitzy helps out over at the campus wellness center. It's a requirement of our scholarships to give back."

I folded my arms over my chest and hid behind a sip of beer. *He volunteers in the pediatric ward?* I did not need to know that.

"I don't think that's what Chessly meant." Callahan smirked.

"Look, I, um, figured I screwed up somehow that night." He scuffed his feet on the linoleum. "Can we talk?" Glancing around at the crowd, he added, "Without an audience?"

My first reaction was to hide behind my usual snark and turn him down. But something about such a big man being so vulnerable in front of his friends had me nodding instead. At my response, Jamaica's eyes almost bugged out of her head. Giving her the tiniest shake of my head, I shut down whatever comment she wanted to make.

The smile that bloomed over Finn's wide mouth was worth my acquiescence. I just hoped the price for it wasn't going to be too high.

Chapter Six

Finn

WHEN I WALKED into the kitchen and saw Chessly standing there, my heart almost pounded out of my chest. Just seeing that girl did weird things to my insides. From the look on her face, the feeling wasn't mutual, and I didn't have a fucking clue how to fix that. All I knew was that I needed a do-over, and this was my first chance at one in the two weeks since we met and hit it off—until I somehow fucked up.

As usual, my timing wasn't awesome, what with me asking for a private conversation in a room full of people, but I never saw her anywhere around campus where I could maybe ask for a few minutes without an audience.

Nodding toward the doorway into the living room, I said, "Let's go somewhere less crowded."

Callahan snorted even as Chessly lifted a skeptical brow. With the heaving crowd in the living room, I understood the irony of my suggestion. But we weren't headed to there.

"Trust me. Please." I dropped what I hoped was a smile and not a grimace.

That skeptical expression remained, but all the same Chessly followed me out of the kitchen. I skirted the dancers taking up the middle of the living room, which was a feat in itself as we wound our way past people drinking, laughing, and making out on the couches and chairs my roommates and I had shoved against the walls. When we reached the foyer, I asked, "Do you have a jacket?"

"I left it in Saylor's car."

"No worries." Reaching into the closet, I pulled out one of my hoodies and handed it to her.

She eyed it narrowly before at last reaching for it and pulling it over her head. It covered her like a blanket, hanging almost to her knees. Hot damn, she looked adorable. I couldn't help how much I liked seeing her in my clothes.

We headed out to the porch where I gestured for her to take the lawn chair in the corner. Leaning against the rail, I gathered my thoughts, most of which were about how damn lucky I was to have another shot at talking to her.

"You had something to say . . .?" she prompted.

Clearing my throat, I said, "Yeah." God, she was so pretty. Before meeting her, I would have said eyes so blue only existed in fairy tales. Her perfect rosy lips were plump and inviting, even in this moment when they were slightly pursed. *Especially* when she pursed them. Her heart-shaped face came to a shallow dimple in her chin. I had an overwhelming urge to run my tongue over that dimple, but I also had the good sense to know she wouldn't welcome that.

She made the "go on" gesture with her hand, a tiny smirk tugging at the corner of her mouth as though she had a clue about what was going through my head.

I clapped my palm over the back of my neck then scratched

the back of my head. "The thing is, I thought when I drove you home after Homecoming that we were connecting. I mean, science nerds, right?" When she gave me nothing, I said, "I thought I was being subtle about taking the long way, but maybe I offended you?"

Busying herself with rolling the sleeves up on my hoodie, exposing her delicate hands, she took her time answering. "That wasn't the problem." She caught my eye. "It was your friends." Seeming to catch herself, she hurried on. "Which is none of my business. You have a right to be friends with whoever you want." When she plucked at the hem of my hoodie, I relaxed. Guess both of us were a little nervous. "But I can't understand what you see in someone like Tory Miller."

"She always seems to be around, you know?"

That brow went up again, and I gripped the porch railing hard enough to leave marks.

"Not really. Maybe you could explain it to me." Though her voice remained steady, I didn't miss the way she white-knuckle gripped the hem of my hoodie where it rested above her knees.

Guess Tory Miller made both of us tense.

"We're not really friends. She's more interested in Callahan than anything."

Her lips thinned. "And that bothers you, huh?"

Putting my hands up to slow down where her train of thought was headed, I yelped, "No!" Clearing my throat, I added with what I hoped was some calm in my tone, "What I mean is that Tory hangs around Bax and me because she hopes we'll hook her up with Callahan." Glancing in the direction of the house, I smirked. "But it's pretty obvious where 'Han's interest is, so I think she's shit out of luck."

Something sad flitted over Chessly's features. "Depends on how bad she wants him."

"What's the deal with you and her? I figured out pretty quick that night she doesn't like you either."

Her gaze slid out to the front yard. "My job is to make sure people follow the rules so everyone can live together in some sort of compatibility. Tory believes the rules don't apply to her. At. All." Her eyes found mine. "The girl goes out of her way to make trouble wherever she goes." Someone opened the door, and loud music and laughter almost drowned out her next words. "I almost lost my job because of her."

I stood straighter. "Come again? Did you say she almost cost you your job? Your RA job?"

"Yes."

Shaking my head, I said, "I thought she didn't live in the dorms."

"She doesn't anymore. But when she was a freshman, she lived on my floor. It didn't take her long to figure out I had her number."

Pulling my brows together, I inclined my head toward her. "What's her number?"

A tiny grin tipped up the corner of Chessly's mouth. "Spoiled rich girl who thinks her daddy's money can buy her out of any trouble she manages to get herself into."

I blew out a breath. "Yeah, you're probably right about that."

Chessly crossed her arms over her chest. "Yet you hang out with her anyway."

"Not recently."

Her brows tried to meet her hairline.

"Sometimes it's easy to get caught up in the flattery, you know? When cute girls keep telling you how much they love to watch you play, it strokes the ol' ego." I blew out a breath. "Guess I needed a reminder about staying humble. Bax and 'Han have been riding me pretty hard about staying away from her and her little band of freshmen." I rubbed my hand over the back of my neck again. "So I've been making a point of studying in the science building instead of the library and being too busy to answer her texts."

"Huh. You gave her your number."

The disgust in her tone had me scrambling not to lose her. "Not one of my better decisions. My friends accuse me on the regular of being clueless about women." I kicked the heel of one foot against the toe of the other. "They might be right sometimes." I stared directly into those eyes I wanted to drown in. "But I'd like a chance to figure you out."

She drew her pretty legs up inside my sweatshirt, resting her heels on the edge of the chair. "Here's your first clue. I'm a woman, not a puzzle."

A laugh snorted out. "Chessly, all women are puzzles to me." Noticing the way she hugged her knees to her chest, I said, "But I think I've figured out that even when wearing my hoodie, you're cold."

"A bit."

"I could sit in the chair and you could have my lap, share body heat while we talk," I offered.

For a second she hesitated, and hope flashed through me that my silly gambit might have actually worked.

Then she shot me down. "This is okay."

Yeah, sometimes I misread the play. But I never stop working. "If you change your mind, the offer stands."

With a smirk, she said, "I'll remember that."

"What did you think of the game?" Of course, what I was truly asking was *What did you think of my play in the game?*

"The Wildcats are fun to watch. Definitely a draw for recruiting people to attend Mountain State." The twinkle in her eyes told me she was messing with me. "Those sacks you had today were impressive."

At her praise, I might have puffed up some. "Thanks. I'm glad you enjoyed them. They're the second most fun play to make."

"What's the most fun play to make?"

"Forcing and recovering a fumble." I grinned. "Let me amend that. A strip sack where I recover the fumble is the most fun play."

"You like being a superhero, huh?"

Shrugging, I smiled at her. "What can I say? I like making life hard for the quarterback. It's what they pay me the big bucks for."

She rested her chin on her knees. "Do you have to be on scholarship to be a starter?"

"No. But usually the guys who earn scholarships are starter caliber when they show up to play. Some guys, like my roommate Danny Chambers, are walk-ons who earn their scholarships by their work in practice that elevates them on game day."

"He's on scholarship too?"

"Not yet, but if he keeps catching everything Patty throws at him the way he has been, I have no doubt Coach will find some money for him."

"What about your other roommates?"

For once I thought first and talked second, toning down my pride in my buddies and me by softening my voice and showing some humility. "Yeah, we all worked hard in high school and keep challenging each other every day in practice."

"Must be tough to do well in school when you put in all that time for football," she mused.

That comment forced me to show off. "We have a standing academic competition in this house."

"Yeah?" She grinned.

"Anyone who finishes a semester with less than a 3.5 GPA has to do everyone else's laundry for the next semester. So far we're all still doing our own."

"Now that's impressive. Yet you have the energy to throw ragers after you win games. Who cleans up afterward?" She dropped her feet back to the deck and hugged her arms around herself.

"We take turns. This week is 'Han's turn. Which is probably why he's hanging out in the kitchen making sure Fitz doesn't overserve anyone." Nodding toward where she rubbed her hands over her upper arms, I said, "You look like you need to warm up." Smiling, I added, "My offer to share the chair is still on the table."

With an answering smile that gave me a shot of adrenaline, she opened her mouth to say something, but a commotion erupted in the foyer and spilled out onto the porch.

In football, especially on defense, timing is everything. If someone even so much as twitches before the center hikes the ball, the refs will call something. If the guy who moved early is on the offense, the refs will call a false start. If the guy moving is on defense, the refs will call offsides. Unfortunately, the refs call me for offsides at least once a game.

Take the night we met. Things with Chessly were moving in the right direction . . .but then Tory Miller showed up. One look at who was behind all that caterwauling assaulting our conversation told me my plans for the rest of the evening were in serious jeopardy.

"Finn said we could come. You can't kick us out just because that bitch Jamaica Winslow is here!" Tory screeched as Johnny Henderson, our buddy from the wrestling team, bounced her and her friends from the party.

Spying me across the porch, Tory switched up her tactics. "Finn! Tell this Neanderthal you invited us." She took two steps in my direction and caught sight of Chessly seated on the lawn chair. "You! What are you doing here? You have no business here!" Planting her hands on her hips, she added, "These aren't your people."

"Tsk, tsk, tsk. Throwing a tantrum as usual, huh, Tory? You're kind of a slow learner." Chessly's modulated voice contrasted Tory's strident tones, inviting me to move closer to Chess.

"Finn! You can't be serious. This person"—she wrinkled her nose as she nodded at Chessly—"is so far beneath you." Glancing around at where we were, she added, "And no fun at all. I mean, she's dragged you away from your own party."

"Tory, you need to go before the neighbors complain."

Out of the corner of my eye, I clocked the subtle shake of Chessly's pretty blonde head, and I figured out my mistake at about the same time as Tory lit into me at the top of her voice.

"What is wrong with you, Finn McCabe? Have you completely lost your mind?" she shouted.

Johnny stepped out the front door. "Everything all right here, Finn? Need some help?"

Before I could open my mouth, Chessly said, "I think I'll head inside, warm up, maybe grab another beer." She aimed that last part directly at Tory.

When it came to women, I might be a little slow on the uptake, but even I could figure out Chessly taunted Tory with her parting comment.

Gracefully, she stood and walked purposefully toward Johnny who was standing in the open front door to the house. Tory stood between Chessly and her destination, and a flash of disaster lit up my brain. Before the two women had the chance to face off, I stepped between them.

"I'll join you."

Chessly glanced over her shoulder, her expression hard to read with the porch light behind her, shadowing her face. "You don't have to."

"That's right, Finn. You don't have to spend time with white trash from the middle-of-nowhere Montana." Twirling a long curl falling over her shoulder, Tory's whole demeanor changed. "You can stay out here with us. I'm sure we can keep you entertained."

The faces of the little troupe of girls standing behind her ranged from worried to speculative. All of them made me nervous.

Sensing the trouble brewing, I gave Tory a smile. "That's a nice offer, but I've been out here for a while. I could use a warm-up and maybe another beer."

I breathed a sigh of relief when Tory and her girls slid sideways to let Chessly and me pass, but I should have known her stand-down from the impending catfight was only a ruse.

Following so closely behind me she almost gave me a flat tire, Tory said, "Since you're going back inside, you can tell your bouncer guy yourself that you invited us."

Ahead of me Chessly gave a snort and kept walking through the door and into the foyer past Johnny, who nodded at her before facing me, his eyebrows pulled together. Sucking in air, I turned and used my size with my forearms on the frame to stop Tory in the doorway.

"Here's the thing, ladies. I'm not the only one who lives here. The other guys insisted on no one under twenty-one." Lifting my hands in a "what can I do?" gesture, I willed them to understand and not push.

Tory's narrow-eyed glare gave me the sense Bax and Callahan knew what they were talking about when it came to the girls who had a thing for football players. "It's not cool to go back on your invite, Finn."

"Like I said, my roommates didn't give me a choice. We're all on scholarship, so we have to follow the rules." I ran my hand over my head and tossed some frat buddies under the bus. "I heard there's a pretty good party going over at the ADRs tonight. Those guys never have bouncers." I winked.

A couple of the girls stepped back, whispering to each other. Tory stayed right where she was.

"We want to party here. With you."

"I'm sorry, but that's not gonna happen. Not tonight." Tossing a glance over my shoulder, I saw Chessly had disappeared to somewhere else in the house. I couldn't do triage in two places at once, so I decided to cut my losses. "See you around, Tory. Ladies." With a salute, I stepped back and shut the door, turning the lock on the handle.

Outside, Tory started screeching again. "Finn McCabe! You

can't be serious. You unlock this door right this minute!" She followed that with pounding and maybe some temper-tantrum foot-stomping.

"Under no circumstances do those girls come back inside. Got it?" I said to Johnny.

"Oh, yeah." He shot me wide eyes. "Glad they aren't wrestling groupies. Sheesh, what a nightmare."

Yeah, I was starting to figure that out too.

"Thanks, man."

Touring the living room, I didn't catch sight of Chessly's golden-blonde head, so I headed into the kitchen. Fitz was still manning the keg and still had Chessly's friend's attention, but other than the two of them and a couple of people waiting in line for beer, no one else was there.

"Have you seen Chessly?" I asked Fitz and Saylor.

"She was here a few minutes ago. Said something about needing a ride home." Tilting her head, Saylor said, "I thought maybe you had that covered."

"I do, if I can find her."

"Maybe she's in the bathroom," she suggested.

Spinning on my heel, I headed through the living room and down the hallway behind the stairs. Knocking on the bathroom door, I called, "Chessly? You in there?"

A thump against the door, followed by a feminine giggle and low male laughter answered me. Still, I knocked again. "Chessly?"

"No Chessly in here, man," the male voice said.

Shit. Where could she have gone?

Making my way back through the party in full swing in the living room, I slipped into the dining room. Chessly didn't come across as someone who participated in flip-cup, but then again, I didn't know her all that well—yet.

When I didn't find her in the dining room either, I headed

back out to the foyer as a bad feeling snaked through my insides. Johnny confirmed it.

Chessly had left the party.

Chapter Seven

Chessly

"WHAT HAPPENED TO you last night? You left the kitchen with Finn, then a long time later, he showed back up there desperate to find you, but none of us knew where you were." Saylor eyed me over her latte.

We'd met up for brunch at our favorite coffee shop a couple of blocks off campus. My friend's demeanor and lack of her usual care with her makeup and hair told me she'd stayed at the party long after I left.

"I caught a ride with Axel and Drake." I popped a bite of cranberry scone into my mouth to preempt additional explanations.

Not that Saylor was in the mood to let me off the hook. "You could have told me you wanted to leave early."

"I didn't want to interrupt whatever you had going with Jeremiah."

A coy smirk tipped up the corner of her mouth as she set her latte on the table, wrapping her hands around it. "I don't usually go for guys his size, but that twinkle tells you something naughty is going on behind those deep brown eyes, and the way he lowers his voice . . ." She shivered, her smirk blooming into a full smile. "Fitz is probably one of the sexiest guys I've ever met." Tilting her head, she eyed me close. "No wonder Piper, Jamaica, and you have a thing for Wildcats football players."

"I haven't hooked up with anyone this year, let alone a football player. Do not lump me in with Piper and Jamaica." I sucked in a deep drink of my Americano and burned the roof of my mouth.

Saylor's laughter at my desperate grab for my ice water made me want to dump what was left of it over her head.

"Methinks the lady doth protest too much," she said with a chuckle.

"Whatever," I grumbled as I ran my tongue over the roof of my mouth.

"So what happened between you and Finn that had him in a dither to find you, and you leaving the party early, hmm?" She picked up her cheese Danish and nibbled around the edge. "The way you spark off him could light up the inside of a cave, so don't pretend something didn't happen."

Because I knew my friend well and I knew she wouldn't stop pushing until I gave her something, I went with a heavy sigh. She wrinkled her nose at me and rolled her hand in the universal gesture for "go on."

Pursing my lips, I shot her a narrow-eyed stare from which she didn't back down in the slightest, forcing me to give in.

"We went out onto the front porch where we didn't have to shout over the music and talked for a while."

"Talked, huh? Is that what the kids are calling it these days?" Over a bite of her Danish, she batted her lashes at me.

Throwing myself against the hard oaken back of my chair, I crossed my arms over my chest and glared at her. "We *talked*. That's all."

A picture of Finn, his T-shirt barely up to the task of covering his massive chest and shoulders, his sculpted arms on full display in the cool November evening, flashed through my brain. Heat rolled over me as I remembered how his suggestion to settle me in his lap had made my lady bits weep. Against my will, of course, because I absolutely was not interested in Finn McCabe in the same way Saylor was apparently interested in Fitz.

Nope. Nope. Nope.

"What did he say that made you leave the party early?"

I glanced around at the funky art on the wall beside our favorite table. This month's student display seemed to be bas-relief sculpture painted in colors completely at odds with the subject matter. Pepto-Bismol-pink paint dots splattered over a water buffalo head as it attempted to emerge from a pool of black water. Random lime-green, electric turquoise, and mouse-gray brushstrokes decorated a llama lounging on a couch. From my seat against the wall, I couldn't be sure if chartreuse and purple flames were revealing or consuming a pea-green rose. The art sort of mirrored my current mood, my intellect at odds with my emotions. Why did Finn McCabe even have to know Tory Miller, let alone know her well enough to exchange numbers and texts?

"It's more what he didn't say." This time I sipped my hot black coffee rather than gulped it. "Someone kicked Tory Miller and her entourage of wannabes out of the party."

"Yeah, that was Fitz. He wouldn't serve them beer, Tory threw a fit, and one of the other players—Dallas Cousins I think—invited them to leave." With a thoughtful expression, she sipped her drink. "Yeah, I'm pretty sure it was Dallas, 'cause the guy was as big as Fitz and could kind of shoo Tory and her girls along by being too massive for them to sneak past. So what didn't Finn say?"

"He didn't deny he'd invited Tory and her buddies to the party when she demanded the bouncer let them back in." I toyed with my scone then popped another bite into my mouth, chewed, and swallowed. "We'd actually been talking about Tory because she ruined what he was trying to start between us on Homecoming."

"What was he trying to start?" An impish grin lit up her face. "Because you had zero interest in him at all that night." She cleared her throat. "Like staring at him the whole time you were at the bonfire."

"What are you talking about? You weren't there."

"No, but Jamaica was, and she said it was pretty entertaining watching the two of you pretend to not be eye-fucking each other every chance you had."

Waving off her comment to avoid lending it any credibility, I continued. "Anyway, he told me he was listening to his roommates and cutting Tory off, but when push came to shove, he tried to play the middle. He didn't want to piss off his roommates by overruling them about letting underage people into the party, and he didn't want to piss off Tory by admitting he'd rather be with me and he shouldn't have invited her in the first place."

With a deep inhale and a slow exhale, I said the thing that had been eating at me since the scene on the front porch of Finn's place the night before. "I can't help wondering if he would have sneaked her and her friends back inside if I wasn't there. If he would have, I don't know, hung out with them."

"That's why you left early. Because Tory's scene forced Finn to choose, and apparently, he didn't." Saylor finished off her Danish, flicking crumbs from her fingers onto her plate before wiping her hands on her napkin.

"You say that like it's a bad thing." I couldn't help the tiny note of hurt that colored my words. "But you know what happened with her last year. You know how toxic and terrible she is."

"Yeah, but I've also seen her turn on the charm at frat parties. The girl knows how to flirt. If that isn't working, she flaunts her daddy's money." Saylor sat back in her hard oak chair and sipped her latte. "Men can be dense when it comes to a pretty woman giving them attention or promising them access to the club. Just sayin.'"

"That's not much of a recommendation for Finn then, is it?" I asked glumly.

"No, but his desperation to find you kind of is."

I spent the rest of the day holed up in my room working on a project for my quantum mechanics class. Usually, the calculations necessary to work through the problem absorbed me, but every time I came close to a solution, Finn's half-grin would flit through my head, or the bashful way he'd kicked his heel against his toe when he talked of being clueless about women or the hope in his eyes when he suggested I sit on his lap to stay warm, and I lost my train of thought. The man was effortlessly sexy in a shy way that drew me to him like the gravitational pull of a black hole.

As thoughts of him continued to interrupt my work, I snapped off the tip of my pencil against my paper, tearing a hole in the page that forced me to rewrite it in the neat standard my professor expected.

I growled at myself for my lack of focus.

Of course, that lack of focus might have had something to do with the fact I was wearing Finn's hoodie. Only after Axel and Drake dropped me off in front of Hanover last night did I clue in that I was still wearing it. Turtling down inside it now, I reveled in the scent of his woodsy cologne and *him*. It was all I could do to stop myself from sucking in the smell of him on the fabric when he dropped it over my head before we headed out to the porch. Giving myself away like that would have been a colossal disaster, especially with the way my evening with him had ended.

Still, I loved how big his hoodie was, how it covered me from my shoulders almost down to my knees. The fleecy inside was soft and snuggly against my skin. I had no idea how it felt to be held in Finn's arms, but in the moment, the next best thing was being wrapped in his clothes.

What was wrong with me?

He had a history with my archnemesis, one that appeared to be friendly at least, more than friends at worst.

The thought soured the coffee in my stomach.

Yet I continued to wear his hoodie right up until it was time to meet Jamaica for dinner before our weekly RA meeting with the dorm supervisor. When I returned to my room late in the evening, I glared at the piece of clothing draped over my desk chair. Yet it seemed I had no willpower when I caught a faint whiff of Finn's woodsy cologne. Slipping the offending item of clothing over my head, I reveled in its softness and the way it made me feel protected somehow.

Gathering my books, I flopped onto my bed to study . . .

. . . And awoke curled up in a little ball inside Finn McCabe's clothes when my alarm went off the next morning.

"Seriously, Chess?" I growled as I stared down at myself. "Seriously?"

I tugged the hoodie over my head and tossed it over the back of my desk chair, slipped on my bathrobe, grabbed my toiletries bag and towel, and headed to the shower. As I let the hot water sluice over my body, I chastised myself for my lack of self-control, my lack of focus. What was it about that one man that had me behaving like a lovestruck adolescent? Never had I worn a guy's clothes even when I was dating someone. No matter how hard I tried, I couldn't make sense of my attachment to that hoodie. It went beyond explanation.

"You okay, Chessly?" Hazel, a freshman on my floor, asked when I stepped out of the shower.

"Of course," I said, but the growl in my response sort of echoed in the tiled space of the community bathroom. No wonder she backed up. Toning it down, I added, "I'm just talking to myself. Don't mind me."

All the way back to my room I was shaking my head at my own ridiculousness. Somehow Finn McCabe had slipped under my skin. The question was, what was I going to do about it?

By the time I'd finished classes for the day, I had a plan. I'd bag up Finn's hoodie and give it to Jamaica to return to him the next time she went over to study with Callahan. But when I ran the idea past her when I met Saylor and her for coffee in the Union before Jamaica's shift at the Sweet Shop, she laughed.

"I heard all about how panicked Finn was after he got rid of Tory and her posse and came looking for you, only to discover you'd left the party." She blew over her coffee and sipped, her eyes sparkling as she traded glances with Saylor. "Whatever happened between you two that night, you're not hiding from it behind me. Especially not after all the grief you've given me about Callahan."

"Jamaica." I injected sternness into my tone. "For a guy who's always laser-focused on executing his assignment during any given play on the field, Finn is woefully indecisive."

My friends traded smirks, and Jamaica said, "That's specific."

"The other night at the party he had the choice between Tory and me. He didn't decide, which is a kind of a decision anyway. I left because I happened to catch Axel and Drake on their way out, and they said they'd give me a ride. I forgot I was still wearing Finn's hoodie until Drake pointed it out as I stepped out of Axel's car at the dorm." I blew out a breath. "It was a silly oversight—one that you can help me fix." I shot her puppy-dog eyes over the rim of my cup. "It's not a huge ask when you're over at their house all the time."

Resting her elbow on the table and planting her chin in her upturned palm, Jamaica shot Saylor an incredulous look. "Can you imagine the disappointment on Finn's face if I hand him his hoodie?"

Mimicking Jamaica's stance, Saylor shot back, "Poor guy. The wild-eyed way he came steaming into the kitchen looking for Chess had everyone feeling sorry for him." She shifted her gaze to me. "Now we're all on Team Finn." Sitting back against her chair, she grinned. "You, and only you, can return the clothes you pilfered from the guy." She shrugged. "Who knows? Maybe he's made the right decision by now."

Chapter Eight

Finn

ONE DAY INTO finals week and I was already getting my ass kicked. Not only did I have exams in every class—exams I had to take early since we'd missed home-field advantage with our midseason loss to the Lumberjacks—but also Coach dropped a new playbook on us during film yesterday. As if I needed another thing to study with molecular biology eating my lunch.

A sigh gusted out of me as I sat on the couch and stared at the game controllers resting on the coffee table. They reminded me of the *COD* rematch I wanted with Enriquè Simms. The guy was too damn cocky, even if he was the biggest asset on the basketball team this season. Didn't look like the rematch would happen until after we returned from Christmas break, what with us traveling to North Dakota for Saturday's semifinal and the basketball team playing a tournament in California over break.

Throwing myself against the cushions, I stared at the ceiling and admitted to myself what was truly bugging me. I hadn't seen, heard from, or heard about Chessly Clarke since that fiasco with Tory Miller following our last house party. Everything had been going well. I even had the idea she might let me warm her up on my lap if we stayed on the porch for a few minutes longer. Then Tory showed up and Chessly disappeared like a phantom in a puff of sweet-smelling smoke.

It made no sense why that girl had me twisted in knots. I hadn't even touched her, for fuck's sake. But something in the way her eyes danced as if she had a delicious secret she'd only share with someone special drew me in. Her snark made me laugh. Then I thought about her hot little compact body, and I squirmed to find a more comfortable position on the cushions. Chessly had it all going for her.

The way she'd sneaked glances my way at the bonfire gave me hope. When she'd given me a second chance at our post-game party a couple of weeks ago and sat with me on the front porch, I'd sensed I was making progress with her. I ground my back teeth together as I remembered how Tory had come along both times and cockblocked the shit out of me. 'Han and Bax were right: that particular jersey chaser was bad news with a capital "B." I'd just been slow to catch on.

Once again, instead of studying something—biology or football—I was thinking about a certain gorgeous physics major when the echoing chime of the doorbell nearly glued me to the ceiling. Scrambling to the foyer, I couldn't imagine who was dropping by at eight o'clock on the Monday night of finals week. I hadn't ordered any food, and none of my roommates were home. Without checking through the small window high up in the door, I jerked it open and blinked.

Did I conjure her with my thoughts?

"Chessly?"

"Hello, Finn." She shifted from foot to foot. "Um, I didn't

mean to keep this so long." Clearing her throat, she amended, "I didn't mean to keep this at all. But—"

A gust of wind swirled snow across my stocking feet, and I stepped back, opening the door wider. "It's freezing out there. Come in."

"I can't stay." She glanced over her shoulder at a car waiting at the curb. "The Uber driver is adding to my fare even now."

"I got it." I slid my feet into a pair of Hey Dudes sitting beside the door. Then in response to the question on her face, I reached for her hand and tugged her inside.

"Finn, I can't stay."

"You have something for me, so the least I can do is offer you some hot chocolate." Without giving her a chance to refute me, I bounded down the steps and out to the curb. When the driver lowered his window, I tugged my wallet from my pocket and handed him my debit card. He ran it through his machine, and I said, "Thanks, man," before tapping the roof of his car twice and jogging back up the walk to the house.

"Did you just send my ride away?" She blinked at me with a mixture of surprise and maybe annoyance.

"He doesn't need to wait out here while you tell me over hot chocolate what of mine you kept but didn't mean to." Gifting her my winningest smile I added, "Here—let me take your coat."

Instead, she handed me the plastic grocery bag containing the mystery item she said she'd kept from me. I dropped it on the floor at my feet and waited for her to unzip her coat.

"You're kind of pushy," she grumbled.

"I'm trying to be a good host by offering you a chance to warm up after coming all this way from the dorms." I let the corner of my mouth tip up and relaxed a fraction when she answered my half-grin with one of her own.

At last she pushed the hood off her head, revealing the cap of silky, honey-colored hair I was itching to run my fingers through.

After she unzipped her coat, I stepped behind her and tugged it back while she pulled her arms out of the sleeves. When I slipped past her to hang it in the foyer closet, I might have accidentally brushed my chest over her side. I mean, the foyer wasn't all that wide for a two people, especially when one of them was my size. The hitch in her breath told me she felt the same spark I did with that brief contact of our bodies.

"How do you like your hot chocolate? Plain or with marshmallows or with a shot of peppermint schnapps?" I asked as I led the way to the kitchen.

"With marshmallows."

I could almost feel her heat as she followed me in.

"But Finn, I don't need anything. Honestly. I only came by to return this because I thought you might need it when you travel to North Dakota this weekend."

When I reached up into the cupboard to grab a couple of mugs, out of the corner of my eye I caught her extending the plastic bag to me again. I set the mugs on the counter and took the bag from her. Pulling out one of my hoodies, I smiled. "You've had this since the Bulldogs after-party."

As Chessly stared at a spot on the counter behind me, her cheeks turned a pretty shade of pink. "Like I said. I didn't mean to keep it."

I tossed the hoodie over the back of a chair at the dinette in the corner of the kitchen and stuffed the plastic bag into the cupboard under the sink. "Don't worry. I have others." Busying myself with filling the reservoir on the coffee maker full of water, I said, "I kind of liked how you looked in it that night."

"Finn." She dragged my name out on a sigh.

"Facts is facts." I shot her a grin as I stepped around her to grab the tin of chocolate powder from the cupboard above the stove. I set it beside the mugs and spooned some into each. "Do you like your hot chocolate more or less sweet?"

It didn't surprise me when she said, "Less."

With a nod I added half a teaspoon of baking chocolate powder to each of our mugs. Showing off, I slipped the coffee pot from beneath the still brewing hot water and slid in a mug without making a mess. When the cup was full enough, I slid it back out and returned the pot to the warmer while I stirred the mix and added a handful of marshmallows to it.

Waggling my eyebrows, I smiled as I handed her the chocolate. "For you, milady."

She answered with an eye roll, but I caught the subtle upturn of her lips as she lifted the cup to them.

In short order, I fixed my own mug of chocolate and gestured for her to go ahead of me into the living room. It didn't escape me how she created more distance by tucking a foot under her ass and sitting so her knee jutted across the cushion between us. An awkward silence descended as we sat on opposite ends of the couch and sipped our drinks.

Chessly broke it. "This is really good. How did you learn to add straight cocoa powder to hot chocolate mix?"

I shrugged. "It's how my dad likes it."

Eyeing me over the rim of her mug, she asked, "What about your mom?"

"Two scoops of chocolate powder and a shot of peppermint schnapps." I shuddered at the thought. "I don't have a clue how she can drink it that sweet."

I liked the way her eyes warmed as she listened to my descriptions.

"What about your parents? Sweet or chocolatey?" I licked some marshmallowy foam from my lip.

All the playfulness that had replaced the awkwardness ran from the room. In trepidation, I watched her pull her shoulders in, protecting herself. For a long second, I thought she wouldn't answer.

"Dad only drinks black coffee." She held her mug in both hands in her lap, adding another layer of protection. "I remember Mom drinking hot chocolate with me when we'd have little winter parties on snowy days, just the two of us, but I don't remember how she liked it."

The waves of sorrow rolling off her pulled me to the middle of the couch where my thigh almost brushed her knee. "Chess?"

"I lost my mom when I was eight," came out on a whisper. Sad eyes found mine. "A car accident on an icy road."

"Jesus, Chessly. I'm so sorry."

Clearing her throat, she said, "It was a long time ago. I don't know why sometimes little things trip me up—like not remembering how she liked her hot chocolate."

A picture of my mom swatting my hand away from the cookie dough when I'd try to sneak some to go with my hot chocolate flashed through my head. "I can't imagine how hard it was growing up without your mom."

A wan smile crossed her mouth. "It was." Her smile warmed. "But Dad's done a good job at being both parents. He's pretty great, actually."

"It's just you and your dad? No sisters or brothers?"

"Just me and my dad." Her eyes dropped to where I was still running my palm over her knee and along the outside of her thigh. I pulled away as though I'd touched a hot stove.

"Sorry." I bumped my knuckles on the bottom of my mug, and chocolate dripped onto my jeans.

A touch of mischief quirked her smile as I brushed at my clothes.

"What about you? Brothers and sisters?"

"One sister. Nikki. She's a senior in high school and a royal pain in my ass whenever I go home."

"Why is she a pain? Did she take over your room or something?" Chessly's eyes danced.

"No. She's smarter than that. But she's totally clueless when it comes to guys." My fingers flexed around my mug. "She dates the dweebs who have no game whatsoever, guys who are going absolutely nowhere. It pisses me off that I have to run one of them off every time I go home."

Her brow shot up. "Overprotective much?"

"My sister's too good for any of the guys in her school—or in any of the schools in our area. She's so damn smart, and she has big ideas for how to run the farm—ideas my dad gives serious thought to."

Chessly's face lit up. "Your sister wants to run your family's farm?"

"Good thing too since I don't want to run it."

"A farm kid, huh?"

I nodded.

"But you didn't like it."

"I didn't say that." I set my empty mug on the coffee table. "The farm was a great place to grow up. And raising food for people is a noble thing to do."

"There's a 'but' in there."

"I feel like I can help more people as a cancer researcher." I shrugged. "After I play myself out in the pros." I draped my arm across the back of the cushions. "What about your dad? Is he a physics guy too?"

Her eyes rounded when I mentioned her major. Why she thought I wouldn't remember everything about our previous conversations was a mystery.

She chuckled. "In a manner of speaking. He owns a hardware store." Lifting her mug to her lips, she sipped more chocolate, and I had an overwhelming urge to learn how hot chocolate tasted on her mouth.

The way girls could make a drink last for days stymied me. The only reason mine had lasted for more than a minute was because we'd left the kitchen to sit in the living room.

"You don't want to run a hardware store?" I grinned. "Who's he going to pass it on to?"

"Probably Piper." An eye roll emphasized her dry tone.

I wrinkled my brow. "Your friend with the purple hair? The one Bax has a major hard-on for?" No matter how hard I tried, I couldn't see that girl within a hundred yards of a hardware store.

"She's job-shadowing my dad over break. It's going to be fun teaching her all about power tools."

"Did not expect that."

Her eyes took on a wicked twinkle. "What, that Piper wants to learn about power tools?"

I might have choked over the vision that suddenly popped into my head of Chessly in nothing but a shop apron brandishing a drill with that same look in her eyes.

She patted my hand where it rested on the cushion. "Are you all right?"

Her impish grin made me think she'd seen directly into my thoughts. My face heated, and I leaned forward to double-check for any last drops of hot chocolate in my mug resting on the coffee table.

"Out of chocolate." I managed to push past the frog in my throat.

Dialing up the naughtiness, she asked, "Talking about power tools really chokes you up, huh?" Her eyes strayed to my mouth, and it was my turn to grin.

"You have no idea."

For a long minute our gazes locked as electric heat sparked between us. I swear, if the lights were dimmed, it probably would have looked like fireworks shooting up from the couch.

Taking a chance, I reached for her mug, which she let go without a fight. Still holding her eyes, I set the mug aside on the table with one hand while I let my other hand drop off the back cushion to land lightly on the top of her shoulder. Slowly tracing the pad of my thumb over her collarbone, I said, "Seeing you on my doorstep made my night." Damn, her skin was so soft beneath my touch. "Thanks for coming over."

The hitch of her breath as I lightly stroked over her skin echoed in my groin.

"Sorry I kept your hoodie for so long," she whispered.

"No worries." My eyes snagged on her plump pink lips. "I liked seeing you in it."

I moved closer, and she let me.

"Chess?"

"Mmm?"

"I'd really like to kiss you right now."

"Okay."

"Yeah?"

A grin ghosted over her lips. Was she teasing me for trying to be a gentleman?

Sliding my hand up the side of her neck, I fingered the silky strands of her hair I'd longed to touch and leaned forward even as I pulled her toward me. We met in the middle, the scent of chocolate on our breaths wafting between us as I stared at her pretty mouth. The slight parting of her lips told me she wasn't teasing me at all. She wanted this kiss too.

Damn. I'd wanted to kiss her for so long, it was all I could do to slow my ass down, keep from doing my usual and jumping offsides. The last thing I needed was to move too fast and have Chess throw the penalty flag.

I brushed my mouth over hers. Electricity crackled between us at the barely-there touch that set my boxers on fire. Pulling back slightly, I caught her blink of surprise, which echoed my own. Again, I brushed my mouth over hers, adding more pressure, and she leaned into the kiss, pressing her lips to mine. The little hum coming from the back of her throat teased a smile from me, but then she fisted her hands in my shirt, hauling me closer, and in a nanosecond, things raced from teasing to serious.

Wrapping my arm around her waist, I pulled her front flush to mine. Taking a chance, I silently asked for another invitation. Running my tongue over the seam of her mouth, I tasted chocolate and sweet woman. When she opened for me, it was my turn to groan as our tongues tangled in a slide-and-glide, chase-and-retreat, nip-and-suck dance that tripped my heart into game speed. It pounded in my chest so hard she had to feel it. Her plush pink lips had been enticing me since the moment I set eyes on her. Having them under mine was as close to heaven as I'd ever come.

Blood roared in my ears as the world telescoped down to this moment with my mouth fused to Chessly's, her hands roaming over my shoulders and up to tug my hair, pebbling my skin. Without breaking the kiss, I slid my palms under her perfectly rounded ass and dragged her across the cushion to slide her beneath me. She flattened her generous breasts against my chest, and I tore my mouth from hers to lick and kiss the lovely column of her neck. She rewarded me with soft moans as she arched up and rubbed those full, round breasts over my pecs. Concentrating on her pleasure kept me from surging into her and giving my rock-hard dick some relief with dry-humping her soft center. Instead, I slid my thigh between hers, putting my weight on it so I didn't squish her into the couch, and nearly lost my shit when she started rubbing her jeans-covered pussy along it. From the feel of things, we were playing from the same playbook.

Her cultured alto voice drew me to her whenever she had something to say. When she moaned her pleasure at my kisses, her pretty tones resonated into me, revving my motor like no other woman had before. Forgetting myself, I gave her more of my weight, pushing her farther down into the cushions. She pushed back against me even as she tightened her arms around me. If we'd been skin to skin, we might have fused together.

I groaned with the ache in my balls and the wild pulse of blood surging through me as both of us deepened the kiss together. One glorious kiss from Chessly Clarke had turned me into a desperate man—one who needed to exert some control over himself to keep from ruining the moment.

Too bad I had no control over the chiming of the doorbell.

Chapter Nine

Chessly

"FINN." I PANTED as he dragged his firm lips up my neck. "There's someone at the door."

"Mmm. The someone already inside this house is the only someone I'm paying attention to right now." He nibbled his way along my jaw then captured my mouth with his masterful one.

How we'd gone from awkward staring to off-the-charts kissing flummoxed me even as I kissed him back with a hunger that would shock me if I stopped to let myself think about it.

Pressing myself into him, I buried my hands in his hair, reveling in the wiry texture of the thick waves and loving the way my curves molded to the hard planes of his chest. He sucked on my tongue, which sent waves of delicious heat through me to pulse in my core. I shifted beneath him in an attempt to close the distance between my hot center and the hardness straining behind the fly of his jeans.

The chimes of the doorbell echoed again

through the living room. Whoever was standing on the other side of the door was determined to gain entrance because this time they didn't let up on the ringer for a full thirty seconds. With a groan, Finn dropped his head on the soft side of the armrest. A soft "fuck" puffed from his lips as he labored to draw in breath.

"You can't ignore whoever it is—not with all these lights on." Glancing around at the three or four lamps scattered on side tables, all of them casting light into the room, I blinked. Before the incessant chiming of the doorbell, I hadn't noticed how bright the room was.

"Whoever it is, their timing sucks," he grumbled.

Such a big man sounding so put-out was kinda cute.

"Cute? I am manly, not cute, Miss Clarke," he informed me, his tone miffed.

Oops. Apparently, I said that out loud.

Laughter danced in his eyes.

"You're cute when you're being petulant," I countered with a grin.

The doorbell interrupted yet again, and he slid back and sat up, gently moving my legs to sit up too. His forlorn expression might have cracked me up except certain needy parts of me commiserated with it.

"Giant pain in my ass," he groused as he adjusted the front of his jeans.

It flattered me that he wasn't trying to hide his reaction to what we were doing. When I squirmed back into the corner of the couch where I'd been sitting earlier, the corner of his mouth quirked up. Apparently, he liked my response too.

The person on the other side of the door laid on the chimes once more, and Finn yelled, "Give it a rest, wouldja? I'm coming." Throwing a grin at me over his shoulder, he said, "Not the way I'd like to be though."

At his words, my eyebrows tried to climb up to my hairline.

His presumption should have irritated me. After all, we weren't even on a date.

Except the evening had sort of started feeling like a date, what with the hot chocolate and conversation—and his sizzling-hot kisses. My body buzzed with the memory of him against me.

When he opened the door, cold air and the sound of high-pitched feminine voices rushed into the house, freezing my libido in a nanosecond.

"Finn! Hi, Finn! We brought you presents."

"We baked all afternoon to give you treats for finals."

"We brought your favorites."

The voices were familiar—and unwelcome. Whoever these girls were, they knew much more about Finn than I did. The guy didn't have a reputation as a player, but I imagined having the adoration of so many people on campus was quite a temptation. And Finn was a guy, a football player no less. It wouldn't surprise me to discover he collected women like he collected game stats.

"Uh, we didn't ask for anything," I heard him say, confusion in his tone.

The group of girls surrounded him as he took a plastic container of what must be his "favorite" cookies. For a fleeting second, I wondered what kind he liked best, but before I could pursue the thought, a freshman I recognized as living in Hanover caught sight of me.

"Hey, aren't you supposed to be in the dorms enforcing quiet hours for finals or something?" she asked.

No wonder the voices sounded familiar. Tory Miller's little band of mean girls had invited themselves over to the football house. I had no business being irritated with them—after all, I'd done the same thing when I showed up unannounced to return Finn's hoodie. But at least I hadn't arrived expecting to stay let alone end up on the couch kindling fires with kisses hot enough to leave scorch marks on my tongue. From the provocative way a couple of these girls were dressed and how they were watching him with calculating eyes, I could tell their plans for Finn's evening included more than sharing cookies.

Deliberately keeping my tone even, I asked, "Hmm, isn't this your first finals week? You should probably be taking advantage of those quiet hours in the dorms."

One of the girls hanging toward the back of the little group of four fidgeted uncomfortably. I recognized her from Jamaica's floor—Penelope, I thought. Clearly, this trip to the football party house wasn't her idea. No doubt she was peer-pressured into coming over by the loud one staring at me from the other side of the couch.

"We studied while the cookies baked," she simpered.

"Of course you did." It was all I could do to hold my gaze steady on hers rather than let loose the epic eye roll her response required.

"It's real nice of you to bring these over, but Chessly has a point—" Finn began but he was interrupted by someone new walking through the front door.

"Hey, Finn. Did you forget our no-party rule for the week before a semifinal game?" Bax asked as he hung up his coat in the closet.

"This isn't a party. I didn't even know these ladies were coming over until they laid on the doorbell."

Finn's tone was defensive, and I almost felt sorry for him, except he'd done nothing about the girl who'd glued herself to his side during this entire exchange. I didn't know if he'd invited the girls over and then forgot when I showed up or if he thought we could all hang out together or what, but their arrival reminded me of the way he chose Tory over me the last time I was here.

The ensuing discussion gained in decibels as the girls insisted they were only offering a much-needed study break. While they pled their case, I fired off a quick text, uncurled myself from the corner of the couch, grabbed our empty mugs, and returned them to the kitchen. After a quick detour to the bathroom down the hall from the living room, I returned to catch the simpering girl giggling and Finn chuckling as she fed him a cookie.

Yep. Time for me to go.

I'd just reached for my jacket after stuffing my feet into my boots when, apparently, he caught on.

"Chess? Hey! You're leaving?"

"This bunch"—I nodded to the girls standing around him in the living room—"reminded me I have a job to do and finals to prepare for." I zipped up my jacket and pulled my gloves from a pocket. "Thanks again for loaning me your hoodie."

He stepped away from the cookie queen. "You don't have to go right now." The pleading in his tone, coupled with a kind of desperation in his eyes, gave me pause.

Then the girl who'd clearly staked her claim on him slipped her arm through his and pulled him close to her side. "Let her go, big guy. We don't need the fun police here."

"Looks like you had other plans that I interrupted." *Fun police, my ass.* Headlights flashed through the window by the door, alerting me to my ride's arrival. "Good luck this weekend, Finn." Glancing past his shoulder, I added, "Bax. Hope you guys start the New Year playing in the national championship."

"Chessly."

I thought I heard a hint of begging in Finn's tone, but he'd yet to shrug out of the clingy girl's hold, so I dismissed it.

"Merry Christmas." I leveled a glance at their linked arms. "Looks like you're starting early." On that parting shot, I jerked open the door and stepped out into the freezing December air.

My Uber was idling at the curb, and I all but ran down the sidewalk to it. As I buckled myself in, some masochistic part of me had me gazing back at the house where I saw Finn standing alone in the open front door. It was monumentally unfair for him to be so damn handsome and to kiss like a man possessed. My mouth still tingled from his kisses. But the evidence proved I wasn't the only woman he enjoyed sharing himself with. In fact, the rather indiscriminate way he spread himself among all the girls told me he understood his major quite well. He had biology and chemistry down pat. Unfortunately, over the last . . . however long I'd been at his house, I'd verified the experiment.

I wanted to lie to myself and say my contribution to his extra-curricular bio-chem fun was inadvertent. My sole aim in dropping by was to return his hoodie. But in the deep recesses of my heart, I couldn't avoid the truth: I'd wanted to see him again, spend time with him. Not only was he athletic and gorgeous, but he was also smart, articulate, and funny. A little awkward too, which was what I think I liked best about him. As much as I hated to admit it, that night at the party was some of the most fun I'd had since I started at Mountain State—at least until Tory Miller ruined it.

From the way I'd left things at Finn's house, she still had her golden claws firmly snagged in the football team even when she wasn't around. She'd trained her entourage of wannabes well. Of course, it helped that they'd set their sights on a player who liked their company and obviously didn't have much in the way of good taste. I had nothing against women showing off their assets—fashion was all about that. What I struggled with was women who thought their bodies were all they had to offer, which was a notion they shouted with their clothing choices.

The clingy girl had paired a plunging V-neck crop top with a leather skirt that barely skimmed the bottom of her butt. Her thigh-high pleather boots were probably the only thing keeping her warm. Even I couldn't ignore the nips-up situation her thin knit top had revealed in the cold air when she walked into the house without a jacket.

A second wannabe, who'd set her sights on Bax the second he walked through the door, appeared to have appropriated someone's cheerleader uniform: a short, tight skirt and a sleeveless crop top. In the generous light of the room, I'd noticed the goosebumps covering her bare legs, which explained her fidgeting. Or possibly her nerves were the problem because Bax had appeared less than thrilled with their rendezvous. At least one of the men had good sense. Plus, from the way he acted in Stromboli's the night of the party, Bax had a serious thing for my friend Piper.

Like the snow swirling in the streetlights, my thoughts churned as the Uber driver carefully navigated the slick streets. Dropping my head back against the seat, I stared at the ceiling of the car.

Cripes. I absolutely did not want to be attracted to Finn McCabe. Not one little bit. I'd thought returning his hoodie would help me expunge thoughts of him from my mind. Then he turned on the sweet with the hot chocolate and what I'd believed in the moment to be honesty. So I'd done the monumentally stupid thing and kissed him.

My body had betrayed me as I gave myself over to his touch. I'd never experienced anything before that felt as right as Finn's big body pushing me into the cushions of the couch. The raw voltage that arced through me when he set his lips on mine had left me soaking wet. My face heated as I thought about the shameless way I'd rubbed myself against him.

I was no different from the girls who dropped by to deliver cookies—among other things, apparently. My excuse was his hoodie, and I'd dressed in jeans and a sweater rather than a boobalicious crop top and short skirt. Otherwise, I hadn't behaved a whole lot differently from the troupe of freshman girls who'd descended on his doorstep behind me. Only after the jersey chasers arrived did I discover Finn's true colors. He liked the attention of all the girls, indiscriminately. I'd deluded myself for a minute into believing I was different from girls like Tory and her wannabes. The sigh that escaped me was one of pure self-disgust.

"Hey, I'm not trying to rip you off." The driver glared in the rearview. "The roads are super slick, so I'm being careful."

"That was aimed at me, not you." I apologized. "Take your time."

Finn came off as such a decent guy, if a bit clueless around women, but that was an act. He knew exactly what he was doing to keep women coming around, bringing all manner of treats, from cookies to kisses. All my life I'd prided myself on my self-control and ability to think rationally. One kiss from Finn had tossed all that pride right off the top of world to splat on the sidewalk in front of his house as I'd all but run away from the scene of the crime. Disgust roiled through me at the way I'd behaved.

My plan had been to drop off the hoodie, hop back in the waiting Uber, and return to my neatly ordered world—the one that would now be free of annoying distractions, like a certain sexy lineman. But when he opened the door, one look at his handsome face and those shoulders that filled his T-shirt right up, and I lost all common sense.

Instead of expunging him from my thoughts, I'd made it so much worse because now I knew exactly how his body pressed to mine could light me up. I knew exactly how his kisses could send lust molecules crashing through my blood. I knew exactly how the groaning sounds he made as I ran my fingers through his hair reverberated deep in my core.

I loved science—the experimentation, the principles, the behind-the-scenes information on how the world worked. But tonight I'd learned why the universe withheld certain secrets. Like what kind of chemistry I shared with a certain football player.

I was such an idiot.

Chapter Ten

Finn

AS I GINGERLY dropped my gear onto the floor of my bedroom, I did my damnedest to ignore my body. After the thrashing we'd received at the hands of the Buffaloes in the semifinal game yesterday, I was a walking bruise. No one on the team wanted to spend one more minute than necessary in North Dakota, so by unanimous vote, we'd loaded the buses and headed home directly after our crushing defeat.

Without the benefit of an ice bath and some light stretching after that beat-down, every part of me hurt. Eight hours on a bus had certainly contributed to the soreness, but more of it was in my head. The resounding silence on the ride home said every person on the bus, from the coaches to the players to the managers was struggling with our loss. Bax boarded right ahead of Coach Ellis wearing one of his more obnoxious T-shirts rather than required dress attire, and Ellis didn't even blink. That was how poorly we responded to the biggest loss of our careers.

The drive from the facility to the house in

Callahan's pickup wasn't any better. Without a word, my three roommates and I had loaded up and driven home, each of us peeling off to our rooms without even saying good night—or good morning, as it were, since we were closer to Sunday than Saturday. Coach gave us the rest of Christmas break off, telling us we'd watch film when we returned. As if watching that season-ending disaster was any way to start the new semester.

All the silence left me with too much time to think. What I should have been thinking about, of course, was how I could have played harder, made more of an impact in the game. What I was actually thinking about was how I'd totally whiffed it with Chessly—again—when she handed me my big chance with her on the night she returned my hoodie. Until the fucking doorbell rang, I'd managed to do everything right—offer her a snack, have a conversation, take my cues from her—which had landed me in the glorious position of kissing the hell out of her.

Then that pack of jersey chasers had arrived with their cookies and their fawning all over me, and I didn't know how to push them away without being rude. Of course, they didn't have any trouble being rude to Chessly and making themselves at home without an invitation. By the time I'd clued in and got my act together, Chess was leaving without a backward glance. I didn't have to be Einstein to know what she thought.

If she'd stuck around for even five more minutes, she'd have witnessed a master class in sending jersey chasers packing. At the start of the semester, Bax was as enthusiastic about all the attention as I was, but since hooking up with his purple-haired hottie—Chessly's friend no less—he'd run out of patience with girls who followed the football team around like it was their job. Throw in the mess Tory Miller had made for Callahan at the end of the semester, and Bax's patience with them had dropped to less than nonexistent. After the debacle with Chess who I'd been wanting to know better for months, I finally figured it out.

About five minutes too late.

Supposedly, with knowledge came power. One night with her had taught me that despite appearances, Chess was no delicate china doll. The strength and resilience of her limbs as she'd wrapped her arms around me and run her heels up and down my hamstrings and the backs of my calves had turned me on like no other woman. The way she'd rubbed her torso along mine said that rather than intimidating her, my size turned her on. The way she'd kissed me back with those whimpers in the back of her throat as her plush lips pressed urgently to mine drove all rational thought from my head. Discovering how well we fit together, how much we turned each other on with only kissing—I mean shit, I didn't even try to palm her tits or slip a hand between her legs—had left me powerless to think of anything other than Chessly Clarke.

That girl had turned me inside out from the second I laid eyes on her. But after striking out with her twice, I didn't have a clue how to make her see I hadn't initiated any of what happened with Tory Miller and the other jersey chasers. It was just bad timing.

Pinching the bridge of my nose, I shook my head. Bad timing seemed to be my thing this year. All by myself I'd given the Buffaloes twenty free yards at critical moments in the game. Their stadium had lived up to its hype as the 12th man, the noise of the fans drawing me offsides multiple times. By the fourth time the refs called me for it, I thought Bax was going to tackle me to the turf rather than go after their running back. No doubt Coach was planning an earful about it when we watched film after break.

Fan-fucking-tastic.

With far more effort than the situation called for, I dropped my dress pants to the floor and pulled on a pair of sweats. I sucked in air as fire licked across my shoulders and down my arms as I shrugged out of my dress shirt and tugged a hoodie over my head. When I stepped out into the hall to hit the head and maybe scare up a bottle of ibuprofen, I heard soft giggles and sighs coming from behind 'Han's closed door. Guess he had company to ease the pain of the semifinal loss. Jamaica's brand of TLC probably worked better than the kind I sought from pain meds.

I closed my eyes as the phantom touch of Chessly's fingertips digging into my shoulders when I'd pinned her to the couch flitted over me. What I wouldn't give to feel her soft body against mine right about now. Dragging my ass into the can, I found a half-full bottle of pain reliever in the medicine cabinet, thank fuck. After downing three tablets and chasing them with a couple of handfuls of water—apparently, the last guy to clean the bathroom hadn't returned the cup we kept by the sink—I wandered back to my room, closed the door, and flopped down onto my bed.

With the way the past week had ended, I thought sleep would elude me. Then my alarm was blaring from somewhere in the middle of my room. Groggily, I located the offending device in the pocket of my pants in a heap on the floor, shut it off, stood, and took stock. Soreness was the order of the day, but at least I could move with some semblance of ease. Good thing too since I had a four-hour drive home after I dropped Bax at the airport.

My plan for a hot shower to soothe away some of the soreness shot straight to hell when Bax stepped out of the steamy bathroom right as I walked into the hall. With a sigh, I headed downstairs instead. The old Victorian we called home came with some perks—like generously sized bedrooms and a downstairs big enough to throw the kind of rager that had made our house famous on Jock Street—but what it lacked was a hot water heater big enough to accommodate four football players who needed twenty-minute showers after games.

Soft feminine laughter alerted me that Callahan and Jamaica were in the kitchen. Rather loudly clearing the morning cobwebs from my throat, I alerted them to my presence a couple of steps before I walked through the doorway.

Callahan glanced away from mooning over his girlfriend where they sat at the breakfast table. "Morning, Finn. Got a stack of pancakes warming in the oven."

"Thanks," I mumbled as I pulled a mug from the cupboard and filled it with steaming coffee.

"You're kind of quiet today, Finn," Jamaica said.

"Losing that game took all the fun out of Christmas," I said. After a fortifying slug of hot caffeine, I grumped at my roommate. "Doesn't seem to be bothering you much."

Jamaica rolled her eyes. "It's a football game, Finn. Not the end of the world."

Turning my head from side to side and rolling my shoulders, I shot back, "Sure feels like it."

Callahan laughed. "Bax skipped breakfast to beat you to the shower."

My eyebrows went up. "Is that right?"

Without another word, I snagged a plate from the cupboard and loaded it with five pancakes from the stack warming in the oven. I parked my ass at the table and proceeded to slather butter over the steaming stack before dousing it with half a bottle of maple syrup. Two minutes later, I was back at the oven for seconds, mounding my plate with another five pancakes.

Feeling her stare, I glanced up into Jamaica's wide eyes. "What?" I asked around a bite of fluffy buttermilk deliciousness.

With a long blink, she shook her head. "Callahan spent more than a minute making those. Did you even taste them?"

Gifting her a closed-mouth grin, I winked and swallowed. "They're to die for. Too bad Bax is going to miss out."

'Han took a turn shaking his head. "You're a piece of work, Finnegan." He walked his and Jamaica's plates over to the dishwasher. "You coming back by the house after you drop Bax at the airport?"

"Nah. I'll head north after I drop him off. I think Danny's sticking around to close up the house for Christmas." I finished off my second plate of breakfast and was contemplating a third when Bax strolled into the kitchen.

Without a word, he headed to the oven to discover I'd left him three pancakes. Glaring, he said, "Really, Finn? Really? Why don't you help yourself to all the food someone else cooked?"

"Hey, if you hadn't hogged all the hot water, I wouldn't have come downstairs to find breakfast in the oven." I slugged back the dregs of my coffee then walked my plate and cup to the dishwasher. "Sucks to be you."

Growling, "Fuck you!" Bax grabbed a dishtowel off the handle on the oven and snapped it at me. Forgetting how much my back still ached, I arched away from his weapon and covered my wince with a laugh as I raced out of the kitchen.

Once I was out of sight, I clamped my hand over my lower back and caught a breath before walking up the stairs. By now the water heater should have reloaded enough for me to enjoy at least ten minutes of heavenly heat. Right as I reached the landing, I caught Danny sliding into the bathroom and closing the door.

"Fuck," I muttered as I veered across the hallway to my bedroom. A hot shower did not seem to be part of my immediate future.

Resignedly, I dragged my duffel bag onto my bed and started filling it with clothes I'd need for a few days back on the farm with the fam. By the time I'd finished packing, I heard Danny head back to his room. With a long-suffering sigh, I took my turn, lathering quickly in the lukewarm spray and praying the gremlins in the basement didn't turn the water to ice-cold before I could rinse off.

The plus of not enjoying a hot shower was I that couldn't succumb to X-rated thoughts of a certain blonde with endless blue eyes who kissed like an angel and moved like the devil.

Or not.

Jesus. Even with cold water sluicing down my back, my dick perked right up at the memory of Chessly's sighs as I'd trailed kisses along her jaw and down the satiny column of her neck. I loved the beauty and symmetry of a perfect reaction, the fizz and pop or the changing of color or scent that denoted chemistry in action. What happened between that girl and me on the couch the other night had been pure chemistry. The way our bodies had heated, the pink flush on her skin, the way the taste of her mouth had morphed from chocolate-and-marshmallow to dark feminine deliciousness in the space of a kiss. Pure chemistry.

Lusty thoughts of gliding skin on skin with a certain smoke show of a physics major left me hard enough to drill concrete. Bracing one hand on the wall at the back of the shower, I wrapped my other hand around myself and—

"Fuuuck!"

Glacial water poured from the shower head, washing away my hard-on in an instant.

I might have emitted several more yelps as I swatted at the controls, missing a few times before I finally ended the water torture I should have anticipated. *Would* have anticipated if a certain woman hadn't distracted my thoughts for about the thousandth time since we met. When I stepped out of the shower, I heard Baxter's laughter ringing outside the bathroom door.

"Sucks to be you, Finnegan."

"Asshole."

But I smiled to myself. Hard not to smile when I had Chessly on my mind. In the scheme of things, I'd won. While I might have endured a substandard shower, I'd enjoyed all the breakfast. Doubt Bax had left even a crumb for that other hot water hog, a.k.a. Danny.

A few minutes later, we gathered in the front foyer to say our goodbyes for Christmas break. That was when Callahan and Jamaica dropped the news that they'd be spending the holiday meeting each other's parents. Behind their backs, Baxter shot me a cross-eyed headshake, but it was all for show. I saw how he'd panted after Piper when we were at Stromboli's last week.

I could relate.

"Meeting the parents, huh? That's kinda serious, ain't it?" I asked as I shrugged into my fleece-lined jean jacket.

"When you know, you know," Callahan said, slinging an arm around Jamaica and pulling her close to his side. "Maybe someday when you give up jersey chasers, you'll see for yourself, Finn."

His tone was all Mr. Rogers patient, and I bared my teeth at him. Bax snorted, and I flipped him the bird.

"Touchy, touchy," he said. At 'Han's questioning brow, Bax added, "I'll tell you all about what went down last Monday when we come back from break." He hitched his duffel bag over his shoulder and joined me at the front door. "Behave yourselves, and don't go getting engaged or some other craziness before you come back."

Jamaica sucked in a tiny gasp, and I glanced at Callahan, who remained stoic except for a tiny tug at the corner of his mouth.

Well, fuck me. If someone had said at the beginning of the semester that one of us in the house would be entertaining thoughts of marriage by the end of it, I would have called bullshit. From the looks of things, I would have lost that bet.

"Did not see that one coming," Bax said as I drove him to the airport.

"Yeah. I didn't think any of us would graduate with a lady in tow. It's bad business when your focus is the pros." I wheeled us through the roundabout a block from our neighborhood and headed down the straight shot to the airport.

"Depends on the lady."

Something in his tone snagged my attention, and I slid him a side-eye. Bax stared out the windshield, but I had the distinct impression he wasn't seeing the passing scenery.

"Chessly's friend has you by the balls, does she?" I chortled at my own joke even as my own pair drew up a little at the sound of her name on my lips.

"She's Jamaica's friend too." He aimed a speculative look at me—one I studiously ignored as I focused on the road. "What the hell were you thinking inviting a bunch of jersey chasers to the house the same night you were entertaining a real woman?"

"For the thousandth time, I didn't invite any of those girls—Chessly included. I was home alone, minding my own business when they showed up out of the blue." Gripping the steering wheel, I willed myself not to rise to the bait. "But I get it. Jersey chasers are bad news."

Settling back against the seat, Bax blew out a breath. "We're a pair, Finnegan. 'Han is so much smoother with women than we are. It's a surprise to see him settling down with someone. You and I are lucky if Piper and Chessly even give us the time of day." He shot me a shit-eating grin. "'Course, after last Monday night, you'll be lucky If you ever see Chessly again."

"Fuck you, Bax."

Out of the corner of my eye, I caught his shrug, which only added to the sinking feeling his reminder gave me.

We were silent for the rest of the ride to the airport. After I dropped him off, I pointed my rig north, cranked up some Drake, and tried to focus my mind on what awaited me at home for Christmas: Mom's incredible food, chores with Dad, and razzing the shit out of my sister, Nikki. But every other mile I caught myself wondering how a certain gorgeous physics major with a smart mouth and all my attention would be spending the holidays.

Chapter Eleven

Chessly

"I'M SO HAPPY you decided to spend the holidays with me. Not to say working at Dad's store is boring"—I slid a glance in my dad's direction as he straightened some tools on a nearby shelf—"but it's much more interesting with you here." I grinned at Piper and touched a finger to the deep purple strands intermingling with her chestnut hair. "The locals apparently go for color."

"Nah. They like testing the new girl."

"Speaking of, did you read up on power tools or something before you arrived?" Crossing my arms over my apron, I leaned against the counter beside the cash register and regarded my friend.

With a shrug she said, "I'm earning credits for this internship with your dad, so I thought I'd better know something about hardware stores." Glancing over her shoulder at my dad and back to me, she added in a conspiratorial whisper, "Plus I wanted to impress him before I wreck his good opinion of me when I corrupt you tonight."

I laughed. "Good luck with that. The Elk Horn isn't exactly a hot spot for debauchery, even on the biggest party night of the year."

"How would you know?" she challenged.

"It's the only place in town that serves food after eight. The entire high school hung out there after ball games on the weekends. They're supposed to kick the kids out at ten, but no one ever checks." Pulling my phone from my pocket, I noted we only had to wait about fifteen minutes before we could flip the "open" sign on the front door to "closed."

Dad walked over to the cash register where Piper and I were talking. As though sensing my thoughts about closing, he said, "Why don't you two call it a night? I doubt we're going to have a rush between now and closing time, seeing as it's New Year's Eve." He gave a little chuckle. "Unless someone without a plunger overflows a toilet tonight."

I shot him a look from beneath my brows. "A visual we did not need, Dad."

His grin only grew.

Shaking my head with a tiny grin of my own, I untied the back of my shop apron and lifted it over my head to fold and stow it on the shelf beneath the register. Following my lead, Piper removed her apron, folded hers much more neatly, and laid it on top of mine.

Dad pulled a couple of twenties from his wallet and handed them to me. "Pick up some pizza on your way home—and save me a slice."

As I took the money, I stood on my toes and kissed his stubbly cheek. "Thanks, Dad. We'll save you two—maybe three." I winked, and he winked back. "The usual?"

"Sure, unless Piper isn't a fan."

My dad in a nutshell: considerate of everyone. No doubt that consideration was what had ensured a thriving business in our small town despite the lure of online retailers offering cheaper prices.

"What's the usual?" Piper asked as we headed back to the break room to retrieve our coats and purses.

"Pepperoni and jalapeño with extra cheese."

"Mmm, sounds delicious. Hope you're picking up two pies."

We walked out the back of the store into the frosty last-day-of-December air, both of us drawing our collars up to our chins. Piper wore a gorgeous gray cashmere scarf and a matching beret, while I snuggled my cheeks lower into my standard knit Wildcats muffler. Our breaths hung in the air as we hustled over to my dad's old pickup.

I fired up the engine, but we had to wait a few minutes for the ancient truck to warm up before I could put it in gear. Gauging my friend's reaction to our vehicle—after all, she drove a new Camaro to deliberately piss off her corporate-raider dad who'd offered her a BMW SUV—I blinked at the dreamy-eyed expression on her face. *Huh.* Who would have guessed she liked old pickups?

Dad liked to walk to work—said the exercise kept his head clear. By the time he'd closed up the shop and arrived home, we'd demolished one pizza and were one slice each into the second.

"Did you leave me any dinner?" he asked as he hung up his coat on a peg by the back door.

"Barely." I set what was left of my piece on my plate and licked my fingers. "Good thing you made it home when you did."

All through dinner Piper and I giggled over the way old Mr. Rehnquist had kept staring at her hair as she helped him find some calk for his leaky shower. "That color exists in nature?" he'd finally asked. "It does. See?" She'd tilted her head to show him her roots, which of course were purple since she'd seen her cosmetologist between final exams. "Be damned. Never seen anything like that." He'd grabbed his tube of calk, paid for it, and tottered out of the store, shaking his head and muttering to himself. I'd almost wrecked myself at the time trying not to laugh. Now my stomach hurt from laughing through the retelling.

Dad's eyes twinkled. "Talking about old Rehnquist, huh?" He settled himself in his chair and slid a slice onto the plate I'd set for him. "The old guy needs a plumber, not another tube of calk, but he says he can buy a lot of calk for what a plumber would cost him." With a shrug he smoothed his napkin over his lap and picked up his slice. "Far be it from me to tell him how to spend his money."

"Even though you've mentioned the names of a plumber or two to him, I bet." I sat back in my chair and eyed what was left of dinner on my plate.

"You can't force someone to see sense." Shifting his attention to my friend, he added, "Made it easy for you to have some fun with the old fella."

"Couldn't help it, sir," Piper said, her eyes dancing. "With as hard as he was staring at my hair, I worried he might change the color with his eyes alone."

A snort escaped Dad's lips, and my friend and I grinned at each other across the table.

"It's been a pleasure working with you, Piper. I gotta admit, when Chessly first proposed the idea of you interning with me, I thought I was getting some free help over the last rush of the holidays." He bit into his slice, chewed thoughtfully, and swallowed. "But you have a great business mind. Starting the day after tomorrow, I plan to implement several of your ideas for streamlining my inventory. Thank you."

"Truthfully, Mr. Clarke, I've learned more from you in a week than I've learned in the past two semesters of business classes." Piper set her plate aside, the crust of her last slice going uneaten.

At her compliment, Dad beamed. "So what are you girls' plans for tearing it up tonight to ring in the New Year?"

I rolled my eyes. "Kinda hard to tear anything up at the Elk Horn, Dad."

"Oh, I don't know. I heard Buzzy asked Shane to bring in his karaoke machine tonight. 'Course, all the caterwauling that will encourage might scare the New Year away from arriving." He chuckled at his own joke.

Speculation gleamed in Piper's eyes. Didn't take a genius to know what my friend was thinking.

"Caterwauling will about cover it if we join the singing," I said.

Dad grinned.

"We'll duet." Piper winked. "And we'll probably be asked for an encore."

I snorted. "There's a reason why you've never heard me sing."

"It's not that bad, honey," Dad said, but he didn't make eye contact.

Glancing across the table at my friend, I said, "My singing is so bad my third grade teacher asked me to be the choir manager for our annual Christmas pageant. I handed all the singers their props and didn't sing a note, even in practice."

"Okay, I'll sing, and you can be my backup dancer."

Dad and I exchanged a smirk.

"That's going to be a whole lot better," I said. "Not."

"Depends on how much alcohol we enjoy before the big event."

Before I could ask, Dad jumped in. "Yes, I'll drive you and pick you up."

I stood to walk my plate over to the sink, stopping to drop a kiss on Dad's cheek on my way by. "Thanks, Dad. You're the best."

"You weren't kidding about how rustic this place is," Piper said as her eyes took a tour of Harlo's "hot spot." She stepped toward the bar to check out the liquor selection on display. "It's cute though. I like it. They even stock my favorite vodka."

Since it was only ten o'clock, the bar wasn't too crowded. Not that I thought a crowd would show up. In the corner of the room to the left of the bar, Shane had set up his karaoke equipment on the tiny triangular dais where bands were said to have played back in the day, like maybe when my parents first moved to Harlo. I couldn't remember a live band playing at the Elk Horn.

Several unoccupied barstools meant we could have our pick. Piper being Piper chose two in the center, directly in the line of sight of the front door.

"Is it necessary for us to be so conspicuous?" I asked as I took my time removing my jacket and draping it over the back of my stool.

"You don't want to sit here? Because these seats guarantee great service."

Her excuse didn't fool me for a second. "Trust me. No one worth impressing is going to walk through that door tonight."

She smiled indulgently at me and called the bartender over to order her usual lemon drop martini. I ordered a beer and settled into my seat.

"This week has been so much fun. Way better than spending it with my family in Aspen," she said as the bartender set our drinks in front of us. Color filled her cheeks. "That sounded bad. I truly enjoyed spending time with you and your great dad."

"Even more than skiing in Aspen?" I deadpanned.

"Don't worry, I'm not missing out. I signed up for a ski class for a PE credit. Between that and weekends, I'll manage lots of time on the slopes this winter." She winked. "I learned so much in the store, and I had a plausible excuse for avoiding my family during the holidays. Win-win." She clinked her glass to my bottle. "Thanks again for letting me crash your break."

I clinked my drink to hers again. "Thanks for making the break way more fun than usual."

Shane interrupted on his mic. "Happy New Year! Time to get this party started. First up is Max Robinson singing Jelly Roll's 'Need a Favor.'"

"It's about to get even more fun," my friend said. The cryptic tone of her voice put my guard right up.

I narrowed my gaze at her. "I'm going to do everyone in this bar a huge favor and *not* sing tonight. Trust me."

With a coy smirk, she lifted her drink to her lips. "We'll see."

Piper opened a tab and refused to let me pay for a single drink. That open tab also meant I never went without a fresh beer in front of me. By 11:30 p.m. the bar was more crowded than I'd ever seen it. Guess word had spread about the purple-haired wild woman entertaining at the Elk Horn, and everyone in town had come to see.

Truth be told, my friend couldn't sing much better than me, but what she lacked in talent she more than made up for in enthusiasm, taking the entire bar along with her for the ride. The night felt like all the nights we'd spent with Jamaica and Saylor when we were freshmen goofing off in the dorms, and before I knew it, I'd agreed to sing with her. Good thing everyone knew the words to "Don't Stop Believin'" so we didn't end up singing it alone.

By midnight she'd talked me into dancing on the tabletops. Why Buzzy put up with that nonsense, I have no idea, but boy howdy, was it fun. Max was back singing again, I swear he sang for half the night, but at least he had a decent voice. I think I remembered him singing in the high-school choir. Anyway, he was belting Luke Bryan and Blake Shelton drinking songs, which made it easy to take the party up a level.

Piper and I cracked up at my bad joke, and that was when I caught Stan Wellington trying to sneak a peek up my skirt. I don't know what he thought he going to see with me wearing leggings, but that move reminded me why turning him down for every date he'd asked for in high school proved I had a strong sense of self preservation.

"Don't you know it's never a good idea to drink and text?" I asked Piper when I hopped off the table and caught her in the act. "What did Saylor and Jamaica think of my mad dance moves?"

"I wasn't texting them." A pretty shade of rose rode her high cheekbones.

With narrowed eyes I asked, "Who were you texting?"

"Um, Wyatt."

"Wyatt? As in, Wyatt Baxter? Wait, when did that happen? Never mind." I snorted. "Did you share our incredible singing with him?"

She laughed. "No—our stellar dance moves."

Grinning, I linked arms with her. "Bet he's glad you finally gave him your number so he could enjoy that."

About then, Stan made his move. Dropping his arms over both of our shoulders, he said, "The countdown to midnight starts in a minute. Which of you lucky ladies is getting the first kiss?"

"Do you play football for the MSC Wildcats?" Piper's words dripped saccharine—something a smart man would have picked up on and backed away from. Slowly.

Stan had never been known for catching on to subtlety.

"I'm a machinist. I work for a living."

Piper stepped out from beneath his arm, turned, and patted him on the chest. "Good for you, sugar. But we only kiss Wildcats." Giving him a little push, she added, "You'd better hurry if you're going to find a soulmate before the clock strikes midnight."

"You always were a stuck-up little bitch, Chessly. Makes sense your friends are just like you," my old classmate snarled.

"I'm not stuck up at all, Stan, but I draw a line at kissing guys who try to look up my skirt without my permission." I might have had a good buzz on, but I wasn't drunk enough for his ridiculousness.

Right then the bar erupted in the countdown to midnight. "TEN! NINE! EIGHT! SEVEN! SIX! FIVE! FOUR! THREE! TWO! ONE! HAPPY NEW YEAR!" As if by magic, confetti dropped from the ceiling. People laughed, toasted, kissed, played with the confetti, or did some combination of all four. For a few minutes, pandemonium overtook the Elk Horn.

Piper and I toasted, threw back what was left of our drinks, and danced in the confetti. By the time the bar closed down a little before two in the morning, we were hoarse from singing at the tops of our lungs even without the mic, and thoroughly wiped out from dancing all night.

While Piper closed out her tab, I called Dad for a ride home. He sounded pretty chipper on the phone, so I guess he didn't really mind about staying up so we wouldn't have to stumble home on foot in a snow storm in the middle of the night.

"I apologize for corrupting your daughter tonight, Mr. Clarke," Piper said as she fell into the cab of truck.

I grinned at my friend, then at my dad.

He returned my grin. "You girls had a good time, I take it."

"You'll probably hear all about it in the store." I giggled.

"You sang, didn't you?" His tone was indulgent as he took his time on the snowy streets.

"And maybe danced on a tabletop," Piper added, like Dad needed that information.

Chuckling, he said, "Yep. Bet I'm going to hear about it for a while."

We tumbled into the house and up the stairs to my bedroom. Piper grinned at her phone, and I snatched it from her hand.

"Ooh, someone has a boyfriend." I sang as I tried to focus on the text on the phone screen.

Bax: Happy New Year, Piper. Hope you were good. Tell Chessly Finn wants to watch her dance on a tabletop in person.

What?

I narrowed my eyes at my friend. "You sent a video?"

Snagging her phone back, she said, "He asked if we were having a good time. So I showed him." A grin split her face.

Tilting my head, I shot her a glare from beneath my eyebrows. But long after we fell into bed, I was still wondering how Finn had spent his New Year's Eve and what it would be like to dance on a tabletop for him.

What was wrong with me for even entertaining such a ridiculous idea?

Chapter Twelve

Finn

O N NEW YEAR'S Eve Bax and I hit the Molly to shoot pool, drink beer, and watch bowl games on their big screen. Danny and Callahan weren't rolling back into town until New Year's Day—not that we could have counted on them to join us anyway. At least Callahan and Jamaica were public about their relationship. Danny was still pretending he was "just friends" with his high-school prom date—like any of us believed him.

I leaned on my cue and swigged a drink of beer as I watched Bax line up his shot. Right as he let go with his stick, I cleared my throat—loudly. Didn't fuck up his aim even a millimeter, damn it. Two balls dropped into their respective pockets, and he stared me down with a sardonic expression.

"That all you got, Finnegan? Lame, dude."

"'Bout as lame as your shirt."

The T-shirt my teammate was wearing for this fine evening read "I am currently unsupervised. (I know. It freaks me out too.) The possibilities are endless."

"Possibilities, my ass." I glanced around the bar filled mostly with dateless guys exactly like the two of us. The few women in attendance didn't hold much promise—not that either of us were in the mood to pick someone up. The server was cute and flirty, and on any other night, I might have tried to make a run at her. But phantom tingles of Chessly's lips on mine haunted me, reminding me of how little I knew about kissing until she showed me and stole away any notion I might have entertained.

With a chuckle, Bax lined up another shot and dropped another ball into a corner pocket. At the rate he was going, that dollar resting on the table was going into his wallet.

Yeah, we played high-stakes pool.

His phone buzzed with a text right as he let go for his next shot. My antics had made zero impact on his concentration, but that vibration in the back pocket of his jeans sent the cue ball careening recklessly toward his target, grazing the seven ball rather than hitting it cleanly. It limped to the side of the table, gently bounced off the board, and rolled to a sad little stop an inch from the edge.

Bax's eyes lit up as he read the text that stole his focus. He snorted a laugh and glanced up from his phone to me. "Piper and Chessly are having a good time tonight—especially Chessly, from the looks of it."

He held out his phone so I could see the video Piper had sent him. Onscreen, I watched Chessly dancing on a tabletop in some bar. She did some hip-swinging move that emphasized her sexy short skirt. Black tights covered her endlessly long legs, and my mouth went dry as I remembered how perfectly those legs had wrapped around me when I pinned her beneath me on the couch.

I grabbed my friend's wrist and poked the screen again for another round of torturing myself as I watched my dream girl entertaining a bar full of people cheering on her dance moves. This time I noticed the douche standing behind the table and obviously trying to see up her skirt. My hand flexed with the need to punch the perverted son of a bitch in the mouth. What the fuck did he think he was doing trying see up my girl's skirt?

My girl?

In my dreams, for sure. But after the way the evening had ended the last time she was at the house, I worried about ever scoring another chance with her.

"It's not that far to Harlo from here," I said as I gave Bax his hand back.

"Right. We already established that in this weather—and in the dark—it'd take hours to make it there. By then the bars will be closed and Piper and Chessly will be—" His lips thinned. "Hopefully, they'll be all tucked in at Chessly's place." He checked his phone again. "Piper says the dude in the background is someone from Chessly's high school class and kind of a dick."

"That much is obvious in the video," I grumbled.

A tiny grin tugged at the corner of his mouth. "Piper's tipsy, but she says they're headed home with Chessly's dad."

At Bax's pronouncement, air gusted out of me. From the looks of things, the girls were having a bigger night out than my buddy and me, but at least they weren't hooking up with assholes from Chess's hometown.

"Maybe it's time for us to call it a night too. This place is making me feel kinda pathetic." I finished off my beer and set the empty bottle on a nearby table.

"We're kinda pathetic." Bax laughed. "We still have a dollar on the table. Shoot your last shot. See if you can win it."

"'Cause I need a buck that bad. Jesus."

Still, I chalked my cue stick, lined up my shot, and banked the ball into the side pocket. Following that success, I ran the table. With a triumphant smirk, I waved the dollar with a flourish and stuffed it into my pocket. Bax rolled his eyes, but I caught his grin as he racked his cue stick.

"You should prolly add that buck to the ten-spot you're leaving for the waitress."

With a sigh I fished it out of my pocket. "Yeah. We might be pathetic, but that poor woman had to wait on all of us sad saps all night."

I slipped my winnings and a ten-dollar bill beneath my empty beer bottle and followed Bax to the door where some girl met him and tried to chat him up. Bax stammered something about it being nice to see her again, but we were on our way out. Her whine of protest was one we'd all heard at some time or other with girls we had no intention of hanging out with. The boys—and a certain hot physics major—thought I harbored an unhealthy interest in jersey chasers, but even I had standards when it came to girls with a propensity for clinging. It took him a minute, but Bax finally dredged up the girl's name. From the sound of it, "Emily" was a first-class clinger.

I knew my friend well. If I didn't step in and fix this, Bax and I would either be stuck with two girls we didn't want to be with, or "Emily" would pop off with a social media tantrum that could do real damage.

In one of my rare moments of smoothness, I said, "Ladies, any other night, we'd jump all over what you're offering. But Coach has us doing a team-bonding thing tomorrow." I added an epic eye roll for emphasis. "He doesn't want us twisting off and getting into trouble on New Year's, you know?" Throwing my arm across Bax's shoulders, I tugged him with me to the door. "Sorry we can't hang out."

The Emily girl seemed only marginally mollified. Her mousy friend looked starstruck, but like her friend, she only had eyes for Bax. The door to the Molly closed on their last protests as Bax and I escaped into the frigid snowy night.

"Let me guess. You had a one-night stand with that Emily

girl," I said as we waited for Bax's truck to warm up enough to defrost the windows.

"Nope. I drunk-kissed her at a party—can't remember which one—and she made sure that even in my inebriated state I could figure out she was a clinger. I didn't even try for second base." He blew on his hands and rubbed them together.

The steam from our breath made it hard for the defroster to keep up, and he revved the engine a couple of times to build more heat.

"Guess that explains why you struggled to come up with her name." I slid him a sly grin. "Might have been easier to escape if you'd told her you didn't have a clue who she was."

"'Asshole' is not a reputation I want to cultivate, Finnegan." His tone had an eye roll in it as he put the truck in gear and took his time pulling out of the icy parking lot. "Good on you to think so fast though. Team-bonding on New Year's Day even sounded plausible to me."

Grinning, we fist-bumped over my quick-witted awesomeness. Then I cranked up the radio, and we drove the rest of the way home to the sounds of Lainey Wilson and Kane Brown, each of us in our own heads.

After the second week of break, I wanted to climb the walls. Bax and I played so much *COD* we finally had to take a break from killing zombies and each other and switch to *Madden*. Hitting the gym on the daily helped to relieve some of the boredom, but more than once I wished our coaches remembered we weren't preparing for a national title. It would have been nice to have spent a little more time at home on the ranch.

Sure, I had no interest in horning in on my sister's domain, but that didn't mean I didn't enjoy checking on the cows, bucking hay, and eating all of Mom's luscious food. Hanging out with my family also meant I had a lot less time to think about a certain blonde physics major with eyes so blue I could swim in them.

It didn't help that following our collective return to the house after Christmas, Callahan and Jamaica spent all their free time holed up in 'Han's room with occasional forays to the kitchen where I caught them on more than one occasion lip-locking while their food came perilously close to burning. Danny wasn't any better, spending all his time outside the gym either at his part-time job at the tire shop or over at his high-school "friend" Taryn's place. From the way he smiled to himself when he thought no one was watching, I could tell he was making progress toward moving from the friend zone to the end zone.

Then today, Bax bailed on me too. Piper had finally given him her number sometime over break—hence the video on New Year's Eve—and she was back in town. Now the king of one-night stands was going on dates, for fuck's sake.

Being the odd man out sucked. Big-time.

I flopped back on my bed, shoved my hands beneath my head, and stared at the ceiling. I'd always thought the inevitability of my friends finding someone special would happen after we finished college. While we played for the Wildcats, we'd all hang out together, party together, have the occasional one-night stands with consenting ladies who knew the score. Common sense said guys with NFL aspirations needed relentless focus on the game, and serious romantic relationships stole some of that focus. I should know after the ay my ex, Hannah, had fucked with my head all of freshman year.

Besides, jersey chasers didn't stop chasing players once they left the college ranks to enter the pros. It stood to reason players should show up to the NFL single until they figured out the league and how all the travel and community service and endorsements expectations would play out. Take advantage of some of the fun before settling down with someone whose life they'd have to uproot if a trade happened or if the player asked for a different opportunity.

Honestly, what was the deal with jumping the gun and pursuing a relationship in college?

Quick on the heels of those dark thoughts, heat warmed my chest and climbed my neck to my cheeks as a sudden memory of Chessly kissing me floated through my head. *Fuck!* Why couldn't I stop thinking about that girl? Hadn't I just laid out all the reasons why I shouldn't give her a nanosecond of headspace?

Punching my fists into the mattress, I sat up and stared out the window at the fat flakes of snow fluttering down outside as though nothing in the world mattered. With all my roommates out somewhere with their women, the house was so silent I could almost hear each little crystal as it joined the others on the ground.

"Fuuuck!"

The word echoed in the unnatural quiet of the house. I tugged at my hair and jumped up from the bed. After pulling my last clean hoodie over my T-shirt, I dropped down the stairs two at a time, stuffed my feet into my boots without bothering to tie them, and headed out the door. Even if I was the only one sitting in our usual booth, at least other people would be around.

Hitting Johnson's number on speed dial as I waited for my truck to warm up, I hoped he and Fitz were bored enough to join me for a beer at Stromboli's. Relief flooded through me when he picked up on the second ring and said they'd beat me there. At least I still had some friends left who weren't mothered up.

As I strolled up to the front door of the pizzeria, I saw Johnson and Fitz headed in my direction from the opposite end of the block. Grinning, I raced for the door, jerked it open, and rushed inside. With a nod to Jason, the bouncer who sat on his stool in the foyer, I kept moving. Behind me I heard my friends jostling as they tried to walk through the door together. Tossing a glance over my shoulder, I shook my head at the sight of Fitz squeezing Johnson against the doorframe.

I slid into our usual booth at the back a second before my friends joined me, Johnson scowling at Fitz as he rubbed his shoulder.

"Tsk, tsk, tsk, Tarvi. When are you going to learn that in close quarters, size trumps speed every time?" I laughed and bumped Fitzy's fist.

"What he said," Fitz echoed.

"Fuckers," Johnson muttered as he slid into the booth. "Where's Bax and 'Han?"

Tilting my head with a narrow-eyed stare, I said, "Out with their girlfriends."

"Wait. Since when does Bax have a girlfriend?" Fitz asked as he signaled a passing server.

After we ordered a pitcher of beer and a double order of wings, I answered Fitz's question. "Bax has a girlfriend since his unicorn turned out to be that purple-haired hottie he dedicated a pick-six to at the end of the season. She's the one who spent the night after our party celebrating our win over the Golden Bears."

Our server appeared with a pitcher and three glasses, and I busied myself with pouring a glass with a perfect head. After passing it over to Fitz, I poured a second and passed it to Johnson.

As I poured my own glass, Johnson asked, "What about 'Han?"

"That's a whole other deal. He and Jamaica met each other's families over break." I shuddered.

Across the table Johnson tapped out a beat on the table and began singing "Another One Bites the Dust."

I shook my head. "I can't figure out what the hell either of them are thinking. They're NFL prospects—why would they want to join the league while dragging a ball and chain?"

A picture of Chessly Clarke flitted through my mind, her

eyes sparkling with sass and her sweet, compact body tantalizing me from beneath my hoodie, and I gulped half my beer down in one swig.

"They get to hang out with hot women on the regular—unlike, say, certain linemen I know." Johnson slid me a sly grin.

Putting some drama behind the lift of his brow, Fitz said, "Hotness isn't the only thing those women have going for them." He drank some beer and ran his tongue over the foam on his lip. "They're smart, funny"—he shot me a glare—"and they ain't chasin' anybody's jersey."

Now Johnson narrowed his eyes at me too. "Speaking of jersey chasers, what came out of your captains' meeting with Coach before break?"

"He agreed to meet with Buzz Miller to thank him for his generosity to the football program over the years." Fitz coughed into his hand. "And to tell him he's welcome to keep contributing to it. But he won't be allowed access to any player at any time for any reason. If he interferes with any of us again, the team will turn down his money." I sat back against the booth. "That mess Tory Miller caused for 'Han and Jamaica at the end of last semester finally tipped it for Coach."

Johnson shifted his narrow-eyed glare from me to his roommate. "I thought the plan was to shut down that particular gravy train now, not allow that asshole to have any more influence."

Fitz patted him patronizingly on the shoulder. "Politics, man. You can't cut the guy off at the knees without handing him an out to save face. He's given the team too much cash." He swigged back the rest of his beer and reached for the pitcher to refill his glass. "But once he has no say in anyone's NIL opportunities, no VIP invitations to team events and whatnot, he'll make up his mind to move on. When Daddy moves on, it's a good bet Tory will move on too. That'll be good for all of us—right, Finn?"

Though I tried not to, I squirmed a bit under Fitz's stern stare.

"I might have had my own problem with her little group of jersey chasers," I mumbled into my glass.

Johnson sat up tall, a wide grin splitting his face. "Oh, this oughta be good."

Jeremiah leaned his forearms on the table. Even when he was teasing, our nose tackle was formidable. "Does it have anything to do with that cute blonde who hangs out with 'Han's girlfriend? The one you get all tongue-tied around?"

I slid down a bit in the booth. "Fuck off, Fitz."

"You can't leave us hanging now, dude." Johnson laughed.

The arrival of our monster-size basket of wings couldn't have been timed better. I piled my plate and stuffed my face with barbecue chicken, pointing at my full mouth when Tarvi said "Well?" as he tried to imitate Fitz's stern stare. Tarvarius was a nursing major, not pre-law like Jeremiah, so he hadn't perfected that I-can-make-you-talk stare Fitz had down pat. When he raised his brow, I stuffed another wing into my mouth and kept chewing.

"You'll tell us eventually, Finn," Jeremiah intoned. "You always do."

Chapter Thirteen

Chessly

I ARRIVED BACK ON campus a few days before the start of spring semester. Good thing I had dorm business, like making new door tags and setting up programming for my floor to keep me busy since my friends had abandoned me. For football players.

Texting Piper to meet up for drinks was a bust. When she came back to town a couple of days into the New Year, she started dating—*dating*—Wyatt Baxter. Stunning. After she texted him with our antics on New Year's Eve, they'd apparently started talking all the time, and things between them were escalating into the realm of Callahan and Jamaica.

Jamaica made it to RA meetings. When I'd walked down her hall to see if she wanted to join me at Pickle Barrel for a sandwich for lunch on my second day back, I'd seen her cute new door tags with a cartoon theme, so she was keeping up her RA duties. The mystery was how she did that when she spent all her time with Callahan at the big old Victorian on Jock Street.

Thinking of that house brought back memories of the last time I'd been in it. I wanted to lie to myself and say those memories didn't haunt me at least once a day, but that hadn't worked all through break. On more than one occasion, I'd had to drag my thoughts away from that night on Finn's couch and how much farther we'd have gone if not for the untimely arrival of that pack of freshmen.

How much farther I'd *wanted* to go.

Crap! What was wrong with me that I was hung up on a guy who couldn't say no to any female attention, no matter how calculating it was? Either he was super naïve or super egotistical with neither characteristic flattering him.

As I tucked the half a hoagie I'd saved from lunch into my dorm fridge, a third possibility popped into my head. Maybe Finn was a genuinely nice guy—one who didn't want to hurt anyone's feelings. That would explain why he struggled to extricate himself from social scrapes with women and never seemed able to make the right call.

After I hung up my jacket and kicked off my boots, I settled against the headboard of my narrow dorm bed and stared out at the snowflakes swirling beyond the window. That third possibility tripped me up, big-time. Because if Finn wasn't clueless, I couldn't write him off. If he wasn't egotistical, I couldn't put him down. I'd never been one of those girls who wanted to tame the bad boy, bring out his inner Boy Scout or some nonsense. I was a sucker for nice guys.

But if he truly was a nice guy, how did that explain his relationship with Tory Miller? When he dropped me off in front Hanover after the bonfire, I'd had the distinct impression he wanted to kiss me. Then Tory showed up, screeching in her most entitled voice, and he'd defended her. When her posse showed up at his house right as we were getting busy on the couch, he'd jumped right on their cookie offering. With his attention all caught up in those girls and their snacks, he'd made it disappointingly easy to call a ride, put on my coat, and leave.

Thunking my head back against the headboard, I ground my teeth at my own stupidity. As a scientist, observation came naturally to me. As a woman, I couldn't help but notice Finn's handsome face and powerful body. Until that night at the start of finals week, my interactions with him had always included other people, specifically other women who found him every bit as attractive as I did. He liked that attention. Of course he did. If he made himself exclusive with one woman, some of that attention would disappear.

Even nice guys liked to be admired. No wonder he couldn't figure out how to straddle the line between pursuing one woman and maintaining the interest of several more. Yet he'd treated me like I was special, giving me his hoodie when he noticed I was cold, playing the perfect host with hot chocolate and conversation when I returned it. The look on his face when he stood in the open door of his house as I walked away—a look that implied I'd taken something else of his when I left—still had me second-guessing myself and my responses that night.

Usually, I liked the quiet of the dorm before everyone arrived for the start of a new semester. The anticipation of new people and classes and possibilities exhilarated me. Today, all I noticed was the weird silence of a mostly empty building and the snow falling straight down. Without a car, I was basically stuck by myself.

"This is ridiculous," I said into the emptiness of my room.

Swinging my legs over the side of the bed, I stood and stretched then pulled out my desk chair. I had a couple of days before the semester began and syllabi for all my classes. Might as well get a head start on my course reading. As I pulled up some articles on my computer, I chuckled to myself. Reading ahead was Jamaica's thing. She'd finally rubbed off on me.

"Finn asked about you when I was over at the house the other night," Jamaica said as we sat in the Union for our afternoon coffee date the first week of classes. "I was so distracted with all the Tory Miller drama during finals, I think I missed the part where the two of you apparently hooked up." Her narrowed eyes demanded I spill all the tea.

"Who told you that?"

"I might have overheard Bax and him talking about it."

"Bax is clueless. I returned Finn's hoodie. Then a bunch of jersey chasers showed up with cookies 'for the boys,'" I added with air quotes. "Bax came home right behind them, and I left. End of story." I busied myself with removing the lid of my cup, blowing on my coffee, and refitting the lid before taking a sip.

She leaned toward me. "You're hiding something."

I gave her my coolest raised-brow response and kept my mouth shut.

My friend didn't buy it. "I'll get it out of you. You know that, don't you?"

With a shrug I said, "Nothing to get out of me. There's nothing going on between Finn McCabe and me." At least that much wasn't a lie.

Giving me a sage nod, she said, "Uh-huh. Famous last words."

I rolled my eyes.

"So, did you hear the big news?" Pure delight colored her tone. Before I could react to the abrupt change in subject, she plowed on. "The football program severed ties with Buzz Miller. He can give them money, but he can't influence NIL contracts, have any access to players or coaches, is barred from serving on any committees associated with the team, and has to issue a public apology to Callahan for all the trouble he caused last semester." She vibrated with giddy excitement.

"Seriously? I can't believe the university would be willing to do that to a major donor."

Jamaica's expression turned grave. "Callahan didn't give me all the details, but the team captains went to the head football coach and gave him an ultimatum. Apparently, this isn't the first time a Miller girl went after a football player with the intention of ruining his life by saddling him with her."

"Wow." I sat back in my chair. "I still can't believe any college administrator would willingly give up alumni cash."

"They will if they think accepting it on Buzz Miller's terms could cost them their jobs. Dr. Dair is on probation, and he lost tenure. He's lucky to still be teaching here after everything that went down last semester."

I laughed. "I hear a certain amount of satisfaction in your voice, you vindictive girl."

"Tory's the one who should be on probation." Jamaica sighed. "Her dad's money still has some influence."

"Guess that explains the exodus of freshman mean girls moving out of Hanover and into Delta Chi this semester." I rolled my cup between my palms. "Can't say I'll miss Tory's crowd. But I will give her props."

At Jamaica's stunned expression, I clarified. "At least she recruits the nasty ones like her, leaving the fun girls behind for us to hang out with. The atmosphere on my floor is already lighter in the first two weeks of the semester than it was at the end of last semester, and I only had two of those girls living in my hall."

"I asked that Tory be made persona non grata at Hanover. Hopefully, Becky agrees and sends her a letter."

"After everything that's gone down with that girl over the past two years, I can't imagine our supervisor doing anything less. Saves her almost as much stress as it saves us." I finished my coffee, stood, and walked the empty cup to a nearby trash can.

"That's enough Tory Miller for one day—or week—or

month. If I never see that girl again, I'll consider myself having lived a charmed life." Hefting my backpack over my shoulder, I glanced toward the loud giggles coming from the main door into the common area of the Union. As though I'd conjured her with my words, in sashayed the devil herself with her little group of mean girls all surrounding one Finn McCabe.

"What was that you were saying earlier about Finn asking about me?" Nodding in the direction of the doorway, I said, "That might be the reason I don't believe it—and why you shouldn't believe anything you hear about Finn and me hooking up."

The man in question smiled at something one of the jersey chasers said to him. Then his gaze snagged on mine, and the smile dropped right off his face, replaced by an expression that looked a whole lot like guilt.

Jamaica stood beside me and shook her head in Finn's direction, her disappointment obvious in the set of her shoulders.

"I think I'll grab a coffee to-go," I said.

"I'd join you, but I'm headed down to the Sweet Shop for my shift."

"Looks like we're both avoiding a scene."

We exchanged a look as Jamaica gathered her things.

"See you at the RA meeting after dinner," she said as she headed to the stairwell on the opposite side of the commons.

I made my way to the back of the short line for coffee and pulled out my phone. Mindlessly scrolling social media let me appear as if I was ignoring Finn and the antics of the girls demanding his attention, while surreptitiously paying attention to him because I couldn't seem to help myself. Yet somehow I missed him moving to stand directly behind me as I placed my order.

"Make that two," he said over my shoulder to the barista behind the counter.

"Name?" the barista asked.

We answered simultaneously.

"Chessly."

"Finn."

"I can buy my own coffee. Thanks," I said letting the frost in my tone crackle in the air.

"Yeah, but I want to buy you a coffee." He smiled that contagious smile of his on purpose.

I fought not to return it. "You buying for all the girls you arrived with too?"

Confusion pulled his eyebrows together. "I'm not with any girls."

"Which totally explains that giggling group you walked in here with." I shook my head and pulled my wallet from my backpack.

Finn beat me to it, tapping his phone on the card reader.

"I'll pay you back." I went to pull some bills from my wallet, but he covered my hand with his.

"No need."

Tingles shot out in every direction from where his calloused palm met my skin, momentarily immobilizing me. Our eyes locked, and I swear I experienced a moment of entanglement. Until this second, I'd thought the orchestrated objective reduction theory of quantum consciousness was closer to science fiction than to physics, yet standing here with Finn's skin on mine, our gazes ensnared with each other, a sensation of awareness I couldn't explain nor deny shuddered through me.

"Finn! Two coffees for Finn!" a barista called, breaking the spell.

Flustered, I stuffed my wallet back into my backpack and stepped over to where two steaming café au laits waited.

"Thank you, but you didn't have to pay for this." After that fleeting encounter in front of the register, my tone had warmed up considerably and without my permission.

"I did if I wanted to talk to you. Which I do." He ushered me in front of him.

"What about your entourage?" I glanced behind him to see the jersey chasers glaring at us as they placed their orders. Curiously, Tory had vanished from the group.

"Chessly, I'm not with them. I came here to do some studying and ran into them at the bottom of the stairs outside. I'm totally not with them." The hitch in his voice pleaded with me to believe him.

"Okay."

He relaxed.

"What did you want to talk to me about?"

Tension returned to his shoulders. "That night before finals. I didn't invite those girls."

"Sure, Finn. Whatever you say." I started walking toward the main doors.

He fell into step beside me. "It's true. I didn't have a clue they were coming over."

Crowding me a little, he forced me to look at him. "And they didn't stay. We thanked them for their cookies and called an Uber to pick them up. If you don't believe me, ask Bax."

"Whatever. It seems wherever you are the jersey chasers will be there too."

"I don't seek them out. They find me." He followed me down the stairs and outside as I headed to the science building.

"Do they have a tracker on you or something?" I chuckled even though my comment wasn't actually funny.

Blowing out a breath, he said, "The next best thing. The college publishes our schedules."

I shot him a side-eye.

"It's true. Something about making sure people know we're student-athletes. Damn invasion of privacy if you ask me," he grumbled.

"Wow. Is that only for the football team or for all athletes?"

"Everyone on an athletic scholarship. If not for the fact that scholarship athletes get more playing time, I'd have taken the full academic one the university offered and walked on the team instead." He sipped his coffee as he ambled down the sidewalk beside me. "Where are we going?"

"*I'm* going to the science building," I said, trying to drop a hint. Then I stopped dead center in the sidewalk. "Wait. You were offered a full academic scholarship?"

The tips of his ears turned red, and I didn't think it was from the icy January air. "Uh, I did okay on the ACT, maybe graduated with a 4.0." He rubbed his hand over the back of his neck. "Are you headed to class right now?"

"No. I like to study in the science building." I resumed walking in the direction of Hillman Hall. "No wonder you're bio-chem," I said under my breath.

"Mind if I study with you?" The hope in his words left me no choice but to acquiesce. Saying no to those puppy-dog eyes he gave me would have felt like kicking a puppy. Besides, he bought me a coffee.

My acquiescence had nothing whatsoever to do with how hot he was or that he played my favorite sport or that I'd just discovered he was super-smart. It certainly had nothing to do with the weird connection that had passed between us in the Union—the one that had left phantom tingles skittering over my skin to center in my core like a gathering storm even as I merely walked along beside him.

Definitely not.

Chapter Fourteen

Finn

RUNNING INTO CHESSLY in the Union was a gift I'd almost squandered when those freshmen surrounded me like a school of sharks. After my conversations with Bax during finals, and Tarvi and Fitz over break, I'd reached the conclusion I needed to back away from a certain group of girls no matter how willing they were to take care of me. Especially with how willing they were to take care of me.

Wanting to know Chessly better also might have had something to do with my change of heart.

Even bundled up in a bright pink puffy coat with the hood tied down tight to her head, she dazzled me. Skinny jeans emphasized her long legs. I remembered all too well how sweet those legs had felt wrapped around my hips on our way to dry-humping on the couch before the jersey chasers' untimely interruption. As we walked along, I reached down and discreetly adjusted the semi that had sprung up at the memory of that night.

When we reached Hillman Hall, I hustled ahead of Chessly to open the door. A tiny smile ghosted over her lips as she gazed up at me when she stepped inside. Stomping snow off our boots on the rug inside the door, both of us gave a little shiver at the change in temperature, from frigid January air outside to the toasty warmth of the building. Then with a purpose, Chessly headed off in the direction of the wide staircase bisecting the lobby and half-jogged up the stairs. I followed, unapologetically admiring the sway of her tight little ass. Probably a dick move and more than a little stupid if she glanced back and caught me, but damn, it was at eye level.

At the top of the stairs, she veered left, and I figured out our destination was the study carrels at the end of the hall outside the physics department.

"That's a miracle," she said as she zeroed in on a table near the floor-to-ceiling windows.

Walking half a step behind her, I asked, "What's a miracle?"

"My favorite table being open at this time of day. Usually, this nerdy grad student snags it. He always shoots me this smug smirk when he's there too, like—"

Out of nowhere, an Ichabod Crane lookalike materialized in front of the carrel right as Chessly let her backpack slide down off her shoulder.

"Hey! We were going to sit here," she protested with an indignant sniff.

If I hadn't been with her already, I would have played with her for that response alone. Apparently, Ichabod had the same idea.

"You should be quicker then." He smirked.

"Or you could be polite," I said, deepening my voice in my best Jeremiah Fitzgerald imitation.

Only then did the guy acknowledge that Chessly wasn't alone. His eyes widened and the smirk dropped right off his lips.

"Oh, uh, sure. Sure. No problem." Clearing his throat, he added with a gesture at the carrel, "You go ahead."

"Thank you," I said. Then, to be certain he'd picked up the hint, I stepped around Chess and pulled her chair out for her.

With a bemused smile at me, she sat down, and I nearly had to step on Ichabod to move him away from the opposite side of the table so I could sit across from her.

"Have a good session or whatever," the guy said as he backed away. As quickly as he'd materialized, he disappeared.

As I set my backpack on the floor beside the table, I said, "I don't think it's a coincidence that guy sits at your favorite table." I shot her my best smile. "Can't say I blame him either."

Her brows came together in confusion. "What are you talking about?"

"Ichabod has a crush on you."

"Ichabod?"

"Yeah. Like the character from 'The Legend of Sleepy Hollow.' I thought everyone read that story in high school." I grinned.

Her face relaxed into a smile as my meaning dawned on her. "Oh, the grad student." She giggled. "He does look a bit like Ichabod Crane, doesn't he?"

"Not your type at all, huh?"

She unzipped her jacket, shrugged out of it, and draped it over the back of her chair. I had to work my ass off to keep my eyes on her face as she revealed her luscious rack in a tight green turtleneck sweater.

"I don't have a type," she said primly as she reached down and opened her backpack. She pulled out her laptop and a notebook and set them on the table in front of her, momentarily distracting me from her gorgeous figure.

"Sure you do, or you would have caught on that ol' Ichabod has a thing for you." Taking a chance, I added, "And you wouldn't have let me join you."

"You think you're my type?"

I could tell she was trying to inject a load of disbelief into the question except it came out kinda breathy.

I grinned. "If those kisses were anything to go by"—I leaned forward—"and they were"—I dialed up the heat in my smile—"I'm definitely your type."

"I've been trying to work out if you have an ego or not." She gave a sage nod. "It seems you have a rather big one."

Laughter barked out of me. "Nope. It's not ego talking here." I snagged her eyes with mine and held them. "It's the scientific method. Make a hypothesis, test the hypothesis, draw a conclusion." Sitting back, I crossed my arms over my chest and didn't miss the way her eyes toured my biceps and shoulders. "Hypothesis: Chessly Clarke is interested in Finn McCabe."

She sucked in air but said nothing.

"Test: Finn invites Chessly to a party and finds a way to spend time with her alone. They have a nice conversation. Chessly leaves the party wearing Finn's hoodie. Will she return it or burn it?" I dropped my forearms to the table and leaned in. "Not only does she return it, but she also spends the evening talking to Finn, drinking hot chocolate, and kissing on the couch." I winked. "Conclusion: Chessly Clarke is interested in Finn McCabe." I gave her a second to refute me. When she remained silent, I whispered, "And Finn McCabe is very interested in Chessly Clarke."

Clearing her throat as she laid out her pencils, she said, "But you're also interested in Tory Miller and the girls in her group." Glancing up at me, she added, "So I'm not seeing your interest in me as special."

Reaching across the table, I covered her hands with mine. "I have zero interest in Tory Miller or any of her little friends." Beneath mine, her hands stiffened. "But my mom raised me to be polite to people, so when they talk to me, I acknowledge them. When they show up at my house unannounced with a tin of fresh-baked cookies, I say thank you and enjoy their hard work."

I rubbed the pad of my thumb over the soft skin on the back of her hand and took a big chance. "I'd also way rather hang out with you than with a bunch of freshmen whose only interest in me is that I play football."

"How do you know that's not my only interest in you?"

Giving her hand a tiny squeeze, I leaned forward, "Because I've kissed *you*." I sat back with a small smile and enjoyed the pink flush sliding up her cheeks.

She tugged her hands away, and I let her.

"I have a project to research for quantum physics. Don't you have any homework?" Her prim tone confirmed what her flushed cheeks had already told me.

My interest in Chessly Clarke wasn't one-sided.

But I let her get away with her deflection. Pulling my laptop from my backpack, I set it on the table and opened it to the syllabus for my physical chemistry class. With a sly glance at my study partner, who studiously ignored me, I navigated to the homework that required some physics, pulled up a couple of problems, and after giving it a few minutes, said, "Since you're a physics major who wants to be a doctor, maybe you can help me with some physical chemistry homework."

Her eyes narrowed as if she thought I was playing her—which I'll admit I kind of was—but she said, "Okay. Let me see."

I spun my laptop to face her, and she pulled it toward her to see what I was on about. "This looks like a standard physics problem. What are you solving for?"

"Y."

She studied the problem for a few minutes, flipped her notebook to a blank page, jotted some notes, and said, "I think if you apply basic calculus reasoning, you can get there by first solving for X."

I'd figured that out too when I worked on the problem earlier, but she didn't need to know that.

"Thanks."

I took my laptop back and worked on the problem while she returned to her project. Even though I remained hyperaware of her, catching her little sighs and feeling her eyes on me from time to time, I still managed to finish all my physical chemistry homework for the next two weeks while we worked together in easy silence for a couple of hours. At last my ass needed a break from the hard wooden chair.

"You in a good place?" I asked.

Lifting her eyes, she asked, "A good place for what?"

"Taking a break, maybe letting Ichabod have a turn at the good study carrel." I grinned.

She sat up straight and groaned. "Argh. How long have we been working?" Pulling her phone from her jeans pocket, she answered her own question. "How did that happen?"

"What? Time?" I laughed.

With an exasperated huff, she said, "Yes. I can't remember the last time I studied for two hours straight with no breaks."

"Well," I drawled. "You did take a few breaks to see what I was doing."

Her narrowed eyes amused me.

"I have no idea what you're talking about," she said with a sniff, but her eyes didn't meet mine. "I've outlined my entire quantum physics project." Almost as an afterthought, she whispered, "All of it."

"I've finished two weeks' worth of problems for physical chemistry." With a quirk of my lips, I added, "From the looks of it, we should study together more often."

Her brow shot up.

"You know, since both of us get so much done when we're together."

She shook her head, but I caught the tiny grin playing over her luscious lips.

Reaching my arms above my head, I twisted from side to side, giving my back a stretch. Across the table, Chessly tested all my good intentions when she pressed her elbows back and arched her back, lifting her tits to the ceiling. I had to remember I was a gentleman so I wouldn't allow myself to drop into a fantasy of her stretching like that in front of me without clothes on. *Fuck.* The more time I spent around her, the prettier she became, which was saying something considering she'd had all my attention since the moment I first saw her.

Clearing my throat, I said, "Would you like to grab a pizza at Stromboli's?"

"Um—"

From the expression that flitted over her features, I worried she was planning to turn me down. Then her stomach did me a solid, rumbling loud enough to be heard down the hall. She slapped her hands over her middle with an embarrassed chuckle.

Grinning, I said, "I'll take that as a yes."

"Fine. Okay. I guess I can take a break for dinner."

"Don't hurt yourself admitting you liked studying with me as much as I liked studying with you."

"Whatever," she said, but she didn't put any heat into it.

We gathered up our laptops, notebooks, and whatnot, repacked our backpacks, and headed out into the frigid January evening. Outside Hillman, we fell into step as I subtly guided her in the direction of the parking lot. Our breaths lingered in the air behind us. She must have been super cold because she didn't move away when I dropped my arm casually across her shoulders, pulling her closer to my heat.

One of the perks of being a big man and an athlete was that I ran hot. While she huddled in her down puffy coat, I managed just fine in a T-shirt and hoodie. We didn't waste time though, walking briskly over the recently plowed sidewalk to the parking lot behind the Union where I'd left my truck.

When I unlocked the passenger door, I noticed her teeth chattering, and I wished I had a remote starter so I could have warmed up my ride for her while we made our way across campus. My old beater pickup probably wouldn't have tolerated one, and I usually didn't care if the cab was a bit chilly. Actually, I preferred it. But that wouldn't do for my date.

Date.

Huh.

I smiled to myself as I cranked the heater to high. What started as a chance encounter in the Union had progressed to a study session that had morphed into a date. Not that I'd mention that. Most of the time when it came to women, I was clueless. But every now and then, I picked up on their cues. What I picked up on with Chess was that she was too polite to tell me no after her stomach had outed her at the precise second I asked her to pizza. As dates went, this one was uninspired owing to its serendipity. Still, I had the common sense to appreciate my good fortune.

"Why did you decide to be an RA?" I asked as I let my truck warm up.

I'd bailed on the dorms the second a room had opened up in our house my freshman year. Turned out, I wasn't a big fan of communal living, and I struggled to understand how Chessly could stand it for going on three years.

She turtled further down into her coat. "My scholarship covers tuition and books. Being an RA means the college pays my room and board. It takes the financial burden off my dad."

Remembering the story of how she'd lost her mom, I put the truck in gear and took my time easing out of the snow-covered parking lot.

"Yeah, but you have no privacy in the dorm."

Turning her head on the seat, she gave me a long, slow blink. "As opposed to how much privacy you have at your place? Jamaica says you all have to lock your doors on party nights to keep people from using your beds for shenanigans. Trust me, I've never had that problem in the dorms."

"It's a minor inconvenience."

She snorted.

"It might be a bigger deal if we had parties every night, but the team takes turns when we win." I signaled and took my time navigating a slick corner. My parents had given me new snow tires for Christmas, and I'd loaded a couple hundred pounds of sandbags in the box, but sheer ice covered the streets. I didn't need my date to freak out if the ass end of the truck decided to take us on a little slide.

"From what I hear, you and your roommates like to host several of those parties a season."

"What we like is to win. The parties are a bonus." I shot her a side-eye. "Most of the time, it's only the four of us at the house, as opposed to twenty or thirty people trying to use the same five showers every morning. Doesn't that drive you nuts?"

With a shrug she said, "You figure out how to schedule. I wake up super early, grab a shower, and study for an hour before breakfast. I'm usually one of only two people in the bathroom then, which means I skip the 7:30 a.m. rush that starts most of the freshmen off on the wrong foot every day." She smirked.

"Yeah, that wouldn't work so well at our place, with three of us sharing one bathroom and Coach Larkin expecting us in the weight room fifteen minutes before training starts." I laughed. "Bax and Danny are even less morning people than I am, so if we didn't shower at the facility after morning workouts, we'd probably start each day with a fight." The thought of us racing to the head and bouncing off each other like a trio of clowns made me grin. "Plus, the water heater in our old house is all the way in the basement. It takes it forever to heat up and then as though it's worked overtime, after about twenty minutes, it stops making hot water. With no warning. If you're the second guy, chances are good you're going to freeze your nuts off before you can rinse off. The third guy is just shit out of luck."

Chessly's amusement warmed my chest, and I discovered I wanted to keep entertaining her so I could listen to more of her sultry alto laughter.

"So your shower arrangements aren't that different from the dorms if your morning routine includes a trip to a locker room full of people all needing to get ready for the day at the same time."

"Except there are twenty-five showers with an endless supply of hot water. I'm never late for class because some moron decided he wanted to spend thirty minutes under the spray, and I never endure a shocking surprise." She laughed again, and I glanced over to see color rising high on her cheeks. Guess all this talk about showering maybe had her thinking naughty thoughts.

I hoped.

It certainly had me thinking about a naked Chessly—preferably in the privacy of the shower across the hall from my bedroom when my roommates weren't home.

It seemed only seconds had passed before we arrived at the pizzeria. By some miracle, an open parking space waited directly in front of the bar. After showing off my expert parallel parking skills, I shut off the engine and turned in the seat to smile at my date.

"I thought you were going to feed me."

Touching two fingers to the side of my ball cap, I said, "Yes, ma'am."

I held the door to the bar open for her and followed her inside. The heavenly smell of garlic and cheese assailed my senses, and it was my stomach's turn to rumble loud enough to make Chessly giggle as she walked in front of me. Without asking, she led me back to the football team's booth, which, surprisingly, was open.

As much as I wanted to slide in beside her, we weren't there yet. Sitting opposite her, I said, "I like everything on the menu here. Pick what you want."

"My favorite is chicken and artichoke pizza with extra cheese."

"Extra-large."

She laughed. "Of course."

I watched in fascination as she tugged off her mittens, unzipped her coat, and stuffed them down one sleeve.

"Why do you do that with your mittens?"

She gave a self-deprecating chuckle. "So I don't lose 'em."

It was such an elementary-school move, and I loved it. Sassy, sardonic, take-no-prisoners Chessly Clarke needed to tuck her mittens into her sleeve. I grinned.

"What's so funny?"

"Nothing." Resting my elbows on the table, I set my chin on my hands and gazed at the gorgeous girl seated across from me. "But you are terribly cute."

Chapter Fifteen

Chessly

"TERRIBLY CUTE? WHAT'S that supposed to mean?" I asked.

"It means I like how you're such a badass physics major who still does what her kindergarten teacher taught her to do after coming in from recess." Finn's warm smile held a hint of teasing.

What was I supposed to do with that?

With all the talk about showers on the drive to the bar, my thoughts kept straying to naked Finn. The effort I'd expended to stop myself from crossing my legs to cover my body's reaction to mental images of water sluicing over his big, sexy body had almost worn me out before we even arrived. I had the idea he'd brought it up on purpose to send my thoughts in that exact direction. Now he was gently teasing me about how I liked to keep my things together. My libido might be suffering from whiplash, and my cheeks were flushed with a heat that had nothing to do with coming in from the cold to sit in a warm bar.

The server's timing was a mercy.

"What can I get you guys?"

"An extra-large chicken and artichoke pie." Finn flashed a grin my way. "With extra cheese, a couple glasses of water, and—"

"I'll have a pint of the chocolate stout," I finished for him.

"Make that two." Finn emphasized his request by holding up two fingers.

"Got it. Anything else?"

With a shake of my head, I said, "I'm good."

"Better add an order of wings with hot aioli." His eyes twinkled. "Bring it first. I don't want my girl here to gnaw off her arm or something."

"Seriously?" I huffed.

He lifted his hands in a what-can-I-say? gesture. "Hey. I'm not the one whose stomach sounded like a jet taking off when we were studying."

Glaring at him from beneath my brows I said, "But you were the one whose stomach sounded like a pride of lions in the jungle on the drive over from the Union."

He grinned at the server. "Yeah, don't wait on those wings."

The guy laughed, gave a salute, and headed back to the kitchen to place our order.

"Gnaw my arm off, my ass," I muttered.

Finn put his hand to his ear. "What was that?"

"A gentleman would have ignored my rumbling stomach, not proclaimed it to the waitstaff." I crossed my arms over my chest and pretended to pout.

"If I'd have ignored your stomach, you might have talked yourself out of sharing a pizza with me, and that wouldn't do at all." His smile was positively puckish, and I couldn't suppress an answering twitch of my lips.

Since the place was about half-full, only a couple of minutes passed before the server arrived with our waters and beers. Grateful, I drank down a healthy swig of my stout, enjoying the bitter tang tickling my tongue.

"You said something about early-morning training. You do that even in the offseason?" I drew patterns in the condensation on my beer glass as my eyes traced the path of Finn's tongue licking beer foam from his upper lip.

Against my will, my core tingled with thoughts of that tongue licking me, and beneath the red gingham-topped table where he couldn't see, I clamped my thighs together.

"The offseason is where the magic happens." He waggled his brows. "Strong, conditioned bodies are more durable and harder to play against."

I chuckled. "Is that you or your coach talking?"

"Both." A cloud fell over his features. "But I could build that strong body equally as easily in the afternoons as in the dark hours of the morning."

Right then, a basket of steaming chicken wings landed on our table, courtesy of a smirking server. "Got 'em to you as quick as I could. Wouldn't want to be responsible for any carnage at your table."

The corner of Finn's mouth quirked up. "It was a near thing, but you did good. Thanks, man."

As I passed an appetizers plate across the table to Finn, I didn't bother to leave the snark out of my tone. "You're hilarious, you are. Both of you."

They exchanged a chuckle, and I seriously considered pulling the basket of wings to my side of the table beyond Finn's reach.

"Don't even think about it, Miss," Finn warned.

"What?" I batted my lashes at him.

"Keeping all those wings to yourself. There's not enough of you to eat 'em all."

I stuck my nose in the air. "You're the one who said I was hungry enough to gnaw my arm off." For emphasis I snagged three wings and put them on my plate. "Just sayin'."

His laughter filled our booth. "Gorgeous, smart, and fun to tease. You're the whole package, Chessly Clarke." Leaning forward, he added in a conspiratorial whisper, "And the way you kiss can make a man forget himself. Just. Sayin'."

That last comment stopped my hand mid-dip and my wing dripped aioli back into the bowl as my gaze took yet another tour of his full lips. His whiskey-colored eyes didn't leave mine as he covered my hand with his, raised the chicken wing to his mouth, and snapped off a bite right at the edge of my fingertips.

"Hey! No fair distracting me like that, wing thief."

He stopped chewing for long enough to toss me an unapologetic grin, finished chewing, and swallowed. "All's fair in love and dinner."

"Love?" I snorted. "You're a piece of work, Finn McCabe," I growled with none of the sarcasm I intended.

"Yeah? Like a Greek sculpture or Michelangelo's *David*?" He sucked some sauce from the tip of his finger and winked. "I can get on board with either."

I drew in a long breath and let it out with a lip-fluttering sigh. "It's the football player thing, right?"

He downed another wing then asked, his tone all innocence, "What is?"

"The over-the-top ego."

Twinkling eyes met mine. "You're the one who said I was a piece of work. I was curious about which one is all." Stuffing another wing into his mouth, he grinned at me around it, his expression utterly unapologetic.

Though I answered with a slow shake of my head, I couldn't help smiling back at him.

In much less time than I would have thought possible, all that remained of the basket of wings was a carnage of bones in the bottom of it. It stood to reason that most of the wings had gone into Finn, but I'd managed my fair share of the lot, much to his amusement.

Right as he dropped the last bones into the basket, the server arrived with a steaming pie.

"Exactly on time, my man," Finn said as the server slid the pizza onto the table.

Eyeing our wing basket, he smirked. "Looks like you were right about arms being in danger here."

With a sage nod, Finn said, "I know, right?" Chuckling, he added, "It was a near thing, let me tell you."

Under the table I gave his shin a little love tap with the toe of my boot.

"Ouch!" He slipped a hand beneath the table to massage his owie. "What was that for? Telling the truth?" Laughter danced in his tone as I tugged the pizza toward me.

"I shouldn't share any of this with you since you barely left me a wing."

The server chuckled at our antics before asking if we needed a refill of our beers. I asked for one. Finn didn't.

"Why didn't you order another beer?" I asked when the server moved off.

"The roads are slick, and I'm driving." The corner of his mouth quirked up as he tugged the pie back to the middle of the table.

Something in his tone told me what he truly meant, and it warmed me from the inside out. If someone had told me I'd end up with Finn McCabe after my usual coffee date with Jamaica today, I would have said they were nuts. Yet I'd spent most of the afternoon and early evening with the guy, and I had to admit to myself that he might not be what I thought he was on the night we met. Or, more correctly, what I thought he was when he dropped me off at the dorm that night.

I pinched off the cheese stretching from my slice to the rest of the pie, wrapping the excess around my finger then sucking it off. Across the table Finn's jaw stopped mid-chew as he watched me enjoy the gooey mozzarella. It was only cheese, but with the way his eyes darkened, it could have been something else. The second that thought entered my head, I shut it down by shoving food into my mouth.

I bit off a massive bite of my slice and immediately regretted it. Extra cheese meant extra-hot, and I panted through parted lips over the searing bite.

"Serves you right for not *blowing* on it first." Mischief danced in his eyes, telling me that his mind had definitely gone to the same place as mine.

For cripes' sake. Why did my mind keep going to naked Finn?

If I weren't careful, I'd give myself away and then I'd be just another football groupie, a jersey chaser. I loved the game, and I was a lifetime Wildcats fan, but I'd be damned if I'd ever stoop to chasing a football player. Even one who kept presenting himself as a genuinely nice guy. Even one as hot as Finn McCabe.

When the check came, I snagged it and pulled out some bills to cover my half. Finn pulled off his ball cap, ran a hand through his thick, wavy hair, mashed his hat back on his head, and spun it backward. A sheepish expression crossed his features as he cleared his throat.

"Um, I have an NIL with Stromboli's."

"I know. I've seen your ads on local TV."

"Yeah, well, I also get a discount on food here." He tugged the receipt from my fingers. "This is the actual price of our meal." He pointed to the small print at the bottom.

I knitted my brows. "Then why list the price everyone else would pay?"

"To make sure the servers receive their correct tips. It's, uh, something we all asked for." He rubbed his hand over the back of his neck as if he was embarrassed about being a decent person who didn't want to stiff the wait staff.

I pushed my money toward him. "Well then, that covers my half of the tip too."

"Chess."

"What's the deal, Finn? My friends and I always split the check." I tilted my head. "You didn't think I expected you to pay for me, did you?"

"I kinda wanted to."

Narrowing my eyes, I said, "This is not a date. It's two people who spent the afternoon studying together having something to eat afterward. That's all."

The wounded look that flitted across his face made me feel like I'd stolen his birthday cake. Before I could process it, he'd replaced it with a sunny smile.

"All right. That means I can plan a proper official date."

"Um—"

"We've hung out together a couple of times. We've already made out once—which, for the record, was a glorious experience." The wattage of his smile as the memory of that night was like a beacon in our booth. "Now we've studied together and had dinner together. The next step is an official date."

The comical way he waggled his brows tugged a reluctant half-smile from me. "I'll think about it."

He pulled out his wallet and added some bills to mine, stood, and held out his hand to me. "You bet you will."

Chapter Sixteen

Finn

EVEN THOUGH I'D put Chessly on notice we were going on an official date, two weeks passed before I had a chance to run into her again. We'd started DMing each other on social media, but she'd kept it light and hadn't given me an opening to ask her out. I had a bad feeling it had something to do with the fact that a certain group of jersey chasers who'd been walking toward her dorm when I dropped her off after our impromptu dinner. They'd glared at her, she'd glared back at them, and then she'd said good night without giving me even half a chance to steal a kiss.

Which I'd totally been planning to do.

I'd stopped by the Union on multiple afternoons, hoping to catch her and coming up empty. I'd checked her favorite study carrel in Hillman enough times that Ichabod, who usually had it, had started to smirk at me with something like pity in his eyes.

It was coming up on Valentine's Day, and I'd decided to ask her to join the gang for a sledding party on the old ski runs outside of town on the mountainside below the Mountain State "M." Callahan and Jamaica were going. I'd heard a rumor in the house that Bax had asked Chessly's other friend Piper, so I thought I had a better than even chance of success for making the sledding party our first official date. Asking her in person rather than over Instagram would only help ensure that success.

When I saw her in line for coffee at the Union a couple of days before Valentine's Day, I knew the gods were smiling on me. I stood at the end of the counter where she had to wait for her drink and studied her. Damn, would I ever get over how pretty she was? Today she was wearing some kind of lavender wool hat with a crocheted flower pinned to one side of it. It looked cute as hell. Something on her phone quirked up the corner of her lush mouth, and I wanted to know what put that expression on her face. Her smooth skin held a faint hint of pink, which said she'd recently come in from outside. The hem of her pink puffy coat grazed the tops of her thighs, hiding her pretty curves, yet accentuating her long legs dressed in skinny jeans.

When she glanced up from her phone, I smiled my winningest smile. "Hello, gorgeous. Long time, no see."

"Finn! You surprised me," she gasped.

"Got a minute?" I asked as we stepped away from the counter.

"Um, I'm actually on my way to class," she said. She sipped from her brew and momentarily closed her eyes in bliss.

"I'm between classes. I'll walk you."

For a second, she seemed to have to think it over—which, combined with this being the first in-person conversation we'd had for so long, worried me.

"Okay."

She started walking, and I fell into step beside her.

"I've looked for you here—and in Hillman—but you haven't been around much these past few weeks." I did my damnedest not to sound pouty, but from the side-eye she shot me, some of my frustration at not seeing her leaked into my tone.

"That quantum physics project I was working on that day—"

"Yeah?"

"It's due next week." She blew out a sigh. "Honestly, it's kicking my ass. My partners and I have been burning all the midnight oil, and the morning oil, and the afternoon oil . . ." She trailed off. "Plus, I was on deck for dorm programming for the past two weeks, which was such sucky timing with classes. I've barely had a chance to breathe." The look in her eyes when she glanced up at me willed me to believe her.

"I get it. I've had a few projects like that, especially in organic chemistry last year."

Tension melted out of her shoulders as she sipped her coffee. "After this weekend I might be able to snag a few minutes to do something fun."

"This weekend is Valentine's Day."

She shrugged. "So?"

"You know the old ski hill out by the 'M?'"

"What about it?"

I shoved my hands into the front pockets of my jeans. "A few times a year the old guy who owns the land lets people come out and sled the big hill the trees haven't overgrown yet. It's lit up and everything."

"Uh-huh."

Damn. She wasn't making this easy. Why I was so nervous to ask her out was an entirely different mystery.

"Valentine's Day is one of the days he opens it up. A bunch of us are heading up there to play, and I thought maybe you'd like to go with me." *Jesus, I sound like a sixteen-year-old.*

Chess stopped in the middle of the sidewalk to look me in the face. "You know what, Finn? That sounds like a blast."

The expression in those stunning sapphire eyes was sincerity itself, and a smile leaped to my face.

"But half the RAs on staff have dates already, which means the rest of us are on call." She started walking again, and it took me a few steps to catch up—literally and figuratively.

"You can't get out of it?" I asked. *Begged* was more like it.

"Afraid not." Her mouth turned down. "There's no one left to cover for me. I'm sorry, Finn." She glanced up at me with wistful eyes. "I bet it's going to be a ton of fun."

"Not as much fun as it would be if you were there."

We stopped outside the front doors to Hillman Hall. Tilting her head she asked, "You don't think you'll take someone else?"

She was fishing in waters that were full of traps—for me.

"Nah. Most of the team goes, and not many of us bring a date." I peeked at her from beneath my brows. "I heard Jamaica's going." Then I frowned. "Guess she's one of the RAs you're covering for, huh?"

"Yep." Tilting her head, she studied me. "You're really not going to ask anyone else?"

I stared down at where I was scuffing the toe of my boot into the snow on the sidewalk. "You were the only girl I wanted to play with." Gazing into her eyes, I said, "Guess I'll have to come up with a different epic idea for our first date."

For a long moment, we stared into each other's eyes.

She blinked first. "Give me some advance notice so I can shift my call if it's my turn."

Well, if that wasn't a green light for pursuing this girl, I didn't know what was. "I'll need your number for that."

Somewhere inside the building a bell rang, signaling two minutes until classes started. "I've gotta go."

I pulled my phone from my pocket and pulled up a screen. "Digits, Chessly."

She rattled off her number, flashed me a quick grin, and

headed into Hillman Hall. Over her shoulder she called, "I'm looking forward to epic."

Long after she disappeared inside the building, I stood on the sidewalk with a stupid smile on my face. Chessly Clarke wanted to go out with me. She was looking forward to an epic date. I'd made her a promise, and I had every intention of delivering.

The Monday following Valentine's Day, my physical chemistry prof decided people weren't taking the class seriously enough. To drive home his point, he assigned quizzes for every class for the next two weeks. By Thursday I was up to my ears in calculus, physics, and chemistry problems all rolled together, leaving me in serious danger of drowning in a sea of red marks, so I sent up an SOS to the one person I thought wouldn't mind helping me. I hoped.

> Me: Hey, you busy this afternoon?
>
> Chess: I need more advance notice than a couple hours for an epic date.
>
> Me: No doubt. And I promise to give that to you.
>
> Chess: So what's up?
>
> Me: This is me phoning a friend. ;) Would you mind helping me with some physics problems? I'll pay you in coffee or ice cream or both. Your choice.
>
> Chess: Both. Coffee before, ice cream after.
>
> Me: Deal. Meet you at the Union in thirty?
>
> Chess: Done.

I'd texted her some videos of a couple of the more spectacular wrecks on the sledding hill on Valentine's Day with a "wish you were here" note. She'd texted back laughing emojis. Other than that, we hadn't burned up each other's phones in the past week. If not for my pouty prof giving me an excuse, I probably would have resorted to barraging her with texts.

"What's with the cheesy grin, Finn? You got a hot date?" Danny teased as he passed through the living room with a load of laundry in his arms.

I swear, our new roommate practically lived in our laundry room. Of course, since he wasn't on scholarship—yet—he had a job at a local tire shop. Guess it was dirty work.

"Not yet. But I'm working on it."

He stopped and leveled me with a glare. "Not with one of those jersey chasers, I hope."

"No, Dad. I've figured out the deal with those girls. Especially since it means less money for my friends for scholarships." It was my turn to level him with my stare.

"From what Callahan told me the other night, some other donor stepped up and offered to fill the void Buzz Miller left when he pulled out of the alumni association in a huff. The guy runs a trucking outfit or something." He shifted his clothes higher in his arms.

"Who?" I asked, suspicion coloring my tone.

Danny smirked. "Jamaica's dad. He's directing the money specifically for football and Letters and Science scholarships—and his donation is bigger than Miller's."

"I hope that means your days at the tire store are numbered." I chuckled. "'Course, the job does give you an extra workout, which can't hurt, Fly Boy."

I had Danny by 80 pounds, but his years as a mechanic in the Air Force had stacked on the muscle. Plus he was wiry as hell, which made him a great receiver—and meant I'd never challenged him to a wrestling match despite my weight advantage. Didn't mean I wouldn't razz him though.

He snorted. "From the way you staggered up the hill with your tube the other night, you should probably join me slingin' tires around in the afternoons."

"Whatever." I flipped him the bird. "I made two runs for every one you made since you had to fool around with your girl at the top and bottom of each one. It's a wonder the two of you managed any tubing at all."

As he headed up the stairs, he huffed out another laugh. "Better get on that date so you can start having your own fun."

Thinking about meeting up with Chessly put a goofy grin on my face. I'd told her half an hour, but I wasted no time in stuffing my shit into my backpack, throwing on a hoodie and heading to the Union. I ended up waiting at the back of the coffee line for ten minutes before she arrived, but I didn't care. Sunshine followed her right into the building when she walked through the door, the sight of her warming me from head to toe.

"Hello, pretty girl. Thanks for agreeing to help me out," I said as she joined me.

She shrugged. "What can I say? I'm a sucker for problem-solving."

But I noticed the rosy glow tinging her cheeks at my greeting.

I moved a little closer to her and dropped my voice half an octave. "Is that right? Care to help me solve another problem I'm having?"

"What problem?" The words came out breathy.

"Figuring out how to spend more time with a certain hot physics major I know."

Her luscious lips flattened into a line. "Is that what your plea for help was? A sneaky way to see me? You don't need to make up excuses, Finn. You can just ask me out."

Putting up my hands in a slow-down gesture, I said, "My physical chemistry prof is on a tear. He's assigned a quiz for every day this week and next with the problems increasing in difficulty at a rate I'm struggling to keep up." I ducked my head. "I truly do need your help."

The barista signaled it was our turn to order. After Chess ordered her usual café au lait and I asked for an Americano, she shot me a look from beneath her brows while we waited for our drinks.

"So this afternoon isn't a date."

"Nothing epic about coffee and studying together." I winked. "And I promised you epic." Clearing my suddenly dry throat, I asked, "Are you on call next Saturday?"

"No." She dragged the word out almost into a question.

For a second I stared down at where I was toeing the linoleum tile, then I glanced up to catch her eyes. Jesus, her eyes were so blue and clear. Staring into them almost made me forget what I wanted to ask. "Got anything else going on?"

"Not yet." A smile came into those stunning eyes.

Damn, my mouth had gone as dry as the Mojave. I swallowed, and asked, "Would you like to go on an epic date—with me?"

"Order up for Chessly," the barista interrupted. "Got one here for Finn."

I grabbed my coffee and scalded the roof of my mouth in my haste to manufacture some spit.

A hint of a twinkle played with Chessly's warm smile before she hid it behind a sip of her latte. Another customer crowded in front of us to grab his drink, and I let my free hand dip to the small of her back to guide her over toward an open table at the back of the room.

We set our drinks down and pulled up chairs opposite each other, the unanswered question hanging in the air between us. But I couldn't take the suspense.

"You up for something epic?"

"After all the buildup, anything less will be anticlimactic

to the point of implosion. You sure you want to promise that?" she challenged.

I relaxed. "Don't you worry. I've had lots of time to think and plan. All you have to do is say yes."

Her smirk stretched into a full smile that threatened to blow my socks off. "Okay, Finn. Yes. I'll go out on an epic date with you next Saturday."

For a long moment, we sat there smiling at each other before I remembered why I'd asked her to coffee.

"Um, we should probably work on—"

"Yeah, we probably should."

Still, neither of us made a move to unload our backpacks until Chessly's friend Piper Maxwell materialized beside our table.

"Here's an interesting pair," she said with a chuckle. "Since when did you two start hanging out together?"

Chess cleared her throat. "Finn asked me to help him with some physics."

Piper crossed her arms over her chest. "Is that what the kids are calling it these days?" she teased.

To emphasize her point, Chessly opened her backpack and pulled out a notebook, a calculator, and some pencils. Raising her brows at me, she blinked twice and slid her gaze to where my backpack rested on the chair beside me.

Taking the hint, I unloaded my laptop, a notebook, and a pencil.

"Huh. From over there"—Piper nodded in the direction of the coffee line—"this looked pretty cozy for a study session."

"Don't you have a class or some corporation to dominate today?" Chessly grumbled.

"For the record, it's about time the two of you started hanging out." Piper laughed. "Maybe now you'll stop putting your grump on every time Finn's name comes up."

I didn't know how to take Piper's comment, so I asked, "I make you grumpy?"

"Only when jersey chasers are involved."

"Ah. Well, you don't have to worry about that. We put out the word we don't want them coming around the house, and Stromboli's hasn't let them through the door since the semester started." I leaned my forearms on the table. "Plus, I've taken up studying at Hillman instead of at the library."

Chessly's wide eyes told me she didn't miss my meaning.

"For the record, the two of you are cute together." A naughty grin accompanied Piper's observation. "Maybe you should study—"

"Piper." No one in a three-table radius could have missed the warning in Chessly's tone.

With a grin, I let my study partner know I kind of agreed with whatever Piper was going to say. The cute way she wrinkled her nose back at me only made me grin harder.

The deep baritone of my roommate's voice interrupted our little standoff. "Hey, babe. Sorry I'm late." Bax threw his arm over Piper's shoulders and brushed a kiss over the side of her head. "Finn. Chessly." He did a double-take. "Wait—are you two here together? I thought after that night at finals—"

It was my turn to shut my friend up. "Chess is helping me with some physics. No big deal." Why was it so hard for our friends—our *friends*, for crying out loud—to admit it was cool if Chessly and I hung out?

Bax's jacket hung open enough for me read today's T-shirt: "I enjoy long romantic walks to the beer fridge."

"I don't get it, Piper. How can a classy girl like you hang out with someone wearing that?" I pointed to Bax's shirt.

He glanced down at it as if he hadn't seen it before then glanced back up and grinned. "Piper appreciates honesty—right, babe?" He tugged her tighter against his side.

She smirked at him. "Absolutely."

I shook my head in wonder. Across the table Chess rolled her pretty eyes.

"We should get going, Piper." Something intimate colored my roommate's tone, and it didn't take a genius to know why he wanted to leave.

"Have a good afternoon, kids," Piper said with that naughty smile again. "Don't get into trouble."

Chessly bared her teeth at her friend while I deliberately took a long drink from my coffee.

When they finally moved off, we exchanged a glance before she broke the silence. "Well, that was awkward."

"Is it going to be awkward for you to go out with me?" With the uncomfortable way she'd acted after her friend arrived, I worried she might change her mind about our date.

"And miss the epic date to end all epic dates? Um, no." The mischief in her smile warmed my chest.

With a nod I said, "Good because we're going to have a great time." After a beat, I winked. "An epic time."

Chapter Seventeen

Chessly

"YOU'RE REALLY GOING out with Finn this weekend, huh?" Piper asked as we met for our Wednesday afternoon coffee date in the Union. "I thought with all the attention he pays to jersey chasers that you'd written him off." The concern on her face forced a confession.

"He's different than I thought."

My friend raised a skeptical brow.

"He's sweet, a funny combination of cocky and awkward." I sipped my café au lait. "And he likes my brain. We actually talk about science when we study together. When you saw us here the other day, he'd invited me to coffee so I could help him with some physics problems."

She sipped thoughtfully from her cup. "Huh. A pair of science nerds together. It does kind of make sense."

I wrinkled my nose at my friend. "Ha, ha. You're hilarious."

"I have to admit, you two are pretty cute together." Her eyes danced. "When we returned to school last fall, you, Jamaica, and I would have laughed our asses off if someone had told us we'd be dating Wildcats players right now."

"It's one date, Piper. We're a long way from you and Bax. Even longer from Callahan and Jamaica."

"With everything you put me through after my one-night stand with Wyatt, you think I'm going to let go of this thing growing between you and Finn?" She shook her head. "Nuh-uh-uh. It's your turn now." Her expression turned positively wicked. "Next week, I'm inviting Saylor and Jamaica to coffee with us so you can give up all the deets about your date."

I rolled my eyes so hard I almost pulled a muscle. "You'll get as much as you gave us about you and Bax."

A tiny secret grin spread over her lips. "We'll see."

Though I looked for him in Hillman a few times, I didn't see Finn at all during the week. Finally on Friday afternoon, I gave in and texted him. It felt weird, like I was being pushy or something, but I didn't want to greet him in jeans and a hoodie if he was taking me somewhere special like Copper with its cocktail dress and suit requirements.

Me: What is the dress code for this epic date?

It took him about half an hour to respond—time in which I wondered if maybe after all the hype, he'd panicked and decided to call off the date. I hated how disappointed the thought left me. After all, it was only one date.

Except I couldn't stop thinking about that night on his couch and the way his kisses had lit me up, how his big body pushing me into the cushions had heated my core, how conflicted I still was about those jersey chasers' interruption. What would have happened if they hadn't showed up when they did?

Finn: Casual. Probably a sweater would be good. And shoes you can play in.

Me: Shoes I can play in?

Finn: No heels. Tennies or something.

Thinking about Jamaica and Piper's descriptions of their Valentine's Day fun on the sledding hill, I asked: **Do I need snow pants too?**

Finn: We'll be inside.

Three little dots followed, so I waited.

Finn: Now stop fishing. I'll pick you up tomorrow at six.

He followed that with a heart-eyes emoji, which dragged a smile from me.

In high school, my friends and I mostly went on group dates, doing activities like skating parties and dances. The few guys I'd dated so far in college had taken me on standard dates to dinner or to the movies or to parties. Knowing Finn grew up in a small farming town in the middle of Montana, I couldn't imagine what he considered an epic date, but my excitement to find out had rocketed to the stratosphere. Anything short of fireworks was going to be anticlimactic.

A thought struck me, and I laughed. If he took me out for pizza and beer at Stromboli's, I honestly wouldn't be surprised. And it would be the funniest joke ever—ratchet up my expectations and then take me out to a bar. After the thought struck me, I kind of warmed to it. Then he texted me.

Finn: Do you have any food allergies?

Huh. Guess we weren't going to Stromboli's.

Me: None. But I'm not a fan of fish.

Finn: Cool. Me neither.

The three dots appeared, disappeared, and then: Six o'clock tomorrow. Epic. Followed by a winky-face emoji. I could absolutely see Finn giving me one of his cheesy winks, which twitched another laugh out of me.

What was it with these guys and their winking? I'd seen Bax wink at Piper from the football field—it was the reason Saylor and I had given her such a hard time about him. I'd also caught Callahan winking at Jamaica—only, the way he did it was panty-meltingly sexy and also a little overwhelming to my taste. Finn's winks were always silly, like he was trying out a move he knew he could never pull off.

So, of course, they worked.

At least on me.

Crap.

Too much of my headspace these days contained Finn McCabe.

I tossed my phone aside on my desk and pulled out a journal article on orchestrated objective reduction theory. The idea of our brains organically connecting to the universe, that we could experience quantum consciousness, allowing us to be in all places at the same time, fascinated me. I wondered if Finn had been thinking as hard about our date as I'd been thinking about it and if that was what had prompted me to step out of character and text him about it.

Determined to put a certain sexy football player and his epicness out of my head, I cued up my Mozart playlist—the one I'd made to improve my math scores—and started reading. Ironically, Orch OR theory took my mind off Finn and our date for the rest of the night.

By the time six o'clock rolled around the next day though,

I was a ball of nerves. Every sweater I owned lay in disarray on my bed. I finally settled on a turquoise boyfriend cardigan over a white T-shirt I tucked into my skinny jeans. Since snow was still blanketing the ground, I opted for my hikers rather than my tennis shoes and hoped I was appropriately dressed for an epic date.

At six on the dot, the front desk messaged me via the dorm intercom system to tell me I had a visitor in the lobby. In the mirror above the sink in my room, I gave my hair one last fluff, slicked a lick of lip gloss over my mouth, grabbed my jacket and wallet, and headed downstairs to meet my date.

With his massive shoulders and six-foot-six height, Finn stood out wherever he went. But in the lobby of an all-women's dorm, even seated on one of the couches in front of the floor-to-ceiling windows, he seemed to take up all the available space. The fact of how handsome he was with his cinnamon-brown hair flirting with the collar of his jacket, his sculpted cheeks, his square jaw, and those laughing whiskey-colored eyes, he couldn't help but grab people's attention. I noticed more than one girl checking him out as she walked through the lobby.

"Hey," I said.

His face lit up as he stood and walked to me. "Hey, Chess." He leaned down and brushed a kiss over my cheek. "Ready for our rocking date?" Leaning in close again, he inhaled and said, "Mmm. You smell nice. Like, really nice."

I blinked at the suave guy greeting me and grinned when he morphed back into Finn.

"Thank you." Smiling, I said, "I gotta admit, my curiosity about what you have planned is dialed to twenty on a scale of ten."

"Then we'd better take care of that."

Gesturing to the front doors, he silently asked me to precede him. Though I'd never admit it aloud, I liked how his dinner-plate-size hand rested on the small of my back as he ushered me to his waiting truck. Inside the cab was toasty-warm, and I slid a sideways glance his way. He'd dressed as he usually did: Wildcats hoodie, jeans, and hiking boots. No jacket even though a cold snap had accompanied the late February snow over the past week. I had a pretty good idea he was sacrificing his own comfort to heat up the cab for me.

"Where are we going?" I asked as I buckled myself in.

"How many times do I have to say it, woman? Quit fishing." The long-suffering look he gifted me cracked me up.

Crossing my arms over my chest, I directed my gaze forward and said, "Fine. I'll quietly await my big surprise." But I couldn't quite suppress a grin.

He didn't bother muffling his laughter. "This is already fun, and the night hasn't even started."

Only a few minutes later, he pulled his old pickup into the parking lot outside the football team's indoor practice facility. Without a word he killed the engine and hopped out, running around to the passenger side to open my door for me.

With a grand sweep of his hand, he said, "Milady."

Consternation knitted my brows. "Why—?"

Waggling his brows, he said, "Trust me."

Putting my hand in his, I stepped out of his ride, and hand in hand, we walked to the side door of the facility. Once inside, we passed several closed doors, which I assumed to be offices as we traversed a long hall. At the end of it, he opened a door to a locker room that smelled like the team might have finished working out for the day only half an hour before we arrived. I wrinkled my nose at the comingled scents of sweaty clothes, menthol, feet, and something nasty I couldn't quite place. The benches were devoid of anyone's gear, so the stench must be coming through the vents in the lockers lining two sides of the room and from the overflowing basket of wet towels outside the showers.

When he caught my expression, Finn said, "Damn. I should have brought you through the long way. Sorry."

We hurried to a door opposite the one we'd entered through and stepped out into a vast space covered in lined AstroTurf. Most of the field was shrouded in darkness except for a small circle of light directly across from us. Once again, Finn's hand rested on the small of my back as he guided me toward the circle of light. As we neared it, I saw a cooler resting beside a red-and-white gingham blanket. A raised pallet covered with a matching picnic cloth and flanked with two large cushions took up the middle of the blanket. The "table" was set for two, with china plates and actual silverware rather than paper and plastic.

"Have a seat," he said as he settled himself beside the cooler.

I sat on the cushion he indicated and watched in fascination as he opened the cooler and started pulling containers from it. Dinner began with appetizers: a veggie tray with hummus. While I helped myself to an appetizer, Finn pulled out two bottles of chocolate stout and two frosted glasses and poured each of us a beer.

"What do you think so far?" he asked.

Though his smile said "of course you love this," his eyes said "I hope I haven't fucked up."

"So far it's a novelty." I crunched on a carrot slathered with yummy hummus. "I've never eaten a picnic indoors in the winter. And I've always wondered what the inner sanctum of the Wildcats looked like." Catching the panic in his eyes, I added, "This beats any picnic I've ever experienced. No wind to cover dinner with dust. No bugs trying to steal bites of food or of me." I settled myself more comfortably on my cushion and smiled. "Real dishes and silverware. Cushions. And no clichés with dainty champagne flutes filled with bubbly—which, by the way, gives me a headache." I clinked my glass of beer to his and sipped. "I had no idea what to expect, but nothing in my wildest guesses included this."

Then, because he deserved it, I got real. "I can't believe how much thought and effort you put into this. You promised a rocking date, and so far you're delivering."

"Whew." A sigh gusted from him before he turned back to the cooler and started pulling out more food. "I didn't know what you liked, so I ordered a little of several things." In a few minutes, a feast covered the "table" between us. Vegetarian New Orleans sandwiches made with garlic roasted peppers and olive relish, succulent meatball skewers, asparagus and peas salad with feta and mint, homemade crackers with a smoky cheese spread, and some sort of tangy pasta salad made with penne, tomatoes, basil, and mozzarella balls. It all had my mouth watering.

"You didn't cook all this yourself," I teased.

"Can you keep a secret from my roommates?" he asked.

With a shrug I said, "Probably."

His narrowed eyes said he was considering withholding his secret.

With an exasperated tilt of my head, I said, "Of course I can keep a secret."

"I could have made all this." He waved his hand over the meal. "It's all food I like. But even though my mom insisted I learn to cook—and I'm good at it—I hate doing it." He spread cheese on a cracker and popped the whole thing into his mouth, chewed, swallowed. "At the house I pretend not to know how, and on my nights to make dinner, I usually pay for takeout." He smirked. "I manage to skip a turn each week 'cause my roomies prefer homemade food."

I laughed. "You're incorrigible!"

He waggled his brows. "You mean smart."

Picking up a meatball skewer from the platter of them, he bit down on the bamboo and pulled the skewer from his lips. My eyes strayed to his mouth, and I grew uncomfortably warm thinking about what it would feel like to have his perfect straight teeth gently bite down on my shoulder—or the inside of my thigh.

Averting my eyes to my own meal, I spooned salad and veggies onto my plate and added a sandwich. "How did you manage to set this up? Or can any player use this space after-hours?"

"Early on I learned to make friends with the equipment and facilities managers. They can make a player's life all kinds of easier." He downed two sandwiches to my one, and I understood the need for such a huge outlay for only two people. "I, uh, started planning this after you turned me down for sledding on Valentine's Day. When I ran my idea by the facilities manager, she loved it as long as I didn't advertise." At my look of confusion, he clarified. "She doesn't want the whole team setting up dates in here every weekend."

"Of course she doesn't. Wouldn't want the Wildcats to get a reputation for being sweethearts." I smirked.

"Exactly."

Finding out he'd put so much advance planning into this evening gave me a pang. For so long I'd thought Finn to be a stereotypically shallow, egotistical football player. Instead, I was discovering he was a man of many layers, and to my shock, I wanted to peel back each one of them.

Turning sideways, I stretched my legs in front of me and sighed. "That was so good. I'm so full I don't think I could eat another bite."

"That's a bummer." He polished off one last meatball skewer and wiped his hands on the cloth napkin beside his plate.

"Why?"

"Because there's dessert." The happiness in his tone reminded me of a six-year-old at a birthday party anticipating cake.

Tilting my head, I blinked at him. "Seriously?"

"Oh yeah." Those two syllables mimicked an orgasmic sigh.

"When you put it like that"—I shifted on my cushion and shot him a flirty grin—"I'll make room."

"Atta girl." Reaching back into his magic picnic cooler, he

carefully pulled out two parfait glasses with special plastic covers on them and handed one to me. Next he passed me a long spoon and said, "Dig in."

I held the glass up to inspect its contents and felt my eyebrows climbing up my forehead. "Is this what I think it is?"

He poked his spoon into his dessert and tasted it, licking the spoon afterward. Watching his tongue curl over his spoon momentarily distracted me, my thighs clamping together at the sudden picture of that tongue curling over certain parts of me.

What's wrong with me? We're only sharing a picnic. On a practice field no less.

Yet the wicked gleam in those whiskey eyes said he knew exactly what thoughts that little move had put into my head.

"If you think it's delicious, you'd be correct."

Was it me, or had his voice dropped?

I dipped my spoon into my dessert and closed my eyes in delight as flavors of fluffy chocolate mousse and sweet-tart raspberry ganache filled my mouth. "Oh my God, how did you know this is my all-time favorite dessert?" My eyes popped open to catch him staring at my mouth.

Shifting on his cushion, his words came out on a rasp. "I took a chance that you might like my favorite dessert."

"It's so good." I spooned another bite and moaned over the textures and flavors filling my mouth.

Finn cleared his throat. "Chessly Clarke, I didn't take you for such a wicked woman."

Only then did I notice his dessert had remained untouched.

"I thought you said chocolate-and-raspberry mousse was your favorite." I pointed at his half-finished dessert. "If you don't want to finish yours, I bet I can make room for it," I teased.

"Wicked, wicked woman," he muttered, throwing me a dark look.

I laughed.

So I wasn't the only one thinking naughty thoughts while we ate our meal. I didn't know what else he had planned for the evening, but I had a good idea I was going to enjoy it.

Chapter Eighteen

Finn

THIS GIRL. CHESSLY killed me the second she arrived in the lobby of her dorm. That oversize sweater made her gorgeous blue eyes pop and emphasized the perfect handfuls of her hips and those long, long legs in her tight jeans. The way her eyes sparkled with curiosity and fun when I played with her on the ride over to the facility told me I'd read her right when I planned our first date.

All through dinner she never let me up, wrapping her plump pink lips over a hummus covered celery stick, groaning with pleasure as she noshed on a succulent meatball, teasing me with her eyes as she dabbed olive relish from her sandwich from the corner of her mouth with her napkin. She'd left me semi-hard from the minute we sat down to eat.

Then she went to work on her dessert, that pink tongue touring those kissable lips, licking off every last taste of the chocolate-raspberry treat, and I thought I'd lose my mind. Before

Chessly, I had no idea sharing a meal with someone could be so damn sexy.

"Next time I'll order two desserts for you." I smiled.

"Next time we could just have dessert for dinner," she said as she set her empty parfait glass on our makeshift table.

I liked that both of us were already talking about another date before our first one was even over.

"You want anything else?" I nodded toward the cooler beside me. "I have a couple more beers in here, but we might want them later since the next part of the evening has the potential to leave us parched."

She blinked. "This isn't it? A romantic picnic in the middle of a football field?"

"Epic, remember?" My lips twitched as I watched her process. "A picnic doesn't rise to the challenge." I started putting away the remnants of our meal—which, admittedly, I'd eaten the lion's share of, but I'd planned for that.

Wordlessly, Chessly pitched in to help. In a couple of minutes, we'd put the picnic away and stacked the blankets neatly on top of the cushions and the pallet I'd used for a table.

She stood when I did, and I said, "Wait right there."

Her brow and the corner of her mouth hitched up, but she said nothing. I jogged down to the other end of the field where I'd set up the rest of our date. Since we only finished dinner a minute ago, I decided we'd start easy. I flipped on the switch for the glow-in-the-dark ring-toss/tic-tac-toe game and jogged back to where I'd left my date.

"What's going on? Have you invited aliens to join us?" she teased.

"Not quite." I slipped her hand into mine and started walking toward the game.

My hand swallowed hers up, but she gripped mine in a way that said she liked holding onto me. God knew I loved touching her. As we strolled up the field, I couldn't seem to stop my thumb from stroking the warm, soft back of her hand. If I hadn't been so tuned in to her, I might have missed the tiny shiver that shook her the first time I stroked over her skin. I didn't even try to stop the smile from stretching my lips at her response to my touch.

When we neared the game, she let go of my hand, and with a delighted laugh ran ahead of me.

"A glow-in-the-dark game!" Turning back to me, she said, "I love playing these."

In her excitement I don't think she clocked that she'd grabbed my bicep and squeezed with both hands. But I noticed—all the way to my cock.

"Let's see who's the better strategist—physics major or biochem major."

"You are so going down, big guy," she challenged. Picking up a handful of glowing yellow rings she asked, "Where is the touchline?"

I'd strategically set up the game so the touchline was one of the painted lines on the turf. Pointing to it, I said, "Here." Then I picked up a handful of red rings and stood beside her.

Right as she pulled her arm back to toss her first ring, I said, "Care to make a little wager on the outcome of this game?"

Stopping mid-swing, she narrowed her eyes. "What kind of wager?"

I touched my forefinger to my lips, pretending to think about it. "If I win, you give me a kiss."

"And if I win?"

"I'll give you a kiss."

Tilting her head, she regarded me with dancing eyes. "So no matter what, when the game is over, there will be kissing."

"Huh." I feigned surprise. "That didn't occur to me until you pointed it out, but now that you mention it, I see your point. The outcome of the game will involve kissing." Leaning down, I brushed a soft kiss over her cheek. "I like this game already, and we haven't even started playing yet."

She blinked, and then a slow smile played over her lush lips.

Focusing her concentration on the glowing green and blue pegs, she wound up and stepped into her throw, ringing one on the edge of the square. Throwing her hands in the air, she did a cute little dance, the remainder of her glowing yellow rings creating a light show as she waved them above her head.

"Nice one," I said before I stepped into my own throw. My glowing red ring dropped over the blue peg beside her yellow ring, forcing her to choose another direction.

She launched her ring for the row opposite the touchline and overshot the game. "Damn," she whispered.

Seeing my advantage, I aimed for the middle blue peg and ringed it.

Suspicion colored her tone. "You've played this game more than a few times, I think."

With a shrug I said, "We like to play lawn games at the house."

After emitting a frustrated growl, she lined up her shot to block me and landed her ring on the peg next up from where she intended.

"Unlucky."

She peered up at me from beneath her eyebrows, her expression daring me to end the game.

Of course I took that dare. After all, the stakes were a kiss. When I dropped my red ring over the peg, lining up three rings across the middle of the square, I turned to her with a grin.

"Pay up."

Her eyes glittered with mischief as she stepped into me. With the foot difference in our heights, I had to lean down a bit to give her access. When she wrapped her hand around the back of my neck, I closed my eyes and puckered up in anticipation of her sweet mouth. But the kiss I expected didn't land on my lips.

Instead, she pressed her luscious lips to the corner of my jaw, lingered for a second, and stepped back.

"There's your kiss."

I should have clocked that warning in her naughty gaze. But when she played with the stakes, she gave me ideas for the rest of the night.

"Thank you." I smirked. "Stay right here."

I set my one extra ring beside the square of glowing pegs and jogged across the field to where I'd set up the next game: glow-in-the-dark cornhole. After I turned on the game's lights, I trotted back to my date. "Let's see how we do with the next one."

She shot me a dubious glare when we walked up to the game. "You play this at every football party, I bet."

"Nah. I'm usually representing the boys at the beer pong table."

Ignoring my comment, she went on. "Plus, your roommate is from Kentucky. I read somewhere that this game originated there."

"Maybe." I shrugged. "I couldn't tell you. But I don't play it as much as you think."

"Hmph," she snorted.

Suppressing a laugh, I said, "Same stakes?"

Shooting me a side-eye, followed by an eye roll and a secret little smile, she nodded.

"Which one do you want?"

Chess walked over to the red-lit cornhole box and picked up the matching glowing beanbags I'd stacked on the edge of it. I picked up the glowing blue beanbags and stood on the other side of the box from her.

"You go first," she said.

I tossed a bag at the illuminated blue box opposite us, landing it on the slope below the hole.

With impressive concentration, she lined up her shot and tossed, landing her bag on the lip of the hole.

"Hmm," I said and lined up my next toss.

She cleared her throat right as I swung through, and I let go of the bag a fraction too late, sending it up in the air to land on the turf at the foot of the box.

"You did that on purpose."

Turning that liquid blue gaze to me, she batted her lashes. "I have no idea what you're talking about."

She lined up her next shot, and right as she swung through, I snorted into my hand, "Cheater."

My antics didn't faze her. She followed through with a perfect toss that dropped the bag through the hole, taking the one clinging to the edge with it.

"What was that?" she asked, her tone all innocence. "I don't see how you can cheat at cornhole."

Without giving her another chance to distract me, I tossed my third bag, landing it beside the first one on the slope of the box. Her next toss landed on the box right above my two bags. My next toss skidded off the end of the box, and hers landed beside it. When we tallied up the points, she had me down five to zip.

"Seems to me you've maybe played this game once or twice," I said as we retrieved our bags from the blue box and set up to aim at the red one.

With a noncommittal toss of her hair, she said, "I might have played it before."

Might have played it before, my ass. Chessly wiped the floor with me, beating me 21-9, and she hadn't wasted any time doing it.

"Remind me to have you on my team at the next party," I said as we stacked the bags on the blue box.

She stood in front on me, an expectant expression on her pretty face, and it was my turn to tease. Leaning in close, I nibbled my way along her jaw to the sensitive spot behind her ear where I lingered an open-mouthed kiss and relished the shiver that stole over her. For an extra second or two, I stayed where I was, inhaling the soft floral scent of her perfume, a smell that shot straight to my groin.

Stepping away from her, I said, "The next game requires a bit more skill, so I think we need to up the stakes."

"Yeah?" came out in a dreamy tone that I liked—a lot.

"Wait here."

I dragged myself away from changing the bet and giving her a kiss for every point she'd outscored me. Instead, I headed for the end zone where I'd set up the ultimate glow-in-the-dark game. Running from post to post, I turned on the lights for glow-in-the-dark Zber my parents had given me for my birthday last year. As I set it up, that thought about extra kisses took up residence in my head. By the time every post and ball was lit up in a rainbow of neon color, I'd decided to up the ante considerably.

Eyeing the end zone, which was now lit up like some kind of shimmering neon obstacle course, Chessly asked, "What are we playing now?"

"Zber." I handed her a brightly lit lime-green disc. Noting the consternation on her face, I said, "It's a kind of frisbee-golf game. You score points for hitting the posts or for knocking off the balls sitting on top of them."

With a sage nod, she said, "Good thing you're a lineman and not a quarterback."

"Why is that?"

"Because I have a chance against you in this game."

I cleared my throat. "Did you or did you not just kick my ass at cornhole?"

She laughed. "My dad's in a league. He likes to practice with me in the back yard in the summer."

"Huh. Funny you didn't mention that before we started."

Her alto laughter rippled through me. "Looks like you're going to get even with this game."

With my lips next to her ear, I whispered, "I plan to get ahead."

She returned a narrow-eyed challenge, and my body tightened in anticipation of the game—and the stakes.

"We'll make this one more interesting, yeah? For every post you hit, I give you a kiss. For every ball I knock off, you give me two kisses."

"What if I knock the ball off the post?"

"I'll give you three kisses."

A tiny smile played over her mouth. "Challenge accepted. You go first."

Not knowing if Chess had even thrown a disc before, I'd set up the course in a wide zig-zag so we wouldn't have to make fancy throws around posts. I'd also made it fairly short because even though I could fling a frisbee for almost the width of the end zone, I doubted my date could. After the shellacking she'd given me in cornhole, however, I had to consider the flaws in my strategy.

Loosely gripping my glowing blue disc, I took aim at the first "hole," a post about ten yards from the sideline starting point, and let my disc fly. It rapped against the post with enough force to send the neon-purple golf ball resting atop it for a ride.

"That will be two kisses, please," I said.

"Nuh-uh-uh. You hit the post, not the ball." She planted her hands on her hips. "And you accused me of cheating at cornhole." Then she pushed up on her toes and left a soft kiss in the hollow of my throat. When she stepped back, her eyes glittered up at me.

Swallowing hard, I said, "Your turn." I led her to the next touchline and stepped aside as she lined up her shot.

Her disc skimmed the top of the ball without hitting either the ball or the post, leaving an open shot for me. Taking careful aim, I let my disc go, knocking the ball from its post with the frisbee itself rather than its momentum.

"This time there are no technicalities. You owe me two kisses."

My mouth tingled with the desire to have her lips on mine, but with the way the games had gone so far, that wasn't in the cards—yet. My body hummed in anticipation of where she would decide to kiss me though.

Reaching up, she palmed my cheeks and tugged me down to her level. Then she planted one soft kiss on my eyebrow and another in the middle of my chin.

A chuckle bubbled out of me at her antics as she stepped away to retrieve her disc. Again, I let her go first, and this time she dialed in on the post, her disc giving it a tap for a point, but not enough to knock off the golf ball resting on it. Following her lead, I buried my nose in the sweet scent of her behind her ear and trailed the tip of it down the side of her neck and across her collarbone, stopping at the hollow of her throat where I planted an open-mouthed kiss. A tiny moan escaped her, and when I stepped back, my heart sped up at the desire darkening her stunning sapphire eyes.

After that my throw was a bit wobbly, but it still managed to hit the mark, sending the glowing white golf ball flying with the disc.

This time, she took my left hand first and brushed her lips over my knuckles before switching her attention to my right hand. Her eyes danced as she stared directly into mine and gave me an open-mouthed kiss in the middle of my palm. Until that second, I had no idea my hands were erogenous zones. White-hot desire shot from my palm, up my arm, into my chest, and down the center of my body to pool in my balls. Something in my expression must have tipped her off, because Chessly shot me a wicked grin before turning away to sashay over to retrieve her frisbee. When she deliberately bent at the waist to grab her disc, my eyes arrowed directly to her sweet ass, and my mouth watered. With her concentration on her next toss, I dropped a hand in front of my zipper and discreetly adjusted myself in my jeans.

On the next "hole," she had some luck at last. Her toss bumped the post right at the top, knocking the little white ball to the ground. Sticking her hand out, she said, "That will be three kisses, I believe. Pay up."

The games had begun as me teasing her, but this girl was a quick study, turning the tables on me so fast. I wrapped one arm around her waist, drawing her front flush with mine, and cradled the back of her head with the other, holding her right where I needed her. Her hands flew to my biceps, and she held her breath as she waited for where I'd kiss her first. After her antics on the last toss, my patience was shot, so I didn't make her wait long.

Kissing that tiny divot in the middle of her chin, I whispered, "One." Then I kissed the corner of her mouth and said, "Two." Her lips parted slightly, and I said, "Three," before I mashed my mouth to hers, eagerly accepting the invitation she'd given me.

In seconds we'd both forgotten the game as our lips fused together, our tongues chasing and tagging each other as though it were the only activity they were meant to do. Chessly's hands found their way to my shoulders, one sliding up to plow her fingers into my hair while she dug the fingers of her other hand into the hard muscle of my back. To my ever-loving delight, she held me as tight as I held her. When she started climbing me, I dropped my hands to her ass, hauling her up so she could wrap those pretty legs of hers around me.

I sank deep into the kiss, losing myself in the sweetness that was Chessly Clarke. Moans from the back of my throat harmonized with whimpers coming from the back of hers as I squeezed her ass and licked and sucked her tongue and nibbled and tugged on her luscious mouth with my lips and teeth. Even as I lowered us to the ground, we kissed each other reckless.

When her back met the turf, her hips started moving. Her kisses had already lit me on fire, so when she rubbed her soft center along my hard length, I wondered for a second if the flames would eat me alive. But I didn't care.

As I dry-humped her, my hand found its way under her sweater and shirt. The warm satin of her skin rippled beneath my touch, signaling to me I could continue my explorations. When I encountered the lace of her bra, I smiled into our kiss. The tight bud pushing at the lace excited me, and I traced over it with the pad of my finger—once, twice, repeatedly, until she squirmed and arched her back, demanding I do more than tease.

Jesus. I wanted this girl more than I wanted air. Then from somewhere on the other end of the field, the sound of a heavy door slamming penetrated the lust roaring in my ears. Against me, Chessly stiffened, and I broke off the kiss, panting in gulps of air as I stared down into her desire-darkened eyes.

"Who's out there?" a male voice I recognized called out.

"Guess our game ended in a draw," I whispered as I rolled to Chessly's side.

"Who's standing at the door?" she whispered back.

"Barney. He's one of the janitors for the facility. Looks like Georgie, the facilities director who gave me the green light for tonight, forgot to tell him."

With a groan, I dragged myself to my feet. My boner made walking a bit of a chore, and no doubt Chess noticed, but I didn't have a choice.

"Hey, Barney!" I called out. "It's me. Finn. Georgie said my date and I could play lawn games on the turf so long as we didn't make a mess."

"Is that what all that glowing is? I thought aliens had invaded for sure." He chortled at his bad joke.

With a half-hearted laugh, I said, "No aliens. Don't worry. We'll clean up and lock the door behind us when we leave."

"You want some help carrying your stuff out? Looks like you could use it."

Chessly jogged up beside me. "That would be nice of you. Thanks." Extending her hand, she said, "I'm Chessly."

Automatically, Barney stuck out his hand. Then his gaze wandered from Chess to me, and a speculative grin split his face. "Sorry for interrupting your evening. I saw a glow of light under the door and thought I'd better check on it." His tone didn't sound sorry. But he'd poked a pin in the mood, leaving me no choice but to go with it.

"That's great, Barney. Thanks."

I spun on my heel and headed back to the games. In only a minute or two, we had everything powered down and gathered up. Between the three of us, we only needed to make two trips to my pickup to put away what had taken me an hour and a half to set up earlier in the afternoon.

In the horseshoe drive in front of Chessly's dorm, I unbuckled, and turned in my seat.

"Epic, yeah?"

Her smile lit up the interior of the cab of my truck. "Epic. Best first date ever. Thank you."

I slid my hand across the back of the seat and moved closer to her. "Thank you for making it so damn fun." Slipping my fingers beneath the hair on her neck, I gave her a tiny squeeze. "How 'bout if you come a little closer?"

She unbuckled and inched over the seat, a naughty tease in her eyes.

"A little closer."

"Is this a new game?" she asked as she moved another inch toward me.

My eyes strayed to her plump, kissable lips. "Nope. This is a 'thanks for the epic time' kiss, a 'let's go out again' kiss, and maybe after that, a good night kiss even though I'd rather not end the evening."

"Before tonight I would never have taken you for a romantic."

I blinked my shock.

Her pretty lips twitched. "What with you being a scientist and all. But you so totally are a romantic."

I moved closer to the middle of the bench seat. "Admit it. You like that about me." I traced the pad of my thumb over the sensitive skin behind her ear and leaned in to whisper, "You like me."

Cupping my cheek in her palm, she stared deep into my eyes. "You're right. I do like you."

The "thanks for a great time" kiss started in overtime. Chess fused her lips to mine, our tongues jumping right back into that game of tag we'd been playing so well together before the janitor interrupted us. As she kissed the breath right out of me, I discovered the possibility I might never be able to get enough of her hot mouth. When she mashed her chest to mine for the "let's do this again" kiss, I wrapped my arms tight around her and held on.

As my hand found its way to the tight round globe of her ass, she retreated a bit, nibbling and lipping my lips and along my jaw on her way to the sweet spot behind my ear. Obviously, she intended for her good night kiss to leave me with heavy balls I'd definitely have to take care of when I returned to the house.

With a sigh, she scooted over to the door. "I had a really good time, Finn."

"Wanna get together tomorrow afternoon to study?"

"Hillman Hall?"

"Or my place."

Chapter Nineteen

Chessly

"YOU NEED AN extra shot of caffeine in your latte, girlfriend?" Saylor's eyes danced as she blew on her coffee. "How was your 'epic' date?" she asked with air quotes.

Since Piper and Jamaica were otherwise occupied, Saylor and I were it for our standing Sunday morning brunch. Didn't mean I'd escape the inquisition though.

"Finn delivered." I cut into my veggie omelet and stuffed my mouth with a big bite of cheesy-eggy goodness, savoring the crunch of perfectly cooked asparagus and broccoli chunks.

"Did he, now?" Saylor's tone demanded more than my four syllable answer.

With deliberate nonchalance, I said, "We had a lovely picnic and played glow-in-the-dark lawn games on the practice field." I picked up my café au lait and sipped.

Her brows rose to her hairline. "Sounds like he put some effort into it."

The phantom pleasure of turf digging into my back as Finn pinned me to it ghosted over me, the memory setting fire to my core. Shifting in my chair, I swallowed another drink of my coffee.

"And it looks like you had a *good* time," she emphasized with a smirk.

"We shared a kiss. Don't make more of it than it was." I dug into my omelet again, a tiny demon in the back of my mind calling me out for my understatement.

"The pink glow on your cheeks and the way you're squirming tell me that's not it. At. All." Putting her elbows on the table, Saylor lifted her drink to her lips with both hands, drank, and leaned forward conspiratorially. "I'm dating vicariously through Piper, Jamaica, and you. Do not leave me hanging."

Shaking my head, I said, "I'm not going to make something up to satisfy your prurient interests, Saylor Davis. We had a picnic, played some fun games, and he brought me home. End of story." I was never one to kiss and tell, but something about telling my friend about my date with Finn felt like a betrayal: an invasion of our privacy. My lips sealed shut at the idea of sharing any more than I already had.

"No, it's not, and you being as closed-mouthed about it as you are is exactly like Jamaica and Piper. None of you are spilling much of anything. It's highly annoying." She sat back in her chair, pouting. Then a sly grin slid over her features. "So that's how it is. After one date you're all in with Finn, aren't you?"

Pulling a face, I said, "I have no idea what you're talking about." But a little voice in the back of my head contradicted me. *You know exactly what she's talking about* it said.

"Fine. I'll wait until Piper and Jamaica join us. Between the three of us, we'll tease the truth out of you."

"Uh-huh. What about you and Jeremiah Fitzgerald?"

Waving a hand in front of her, Saylor said, "He's a monumental flirt."

"Sounds like someone else I know." I grinned.

She batted her lashes at me. "We did a lot of flirting and had fun, but when he kissed me"—she made a fist and flicked it open—"poof. Nothing. Zero chemistry. For either of us." Checking her nails, she added, "Sad, really. His voice alone could cause orgasms. Then he smiles and lights up the room. Plus, he's super-smart. I bet he ends up on the Supreme Court someday."

"So why aren't you two dating?"

"Like I said. Zero. Chemistry." She sighed. "Some other girl is going to get very, very lucky."

My mind wandered to the way Finn had teased me with little kisses anywhere but on my mouth, and how the anticipation had made my heart race almost out of my chest when he won his "points." When at last he'd pressed his mouth to mine, I thought I might self-combust with lust. From the sounds he'd made and the way he'd ground into me, my kisses had a similar effect on him. Our chemistry was the kind known for causing explosions.

A throat clearing across the table returned me to the present. "You wandered off on me again." Saylor smirked. "You haven't told me anything about last night, have you?"

"I told you everything," I lied. "As much as there is to tell anyway."

"I don't believe you, but you're digging your heels in, so I'll give it a rest—for now."

When I returned to the dorm, I hung out at the front desk as a distraction from spending the rest of the morning reliving each moment of my date with Finn. Though gorgeous, smart, and supremely athletic, it turned out his true asset lay in a romantic nature I never would have guessed before last night. The guy was such a gentleman who obviously wanted to impress me, but also cared that I'd had a super time. From the thoughtful way he'd arranged our picnic and chosen the food, to the fun surprise of playing games together, he'd gone out of his way to show me he had more going on than just a handsome face and superior football playing skills.

Finn's vulnerability in showing me his romantic side told me how attracted he was to me every bit as much as his kisses did.

Aaand, I was back to thinking about his panty-melting kisses again. *Ugh!* The way the man had used his sexy mouth to drive me straight out of my head topped the list of his other fine qualities. I had no idea what I expected, but I certainly never anticipated the way he could make me lose myself in his touch. I mean, I should have had a clue after that night during finals when I found myself pressed into the cushions of his couch by his deliciously hard body. But last night during our date, he'd upped the ante with his teasing, the anticipation of when he would finally put his lips on mine driving me to distraction. At the memory of those hot kisses, coupled with the pleasure of his hard length behind his fly rubbing along the fly of my jeans, my skin tingled and my core pulsed a naughty rhythm.

"Are you trying to memorize the entire schedule for March?" Jimmy asked, a bigger question drawing his brows together.

With an embarrassed little huff at being caught daydreaming about night things, I said, "Nope. Trying to remember if I set up a program for my floor on the Wednesday before St. Patrick's Day." Deliberately, I set the calendar back in its spot behind Jimmy's chair and pulled up the chair next to his.

Lots of students took advantage of work-study jobs like desk-clerking because they could basically get paid for studying for classes. The desk-clerk positions in the women's dorms were especially sought-after since those dorms tended to be quieter than the men's or the co-ed ones, and the male clerks liked the opportunity to meet women somewhere other than at bars or on dating apps.

Jimmy Anderson was our standing Sunday desk clerk—had been since my freshman year. Not once in the time I'd known him had I ever seen him hit on one of the residents or even strike up a conversation that could be remotely construed as flirtatious. A graduate student in astrophysics, he had a plan for joining NASA and working on the team that put people on Mars. Usually, we talked physics, and more than once, he'd helped me out of a jam with a problem or a project. But the way he was looking at me this morning told me he had serious concerns about my mental state.

"What are you working on?" I asked with a nod to the books spread over the counter separating the desk area from the lobby.

"Quarks." The frown between his brows didn't ease. "You sure you're all right?"

"Positive."

His question had me rethinking my big idea to hang out at the front desk, but the arrival of a couple of freshmen who lived on my floor last semester preempted my scramble for a graceful exit.

"We're here to pick up some friends—from 2C and 3B." Chelsea Vonda, one of the nastier girls who'd eagerly joined Tory Miller's posse last semester, curled her lip in my direction. "We're saving them from dorm life," she added as though she were some sort of hero.

The girls they were picking up lived on mine and Jamaica's floors. That couldn't be a coincidence.

Jimmy pointed to the old rotary phone sitting on the end of the counter. "You know the drill. Dial their room number and wait for them to come get you."

"It's such a dumb rule, especially for women," Chelsea's companion said with a less intimidating sneer. Apparently, she was still in training.

"It's basic safety protocol. Presumably the reason certain

women choose to live in Hanover." From his tone, I picked up that these girls didn't impress Jimmy any more than they impressed me.

"Whatever." Tossing her heavy brunette locks over her shoulder, Chelsea picked up the receiver and dialed a number. "We're here." With a nod she pressed the peg down on the phone cradle with her index finger and then dialed a second number. "We're waiting in the lobby."

Curious to see who the Delta Chi pledges had in their sights for recruitment to the mean-girl sorority, I stood and checked my mailbox, which gave me a reason to linger without having to engage with them. A few minutes later, Josie, the sweetest and quietest girl on my floor, rounded the corner into the lobby. My eyes about bugged out of my head when I saw who they'd set their sights on. Were the Delta Chis trying to clean up their ugly reputation, or were they targeting the sweeties because they'd run out of girls like themselves? Why would Josie go with them? Perhaps she and I needed to talk later.

Another girl I recognized from seeing her around the dorm entered the lobby from Jamaica's floor. The dorm was built in the shape of an "H" with the lobby as the crossbar, which made it easy to discern the general area in which a resident lived based on the side she entered or exited the lobby. Though I didn't know her personally, her demeanor gave away her type: sweet, wholesome, maybe a little naïve. Her light blonde hair fell over the side of her face when she ducked her head in greeting.

Something was up. I'd have to talk to Jamaica about her resident too. Looked like the four of us should go out for coffee or something.

I didn't have a problem with the sororities in general. For the most part, they were fancier dorms with more rules than Hanover, each filled with like-minded women. Since I belonged to the women's physics sorority, I actually understood the appeal of such social organizations—except for Delta Chi. I knew about their reputation for nasty from my first campus visit, through freshman orientation, to the mess Tory Miller had put me through last year and the mess she'd put Jamaica through last semester. Nothing but trouble lived in that house, which only made the current scene with Josie and the other apparently sweet girl walking out of the lobby with Chelsea and her friend worrisome.

Jimmy interrupted my thoughts. "Can't imagine what those two want with the nice girls. Hope they're not planning something like a scene out of *Carrie*."

I gasped. "You've seen *Carrie*? Which one—the classic from the seventies or the one from 2013?"

He shot me a look. "The original, of course. Remakes never bring anything new to the table."

"Agreed. I watched Sissy Spacek in Brian de Palma's version after watching Chloë Grace Moretz, and there's no comparison."

"All irrelevant to what just walked out the door of this place together."

I sighed. "I was thinking the same thing. Looks like Jamaica and I will have to plan an intervention. Unless Josie and the other girl *want* to join Delta Chi, which is truly hard for me to believe."

"I was thinking it more than coincidental those two had come for girls from yours and Jamaica's floors." Jimmy's brow lifted. "Tory Miller's had it in for you guys since the day she walked into this dorm. Watch your back, Chessly."

Chapter Twenty

Finn

"HOW DID YOUR 'epic' date go last night, Slick?" Danny asked as he leaned against my bedroom door.

Picking my dirty socks off the floor, I balled them up and slam-dunked them into my dirty-clothes hamper. "Nailed it."

"On the first date?" His eyes rounded in surprise. "Didn't see that coming."

"I didn't nail Chessly. Jeez. Give me some credit for being a gentleman." I shook my head in disgust. "I nailed the date." A grin ghosted over my mouth at the memory of Chessly's expression when she saw the picnic I'd laid out on the turf. "I showed my lady a real good time."

Giving me a slow clap, he said, "Good for you, man. You gonna see her again?"

"Studying together this afternoon."

"'Studying'?" he asked with air quotes. "Great euphemism."

"Because we *are* studying." I rolled my

eyes as I shouldered past him into the hall on my way to the stairs. "Chess has a big quantum physics midterm, and my asshole physical chemistry prof is still assigning daily problems and quizzes."

I dropped down the stairs two at a time with Danny right on my heels. When I reached the bottom, I heard giggling coming from the kitchen.

"Sounds like someone has company this morning," I said.

Behind me Danny chuckled.

The two of us walked in on Jamaica and Callahan nose to nose, smiling at each other. She sat on the countertop with her legs wrapped around him, the two of them oblivious to our presence until I cleared my throat—loudly.

Simultaneously, they turned their faces toward the doorway though the sides of their heads remained touching. "Good morning, Finn. How was your hot date?" Callahan asked before he put a little space between him and his girl.

"Epic. As promised." I grinned.

Jamaica's lips twitched. "Chess thought so too?"

The memory of my sweet girl grinding against me as I'd pinned her to the turf surged up in my brain, leaving a heaviness in my balls. "Yeah, pretty sure she had a good time." I hid the rasp in my voice with a deliberate walk to the fridge. "We got any burritos left?" I glanced away from the open door to the fridge to catch my friends smirking at each other. "What?" I asked.

"I can't decide if you're lying to us or—" Callahan stopped and exchanged a knowing glance with Jamaica.

"Or?"

Whatever he saw on my face spread a cheesy grin over his. "Or you had an epic date last night."

"It's what I keep telling you assholes." Clearing my throat, I added, "Not including you in that, Jamaica."

She laughed. "I didn't think you were."

Danny stepped around me to peruse the contents of the fridge. "Doesn't look like we have any burritos left. Who's up for biscuits and gravy?"

Jamaica pushed off the counter to land practically on Callahan's toes. "I'll make the biscuits if you make the sausage and gravy," she said to Danny.

Just like that the conversation moved from Chessly and me to breakfast, but I wasn't stupid. At some point I could expect an ambush when they thought I wasn't paying attention.

It came near the end of the meal. As I sopped up the dregs of the gravy on my plate with the last biscuit I'd won from Danny in a spirited game of Rochambeau—because he always went to scissors, which made it easy to beat him—Callahan slipped in a sly question.

"Girls talk, you know. Wonder what Chessly will tell my girl when they meet for coffee?"

"That I showed her a good time and was a complete gentleman while I did it." I stood and walked my plate over to the sink where I rinsed it and put it in the dishwasher. "Fuck's sake. The way you guys act, you'd think I don't have a clue how to treat a woman." I grabbed the now empty frying pan off the trivet in the middle of the table and went to work washing it. Since my buddies had done all the cooking, the cleanup was on me. Their commentary made me want to finish in record time so I could escape to my room to avoid any more of it.

Bax must have spent the night at Piper's, so at least I was spared his bullshit. Could have done without Danny following me to my room, though.

"So your date is coming over to study today?" he asked, mocking me with the corner of his mouth as he crossed his arms and leaned on the doorframe to watch me strip the sheets from my bed. "Totally explains the need for clean sheets."

"It's Sunday, asshole. I always wash my sheets on Sunday—

that is if *someone* lets me have a turn with the washer." I shot him my own mocking grin. "You got a thing for appliances? Seems like you spend a lot of time in the laundry room."

"Ha, ha. You're hilarious, Finnegan."

Pulling a set of clean sheets from the bottom drawer of my dresser, I motioned to him. "If you insist on razzing me, you could make yourself useful, at least."

"Fuuuck." He pushed away from the door and dragged his ass over to the side of the bed. "The one thing I promised myself after I left the Air Force was I'd never make a bed again if I didn't have to."

I snapped the bottom sheet across the mattress, and he grabbed a corner with enough force to pop the fabric out of my hand. Snagging the elastic corner again, I pulled it over the edge of the mattress and tucked it in. In about a second flat, we had the bottom sheet pulled so tight over the mattress we could have bounced a quarter off it.

"Guess that explains your bed." I flicked the top sheet over the mattress and smoothed my side of it.

Even after stopping to flip me the bird, Danny was way ahead of me, his side looking utterly perfect. I tossed the blankets across, and in about five seconds, he'd smoothed them out and folded a perfect hospital corner at the bottom of his side. I stopped for a moment to stare at his work before finishing my side.

Clearing my throat, I asked, "Was there a prize for being the fastest at making your bed?"

"Our sergeant usually rolled us out of bed about two minutes before he demanded we be on the parade ground—dressed in fatigues with our beds made and our teeth brushed. Last one to muster got twenty extra push-ups during PT."

I blew out a breath. "Fuck, man. Your sergeant sounds like a bigger hard-ass than Coach Larkin."

"Larkin's a teddy bear compared to my CO, trust me."

Standing at the bottom of the bed, I snapped my comforter across it without asking for Danny's help, but he gave it anyway. I wasn't a big fan of making the bed either, but with my teammate's help, the job took about a tenth of the time it normally took me.

"Before today I thought you were kind of a slob, but now I get why your bed's a disaster. I wouldn't appreciate the daily reminder of all that military fun either."

I gathered up the dirty sheets and stuffed them on top of my smelly workout gear in my hamper. The faint stench of sweat had started to sneak out into my room, telling me I was a day or two past when I should have done laundry.

"Thanks for the help," I said as I carried my dirty clothes out into the hall.

"You still haven't answered the question," Danny said as he followed me.

"Like I told you earlier, we're studying together. We do that often, actually."

He narrowed his eyes. "I've only ever seen Chessly here with Jamaica. When have you two been studying together?"

I headed downstairs. "Since the beginning of the semester. But we usually meet up in the Union or Hillman."

"Yet today she's coming over here? That must have been an epic date last night."

I heard the laughter in his voice as he followed me through the house to the laundry room.

"Don't you have something better to do than follow me around today?"

He watched me load my sheets into the washer, measure out laundry soap, and turn on the machine. "Nope. Sundays are my day off from the tire shop. Thought maybe you'd want to get your ass kicked in *Madden* this morning."

Bax and I usually played *COD* together against a bunch of guys online. Of course, that activity slowed way down after he started seeing Piper. Danny, on the other hand, hardly ever wanted to play *COD*, opting for *Madden* instead. He said after his military service, first-person shooter games stopped being as much fun.

Didn't matter today, though, because I was busy. Grabbing the vacuum from its closet beside the dryer, I said, "Don't have time to beat up on your donkeys, my man."

How a guy as cool and badass as Danny Chambers could be a fan of the Denver Broncos mystified me. He'd had to master the video game for a chance to compete with the rest of the league, given the lack of premier players available to him since he always chose his favorite team.

"Chicken," he taunted, which on any other day might have been enough to goad me into playing a game with him, but I had bigger things on my mind.

"Busy." I headed upstairs with the vacuum and shut off his noise with the machine's whine as I went to work on the carpet in my room. Since my space wasn't the size of Callahan's master suite, and it wasn't my turn to clean our communal bathroom, my chore only took a few minutes. It helped that I'd tidied up earlier.

Satisfied I wouldn't embarrass myself with being a slob in front of my girl, I returned the vacuum to its designated home and stepped into the kitchen to check out what, if anything, we had for snacks. I already knew Chessly liked hot chocolate with marshmallows, and checking the pantry, I saw we had plenty of both. I also spied a bag of peanut M&Ms and several bags of chips, so snacks were covered.

Back in my room, I couldn't settle in to make a head start on my homework, even after I promised myself I'd do exactly that—give myself a little cushion in case studying with Chessly led to other things. Not that I was planning on other things per se, but it didn't hurt to be prepared.

I snort-laughed at myself. Who was I kidding? The question

wasn't *if* I was going to spend quality time kissing Chess, but *how much* time I'd be spending with my lips locked with hers. No wonder I was so antsy.

But it was only noon. I had to give her time for lunch before I texted her to ask if we were still on. I mean, of course we were still on, but it didn't hurt to let her know I hadn't made any assumptions, my thoughts of kissing her notwithstanding.

I dropped to the floor and knocked out forty push-ups. When that barely calmed me, I added thirty squats. Then I remembered my laundry and jogged downstairs to move it. After I jogged back up to my room, I settled myself down enough to sit at my desk and solve five of the twenty problems Professor Fox had dumped on us "to keep us out of trouble" over the weekend. The guy was a peach.

When I checked my phone again, it was after one, which gave me the green light to text Chess at last.

Me: You still up to study together this afternoon?

I kicked back and waited as the little dots waved across the bottom of the screen.

Chessly: In the middle of something. Text you in thirty.

The fuck? I had to wait another half hour to see if we were still on?

Tossing my phone across my desk, I headed downstairs. When I'd scanned the fridge for burritos before breakfast, I'd noticed someone had left half a pizza behind, and I decided it had my name on it. I shoved down several slices of meat lover's and topped it with a beer then returned to my room. A text waited on my phone.

Chess: Do you want to study here or at Hillman?

Me: My place. I'll be over in ten to pick you up.

She didn't need time to think about it and back out. Though she was majoring in physics, she needed reminding that we had chemistry, lots of combustible chemistry. Less than a minute after I texted her, I was backing down the driveway in my truck, headed to her dorm.

When I arrived, I walked past a couple of girls I recognized as running with Tory and her band of jersey chasers. Not wanting to be rude, I gave them a chin tip when they smiled at me, but I kept moving to the phone at the end of the desk. Dialing up her room number, I waited for her to answer.

"Hello?"

"Your carriage awaits, milady."

"You sure? We can always study here. I think the Passion Pit is open."

Was it my imagination, or did she sound a little nervous? What would she have to be nervous about?

"As intriguing as the Passion Pit sounds, I left my books back at my place."

A tiny sigh puffed through the line. "Okay. I'll be down in a few."

She clicked off, and I wandered over to a row of vinyl couches lined up in front of the wide windows overlooking the drive where my pickup waited. I sat on the end of a couch and glanced around the lobby.

Big mistake.

Those jersey chasers took my lack of occupation as an invitation and parked their asses right beside me.

"Hey, Finn. We've missed you at the library." The girl wore a Wildcats jersey over a short skirt. How had I missed that?

"Yeah, Finn, where have you been?" Her friend stood in front of me, twirling her hair and blocking my view of where Chess would arrive from.

"Ladies." I cleared my throat. "I don't want to be rude, but could you back off, please? I'm waiting for someone."

Hair twirler stuffed her hands on her hips. "Who are you waiting for?" The edge in her tone was at odds with the conversation.

"Look, Sally."

"Sadie."

"Right. Right. Sadie, could you give me some space?"

"I hope you aren't here for that witch, Chessly Clarke. Someone said they saw you with her in the Union last week," Mia, the clinger beside me said.

Seeing no way around it, I stood, forcing both girls to give me the room I'd asked for. "Nice seeing you. Have a good day."

I strolled over to the desk, leaned against it, and pulled out my phone. Right then, Chess rounded the corner into the lobby, and my heart did a little happy dance.

I couldn't help the smile stretching my lips. "Hey, you. Ready to go?"

Her answering smile stopped halfway as she glanced past me. "Um—"

"Seriously, Finn? You've been ditching us for her?" Mia sneered.

Hurt flickered over Chessly's features before she composed her face into something bland. The first expression gave me a pang. The second one terrified me.

Taking a step toward her and lowering my voice, I said, "Chess. Do not let these girls wreck our afternoon before it even starts."

Her eyes found mine, and whatever she saw there must have reassured her I meant it because she squared her shoulders and said, "I hope you have snacks 'cause I missed lunch."

Slipping her hand in mine, I turned and walked right between the two jersey chasers who seemed to want to block our exit but stepped aside once they figured out I wasn't going to stop moving.

"She can't possibly be any fun, Finn," Sadie said as I passed by her.

My mama raised me to be polite, especially to girls, but I guess some of them didn't appreciate it enough to return the favor. Still, rather than engage, I kept walking. It wasn't until we were outside the building and halfway to my truck that I caught on that Chessly was having to double-time to keep up with my stride.

"Sorry," I said as I slowed down. "Those two ambushed me the second I hung up the phone with you. I had to work to remember their names even, so don't go thinking I have something going on with them."

I shot her a you-have-to-believe-me look as I opened the passenger door to my truck for her.

She remained quiet as she climbed in, and I worried about that too.

It had taken way too much time and the hell my best friend had gone through last semester for me to catch a clue about Tory Miller and her bunch of jersey chasers. The little scene in the dorm lobby only confirmed my roommates' wisdom in staying far away from those girls. That politeness my mom had drilled into me when I was growing up had its place, and for the most part it had served me well. But maybe I needed to put it aside in certain circumstances. The idea didn't sit well, but given a choice between sneering freshmen whose only interest in me came from the fact I played football and the hot woman currently seated in my ride, there was no contest. Now I needed to convince her of that.

Chapter Twenty-One

Chessly

"WHAT'S YOUR PREFERENCE for lunch? We can call it in and pick it up on the way to my place," Finn said as he swung up into the driver's seat of his truck.

"I don't know. Have you eaten?" I stared at his big hands as he buckled himself in. Those hands fascinated me, especially when they touched me.

"I ate half a pizza about an hour ago for a snack, so I could do with lunch."

That grin should probably be added to an infectious disease list. As much as I wanted to ignore it, to my disgust the corner of my mouth twitched. "You ate half a pizza as a *snack*? Wow."

He patted his fit abs. "It takes calories to keep this motor running."

Though I shook my head, I couldn't help but smile at his ridiculousness. "I could go for a Pickle Barrel."

His grin ratcheted up several watts.

"Excellent plan. Their subs are my favorite." Putting the truck in gear, he added, "And their monster cookies—mmm, mmm, mmm. I might have to order a couple of those."

"You have kind of a sweet tooth, don't you?" I asked as I watched his beautiful hands expertly grip the wheel.

He slid me a side-eye. "After one taste of you, I might have developed one. Yes."

My eyes roamed the ceiling of his pickup. "Where do you pick up these lines?"

Tapping the side of his head with his index finger, he said, "I don't use all this massive brainpower solely to solve chemistry problems."

"Uh-huh. Don't quit your day job."

My sardonic tone pulled a laugh from him. But maybe he picked up on the little shiver that stole over me at his words.

The Pickle Barrel was a tiny hole-in-the-wall only about a block from my dorm. Its size and location were two reasons I frequented it to the point the sandwich makers knew my order the second I walked through the door.

"Half a Beach Comber, hold the onions!" called the skinny girl whose name tag read "Anna" from her place behind the register.

Finn glanced around the space. Both indoor tables were weirdly empty on a Sunday afternoon. He looked back at me. "Is that your order?"

"Yes." I peeked at him from beneath my brows. "I might get that every time I come in."

He smirked. "Alrighty then." Stepping up to the register, he perused the colorfully scripted menu on the chalkboard behind the counter and said, "Add a full South of the Border Cheesesteak and three monster cookies." He pulled his wallet from his jeans pocket.

"Anything to drink?"

"Got it covered." He turned to me. "Unless you have a regular drink too?"

"I'm good," I said, pulling my wallet from the pocket of my hoodie.

Swamping my hand with his, he pushed it and my wallet back toward my waist. "I got this."

"We're studying together. It's not a date," I protested. "You don't have to pay for my lunch."

"Not up for debate, babe." He tapped his card on the reader and put it back in his wallet.

Shaking my head, I mumbled, "Not necessary."

Putting a hand to his ear, he asked, "What was that?"

I crossed my arms over my chest. "Thank you."

His gorgeous whiskey-colored eyes warmed. "You're welcome."

As we headed over to his place, the heavenly scent of sautéed peppers and cheesy meat from his sandwich permeated the interior of the cab, causing my stomach to rumble.

"Is this a thing with you?" he teased.

I crossed my arms over my middle and willed my stomach to be quiet. "Asks the guy who eats half a pizza for a snack."

"Point taken." He smirked.

A few minutes later, he swung his truck in behind another truck already parked in the long driveway fronting the old Victorian where he lived. A Mustang was parked beside it, and I couldn't decide if I was glad or not that two of his roommates were home. The hand-holding and buying me lunch felt more like a date, but the presence of roommates signaled "study session only."

Finn grabbed the bag containing our lunch and hopped out of his truck, jogging around the front of it to open my door for me even before I'd unbuckled my seat belt.

"Thank you," I said as I snagged my backpack from the floor at my feet and followed him up the steps into the house.

In the foyer he toed off his boots and set them neatly on a rug in front of a closet, so I did the same. Then he led me through the eerily silent living room to the kitchen where he set our lunch on the table in the corner. Glancing over at me, he said, "Oh, hey. Let me grab those for you."

He tugged my backpack off my shoulder and held out his other hand for my jacket then disappeared back into the living room. A few seconds later I heard the creak of the stairs as he jogged up them. Guess we were studying in his room. A door closed, and next I heard him thunder back down the stairs. For a big man, he was deceptively quick.

When he reentered the kitchen, he headed straight to the fridge. "What can I get you to drink? A beer? An energy drink?" He pushed something around on a shelf. "Looks like we have some orange juice left."

"Water's fine, thanks."

He closed the door of the fridge and pulled two glasses from a cupboard above the sink, filled them from the tap, and set them on the table. Then he rummaged in the pantry beside the fridge and pulled out a jumbo-size bag of chips, setting it on the table beside the bag of sandwiches.

Nodding to a chair, he said, "Don't wait for me, babe. I wouldn't want you to faint from hunger with lunch in easy reach."

I narrowed my eyes at the mischief tipping up the corner of his mouth. My stomach chose that moment to let loose a cascading series of rumbles and gurgles that filled the kitchen. He snorted a laugh and slid across the floor on his stocking feet to pull two plates from the cupboard, setting one in front of the chair he'd indicated. The guy was such a big goof.

"Like I said, Chess. Dig in before you die of starvation."

"You're hilarious."

"I'm not the one packing around a lion inside me clamoring to be fed."

Wrinkling my nose in his direction, I sat at the table and reached for the bag of sandwiches. Even though my stomach had been the one making all the noise, Finn attacked his cheesesteak, devouring half of it before I'd swallowed three bites of my turkey sub.

When he put his sandwich down for a drink of water, I gestured at the remains and said, "Looks like I'm not the only one who needed lunch."

He tore open the bag of chips and shook a pile onto his plate. "Sorry." The tops of his cheeks took on a ruddy hue. "My mom's always calling me out to slow down, but in this house, you get conditioned to eat up before it's gone." For the next few minutes, he made a point of eating one chip at a time.

"Where are your roommates? At least two of them are home, yeah?"

"Danny has Sundays off from his job." With a smirk, he added, "I imagine your best friend is studying in Callahan's room with him."

"And we're studying in yours?" The thought of being alone with him in a room with a bed in it left me a little breathless.

His eyes dipped to my mouth. "That's not a problem, is it?" With a blink his eyes found mine. "I mean, we can study down here, but we'll be interrupted and distracted, probably more than once."

I was already distracted, and we hadn't finished lunch.

Sliding my tongue over my lips, I said, "Probably better to study without interruptions or distractions."

When his gaze strayed to my mouth again, my skin flashed hot, and I seriously wondered what I'd been thinking when I dressed in layers for the day.

Needing a detour from the direction my thoughts had gone, I picked up my sandwich and filled my mouth with turkey and Italian sausage sub goodness. Finn's eyes remained on my mouth. I stilled in mid-chew as he lifted his hand to my face to gently brush something from the corner of my lip.

I blinked, and he said, "A shred of lettuce escaped."

The ghost of his touch rippled over my skin, and I did my damnedest not to let him see my response. The fleeting dimple in the side of his cheek told me I hadn't kept that to myself. Swallowing my bite of sandwich, I said, "Thanks."

A secret smile revealed that dimple again as he turned his attention to the remnants of his sub. We finished our meal in a charged silence broken only by sideways glances and heated cheeks (mine) and little grins (his). It was like sitting near my sixth-grade crush in the school cafeteria all over again.

As Finn cleaned up the kitchen after lunch—he insisted I didn't need to help with sliding plates and glasses into the dishwasher—Danny wandered into the kitchen, rubbing a hand over his chest. "Hey, you bought lunch? Didja pick up any extra?" Doing a double-take, he said, "Hey, Chessly. I didn't see you there." Returning his attention to Finn, he repeated, "Didja bring home any extra?"

"Sorry, dude. You're on your own." Finn smirked then lunged for the bag containing the monster cookies we'd left on the table.

"Story of my life this weekend," Danny grumbled as he wandered over to the fridge.

Chuckling at his friend, Finn caught my hand in his and led me from the kitchen. In my experience study partners didn't hold hands, but Finn's warm, calloused hand engulfing mine felt so exactly right I couldn't protest.

"Behave up there, kids," Danny called after us. "My room shares a wall with yours, Finnegan."

Even while holding a bag of cookies, Finn managed to flip Danny the bird and kept walking, his long-legged stride forcing me to double-time to keep up as we crossed the living room to the stairs. At least he slowed down as we climbed up the steps to the second story of the house. Stopping outside a door opposite the bathroom, he motioned for me to go ahead of him into his room.

I didn't know what I expected when I entered his private domain, but the perfectly made up king bed and the tidy floor surprised me. Of course a man his size would need a big bed. A squeak of a giggle escaped me as I thought about him trying to fit his tall, broad frame into a narrow dorm bed. The fresh scent of clean laundry and Finn's woodsy cologne, which left me a bit light-headed whenever he moved in close, permeated the air. It was all I could do to stop myself from sucking in a massive noseful and savoring it inside me for a minute.

My backpack sat on the floor beside his desk in the corner on the same wall as the door. His books were stacked neatly on top of the desk, but short of me sitting on his lap on the lone chair tucked beneath it, there was nowhere for me to work.

Turning to share my observation, I ran *smack* into the brick wall masquerading as his chest. Automatically, his arms wrapped around me, and I had no idea what to do.

"Whoa there, Speed Racer."

The laugh in his voice vibrated through me, sending tiny jolts of electricity arcing through my veins.

"Um," I said into his chest, "there's only one chair." At last I glanced up at him. "Maybe we should try the kitchen after all."

"Most of the time, I spread out over my bed, so you can have the chair and the desk—unless you want to flop down on the bed too." He grinned down at me. "I'll make room."

Pulling out of his embrace, I wandered over to the desk. "This is good." I frowned. "Why do you have it pushed against the wall? Why not over here"—I pointed to spot below the window—"where your body doesn't block out the natural light?"

"When I located my desk by the window, I never did any work."

My brow slid up.

He chuckled. "Step over there and look outside."

I did as he suggested and immediately figured out the problem. His window faced the street. Across the road from their house was another old Victorian whose front porch was teeming with people even though it had started to snow on this fine February Sunday afternoon.

"The basketball team won an away game yesterday. We're supposed to be over there helping them celebrate. If my desk looked out on that, the temptation to stroll over to play flip-cup would be damn hard to ignore." Stuffing his hands in the front pockets of his jeans, he explained, "With my desk facing the wall, I can pretend I don't know what's going on across the street, so I won't feel like I'm missing out when I'm plowing through a mountain of unnecessary physics problems purely designed to stroke my prof's fragile ego."

I let the corner of my mouth tip up. "Guess we should tackle those problems so you can show off in class tomorrow."

I hefted my backpack onto the edge of his desk and unzipped it, pulling out my laptop, my notebook, and my own physics book, stacking my gear beside Finn's before returning my bag to the floor. Taking the hint, Finn stepped up beside me and snagged his books from the desk to deposit them in the middle of his massive bed. His eyes danced wickedly as he hopped up onto it and stretched out, his back resting against a mass of pillows piled against the headboard. He reached over to the nightstand where he'd deposited the bag of cookies and pulled one out. Breaking it in half, he said, "You want some?"

Planting my hands on my hips, I said, "You're offering me half? I want the whole cookie."

His eyes heated. "Me too."

Somehow I didn't think he was talking about sweets.

While taking a man-size bite of one half while holding up the other and crooking his finger, he motioned me to the side of his bed. I took a step in that direction then abruptly changed course and raced to the nightstand with the idea of snagging the bag with the other two cookies in it.

Finn must have figured out my intention the moment I made it because he managed to grab the bag and toss it over his body to land it on the bed on the other side of him a second ahead of me reaching the nightstand.

With a magnanimous wave, he offered me the half a cookie again. "We're sharing, Chessly. Catch up." Those incredible eyes of his teased me as he watched me over the top of the second bite of his half.

Baring my teeth at him, I snatched my treat and retreated to the foot of the bed where I leaned a hip against the mattress and savored a bite of nutty, chocolate-and-butterscotch-chip delight. As we ate our dessert, we watched each other, wheels turning in both of our heads. I worked to devise a distraction that would allow me a shot at stealing that bag so I could enjoy a whole cookie. No doubt he was thinking about how he was going to deny me my goal and remain in control of our treats.

As I finished off my half, Finn swung his long legs over the side of the bed, giving me a better shot at hopping up there and attaining my goal. But right as I made my move, he wrapped his hands around my waist. I landed on his lap with a squeak, and he laughed.

His gaze zeroed in on my mouth. "You're kind of messy, you know that?"

"I am not," didn't come out as forceful as I intended—not with him staring at my mouth like it was second dessert.

Leaning in, he touched the tip of his tongue to the corner of my lips, teasing and licking my skin as I closed my eyes and held my breath. Tiny tremors rippled over my cheek as my body tightened in anticipation of what he'd do next. When he pulled back, I lost myself in the dark depths of his eyes, their whiskey-colored irises rimming the black pools of his pupils.

"You had a little chocolate there." The hoarse sound of his voice shot straight to my center.

"Oh," came out on a whisper.

"Looks like a little butterscotch got left behind here." He licked the opposite corner of my mouth—the barest of touches that made my blood bubble in my veins.

Somehow, my hands had found their way to his wide shoulders where I gripped him out of fear I might melt into a gooey mess right in the center of his lap.

Then he brushed his lips over mine, and I melted all over him.

Chapter Twenty-Two

Finn

THE PLAN WAS to study together. Honest.

But when Chessly challenged me about the cookies and made her move to steal the bag, all my focus shifted.

Damn, but she was sweet. When she wiggled around in my lap to straddle me, I forgot all about cookies and homework and the thin wall separating my room from Danny's. She wrapped her arms around my neck and pressed her full titties to my chest, and I lost all coherent thought except for one: kiss the hell out of this girl and show her why she wants to be mine.

In about a minute, it seemed, teasing kisses turned volcanic when she opened her mouth and let me inside. Her whimpers and breathy moans turned me inside out. I squeezed the perfect handfuls of her ass and urged her closer. Trailing my fingertips along her spine until I held the back of her neck, I relished the shivers that pushed her body closer to mine, the needy sounds coming from the back of her throat as she started to grind herself on me.

Slowly, carefully, I eased back, taking her with me until I was lying on the mattress beneath the sexiest girl on the planet. All the while, I kissed her, first nibbling and nipping her full bottom lip before soothing it with my tongue. Then she took advantage, sucking on my tongue, and it was my turn to grind against her. At last we needed air, and Chess pushed up on my chest, gazing down at me with dazed eyes.

For a long minute, we watched each other as we panted in much-needed oxygen. She blinked, and her focus shifted to somewhere above my right shoulder. I figured out her a move a split second too late.

Snatching the bag of cookies, she rolled off me with clear designs of escape, taking my favorite treats with her. She made it to the edge of the bed before I had her around the waist, hauling her back up onto my chest.

"What do you think you're doing, thief?"

"Thief? *Thief?*" she squeaked. "At least I'm not a cookie hoarder."

"Yeah? So you're sharing?" I tightened my arms around her belly.

"Uh, sure," she drawled, her tone lacking any vestiges of sincerity.

In one quick move, I slid her onto her back and fell on top of her, careful not to squish the air out of her. Pulling her wrists above her head, I said, "I'm not sure I believe you."

Even with my hand pinning her wrist to the comforter, she didn't loosen her grip on the cookie bag. Those gorgeous sapphire eyes that haunted my dreams sparkled up at me with equal parts teasing and desire. I imagined mine communicated the same message. "I'll split with you just like you split with me—one third for you, two thirds for me."

"It was fifty-fifty," I corrected.

Narrowing her eyes, she said, "Calculus isn't your struggle, Finn. It's fractions."

She bucked her hips in a vain attempt to push me off her,

but the move sent my mind in another direction. Leaning down, I nosed my way along her jaw to the corner where I nibbled for a bit before kissing my way down the column of her neck.

Another half-hearted buck of her hips accompanied a breathy "Finn."

"Mmm?" I kissed my way back up to the hot spot behind her ear.

"If you let go of my hands, I promise to share." Her breathy tone said cookies weren't truly on her mind.

I let go of her free hand and she promptly slid her fingers into my hair. My free hand found its way to her waist, my fingers slipping beneath her sweatshirt to find warm, silky skin.

An "Oh!" escaped her, the sound goading me to explore. When I encountered the smooth satin of her bra, her earlier bucking against me morphed into a sensuous, languid writhing, accentuated with moans and my name on a sigh. *Fuck*, this girl's sounds alone were enough to get a guy off.

"Can I take this off of you?" I tugged on her sweatshirt.

"Yes," came out on a puff of air.

She lifted her shoulders off the mattress as I slid her clothes from her body. Then I sat back and looked my fill. Chessly Clarke lying in the middle of my dark blue comforter in her plain white bra ranked as the hottest sight I'd ever seen.

"Why are you staring?"

I put my hands on hers to stop her from covering herself. "Jesus, babe. You are fucking gorgeous."

Sliding down her body, I rained kisses down her neck, across her collarbone to the hollow of her throat where I licked and nibbled, drawing more of those breathy sighs from her. I kissed along the perfect swells of her breasts above the fabric of her bra, and she started moving again, her hands buried in my hair as she held me to her. Taking a chance, I slipped a finger beneath the band, rubbing and petting the tight bud I discovered.

With surprising strength, she pushed me up long enough to reach behind her back and unclasp her bra. When she lay back down, my mouth watered at the sight of her full tits topped with a pair of dusky-pink nipples I just had to taste.

"Finn!" she cried out. "Oh!"

Chess tugged on my hair, alternately pulling me from her and pushing me close. *Damn*, I loved how she couldn't stay still beneath my touch. Then she grabbed a couple handfuls of my hoodie and grunted, "Off!"

I pulled off her nipple with a little pop as I sat up. Reaching behind my neck, I tugged my hoodie over my head and tossed it to the floor behind me. "This too?" I pointed to my T-shirt.

She growled and I laughed.

My T-shirt landed somewhere on the floor. Then it was my turn for my skin to ripple and shiver beneath her busy fingers as she explored my belly and pecs. Echoing my earlier sentiments, she said, "Finn, you are fucking gorgeous."

If I hadn't already been so damn hard, the rasp in her voice, the touch of her hands on my body, and the dark pools of her eyes, which had turned to smoke at seeing me half-naked, would have left me as hard as cement. As it was, I harbored a real fear the fly of my jeans would soon be no match for my cock.

As if she heard my thoughts, Chessly dropped her busy hands to the button of my jeans. With an impish little grin, she asked, "May I?"

"Yes. Please." My voice sounded rough in my ears.

I might have breathed a sigh of relief when she slowly lowered the zipper, except her knuckles grazed my length, and impossibly, I grew harder. *Fuck*. I was on fire for this girl.

Covering her hands with mine, I stopped her progress and said the one thing I did not want to say. But it needed to be said. "Are you sure you want to go where this is headed?"

She stared deep into my eyes and said my favorite word in the English language. "Yes."

In a hot second, I was off the bed and shoving my jeans and boxers off my body and onto the floor. My girl's eyes rounded when my dick popped free of my clothes, then she got busy with the fly of her jeans. I would have liked a look at her panties, but she lifted her hips and pushed them down her thighs along with her jeans. When she reached her knees, I stepped in and helped her finish undressing. Then I reached a hand to her and pulled her up to stand in front of me.

As bad as I wanted her, I wanted our first time to be epic, something she would remember forever. That meant taking my time with her even though my body was screaming for release right fucking now.

I ran my fingers through her hair and held her as I brushed my lips over hers. She gripped my hips but otherwise didn't move as I deepened the kiss. Fire licked over my skin as our mouths mimicked what my body longed to do with hers.

Gliding her hands up my sides, she found her way to my pecs then up over my shoulders. When she pressed her glorious body to mine, she left me with no choice but to wrap her in my arms and press her to me, shoulders to thighs. Still, I kept kissing her as my hands roamed the lovely curve of her back. In a perfect world, we could stand here forever kissing and holding each other, absorbing each other. No one I'd ever held had felt as made for me as Chessly Clarke.

Her antics on the bed earlier should have prepared me, but when her thigh came up and brushed the outside of mine on her way to hooking her calf over my hip, I lost a bit of control. Cupping her ass, I urged her to wrap her legs around my waist. When her hot center came into contact with the head of my cock, I let out a curse and stepped closer to the bed. After tearing my mouth from hers, I reached out and jerked the comforter and the blankets down to the foot of the bed. She clung to me as I climbed with her onto the middle of the mattress and settled myself in the most beautiful place in the world: between Chessly's thighs.

"I've been dreaming about this since Homecoming," I said as I nibbled along the side of her face.

She dragged her nails across the tops of my shoulders, and I kissed my way south to her pretty tits. Those sounds I loved coming from her lips intensified as first I sucked one hard peak into my mouth, giving it loads of attention with my lips and tongue before gently tugging with my teeth. Crying out, she arched up into me, telling me she liked what I was doing. So I repeated it on her other breast.

Rubbing her slick center along my length, she whispered, "Please."

Oh yeah, I liked that.

Licking and kissing my way down the center of her smooth belly, I headed to my prize. When I reached the apex of her thighs, I stopped for a second to breathe in the heady perfume of her arousal, the scent going straight to my dick. Diving in, I licked and sucked the tight nub of her clit, and her hips went into overdrive as she started to chant my name. I threw my forearm over her, stilling her movements while I redoubled my efforts to drive her right out of her mind.

She added keening sounds to the symphony of moans and whimpers and sighs, her response to my touch driving me wild. I slipped a finger inside her sweet pussy, and her hands shot to my head where she grabbed fistfuls of my hair and tugged.

This girl.

I added another finger to the hot, wet heaven of her body, pumping in and out in rhythm with my tongue on her clit, relishing her taste, her desperate sounds, the pull of my hair in her hands. Without warning she clamped down on my fingers and came apart. Her body bowed as she cried out my name to the ceiling, her fingers clenching and unclenching in my hair. I took a second to grin against her luscious slit. Then I took my time, gently kissing and petting her back down to earth.

I climbed up her body and rested on my forearms on either side of her shoulders. "You liked that?"

Lazily, she grazed her nails up and down my sides. "You couldn't tell?"

Grinning, I said, "Good, 'cause we're still in the first half. There's a lot of fun left on the clock."

Rolling off her for a second, I pulled open the drawer on the nightstand, retrieved a condom, and wasted no time suiting up.

"I would have done that for you." She pouted.

"Next time."

I kissed and nipped my way up her thighs—first one, until I reached the sensitive crease where it met her hip, then the other. All the while, I ghosted my fingers over her luscious pussy until she let out a growl and tugged on my hair—hard.

"If you don't put that impressive phallus of yours inside me right now, I'm going to . . . to—"

Glancing up at her from my happy place between her thighs, I asked, "You're going to what?"

"I'm going to eat all the cookies."

"Not a problem, babe. I'll have you for dessert."

The cute way she growled my name would have cracked me up except for the naughty dare that came into her eyes the second before she put her hands on her tits. When she went to town rolling and tugging those pretty girls for my viewing pleasure, I had no choice but to give her what we both desperately wanted.

Grasping my dick, I rubbed the tip over her clit, and she leaned up on her elbows to watch. Then she rolled her hips—a not-so-subtle request for me to stop teasing. I didn't know what turned me on more, her stunningly responsive body or her impatience to have me inside her. I'd dreamed about having sex with

Chessly, but the reality was so much hotter, and I hadn't even made it inside her yet.

Then I pushed in and, oh, *fuck.*

"Chess, are you okay? You're so incredibly tight. Jesus."

Widening her thighs and tilting her hips, she invited me deeper. "There is a lot of you, Finn." She let out a tiny satisfied sigh. "And you feel amazing. Keep going."

I pulled out a bit and thrust in deeper. Her tight heat gripping my cock drove all rational thought from my head. Thrusting again, and yet again, I seated myself to my balls inside her utterly perfect pussy. When she started pulsing around me, she left me no choice but to move, and soon I was pounding into her. She flattened her hands on the headboard, those sounds coming from her spurring me on.

"Chess, come, please. Please, baby, I need you to come."

"Clit," she ground out through her teeth.

I pressed my thumb to that sweet little nub and watched in wonder as she climaxed like Fourth of July fireworks. Her eyes held mine for a long second before she arched up, her head fell back, and she keened my name directly into the wall behind the headboard.

A couple of short thrusts later, I shouted my release to the ceiling and collapsed on top of her, my breath sawing in and out of me like a freight train. As the aftershocks rolled through her, she clamped down hard on me, forcing me to move again inside her, and I swear I experienced a second mini-orgasm.

Holy fuck.

Catching the sound of Chess sipping air, I groaned and rolled onto my back, taking her with me. I wasn't ready yet to pull out and end the connection I'd forged with this girl. Never in my life could I have prepared for the way she wrung me inside out then pulled me back into shape better than I was before.

When our breathing returned to something resembling

normal, I rolled her to my side so I could tie off and trash the condom. Then I cuddled her close, my fingers drawing lazy patterns on the soft skin of her arm. After all the noise we'd been making, the aftermath in my room was weirdly silent.

"I didn't plan for this to happen today," I whispered into the quiet.

"Me neither," she whispered back.

Tipping my head up to look into her face, I asked, "Are you sorry?"

She huffed out a laugh. "Not even a little bit."

Letting my head drop back onto the pillow, I relaxed. "Me neither." I grinned. "You're incredible, you know that?"

"Confession."

I tensed again.

"That's the first time I've ever come when a man's gone down on me."

I tipped my head up to look at her again. "For real?"

Nodding against my chest, she said, "For real. I've never really even enjoyed a guy going down on me." She traced her fingers through the hair on my chest. "Until you. That was—wow. And then you topped it." She mumbled the next part, but I heard it anyway. "I have no idea what to do with you now."

Chapter Twenty-Three

Chessly

AFTER THE MOST epic sex of my life—he hadn't promised that, but he'd certainly delivered—surprisingly, we fell back into the easy friendship we'd been forming over the past few months since the semester started. One might think from watching and listening to us that we were an established couple rather than whatever we were. I hadn't figured that out yet.

Sex like we'd experienced required recharging, so we'd enjoyed a little nap. Sleeping next to Finn gave me another surprise. Cuddled next to his big warm body felt natural and safe. I woke up first and had to use the bathroom, so I gathered up my clothes and quietly dressed. In the process, I found the bag of cookies, and when I checked inside, to my shock they were still intact. I set them on the desk and slipped from his room.

The house was blessedly quiet, and I wondered if his roommates had gone out or something while we'd spent the afternoon studying each other rather than physics. A giggle escaped me as I reassessed that thought. Studying with Finn gave physics a whole different aspect.

When I returned to his room, I discovered him seated at the desk in his boxers and jeans happily chowing down on a cookie. A whole cookie.

"Hey!" I lunged for the bag.

He grinned around a mouthful of sugary yumminess and snatched the bag from my reach. Swallowing, he smirked and said, "You weren't planning to keep these to yourself, were you, thief?"

"They were tangled up in the blankets and my sweatshirt. You're lucky I even found them." I held out my hand. "Give over." A thought struck me, and I gasped. "Unless you ate them both already. I was only gone for a minute!"

He nibbled a bite from the mostly intact one in his hand. "Pickle Barrel makes the best monsters." His eyes flashed with mischief. "They're my absolute favorite." Smirking, he nibbled another bite. "If you want some of this, it's going to cost you."

Planting my hands on my hips, I said, "What is it going to cost me?"

"A kiss." Pondering for a moment, he added, "Maybe two."

"Finn." I stretched his name into three syllables.

"Chess." He mimicked me, the expression in his eyes positively wicked.

Stepping into his space, I leaned down and aimed for his cheek, but at the last second, he turned his head and my lips landed on the corner of his mouth. The next thing I knew, I was seated across his lap, his skin warm beneath my hands where they landed one across his massive shoulders, the other on his impressive chest.

"Here you go." He offered me a bite of the cookie in his hand.

I chomped a big bite and had to use my thumb to catch the

crumbs threatening to tumble out of the corner of my mouth. He laughed and bit into the soft and crunchy treat. When I swallowed and grabbed his wrist with the intention of taking another bite, he tightened his arm, denying me my goal.

"Nuh-uh-uh. You know the price."

"You're something, you know that?" I meant to call him out, but my words lacked heat.

"As much as I love these cookies, I've had a taste of you, Miss Clarke, and you're my new favorite treat." His gaze strayed to my mouth. "I have a feeling I'm never going to get enough of you."

His words shot straight to my center.

Trying to cover my response to him, I straightened my back and said, "I can't believe how demanding you are."

If anything, his focus on my mouth intensified, drawing me to him. This time I brushed my lips over his and nibbled at the corner before pulling away.

"Bite."

"I always say, 'give the lady what she wants.'" He tugged my lower lip between his teeth before soothing the sting with his tongue.

I intended to call him out for mistaking my meaning on purpose, but when he pressed his lips to mine, I forgot. Wrapping my arms around his neck, I kissed him back, slow and easy, lips on lips, tiny nibbles.

"Mmm," I moaned.

"Better than cookies," he said against my mouth.

That word reminded me and I pulled back. "I still want my cookie."

Laughing, he reached behind him on the desk and handed me the bag. Greedily, I tore open the top to find the last cookie. I sunk my teeth into the treat and savored butterscotch, chocolate, brown sugar, and walnuts. A second bite added raisins, and I pulled a face.

"Let me guess. You found a raisin," he chuckled.

"These"—I turned my cookie from side to side, inspecting it—"would be perfect if not for the occasional raisin ambush." Seeing another of the offensive fruits sticking out from where I'd taken my previous bite, I tugged it free and dropped it on the desktop.

"What did raisins ever do to you?" He smirked.

"They have no business in cookies and everyone picks them out of trail mix."

His brow lifted.

Narrowing my eyes at him, I said, "Admit it. You pick them out of trail mix."

He squeezed my hip and grinned. "Possibly."

"Absolutely," I affirmed. "The only way to eat raisins is in Bridge mix when they're smothered in chocolate," I said and savored another raisin-less bite of my cookie.

Finn's laughter rang through the room. "You're something else, Chess."

I shot him an incredulous look. "What?"

Shaking his head, he said, "Eat your cookie."

His eyes danced as I picked another raisin out of my treat and pulled another face when I missed one in the next bite. Meanwhile, he finished his cookie, raisins and all, like a barbarian.

He traced his fingers down the side of my face, tucking my hair behind my ear and lulling me into not paying attention. Then he pounced, pulling my hand away from my mouth at the last second and stealing my last bite.

"Hey!" I yelped.

A hard kiss shut me up before he leaned back and, grinning the whole time, finished chewing and swallowing my cookie.

"You are a menace."

His eyes sparkled. "You are fun to study with."

"Finn." Tilting my head, I stared at him from beneath my brows. "We have yet to study anything today."

"Not true, babe. We've learned lots of things about each other this afternoon. For example, I learned you don't like to share your cookies." He cut off my protest with, "But cookies taste delicious on your lips." Smiling, he added, "Other parts of you are delectable all on their own. Honestly, Chess, you're kind of a feast."

It was the weirdest—and quite possibly the sweetest—compliment I'd ever received.

Staring at his gorgeous, heavily muscled bare chest with its dusting of light brown hair, I said, "We should actually crack open a book, huh?" My voice might have cracked on my suggestion, drawing a chuckle from him.

Then he urged me to stand, and reluctantly, I slid off his lap to stand beside the desk. He retrieved his plain black T-shirt from where it had landed on the floor during our previous activities, and I mourned the loss of the view when he pulled it down over his torso. With a cursory tug, he mostly righted the blankets and the comforter, revealing his books, which had somehow ended up at the foot of the mattress. Gathering them up, he set them on the nightstand and turned back to me.

"I usually stretch out on my bed when I work, so feel free to use the desk."

When I sat down and pulled some books from my backpack, I truly didn't think I'd manage to do any studying with the hottest man in the world stretched out on the bed behind me. But though we'd been distracted earlier, this wasn't our first rodeo. Studying together in Hillman on multiple occasions had apparently prepared us to study quietly in Finn's room after having epic sex. Either that or epic sex had powered up my synapses.

The rest of the afternoon flew by as I finished nearly all of the last sets of problems for my quantum physics midterm. When Callahan banged on Finn's door, I squeaked, almost taking my chair with me as I leapt for the ceiling at his decibel-shattering interruption of the silence.

"Finn! Move your truck! I gotta take Jamaica back to the dorms."

Checking the time on my phone, I hissed a curse. "I need to head home too. We have our weekly RA meeting in thirty minutes."

"Finn! You awake?" Callahan shouted.

Finn swung off his bed and opened the door. "Dude. Calm your ass down. If you want, I can drop Jamaica off when I take Chessly home."

Callahan's mortified expression cracked me up. "I drive my girl, Finnegan. But if *you* want, I can take Chess with us." He poked his head into the room and shot me a confused look. Apparently, he thought we were busy doing other things.

At Callahan's suggestion, it was Finn's turn to express mortification. "Negative, Ghost Rider. I'll be driving Chess. Give us a minute to gather up her stuff." He let the door click shut in Callahan's face.

"That was kind of rude to do to your roommate." I smirked.

"Didn't want to waste more time arguing with him when I could be doing this with you." He tugged me up from the chair and pulled me in close before brushing a kiss over my lips. "Did you get much done?"

"Almost all of it. You?"

"Every last problem." His gaze dropped to my mouth again. "Wish you didn't have to leave. I could feed you supper and we could watch a movie or something."

I snorted. "Or something."

"Seriously, Chessly. Today was a best day ever." Palming my cheek, he slid his long fingers into my hair. "This weekend has been the best one I can remember in a real long time." He ghosted another kiss over my mouth. "When can I see you again?"

"Like. for a date?"

"Date, study session, hanging out." He rubbed his thumb over my cheek then stared hard into my eyes. "I want to spend more time with you."

"I have some free time tomorrow afternoon before my six o'clock lab. We could meet at the Union." Somehow my hands had found their way to his back where I mapped the muscles beneath his T-shirt. *Damn*, but the man was built. Standing this close to him and breathing in faint notes of clean sweat from our earlier activities, and something woodsy and citrusy on his T-shirt, had me tightening my center and wishing I could take him up on his offer of dinner and a movie—or something.

For the first time in my life, I was seriously contemplating skipping work. Of course, Jamaica heading back to the dorm took that option right off the table.

A naughty thought tipped up the corner of his mouth. "I think I can find us a quiet corner somewhere in the Union."

"Finn . . ." I warned.

"Our trainers ride our asses about eating sugar, but I've tasted your kisses, Chess, and now I'm a sugar addict. No doubt I'm going to need a fix when I see you tomorrow."

When he dropped his killer smile on me, all I could do was give him a dopey one back. The man was utterly lethal to my common sense. From his expression, no doubt R-rated plans were developing in his sexy mind. The scary part was, I was pretty sure I'd be going along with them.

"You finally gave in, huh?" Jamaica shoulder-bumped me as we walked down the hallway from our dorm supervisor's apartment after our weekly meeting.

"Excuse me?"

She laughed and linked her arm with mine. "When Callahan and I came downstairs from his room, Danny was slumped on the couch, whining about all the noise coming through the wall of his bedroom."

I was surprised the hot flames licking my cheeks didn't set my hair on fire.

Giving my arm a squeeze, she said, "No one's judging you." She squeezed me again. "It was past time you put Finn out of his misery."

I wrinkled my brow. "What are you talking about?"

As she explained, we took our time climbing the stairs to lobby of the dorm. "The poor guy's been mooning after you for months, even with all your sarcasm and snark." She slid me a side-eye. "Maybe *especially* because of your sarcasm and snark. I've heard him go on and on about how smart you are. It's obvious you impress the hell out of him." Smiling at me, she added, "Callahan is always complaining about Finn's lack of finesse and discernment when it comes to women, but I don't think that was ever the problem."

When we reached the lobby, I faced my friend as my brows took a trip up to my hairline.

"Finn's problem is he's such a nice guy that he gives everyone the benefit of the doubt." For a second a dark look clouded her features before she smiled again. "But he actively worked for your attention. He's had a thing for you ever since I let him take you home on Homecoming."

"You let him?" I snorted.

Her nose went up in the air. "If you recall, I grilled him on his intentions and demanded he take the best care of you."

Memories of my afternoon with Finn swamped my mind and the words slipped out without my permission. "He definitely did that."

A naughty grin spread over her features. "You will notice I'm not grilling you about your 'study session' this afternoon." Her one-handed air quotes were ridiculous.

Shaking away thoughts of Finn's body and how he'd used it to light up my world, I asked, "I did notice. Why is that?"

"Because I expect the same courtesy from you from now on since both of us are seeing Wildcats players."

I couldn't mistake the meaning in her tone. With the way Piper, Saylor, and I had razzed Jamaica about her relationship with Callahan, I deserved the hard time she was so obviously holding back from giving me.

"I wouldn't say Finn and I are *involved* . . ." I stretched out that last word like a rubber band.

My friend's "Huh" snapped it back at me. That sparkle in her eyes told me I should have kept my mouth shut. "You sure you want to deny that? According to Danny, you and Finn spent most of the afternoon *involved* with each other."

"I thought you said we were going to show each other some courtesy." I pouted.

"But also honesty."

We wandered over to the front desk. Jamaica checked the on-call schedule while I slipped inside the office to check my mailbox for this week's silly postcard from my dad—a running gag he'd started on my first day at Mountain State.

"No mail deliveries on Sundays, Chessly," the desk clerk reminded me.

"Oh, yeah. Sorry. I forgot what day it was."

"Finn made you forget everything but your own name, huh? Impressive," Jamaica teased when I rejoined her at the front of the main desk.

My eyes spun in their sockets. "You're hilarious."

Her smile softened into something genuine. "It's okay, Chess. I know how it is."

Chapter Twenty-Four

Finn

"LOOK AT YOU, all bright-eyed and bushy-tailed this morning," Bax drawled as he wondered into the kitchen in the Monday-morning darkness. "Heard you were 'studying' a certain cute blonde rather closely in your room yesterday afternoon."

"Wanna know what I think of your air quotes, Bax?" I flipped him the bird and he snorted a laugh.

Shooting me a narrow-eyed stare, he tossed my description of his girlfriend Piper Maxwell back at me. "Seems unicorns really do exist."

"Fuck off." I reached into the fridge and pulled out four foil-wrapped breakfast burritos, lining them up on the baking sheet I'd set on top of the stove. Then I slid them into the pre-heated oven to warm up.

Should have known ignoring him wouldn't work. "Yep, looks like you found your very own unicorn. I didn't think there was a woman out

there who would put up with a D-end who sucks at *Madden*." He laughed at his ridiculous observation.

Facing him, I said, "I kick your ass in *Madden*, in *COD*, in every game we play all the fucking time."

"Keep believing that, Finnegan." He smirked. Crossing his arms over his chest, Bax sobered. "About damn time you hooked up with her, man." My roommate helped himself to the coffee I'd brewed first thing after I came down to the kitchen. Staring at me over the rim of his to-go mug, he said, "Well? Are you and Chessly a thing now?"

I ran a hand through my hair and then nudged him away from the counter to grab my own mug of joe. "Fuck if I know. When I tossed the idea out to her, she didn't say anything."

Bax huffed out a glum-sounding breath. "That's one more difference between defensive and skill players off the field too. 'Han and Danny say one thing or put on one move, and the girls fall all over them. The two of us have to work at it, exactly the same as when we're in the game."

I blew on my beverage and swigged some down. "I'm meeting her this afternoon for coffee or whatever."

Bax waggled his brows. "'Whatever' sounds like a good start."

With a snort, I clarified, "We're meeting in the Union. Not the most conducive place for 'whatever.' Which I think is why she chose it. I've scoped out the study carrells in Hillman, and I'm pretty sure the one tucked back in a corner on the third floor no one has ever used, but when I suggested we could meet there, she shot me down."

"From what Danny said, you showed her an excellent time in your room yesterday. Bet you can remind her." He popped his fist on my bicep. "I have faith in you, Finnegan."

"Danny has a big mouth."

Bax laughed. "This house has thin walls."

"And you ladies have nothing better to do than gossip."

"What are we gossiping about?" Callahan asked as he walked through the kitchen door and made a beeline for the coffee pot.

"*We* aren't gossiping." I stared pointedly between my roommates. "But *you* old hens sure seem to do it often."

They burst out laughing.

When he'd finally managed to control himself, Callahan said, "You flipped us so much shit, worked your ass off to hook us up with jersey chasers even after we told you they were bad news, and now it's your turn, you want us to back off?" He coughed into his hand. "Bullshit."

Bax raised his mug, and Callahan clinked his to it.

Assholes.

"Look, I don't know how many times I can apologize for inviting those girls over here. I honestly thought you liked them since you all flirted with them at parties and such. Until the mess Tory caused last semester, I'd never seen that side of her." The timer on the stove rescued me for a minute as I shut it off and pulled our breakfast from the oven. "Well, except whenever she was around Chess." My mouth turned down. "I probably still have some work to do there."

"Maybe you should address that issue before you start 'whatever' with her on your date this afternoon," Bax suggested with his infernal air quotes.

Before I could tell him to mind his own damn business, Danny interrupted. "Seriously, Bax?" he asked as he straggled in to breakfast dead last—a habit I'd noticed since the semester started.

"What?" Bax asked, confusion wrinkling his brow.

"The shirt. Bet Coach Larkin flips you all kinds of shit for that one." Danny grinned and helped himself to what was left of the coffee.

Before Danny's observation, I hadn't paid any attention to Bax's T-shirt du jour. When I read "Every once in a while, someone amazing comes along . . . and here I am," I cracked up.

"Yep, Larkin's going to flip you all kinds of shit over this one." I laughed, glad for the distraction from thinking about a conversation I knew Chess and I still needed to have.

My friend glanced down at his shirt and shrugged, the corner of his mouth twitching. "Nothing wrong with truth in advertising."

Callahan chuckled. "You're a piece of work, Baxter." Reaching past me, he snagged a burrito from the pan. "You riding with me, Finn?"

"Yeah."

"You riding with the awesome one?" Bax asked Danny with a smirk.

Danny shook his head, but he was smiling. "How could I pass up such an incredible opportunity?"

Since Danny had lightened the mood, I decided it was in my best interests to refrain from calling his ass out for sharing what he overheard coming from my bedroom when Chess was over. We jostled our way through the front door and out to the trucks. Normally, my motor ran hot, but this fine February morning in the arctic darkness of a late winter cold snap, I was pretty damn glad to ride with my friend, whose pickup sported a remote truck starter.

I climbed into the warm interior of 'Han's truck, buckled up, and unwrapped my sausage-and-egg burrito. If I was harboring any delusion that the conversation about a certain gorgeous blonde I'd hung out with over the weekend had passed, Callahan shot me down the second he slid in behind the wheel.

"'Bout time you stopped mooning after Chessly and finally impressed the woman." Checking his mirrors, he put his pickup in reverse and cautiously backed down the slick driveway.

"Jesus, fuck. We weren't that loud," I grumbled into my breakfast.

He smirked. "Just saying. You must have shown her a good

time Saturday night since she voluntarily spent most of Sunday with you."

"If you want to know about my date on Saturday night, ask." I stuffed my face with a manly bite of breakfast, not caring how at odds my words and actions were.

"All right, Finnegan. What did you do to impress the lady who, from what I've seen, is pretty tough to impress?" He wheeled through the roundabout a block from our house then peeled open his breakfast on the first straightaway after it.

"You gonna gossip about this too?" I growled. "I picked up a catered picnic dinner, and we played lawn games on the practice field. I showed her a good time."

"Niiice, Finn." My friend held a fist out for me to bump. "I've lived with you for three years and had no idea you were such a romantic."

"Fuck off, 'Han."

"I'm serious. You put some effort into that date. No wonder Chessly wanted to spend more time with you." He cleared his throat. "But I'm glad I don't share a wall with your bedroom."

"You and Danny are first-class assholes." I slid him a side-eye. "Anytime you want to trade rooms, I'm all over taking the master at the end of the hall."

"Nah. My lady and I are pretty happy the master bath shares a wall with Danny's room."

"And happy having another bathroom between your room and Bax's."

He laughed. "That too."

A thought occurred to me—something about Bax's earlier comment about defensive players versus skill players. With a dramatic sigh, I said, "Sorry you assholes are all jealous of my mad skills pleasing my lady. You'll have to get over yourselves, though, because I have plans to keep pleasing her."

When I arrived at the Union, about ten minutes ahead of when Chess said she'd meet me, I noticed the short line for coffee and decided to take advantage. Since she'd ordered a café au lait the last time we hung out here, I figured I was safe with that. By the time the barista had finished my order—I'd added a couple of cranberry scones because lunch went down over an hour ago—I glanced up to see Chessly walking through the door.

Carrying two drinks and a bag of treats, I wound my way through the tables in her direction. When she caught sight of me, she kick-started my heart with the smile that lit her face.

"Hey." I didn't even try to hold back my answering grin.

"Hey." For a long beat, we stared into each other's eyes before she dropped her gaze to my hands. "Whatcha got there?" She nodded toward the treats.

"A coffee for the lady," I said, handing her the drink. "And something to keep your stomach from grumbling through your lab since it falls right at dinnertime."

She wrinkled her nose at me. "You're never letting me live that down, are you?"

"Depends on how often it happens." I grinned.

Narrowing her gaze over her latte, she sipped and closed her eyes. Her moan of pleasure shot straight to my dick.

I cleared my throat and said, "Let's find somewhere to park our asses."

Laughter rang from her. "Oh, Finn, you're so romantic."

Heat climbed my neck to my face, and I turned away to scan for an open table. The place was mostly open for a Monday afternoon, so we had our pick, but I was looking for somewhere with a hope of some privacy.

"Not many good tables today. Wanna try the lounge?"

The college had furnished the old-school lounge adjacent to

the cafeteria in the Union with deep couches and comfy chairs placed in front of a fireplace I didn't think had been lit in fifty years. It was a pretty high traffic area seeing as it connected the cafeteria to some offices behind it, but I hoped one of the love seats facing the windows might be open. Even with people passing through, we'd have more privacy than any table in the café.

The secret smile on Chessly's face told me how transparent I was, but also, she was smiling.

I stepped beside her and casually dropped my hand to the small of her back, ushering her a bit in front of me in the direction of the lounge. "How was your day so far?"

"Same ol'. Yours?"

"Mmm? The usual." *Keep it together, Finn. Do not make this fucking awkward.* "Coach Larkin amused himself at Bax's expense, which was highly entertaining." I snorted at the memory of Larkin saying, "Here I am," on every pass he made by our stations until Bax was powering through his sets like a damn bull in an arena. "Kind of started the week off right." I grinned.

"Let me guess. Bax was wearing one of his interesting T-shirts."

"Got it in one." I winked. "Danny warned him before we left the house, but Bax is Bax. He wears those shirts like a dare and a badge of honor all at the same time." I grinned down at her. "I don't know how your classy friend can date him."

The corner of Chess's mouth tipped up. "Piper's pretty good at hiding her inner redneck behind that trust-fund-baby façade, but don't let it fool you. She's one hundred percent perfect for your roommate."

As I'd hoped, there was an open couch—one of the deep ones facing the windows. With the absence of leaves on the bushes outside the building, anyone who glanced toward the windows could probably see through the branches, but no one walking by ever looked over. I was counting on that as I set my coffee and the bag of treats on the table in front of the sofa and my backpack on the floor beside it then sank down into the cushions.

Beside me Chessly followed suit, though she didn't sit as close to me as I'd hoped. *Patience, old son. We're still only in the first half,* I reminded myself.

Leaning back, she sipped her coffee, the sapphire pools of her eyes sparkling over the rim of the cup. "So what's in the bag? Monster cookies?"

The memory of her sitting on my lap yesterday—and how sharing cookies had led to sharing so much more—flashed through my head. I leaned forward with the obvious goal of snagging the bag of scones, but what I needed was a distraction so I could adjust my junk. How the mere mention of those cookies could cause a semi told its own damn story of how easily Chessly could wind me up.

"We have to save monster cookies for private treats." I let my voice drop as I sat back against the cushions and enjoyed watching her squirm further down into the couch. "Plus, the Union doesn't have monster cookies on offer. I hope cranberry scones can help you with that stomach problem you have."

"What stomach problem?" she squeaked, her tone indignant.

"The one where I always seem to catch you when you're hungry."

A pretty shade of rose bloomed over her round cheeks as she set her coffee on the table and reached for the bag in my hand.

"Nuh-uh-uh. If you want your share, you're going to have to come over here."

Her brow knitted in confusion. "I'm sitting right beside you."

Shaking my head, I said, "Not close enough."

"Finn," she hissed, her eyes darting from side to side. "We're in public."

"People sit next to each other in public all the time, Chess. Especially people who like each other." Taking a chance, I whispered, "I like you a lot."

For a second she blinked those beautiful blue eyes at me. Then she pushed herself up off the cushion to slide herself over, but she got a bit carried away and almost landed on my lap. A tiny puff of air escaped her lips as her body collided with mine, and she stared up at me with a combination of surprise and something else—something dark and interested. It was all I could do not to swoop in and steal a kiss, but the loud conversation of some people walking through the lounge at that precise second preempted me.

With all the fanfare of a professional chef presenting his masterpiece, I pulled a scone from the bag and handed it to her. Her snorted laughter at my antics warmed my chest as she plucked the treat from my fingers. When she settled in tight against my arm to nibble at her pastry, I had no choice but to wrap my arm around her shoulders and pull her in close to my side. A happy sigh escaped her—one I hoped had more to do with me snuggling her and less to do with how much she was enjoying the scone.

"How did your class with Professor Ego go today?" she asked between bites.

"Everyone—I mean *everyone*—finished all the problems he assigned for the day. Which from the way he acted, kind of irritated him." I grinned at the memory of his sour grimace in class. "So he was kind of at a loss as to what the day's lesson was since we'd all also pretty much aced the quiz."

"How do you know you aced it?"

"His program grades everything in real time. I always know my quiz scores before I leave class." I chowed down half a tangy, buttery scone, swallowed, and said, "One of his pets in the front row requested he lecture on anatomical physics because they had a question from the reading. Since learning about anatomical physics is the reason we all signed up for the class, they kind of stuck him. Of course, our dear old prof has decided he's made his point, so there won't be any more quizzes this week." I rolled my eyes. "I did all those extra problems for nothing."

Twinkling up at me, she grabbed the bag from my hand and extracted her second scone. "I don't think you wasted your time. If he throws another tantrum, you're ahead. If not, you know more now than you did before the weekend."

"Thanks for the pep talk, Miss Suzy Sunshine."

With a playful little nudge, she said, "You're welcome."

A familiar voice I hadn't heard in two years and had hoped never to hear again floated through the lounge. I couldn't help the way my body tensed as that voice drew nearer, and Chess glanced up at me with a question in her eyes. With any luck, the owner of that voice wouldn't notice us here and would keep walking.

Nope. The sound stopped directly behind our couch.

"Finn? Is that you?"

Surely only the top of my head was visible above the back of the cushions. How could she recognize me from that? Then I remembered which ball cap I'd tugged on this morning. *Fuck.*

Hannah stepped around the end of the couch. "It is you."

Lifting my eyes to her, I tried not to cringe when I caught her catty smile. "Hello, Hannah," I said with exactly zero expression.

Dialing up the wattage of that vicious smile, she asked, "Who's your friend?"

"No one you need to poison," I mumbled.

Beside me Chessly stiffened.

"What was that?" Hannah asked with a smirk directed at the friend I hadn't noticed standing slightly behind her. Returning her attention to Chess, she said, "She's cute. You must have managed to figure out how not to be awkward—or how to hide it better." She laughed derisively then directed a conspiratorial comment at Chess. "He's a farm boy, you know. They can't help their lack of sophistication—or finesse."

"Don't you have somewhere important to be?" I fought a losing battle with keeping the irritation out of my question.

"Always. But I had a minute to say hello to an old friend."

Waving a languid hand in Chessly's direction, she said, "Good luck. You'll need it."

Hannah waited a couple more seconds, but when I didn't rise to the bait, she turned to her friend and moved on. Of course, she pitched her voice for our ears as she moved through the lounge. "I don't know what I was thinking when I dated him freshman year. He was totally clueless in the . . ."

Mercifully, the rest of her words faded into the hallway on the other end of the lounge. But it didn't take a genius to know what she'd told her friend.

Resting my elbows on my thighs, my hands clasped between my knees, I stared unseeingly out the window. It had taken three years after the disaster of dating Hannah Stowell to gather up the courage to ask someone else out rather than just hook up with a willing jersey chaser. Her words—her *pronouncements*—about my lack of finesse, my awkwardness, my size, explained why I went for the jersey chasers who didn't dwell on those things. Their focus was my spot in the starting lineup—and my proximity to pretty boys like Callahan O'Reilly and our previous roommate Deshaun Green, to be honest. But the jersey chasers' attention made me feel special, like I could maybe still attract a woman.

Hannah was the reason it had taken so long and why I was trying so hard to do things right with Chess. I'd managed to avoid my ex for years, yet only one day—one fucking day—after the most glorious weekend of my life—she'd showed up out of nowhere to shit on everything.

The pressure of a hand on my bicep and a soft voice calling "Finn?" dragged me up from the depths of my dark thoughts. I reached for my coffee, stalling the inevitable with a long drink.

"Finn? Who was that girl?"

"The biggest mistake of my life."

"You dated her?"

I dared a glanced in Chess's direction. "Freshman year. I

thought she was perfect. Apparently, she still sees me as a buffoon. An awkward *farm boy*." I finished my coffee and crushed the paper cup in my fist. "Maybe you think that too."

Chess increased the pressure on my arm. "Hey. Look at me. I'm not her."

"But how soon till you will be?"

Her head snapped back as though I'd slapped her. "M'kay." In one smooth move, she snagged her backpack from the floor and stood. "Thanks for the coffee and the scone."

I closed my eyes and railed at myself. *What the fuck are you doing, man?*

But I was too slow.

Without another word, she spun around the end of the couch and was out the door of the lounge before I could drag my ass off the cushions.

"Chess!" I called after her, but she didn't slow down.

And she didn't look back.

Chapter Twenty-Five

Chessly

STROMBOLI'S WAS UNNATURALLY quiet for a Thursday night. Then again, the Wildcats were starting spring practice tomorrow, so none of the players were in the bar. That meant none of their entourage who seemed to know their every move were hanging out either.

Not that any of that mattered.

Since we knew none of the team would be in the pizzeria, what with two of the four of us dating Wildcats players, we helped ourselves to their designated booth in the back. Piper had picked up Saylor on her way to the dorm to grab Jamaica and me. When the conversation centered on Saylor's latest to-die-for winter ensemble of a black-and-tan duster, fleece-lined tan lace-up boots, and an off-white beanie with matching gloves, I breathed a discreet sigh of relief. I should have anticipated they intended for that conversation to lull me into inattention, giving them a chance to pry out none-of-their-business info on the state of things between Finn and me.

We'd barely slipped off our coats when Jamaica, the traitor, launched the first salvo. "Finn has been moping around the house all week like someone stole his birthday. Know anything about that, Chess?"

"Couldn't tell you. Maybe his professor reinstated the daily quizzes and he didn't study." I grabbed a menu from the end of the table and pretended to read it.

"Wyatt is worried about him. Says he won't come out of his room to play video games and barely shows up for dinner," Piper chimed in.

Ducking my head deeper into the menu, I shrugged. "Like I said, I have no idea what's going on with him. I haven't seen him since the weekend."

Saylor's stare bore into me. "I think that's the point these two are trying to make. You haven't seen him since the weekend, since the epic date he promised you. From your description at brunch on Sunday, the man delivered. What gives?"

"Danny grumbled all evening on Sunday about the noise coming from Finn's room during your afternoon 'study session,'" Jamaica added. "From what he said, Finn showed you a good time then too." Leaning her forearms on the table, she added her stare to Saylor's. "According to Callahan, since the weekend, you haven't returned Finn's texts or DMs on Instagram. Seriously, Chess. What happened?"

Flopping back against the leather booth, I blew a breath at the ceiling. Knowing my friends as well as I did, I had no choice but to give them something or they'd never let up. "We met at the Union Monday afternoon between classes. He bought me coffee and a scone." A pang zinged my heart at the memory of Finn remembering my favorite beverage and his teasing about me skipping meals only to be starving later.

"Sounds like he royally screwed up." Piper's tone was as dry as sand as she shot a massive eye roll across the table at Saylor and Jamaica.

"We were having a nice conversation when this girl walked up and started insulting him." Closing my eyes against the image of big, strong Finn trying not to turtle in on himself, I forced away another pang. "Turns out, he dated her, and from what I gathered, it didn't end well." Shaking my head, I added, "Anyone could have predicted it wouldn't end well considering how sweet he is and what a fucking bitch he dated. She reminded me exactly of Tory Miller."

"So what's the problem? Why aren't you talking to him?" Jamaica asked, her eyebrows knitted in confusion.

"Because he wrote me off before we even had a chance to see where things might go with us."

As I said the words, I was working my ass off to stem the tears that threatened to fall every time I thought about his cruel question. *"I'm not her." "But how soon till you will be?"* Obviously, Finn thought the same of me as he did every other girl in his orbit. No doubt it would make zero difference if I told him how I saw him. He wouldn't believe me. So what was the point? Better to cut my losses before I gave him any more of myself than I already had.

"*He* wrote *you* off?" Jamaica's voice climbed half an octave on the question. "He's been mooning after you since we introduced you on Homecoming."

"Yeah, well, the second I asked him about his ex, he pushed me away, said I was probably just like her—or I would be." I leveled my friend with a look. "So yeah. He wrote me off, comparing me to the mean girls he apparently prefers to date."

Mercifully, the server chose that minute to ask for our order. We started with drinks, but since we always ordered the same pizza whenever we came in, Piper took on the leadership role and ordered it for the table without consultation. With the way our conversation was going, I doubted I'd want much of whatever she decided to order anyway.

Jamaica reached her hands across to me, palms up. If I took that invitation, I'd probably embarrass all of us by bursting into tears. But I also couldn't leave my friend hanging. Gingerly, I dropped my hands into hers and nearly lost it when she gave me a loving squeeze.

"I don't think he wrote you off, Chess," she said. "Maybe seeing his ex in the same space with you threw him. Maybe he panicked."

"Maybe last weekend was only a hookup, nothing serious," I countered.

"How would you know when you're not communicating with him?" Saylor asked, her tone verging on sour. "I've never known you to show an interest in a guy past a few dates. A guy scratches an itch and you move on." She tapped the tabletop with her fingers. "You always say you have goals—goals that will be easier to meet if you aren't carrying baggage." She raised a brow. "Is that how you see Finn, as baggage?"

When I reared back at Saylor's ugly question, I almost jerked Jamaica's arms from their sockets. "No! God no. Sure, before he started talking to me, I wouldn't have said Finn was my type." Leaning my elbows on the table, I cupped my face in my hands. "Now I think he might be, but I'm not his."

Piper rubbed her hand over my back. "This is a blip, Chess. A misunderstanding."

Tilting my head, I let my side-eye speak for me.

"I mean it. The way Finn was always asking Wyatt about you after Wyatt and I got together—" she glanced across the table to Jamaica—"and the way he asks Callahan about you—"

"The way he finally caved and asked me what you like before he asked you out," Jamaica added. "The man's got it bad for you, girlfriend."

"You didn't see his face, hear his words when he wrote me off." I sniffed back the tears that were now in real danger of falling because of my friends' concern. "I don't know what I said wrong, but whatever it was, he sees me the same way he sees every other girl he's hung out with." Trying out a smile that hovered more on wobbly than confident, I said, "Better to learn that now than in a few months when maybe he's talked me into rethinking my goals. I mean, I'm headed to med school and he's headed to the NFL. Whatever might have happened between us probably wouldn't have worked out long-term anyway."

Saylor tsked. "Here you go again, not giving the guy a chance."

The server arrived with our drinks—a pitcher of beer for Jamaica, Saylor, and me to split and a lemon drop martini for our more refined friend, Piper, who never drank beer if she could help it. Saylor jumped right in and did the honors, pouring each of us a glass with a perfect head. Normally, I'd truly appreciate her handiwork, but even though the night had barely begun, I was already drained and wished I'd begged off. Then again, the entire gathering had all the hallmarks of an intervention, so I doubt my friends would have allowed me to skip.

I sipped my beer, more to have something to do to avoid talking than because I actually wanted to drink it. A soccer game was playing on the big screen behind the bar, and from where I was sitting on the end of the booth, I had a distorted view of the action. The blue team scored a goal on the red team, and a trio of guys seated at the bar let out a collective groan that drew my friends' attention.

Turning back to the table, Jamaica said, "With spring ball starting tomorrow, the guys are going to be completely immersed in football. Callahan said we could maybe see each other on Sunday night after our RA meeting."

"Yeah, Wyatt said pretty much the same thing." A secret

smile tipped up the corner of Piper's mouth. "But knowing him, I'll see him before Sunday night."

"Excuse me. I need to use the ladies' room." When Jamaica started to rise to join me, I added, "It's quiet in here tonight. I'm fine going alone."

Without waiting for a response, I headed down the hallway to the restrooms at the back of the bar. All that talk of my friends hooking up with their hot guys—guys who shared a house with the one man who'd ever slipped under my skin—had left me needing a moment to myself. They must have figured that out since none of them followed me.

I turned on the cold water and ran my wrists beneath it, the action simultaneously cooling me off, soothing me, and taking my mind off the tears that had been hovering near the surface on a continuous basis since Monday afternoon. Finn hadn't said anything about spring ball starting this week, but maybe he'd decided hanging out with me would be too big of a distraction from preparing for his last year as a Wildcat. The team had made it to the semifinals this past season, and everyone had high hopes that even with the quarterback graduating, they had a chance to move past the semis and into the national championship.

A goal like that would require a player's full focus. I could respect that, especially if that player also majored in bio-chem. Yet his friends seemed to have time for their girlfriends, school, and football.

My reflection stared back at me from the mirror above the sink, reminding me I didn't know Finn well at all. Yeah, my fingers had traced every shadow and curve of his muscular body, and I knew how he pulsed and swelled inside me when he came. I knew the faintly sweet masculine taste of his mouth when he kissed me like he needed my air to breathe. I knew the diabolical way he could use his tongue on me to give me pleasure I'd never experienced with anyone else.

I knew someday he wanted to find a way to stop little kids from suffering the ravages of childhood cancers.

But I didn't have a clue if he even wanted a relationship. Perhaps that encounter with his ex had reminded him that he didn't have the time or the energy to give to someone else right now. If that was it, he could have just told me. He didn't need to be an ass about it, lump me in with mean girls I'd never in this lifetime want to be associated with.

I dried my hands and stared myself down in the mirror. "You're better off without him."

If only I could convince my stupid heart to believe that after it went and fell for him even before he showed me the best time of my life.

"Better now?" Piper asked as I slipped in beside her in the booth.

While I'd been attending my pity party in the ladies' room, our pizza had arrived. I maneuvered the spatula beneath a slice and slid it onto my plate.

"I will be if we can talk about something else."

Lucky for me, I was on call in the dorm over the weekend. It was the perfect excuse not to head to the stadium with Piper, Jamaica, and Saylor to watch spring practice. Since she'd started dating Callahan, Jamaica had replaced her aversion to all sports with an avid interest in football. It was kind of cute. Piper, Saylor, and I had attended most of the Wildcats' home games together since our freshman year, but the idea of watching Finn tear it up on the field when I knew he'd lost interest in me would have been too much. Still, I couldn't help but wonder how practice was going.

Determined to take my mind off a certain football player, I cued up some Mozart on my phone and went to work on a set of calculus problems for my Physics 3 class. I had no idea how calculus was going to help me solve ligament and muscle injuries as a specialist in sports medicine, but I liked the elegance of the math, and usually I enjoyed the challenge of solving the problems. Yet even with my math music playing in the background, I couldn't stop my mind from straying to a certain defensive lineman and how he was faring in what was essentially the first practice of the season.

At last I gave up and headed to the Passion Pit in the basement of the lobby. One of the other RAs hosted a regular Friday night pajama party for her floor, but everyone in the dorm was invited until all the seats filled up. When I arrived in the common area, Rosie was cueing up the movie. As the opening credits for *He's Just Not That Into You* rolled across the screen, I had to stifle a moan. If I wasn't already inclined to believe in Orch OR theory, I'd experienced enough coincidences to push me into believing it.

Moving as discreetly as possible, I let myself out of the room and headed up to the lobby. Perhaps I could cover for the desk clerk, who could probably use a break right now. When I reached the top of the stairs, I saw Saylor standing at the desk, her hand poised over the phone to call for a resident to escort her to their room. It didn't take a genius to know who she wanted to visit.

"Hey, girlfriend. Thought you were watching football," I said as I stepped around the top of the stairs.

"Practice finished up a while ago. Piper had her car, so she said she'd give J a ride back here after they said good night to their guys." She linked her arm through mine. "I have a bottle of wine tucked into my purse," she whispered conspiratorially as we headed down the hall.

"What are we celebrating?" I asked as I keyed us into my tiny single room.

"It's more commiserating, I think." She pulled the bottle from her purse and set it on my desk before slipping off her gorgeous duster and hanging it over my boring puffy coat on the back of my door.

Making herself at home, she pulled two water glasses from the cupboard above my sink, unscrewed the cap on the wine, and poured two generous glasses. After handing one to me, she made herself comfortable on my bed, leaving me to sit on my hard desk chair.

"Okay, why are we commiserating?"

"We're feeling especially sad for one Finn McCabe who couldn't seem to do one thing right in practice this evening. From what I could see, his coaches did nothing but ride his ass from the second drill through the short scrimmage at the end." Shooting me a stare that spoke volumes, she tipped her glass and sipped. "Anyone with eyes could see the poor guy's head was absolutely not in the game." After another sip, she continued in a conversational tone. "He did pretty well in the first drill, then he glanced up in the stands, noted the three of us sitting together, and proceeded to fall apart for the rest of practice."

The wine in my mouth tasted like vinegar. "Why are you telling me this?"

"Of the four of us, you are hands down the smartest when it comes to the books. Jamaica has a 4.0 because she works her ass off for it. Likewise, Piper and I work to maintain our GPAs and our scholarships. But you . . ." She gestured languidly with her glass. "You solve advanced calculus problems to relax. Yet when it comes to a certain hot Wildcats player, you are about as bright as a box of rocks."

"Excuse me?" My voice and my eyebrows rose in unison.

"I don't know what happened in the Union on Monday, but I think you need to give Finn another chance, let him explain himself at least. Because from what I saw on the field today, the guy's a wreck. And if he doesn't get his head back in the game, one of two things is going to happen. Either he's going to lose his starting position or"—she stared me down hard—"he's going to get hurt." She sipped from her glass. "You don't want to be responsible for either one."

Her words came like punches to the gut. I set my wine on my desk and glanced out the window above it into the dark.

Saylor sat forward, her hand coming down on my forearm to give it a reassuring squeeze. "Just answer his texts, huh?"

Huffing out a mirthless laugh, I asked, "Is that why you brought the wine? To fortify me for reading Finn's texts?"

"Nah. I brought it because it's Friday night and you're stuck in the dorms and can't come out to play with me." Her lips curled up in a naughty grin.

"Uh-huh. Whatever."

"Wait. You haven't even read his texts?" She sat up so fast she almost sloshed wine all over the secondhand area rug I used to cover the cold linoleum floor.

"Look. He made himself clear when he lumped me in with all the bitchy girls he seems to prefer to hang out with."

"Chess. You're making excuses." Tilting her head, she stared at me through narrowed eyes. "You're into him—like all in with him—aren't you?"

With a shrug, I maintained my gaze on the darkness gathering outside the window. "Doesn't matter. When he looks at me, he sees his ex. Never mind we're nothing alike. She's a tall brunette with dark brown eyes, and she dresses like she works in finance—red power suit with pantyhose and heels." Turning my attention to my friend, I added, "The only thing the two of us have in common is we both went out with Finn McCabe."

Saylor patted my knee and said nothing.

"Honestly, I can't imagine why he'd want to date me when she's apparently his type."

"Honey, she's not his type. That's why he worked so hard to impress you." Giving my knee a squeeze, she said, "These past few weeks since the two of you started hanging out, you've been happier than I've ever seen you." Standing, she drained the dregs of her wine and set her glass in the sink. As she shrugged her coat on, she said, "Read his texts. Think about talking to him at least before you run away."

Chapter Twenty-Six

Finn

"**P**ULL YOUR HEAD out of your ass, McCabe!" Coach Ainsworth shouted. "Jesus. Did you forget every fucking thing about football in your two months away from the field?" Turning away in disgust, he yelled, "Jones! Get over here and show the *senior* how to play D-end."

Seth Jones, a redshirt sophomore, trotted over from the sideline and lined up in my spot. The scout team quarterback lined up behind center and called the signals. When the center hiked the ball, Jones shot off the line like a rocket. In the end he was no match for Donahue, our massive left tackle, but he sure as hell ran the defensive play better than I had for the past two days.

Beside me, Ainsworth said, "Think you can do even that much, McCabe?"

"Absolutely, Coach."

Guess I didn't have enough enthusiasm in my tone because he said, "Jones. Stay in there."

If I'd still had a heart, it probably would have dropped right out of my chest at seeing the ease with which Coach replaced me. But I'd been walking around like a zombie for two weeks, and I didn't have a clue how to turn it around.

Jones took my place for four more plays before Ainsworth let me back in, this time as part of the second string defense against the third string offense. Even in my semiconscious state, I figured out I had to bring it if I wanted to get on the field at all. When the center hiked the ball, I blew through the double-team the tackle and guard had set and barely managed to check myself when I ended up alone in the backfield with a terrified freshman QB. Instead of laying him out like I would an opposing quarterback in a game, I picked him up and set him down gently. It wouldn't do to injure the guy after all my other fuckups lately.

"That's what I'm talkin' about, McCabe! The question is, can you do that against guys your own size?" Ainsworth asked.

Yeah, I shoulda figured one good play wouldn't let me out of Coach's doghouse. For the rest of practice, I played with the second string, which did fuck all for my attitude. I had three or four more years' experience and time in the weight room over these players, so while I couldn't exactly mail it in, I didn't have to work at full speed either in order to look good. At least I'd started remembering and running the plays, so Coach could stop riding my ass about missing assignments.

After practice I braced my hands on the wall of the shower, letting the hot water run down the middle of my back and blanking my mind. The latter had become my go-to coping mechanism since that awful afternoon when Chess walked out of my life.

"You gotta fix this, Finn," Bax said as he stepped under the spray in the adjacent shower. "Coach isn't going to let you ride on last year's play."

Turning my head to the side, I regarded my friend. "Yep. Got that all figured out, Bax."

The shower head on my other side came on and with it I

heard Callahan's voice. "Seriously, Finn. What the fuck? You didn't screw up like that when we were freshman, for fuck's sake."

Great. As if Ainsworth's attempts at humiliation on the field weren't enough, my buddies had decided to berate me in stereo.

"Don't you two have someone better to do than to ride my ass?" I growled.

"There it is," Bax said.

"As a matter of fact, Finnegan, both of our girls are worried about you too," 'Han chimed in. "For the record, Jamaica says your lady is walking around in as thick a fog as you are."

"For the record, I don't have a lady." Though I wasn't ready to give up gallons and gallons of glorious hot water, I didn't need my friends bullshitting me about how bad off Chessly was. Against my buddies' advice, I'd barraged her phone with texts begging her to talk to me, to let me explain what seeing Hannah had done to my head. But I'd said the unforgivable. Even a dumb fuck like me could figure that out.

I stepped out of the shower and toweled off as I walked over to my locker. Not needing any more of my roommates' observations, I wasted little time dragging on my boxers and jeans and pulling a hoodie over my head. By the time they'd joined me on the bench, I was lacing up my boots.

"You riding home with me?" 'Han asked as he tossed his towel in the bin at the end of the row of lockers.

"Nah. I got some studying to do. Think I'll head over to Hillman where it's quiet."

"It's Thursday night, dude. Our place is quiet," Callahan protested.

"Uh, not as quiet as you think." I tossed my duffel bag over my shoulder and piggybacked it with my backpack. "You have a nice evening."

"Finn." There was a warning in 'Han's tone, but I ignored it and kept walking right out the door of the locker room.

And right into Coach Ainsworth.

He threw his arm across my shoulders. "McCabe. Walk with me to my office."

As if I had a choice.

He closed the door and gestured for to me to take a seat in front of his desk. Taking his time, he shuffled some papers and set them aside then leaned back in his chair with his hands behind his head. "You wanna talk about it?"

"Coach, I know the plays."

"You're carrying a 3.9 GPA in bio-chem. No question you know the plays." He sat forward, resting his forearms on his desk. "The question is, where the fuck is your head?"

Closing my eyes at his penetrating stare, I hauled in a breath, let it out slowly, and returned his gaze. "Just having a rough couple weeks, Coach. I'll get it together."

"That's the thing, Finn. I'm worried about you getting your shit together. You hardly reacted when I pulled you out today, and that's not like you at all."

"I sacked your QB three plays in a row." I defended myself and immediately wished I'd kept my mouth shut.

With a snort, he said, "The third string freshman who walked on this spring. You should have been drilling our second-best guy, and you couldn't get past Donahue, who you've owned for the past year." Running a hand over his head, he sighed. "I don't know who put out your fucking fire, but you need to move past that shit." He pulled up short. "It's a woman, isn't it? Fuck. Some little co-ed is fucking with your head, isn't she?"

"Nope," I answered honestly. Chessly hadn't done one damn thing to my head. I did that all by myself. "All the fucking up is on me. Like I said, I'm working on it."

He stood from his chair, which I took as my cue to leave. "Show up tomorrow ready to play, or I'm starting Jones in the scrimmage this weekend. Got it?"

I nodded. "Yes, sir. Understood."

Though I wanted to slam the shit out of his office door when I walked out, I held back and left the damn thing open as I headed down the hall and out the doors of the facility. It wasn't Coach's fault I hadn't been practicing like a starter. Nope, that was all on me too. Jesus. I didn't suck this bad even after Hannah told me what a big, dumb, awkward fuck I was when she ended it with us. That said everything that needed saying about how I felt about Chessly.

Even as my eyes registered the tree-lined sidewalk and rows of buildings between the facility and campus, what I couldn't stop seeing was the devastation on Chess's face when I'd accused her of being like Hannah. It was a knee-jerk reaction to that witch who'd made me feel about an inch tall for most of our relationship and for too long after it ended.

Intellectually, I could work through my ex's comments and label them for what they were: emotional abuse meant to strip me of all my self-confidence. If I'd played along like a good little boyfriend, we'd probably still be together, but I wouldn't have a single NFL prospect. When I wouldn't let her penetrate my game, she attacked my skills in the sack. The year of celibacy following our breakup only ended when the jersey chasers came along and made me feel better about myself.

After what Tory Miller put Callahan through last semester, I saw where my experiences with her and her girls weren't real either. But what went down between Chessly and me that glorious weekend? Nothing fake about that at all. She was as into me as I was into her. Maybe some girls fake it with guys sometimes, but there was nothing fake about her expressions as she'd stared into my eyes and let go when I was inside her. The playfulness during our date, and again after we'd rocked each other's worlds in my bed, was real too. Never before had I felt so relaxed, so able to be myself, as I had with Chess.

Jesus, I missed her something fierce.

As usual, I started scanning every study carrell in Hillman the second I walked through the doors. As usual, she wasn't in any of them. Guess she'd found somewhere new to go for quiet study time. But like a sucker, I headed upstairs to her favorite carrell only to find the geeky guy sitting there again—as usual. He nodded to me as I strolled by, his expression one of commiseration rather than ridicule, which told me what a pathetic sap I'd become.

I threw myself into a chair in a carrell at the end of the hallway, one beside the floor-to-ceiling windows facing the Union. I didn't bother unloading my books from my backpack and pretending to study. Instead, I pulled out my phone and stared at my texts, willing her to respond to even one of them. But exactly like the other thousand times I'd checked, mine were the only ones onscreen. At least she hadn't blocked me—yet. Pathetic sap that I'd become, I took comfort in that.

Out of the corner of my eye, I caught a flash of bright pink and all but pressed my nose to the glass. A blonde in a puffy coat was trudging up the steps of the Union. I didn't need to look twice to know it was Chess. Shoving my phone in my pocket, I snagged my bags and wasted no time racing down the stairs and across the courtyard into the Union.

I was out of breath when I slid through the doors into the cafeteria, scanning the place with a laser focus. She wasn't in line for coffee, and I didn't see her seated at any of the tables, so I speed-walked through the space and into the lounge on the off chance she might be there. I slowed down enough to check out every couch, love seat, and wingback chair in the room, but with the exception of some bearded guy in a tweed jacket sitting in front of the cold fireplace, the room was deserted.

Wasting no time in passing the offices lining the hallway on the other side of the lounge, I made my way to the stairs, dropping down them two at a time to the lower level. I couldn't imagine why she'd be down in the gaming area, but maybe she was meeting someone. The idea gave me heartburn, but I shoved it down and kept moving. Checking out the bowling alley, I only saw a couple of pairs of players flipping each other shit as each team rolled gutter balls. The usual gamers manned the foosball table and the video games. Nowhere did I see that distinctive coat or that perfect blonde hair.

When I rounded the corner to the Sweet Shop, I thought I caught a glimpse of her inside. Slowing my ass down, I worked to steady my breathing so I wouldn't come across as a total stalker and strolled up to the shop. Inside, the store was tight, and I accidentally knocked over a display of monster-size chocolate bars on a table to the left of the door.

My face heated as I dropped my duffel and pack and knelt to pick up the mess. A pair of feet came into my peripheral view, and I glanced up into Jamaica's laughing eyes.

"Don't worry about it, Finn. I'll get that."

"Sorry. I didn't mean to make a mess of your place." I stacked the chocolate back on the table and hoped I hadn't broken too many of the bars. "But, fuck, this place is kinda packed."

The whole store was about the size of my bedroom. One wall toward the back was stacked from a waist-high counter halfway to the ceiling with long tubes filled with a rainbow assortment of candies. In front of it were rotating displays holding bags of everything from gummy worms to cinnamon bears. How one weaved through the tables with their stacks of chocolates and fancy boxes of who-knows-what without knocking something over was more of a mystery than my clumsiness at accidentally knocking off a display with my backpack.

"What brings you to the Sweet Shop? I don't think I've ever seen you in here before." She rearranged the chocolate on the tabletop.

I rubbed the back of my neck and tried to come up with an excuse since we were the only people in the store. I guess the pink-puffy-coated blonde I thought I'd seen had been a figment of my imagination.

Jamaica stopped messing with the chocolate to give my forearm a fleeting squeeze, her tone soft and sad. "She was here a few minutes ago to drop off a Pickle Barrel for me since I'm working a double today."

We both knew who she meant.

"Fuck." Shoving my hands in my pockets, I caught myself. "Sorry, Jamaica."

"No apologies needed, big guy." She patted my shoulder. "If it's any consolation, she's as much of a hot mess as you are."

"Not helping."

Her brow shot up and her eyes took on a wicked gleam. "But I bet I *can* help."

"Look—"

"You still going to be on campus in a few hours?"

I shrugged. "Dunno. Probably. Why?"

"I get off at nine. Meet me here and walk me home."

"Uh, you sure about that?" I rocked on my heels. "I don't want to get crossways with Callahan. I might outweigh him by thirty pounds, but under the right circumstances—like me walking his girl home—he's damn likely to kick my ass."

"He won't mind. Trust me." She patted my shoulder again. "Meet me here at nine or a little before." She picked up my duffel and my backpack, handing them to me with one hand while making a shooing motion with the other. "Go on. Grab some real food, maybe do some homework, and show up back here on time."

"Why—?"

"I've got a plan, Finn. One that's going to fix this one way or the other. Trust me." For such a compact woman, she demonstrated impressive physical strength when she turned me and pushed me out the door.

Turning back, I said, "But what if I wanted to buy some candy?" I let a grin ghost over my mouth.

"You didn't though. See you in a couple hours."

I was leaning against the wall across the hallway from the Sweet Shop when Jamaica locked up a few minutes before nine.

"Hello, Finn." She smiled. "Two things I appreciate about you. You're dependable and you're on time." She linked her arm with mine and started walking toward the stairs.

"Yeah? Tell that to my coaches next time you see 'em, wouldja?"

"Okay, sometimes you're early." She smirked.

"Ah, come on, Jamaica. You don't even know all the rules to football well enough to take shots at me for being offsides," I grumbled.

"Callahan's taught me so much about the game. You'd be surprised what I know." She let go of my arm to climb the stairs.

At the top, I opened the door for her, and we stepped out into the humid air that said spring was on its way. Darkness had descended while I'd been inside the Union downing a mediocre pepperoni pizza and finishing some homework for my organic chemistry class. The one thing that hadn't suffered in my involuntary hiatus from Chessly was school. Somehow I'd managed to keep my grades up—probably because burying myself in my classes was my only escape from thinking about her.

"So what's your plan, Batman?" I asked as we headed across campus to her dorm.

"You know how in our dorm you have to call a room from the lobby and wait for the resident to escort you?"

"Yeah?"

"The rule only applies if you arrive on your own." The smile she gave me was so conspiratorial, I wondered if we were about to commit a crime. "If, however, you show up with a resident of Hanover who walks you to a certain person's door and knocks, you can bypass the system. When the resident opens the door, there you are."

"If she doesn't invite me in, will alarms go off alerting the police to come arrest me?" I wasn't entirely joking with the question.

"She'll invite you in." Somehow, her enigmatic tone did little to reassure me.

When we arrived in the lobby, Jamaica waved at the desk clerk who waved back as we kept walking. Since I'd never been to anyone's room in this dorm before, I stayed one step behind her and paid attention to my surroundings. A mural of mountains and mountain sports decorated the walls of the hallway she led me down. Outside of each doorway hung a corkboard, each of which said something about the people living behind the doors— photos, notes, girly trinkets with feathers and flowers.

While I was busy checking out the floor, I forgot to be nervous. Then, abruptly, we stopped at a door that was recessed into the wall. In the tiny entryway, I noted a whiteboard about twice the size of a standard notebook with Chess's schedule neatly written on it, along with the hours she had available for residents.

"Are you sure she's even home?" I whispered to Jamaica as she raised her hand to knock.

Jamaica's eyes glittered up at me. "She's here."

"But what if she—?" I swallowed hard. "What if she kicks me out? Are you going to escort me back to the lobby?"

"She won't kick you out."

Before I could ask how Jamaica could be so sure, she rapped hard on the door twice.

A muffled "Just a sec," filtered through the door. Then before I had a chance to figure out what I was going to say, Chess swung the door wide and stared. "Finn?"

I nodded.

"How did you know which room? How did you get past the front desk?"

I glanced around and behind me, but my escort seemed to have disappeared like magic. "I don't know where she went, but Jamaica brought me here."

Chess planted one delicate hand on her hip, her eyes narrowed. "Of course she did." For one terrible second, I thought she was going to leave me alone in the hallway. Then she opened the door wider and said, "You'd better come in. I don't need to get reported for having an unescorted man at my door."

After I stepped into her room, she closed the door behind me, and for the first time in two long weeks, I was in the same room with the woman who haunted my dreams and most of my waking moments too.

Chapter Twenty-Seven

Chessly

THE ABSOLUTE LAST person I expected to see on the other side of my door was Finn McCabe. More than anything, I wanted to wring my best friend's neck for dropping him at my door.

Or hug her.

I wasn't completely sure.

God, he looked wonderful, all broad and strong and gorgeous. *Why did he have to be so handsome?* He took up so much damn space in my shoebox of a room. And he smelled so good, like outside and something distinctly *him*. But as I looked closer, I noticed the dark circles under his eyes, the beard stubble, the kind of defeated posture that squeezed my heart.

For a long moment, we took each other in. Then I asked, "Why are you here?"

"I need to talk to you, but you won't return my texts or DMs."

Truthfully, I hadn't opened any of his messages. I was too afraid of what they would do to me.

Remembering my manners, I reached over and pulled my desk chair around for him. "Please, have a seat."

I grabbed a pillow and pulled it to my chest as I sat against the headboard on my bed. Drawing my knees up, I wished I'd had some kind of warning he'd be coming by tonight. I would have been dressed for the occasion at least, rather than wearing a ratty old pair of tights, an oversize Balefire T-shirt, and no bra.

"Are you a fan of the band?" He nodded in the direction of my shirt.

"Yeah. They're awesome."

He ran a hand through his hair, leaving it sticking up on one side. "The director for our last NIL commercial shoot for Stromboli's comped us tickets to their show at the fieldhouse next month."

"Lucky you. I heard their shows are epic." I desperately wanted that word back after it slipped out to remind me of the best date of my life. Snuggling my pillow closer, I bit my lip and tried to calm myself down.

"Chess. I'm sorry. Until that day at the Union, I hadn't seen my ex in almost three years. Hearing her say those things—fuck, it dredged up so much shit." He blew out a breath. "I reacted badly." Clasping his hands between his knees, he stared down at the floor and then found my eyes again. "You didn't deserve that."

"Thank you," I whispered.

"You're nothing like her. Seeing her again put me back in a dark place. If I could take those terrible words back, I would in a heartbeat." His body seemed to vibrate with intensity, as though he was willing me to believe him. "You'd never treat anyone the way she treated me. You'd never say those things. I know that." Those gorgeous whiskey eyes pleaded with me. "You're the most incredible woman I've ever met. That weekend we spent together was the best time I've ever had." He reached out then dropped his hand. "Hannah's right about one thing—I fuck up with women. I try hard not to, but I'm not cool like Callahan or lacking a give-a-shitter like Bax or experienced like Danny. But I think I could get it right more times than I fuck it up with you if you'll give me another chance."

I'd never heard Finn say so many words in one go. But it was the way he held himself, like he was willing me to see him, hear him—the real him, the man who was laying his heart on the line—that crashed through the walls I'd built to protect myself from him.

Still, I needed him to know. "I'm not a jersey chaser or a mean girl like your ex, or Tory Miller. When you said I'd eventually be like them . . . It hurt so much that you could think for a second I could act like them, devastate people the way they do every time they open their ugly mouths."

"I know, Chess. I know. You're sassy and sarcastic, but never mean." Air gusted from him, then he whispered, "When I'm with you I feel seen—and safe."

Unfolding my body from my perch on my bed, I stood and stepped over to him, seating myself on his lap. I wrapped my arms around his neck and rested my head on his shoulder. For a second, he hesitated, then he enfolded me in his massive arms, hugging me tight as he buried his face in my neck.

"These past two weeks without you have been the longest of my life," he said into my skin.

"I know."

Pulling back, his gaze seared into mine. "While we might have only had one real date, I'm all in with you. You have to know that."

A smirk tugged the corner of my mouth. "What about all our study dates? Don't those count?" An awful thought invaded and I asked, "Or were you seeing other girls after we started studying together?"

"The jersey chasers gave me attention at a time when I needed it. They also didn't demand anything of me."

I tried not to stiffen at his words, but he was talking about Tory Miller and her posse of mean girls, and I couldn't help it.

"But since that night we hung out on the front porch of my place, I haven't spent time with any other girl."

I relaxed, yet his expression remained dead serious.

"Ever since I first saw you the night of the bonfire, you've been it for me." He reached up and tucked a wayward strand of hair behind my ear. "Our date weekend sealed it." His eyes followed the movement of his hand as he smoothed his fingertips over my skin. "You're someone special, Chess. Someone I want to spend all kinds of time with."

Tiny goose bumps broke out over my body at his words and his touch, and I snuggled in closer to his chest.

"Does this"—he gestured to me sitting on his lap—"mean you forgive me? That you're willing to let me prove I know how to talk to you, how to treat you?"

I kissed his neck and enjoyed the way he trembled beneath my touch. "I think you're pretty damn special too, Finn McCabe," I said into his skin. "I don't know how this is going to work out for us considering the plans we have for after graduation, but I can't seem to stop myself. I'm all in with you too."

When he covered my mouth with his, it was glorious. No one had ever kissed me the way Finn did, like he couldn't—wouldn't—ever be able to have enough of me. At some point while we were devouring each other, I turned, or he turned me to straddle him, and the glorious friction of my center sliding up and down along his shaft heated me from the inside out. Then cool air rushed over my skin as I tugged my T-shirt off.

Finn groaned as I exposed myself to his gaze and his touch. When he covered my breasts with his big, calloused hands, I couldn't help but to arch into him as he kneaded and squeezed my sensitive flesh.

"Fuck, Chess. You're so perfect. Do you even know how perfect you are?"

The question was rhetorical as he buried his face in my cleavage. Then he plumped and kissed my curves while his thumbs rubbed and teased my nipples, needy for his mouth on them, which he denied with a chuckle when I squirmed in an attempt to make him give me what I wanted. When at last he sucked one turgid peak into his mouth, I moaned his name so loud, I was sure anyone walking in the hallway outside my door would have heard me.

Transferring his attention to my other breast, he teased me with the tip of his tongue before gently closing his teeth and tugging, following the tiny nip with a long, deep kiss. I kneaded and squeezed his shoulders as I dry-humped him, desperate for the additional delights his attention promised.

Instead, he pulled off me, clamping his hands on my hips to still my movements. Tortured eyes stared into mine.

"When I left the house this morning, I had no idea my day would end here with you back in my arms. As bad as I want you"—he pumped his hips—"need you," he rasped, "I didn't come prepared. At. All." He gritted his teeth. "Fuck."

My body was on fire for him, and while we could take care of each other in many ways, the one I wanted was Finn inside me.

Leaning in, I kissed him, making promises with my mouth I intended to keep.

"Chess," he groaned. "We have to stop. I don't have any protection with me."

"I can fix that." Reluctantly, I slid off his lap and pulled my T-shirt back on over my head.

A rueful chuckle accompanied the once-over he gave me.

"Covering up that gorgeous rack of yours fixes jack shit, babe. I know you're naked underneath that shirt."

"Hold that thought."

I slipped out the door and hotfooted it down the hall to the communal bathroom where to my relief, I discovered the condom basket still contained a few packets. For a second I debated before snagging three and hustling back to my room. Finn remained seated where I'd left him, one hand covering his glorious crotch. From what I could tell, he was trying to talk himself down, which wouldn't do at all.

Turning the lock on my door, I said, "Dorm furniture isn't as sturdy as the nice stuff you have at your place, but if we're careful, we can still have a good time."

"What?" he began before I thrust the handful of protection at him. A smile like daylight lit up his face as he reached for my offering, setting the condoms on the desk beside him. "Come here, you resourceful girl." He patted his lap. When I straddled him again, he said, "Where were we? Oh, yeah, I remember." Without ceremony, he whipped off my T-shirt and covered my breasts with his hands. "I believe my mouth was here"—he suckled one excited nipple—"and your hips were doing this." Clamping his hands over my hips, he lifted me up and down until I took over.

In seconds, I was clawing at his hoodie, silently demanding he take it off. He reached behind his head and dragged off the offending clothing in the cool way guys do. I grinned as a second later his T-shirt joined it on the rug.

Desperate to feel his skin on me, I flattened my chest to his and dove in for a kiss. Our tongues stroked each other as I ran my hands over his shoulders and up into his shaggy hair. Tingles chased up and down my back wherever his calloused hands smoothed and caressed. Then they found their way inside my tights, kneading and squeezing my ass as much as the body-hugging fabric would allow.

At last we came up for air, smiling at each other as I ran my fingers through his hair and he continued to fondle my butt.

"I love the way these pants or whatever show off your gorgeous ass"—he glanced down—"and these delicious long legs of yours, but I'd like 'em better if they were on the floor."

"Only if your jeans join them," I sassed.

I slid off his lap and pushed my tights and panties down to the floor. He unlaced his boots, kicked them off, then stood and shoved his jeans and boxers down to join the rest of our clothes on the rug.

Running his hands up and down my arms, he stared deep into my eyes. "I missed you so much. Until you opened the door tonight, I was only breathing half the air I need." Sliding his hands around my waist, he tugged me close, our bodies touching from chests to knees. "Tonight I took my first full breath in two weeks." He ducked his head to run his nose along the column of my neck. "Because I need you like breathing. I didn't see that coming until you walked away."

Soft kisses along my skin raised goose bumps over my body.

Against my lips, he said, "You're it for me, Chess."

I couldn't stop the moan that bubbled up from my throat as he kissed me slow and easy. His unhurried savoring after so many days apart came close to driving me straight out of my head, but intuitively, I understood he needed this, needed to take his time with me no matter how badly I ached for him. Especially with the way his hard shaft rubbed against my lower belly, the promise of so much pleasure so close to where I needed him most.

As though he'd read my mind, he stepped us over to my narrow bed and pulled me down to lie on top of him. "I want you so much, babe. But if I take the lead, we're likely to break something." A self-deprecating chuckle escaped him, and I smiled.

Sitting up to straddle him, I smirked. "So that's your way of getting out of doing the work, huh?"

"Just taking care of the furniture." He thrust his hips up a couple of times. "Does this bed have any springs in it at all?"

I snorted. "Barely." Stretching my arms over my head, I gave him a wet dream's view of my body before I reached behind me to retrieve a foil packet from where he'd dropped them on my desk.

His busy hands covered my breasts, plucking and kneading and driving me wild. I wasted no time tearing open the packet. Then it was my turn to tease and play. Fisting him with one hand, I enjoyed his hard length. I held him right where I wanted him as I rubbed my clit over the head of his cock.

"Chessly," he warned through gritted teeth. "Be careful."

"I'm always careful." With a secret grin, I rubbed my wet center along his length. When he groaned and clamped his hands over my hips, I stopped and smoothed the condom over him. "See how easy that was?" I asked.

He answered with a deeper groan. "If you don't sit on me properly in the next two seconds, I won't be responsible for what happens to this bed. Fair warning."

It occurred to me it would be fun to tease him, and on any other day, I probably would have. But I was as desperate as he was to reconnect, to feel him moving inside me, to know the pleasure I'd only ever experienced with him.

Positioning him at my entrance, I slid down his shaft slowly, savoring the sensation of Finn filling me full. When I was seated, I couldn't stop pulsing around him. "Oh, oh, *Finn*! You feel so good."

Sweat broke over his brow as he gritted out, "Move, babe. For the love of all that's holy, *move*."

His eyes glittered up at me, and he put his hands on my breasts. Rubbing, tugging, twisting, he teased my nipples, arrowing sensation straight to my pussy. It wasn't long before my long, languid glides up and down his shaft had shortened in duration and increased in intensity.

"That's it, Chess. Ride me."

The pleasure built as I rode him faster until rivulets of sweat chased each other down my spine, and air sawed in and out of my lungs as I chased my release. When I couldn't move fast enough for either of us, Finn dropped his hands to my hips and took over from beneath me.

"Hands on your titties, babe. The girls need more attention."

When I hesitated, his brow shot up in challenge. Then I remembered how he'd put himself out there by showing up at my room in the first place, and I covered my breasts with my hands.

"Play with them like I was playing with them," he commanded.

Diving deep and channeling my inner goddess, I did as he wanted and watched in wonder as his eyes turned black with desire while he thrust up into me harder, deeper.

"That's it babe." He smiled. "Your pussy likes it when someone is playing with your tits."

Under us my narrow dorm bed protested the vigorous workout we were giving it. But I was too close to bliss to care. And then Finn pressed his thumb to my clit, and I clamped both hands over my mouth to muffle the scream that erupted as the mother of all orgasms exploded through me. A few seconds later, Finn let out a shout, his body going rigid as he held us both off the bed.

Slowly, I floated down from outer space to lie across his broad chest as the aftershocks rippled through me. His heart pounded against mine in a mirror rhythm, and I kissed the space where his shoulder met his neck. Leisurely, he traced his fingers up and down my spine as the sweat cooled on my skin.

"For the record," he said, "two days is too long to go without this, Chess. Never mind two weeks. My heart is still racing in my chest from what you just did to me, and already I'm thinking about doing it again."

"Mmm," was all I could respond.

"But I have to be up at the butt-crack of dawn for morning lift, so as much as I want to stay here with you and use up all the condoms, I can't."

Resting my chin on my stacked hands, I stared at his sculpted lips and said, "I have an eight o'clock quiz, so as much I'd like to entertain you all night, I can't."

Groaning in unison, he lifted me off him to stand and stretch. He tied off the condom and tossed it in the trash beside the bed. Pointing at the two unused packets on the desk, he said, "We'll leave these here for emergencies, but from now on we're playing at my place." He pushed on a spot on his lower back. "I'm too big for the kiddie bed the university gives you to sleep on."

Wrapping my arms around his waist, I massaged the spot where his hand had been. "Poor thing. Did you get a cramp?" I teased.

"Be nice."

"I thought I was being nice."

He smiled down at me. "Yes, you were very, very . . . nice. The fucking nicest." For a long minute, he hugged me hard. "Can you come over to my place tomorrow night after class? Or are you on call?"

"I'm not on call."

Clearing his throat, he said, "Will you stay the night?"

Hugging him back I said, "How can I pass up that king-size bed?"

CHAPTER TWENTY-EIGHT

Chessly

IT WAS AFTER midnight by the time Finn and I had dressed again and I'd walked him to the lobby. Before he stepped out into the night, he wrapped me tight in his arms and kissed the hell out of me. When I headed past the front desk in the direction of my room, the front desk clerk gave a low whistle, and I flipped him the bird. But my face was so hot, I was sure I could have fried bacon on it.

Too keyed up from my unexpected reunion with the great big guy I didn't see coming, I decided I owed him the courtesy of reading his texts. Flopping back on the bed that now smelled like him and us and sex, I closed my eyes for a minute, gathered my courage, and opened the text screen.

He'd started texting immediately after I left the lounge in the Union that awful day.

> Finn: Chess! I'm sorry. I'm so fuckin sorry. I didn't mean it.
>
> Finn: Please believe me.

Finn: Can we talk? Please?

Later that same night he wrote:

Finn: I was a dick. Tell me off or whatever you need to do. I deserve it. But please talk to me.

The next morning he said:

Finn: Chess, you have a right to be mad. I said a terrible thing. I didn't mean it.

Finn: You're not her.

Finn: Please.

For the rest of the week, he'd sent more texts with various iterations of the same message, his desperation becoming more intense as the days wore on. The second week the tenor and content of the messages changed, as though he'd resigned himself to me dumping him, but he couldn't stop hoping for a different outcome.

Finn: I miss you so much.

Finn: I fuckin MISS YOU.

Finn: Guess you're not hanging out in the Union anymore?

Finn: Looking for you in Hillman.

Finn: I can't help it. I look for you everywhere.

Finn: The graduate geek has had your carrell every single day this week.

Finn: Jesus. I miss you so much. Is it possible for a literal hole to open up in your chest? It's a question of physics only you can answer for me.

Every word I read made my heart hurt until I had to check my chest for the bruise that must be covering it. Tears spilled over, blurring the screen as I read the texts that had come in during the afternoon before he showed up at my place.

> Finn: The geek stopped laughing at me today. Guess I'm that pathetic now.
>
> Finn: The geek is the lucky one. He's never heard you laugh.
>
> Finn: He doesn't know how you don't like to share your cookies.
>
> Finn: He's never heard you come. Lucky bastard. He doesn't have a clue how good he has it.
>
> Finn: I fucked up in practice again. Coach demoted me to second string. I wish I could give a shit about it.
>
> Finn: I miss you.

By the time I'd reached the last one, I was openly sobbing and wishing so hard that he was back here in my room where I could hold him. Just hold him and show him I'd forgiven him, show him how much I regretted being too prideful to listen to him like my friends had begged me to do. *Shit.* He'd been playing so poorly in spring ball that he'd been demoted? He wasn't a second-stringer: he was headed to the NFL. He'd been so excited for practice to start again. Had I done that to him—stolen the fire and joy from the game he lived to play?

I was so hurt that he'd lumped me in with a bitch like his ex, but now I had to wonder if he hadn't been right. Who treated a man as soft-hearted and generous as Finn McCabe the way I'd treated him: by ignoring him and not giving him a chance to apologize?

Me: What time do you practice?

Finn: During your lab.

Finn: I can pick you up from Hillman after we're both finished.

Me: I can make up the lab.

A sharp rap on my door at 7:30 a.m. put a big smile on my face that faltered the second I opened the door to find Jamaica on the other side.

"Expecting someone else?" she asked, with a feline grin.

Grabbing her by the wrist, I dragged her into my room and shut the door. "That was a neat trick you pulled, J."

She snorted. "You're welcome." Her eyes sparkled without a shred of remorse. "I take it the reunion went well."

"I think sometimes I can be a bit pigheaded." Deliberately, I didn't look at my friend as I gathered my books and stuffed them into my backpack.

"Only sometimes?" she teased. "You still haven't answered the question."

"Let's just say, I'll be sitting beside you in the bleachers this afternoon watching the Wildcats practice." I slipped my jacket on and went in search of my gloves.

Grabbing me from behind in a hug, Jamaica said into my back, "I'm so happy you two worked things out. It's been hard watching you both suffer for the past couple of weeks."

Facing her, I slipped on my gloves. "What are you saying? You've barely even seen me."

"My point exactly. You've been holed up in here rather than showing up for coffee with the rest of the gang, or dropping by the Sweet Shop when I have a shift, or hanging around to talk after RA meetings." She handed me my backpack. "You're not a recluse, Chess, except for maybe when your heart is breaking."

Gifting my best friend a long look, I finally gave in and pulled her into a hug. "I don't know what led to you dropping Finn off here last night, but thank you." Pulling my door open, I ushered her out of my room ahead of me so I could lock up. "Now you can go gossip about me to Piper and Saylor while I ace a quantum physics quiz."

She laughed.

"And I'll see you guys later this afternoon at the field. Finn needs me to cheer my throat raw for him. You can help."

"What—?"

"I'll explain later."

I left Jamaica in the lobby with a perplexed expression.

When I arrived at the stadium, I didn't quite know what to expect. Though I was an avid Wildcats fan, I only ever attended games. Until I'd met Finn and his friends, I had no idea people watched practices if they were open. Sometimes, coaches closed them, which apparently ticked off certain fans who kind of thought they owned the team—like certain alumni donors.

Jamaica, Piper, and Saylor were already in the stands when I arrived. The day had turned chilly, a threat of spring snow in the air, so I'd stopped back at the dorm after my last class to deck myself out in warm boots, an extra sweater, and my Wildcats beanie. I'd emailed my professor that I couldn't make my lab, which I knew wouldn't be a problem since I was allowed one excused absence that I'd yet to use. After reading Finn's texts last night, the only place I wanted to be this afternoon was here cheering him on.

"About time you joined us again," Piper said as I sat on the edge of the blanket they'd laid over the cold metal seat.

"Hello to you too." I grinned.

"Finn is over there with the subs. Would you know something about that, Chess?" Saylor said, her raised brow emphasizing her censorious tone.

Turtling down into my jacket, I said, "He mentioned something about being demoted. But I'm sure it's temporary." *I hope.*

"It'd better be. That sophomore who's playing ahead of him is about a half-second slow off the line," she said, returning her attention to the field.

"Who are you here to watch, Saylor? Have you been holding out on us?" I asked.

"I'm here as an annoying fifth wheel to you three and your hot Wildcats. I also happen to be a fan." She sniffed.

Noticing the sparse number of other fans in the stands and the marked absence of noise coming from those fans, I asked, "Are we allowed to cheer?"

"Bad form," Jamaica said. "Callahan says in games it amps the team up. In practice it distracts them, which the coaches frown on."

"But how will Finn know I'm here supporting him?" After discovering his current situation and the probable part I'd played in it, I needed him to know I was here for him.

"Don't worry, Chess," Jamaica said with a grin. "He knows you're here." She gave a slight nod toward the field where Finn stood beside one of the coaches, but his focus wasn't on what the coach was saying. He was smiling at me.

With a discreet wave, I smiled back at him. A minute later he lined up where the sophomore had been and ran the play like a rock star. Instead of smashing the quarterback into the turf, he picked him up and set him gently back on his feet for what obviously should have been a sack.

"I take it it's also bad form to sack your own quarterback." I smirked.

"That's why the QBs wear red jerseys, so our defense doesn't lay them out," Jamaica said in a sage tone that cracked me up.

"Six months ago, you didn't have a clue about football. Now listen to you, Miss Football Analyst." I laughed.

Jamaica stuck her tongue out at me, and I laughed harder.

As practice wore on, Finn continued to play with the second string D-line, popping the happy mood from last night's reunion like a balloon. My inability to listen, to give him a chance to fix things, had obviously messed with his head to the point he truly had stopped caring about his sport like he'd said in one of those last texts. Watching him tear apart the second string offense today, seeing his fire and skill go unchallenged by the other players, did nothing for my conscience.

At least the coaches seemed to praise his play. From where we sat in the stands, I couldn't hear what they were saying, but their body language conveyed appreciation for Finn's efforts. Maybe he'd had a chance to win back his starting position before the team's spring scrimmages. No matter what, I had some apologizing to do.

As darkness descended on the field, the temperature dropped several degrees, which had the four of us cuddling together under a second blanket Saylor had thought to bring. The players' breath evanesced into the stadium lights, which came on as the sun went down. Their sweaty heads steamed in the cold whenever they removed their helmets on a break in play. Right when I thought I'd have to cry uncle and head back to campus and somewhere warm, the coaches called an end to practice. The players jogged off the field in the direction of the locker room, and my friends and I all sighed in relief.

"I'm frozen," Piper announced.

"Me too." Jamaica's teeth chattered.

"I vote the Union and hot chocolate," I said as we descended the stairs to the concession area beneath the stands.

"We're headed to Stromboli's, Chess," Piper said as though I should have already known that. "The guys are meeting us there."

"Oh. I'm out of the loop."

"By choice," Jamaica scolded.

Sliding her arm through mine, Saylor dragged me ahead of our other friends. "Don't mind them. They're just pissy about their front-row seat at the Finn Implosion Show these past couple of weeks, what with how much time they spend on Jock Street." Her tone might have been nonchalant, but she chose her words to sting.

Bruised already from my own conscience, Saylor's words only pummeled my heart harder.

"He compared me to women like his ex-girlfriend—like Tory Miller. If that's the way he saw me, then I didn't see the point of us spending any more time together," I said in my defense.

"But you couldn't give him a pass for maybe reacting to the moment?" Saylor's tone had lost all its previous lightness.

"Jamaica escorted him to my room last night after her shift at the Sweet Shop. He didn't leave until midnight." I left it there, disengaging myself from Saylor's hold on my arm as we neared Piper's car.

"About time."

Yep. I had so much making up to do.

Chapter Twenty-Nine

Finn

"**WHAT THE FUCK** time did you roll in last night?" Bax asked as I strolled into the kitchen to grab breakfast the morning after my reunion with Chessly. I rarely overslept, but after going a couple of rounds with Chess and trying not to break her bed while doing it, I'd come home and slept like a stone. When my alarm went off, I didn't.

That meant I'd barely had a chance to gather up my books and shit in time to catch Bax for a ride to the facility.

"Late. Thanks for waiting for me."

I snagged the hot breakfast burrito he handed me as we hustled out the front door.

"What's your story? You're usually the one who bangs on my door in the morning, not the other way round."

I didn't even try to stop the grin that spread over my face. "Chess and I are back on speaking terms."

Sliding me a sly side-eye, he asked, "Do you mean speaking, or do you mean *speaking*?"

"Yes." I bit into my breakfast to stop myself from saying more. My roommates had a way of getting things out of me that were none of their business.

Instead of pressing me for details, he lifted a fist for me to bump and left it at that. I guess he'd figured out Chess was too special to discuss—kinda like the agreement we'd come to about his girl.

He might have broken a few laws on our way to the facility, but at least we were on time to lift. We'd all learned from Bax being late to weight training once that it was way better to show up drunk than to show up late. Coach Larkin's punishment for tardiness—an extra half hour of burpees and laps on the track—wasn't worth oversleeping.

Being on time did fuck all for Larkin's attitude toward me though. He started in on me the second I walked into the weight room.

"Good morning, McCabe. If you're planning to mail it in here the way you've been doing out on the field this week, you might want to skip ahead and go on out to the track."

Clearing my throat, I said, "Don't worry, Coach. I've pulled my head out of my ass."

"We'll see," he growled.

I stepped over to the hand weights, picking up fifty pounds in each hand, and started warming up. Coach stood behind me, watching my form and counting my reps as though I were a rookie or something. He nudged Bax out of the way when it came time to spot my bench presses. When I asked for two additional forties above my usual weight to be added to the bar, he made a harrumph sound and started counting. By the time I'd finished the circuit though, with him bird-dogging every exercise and every rep, I think he'd figured out I was serious. My focus hadn't wavered once.

"The question is, can you manage the same concentration on the field this afternoon?" was all Larkin said as I walked out of the weight room, second to last ahead of Callahan.

I deserved that. For the past couple of weeks, I hadn't given anyone my best. In a sport that was all about "what have you done for me lately?" my production merited Larkin's disapproval and Ainsworth's pissed-off attitude. I'd dug a hole for myself, and it was going to take time and a whole bunch of effort to climb out of it. At least I'd stopped digging.

A picture of Chessly, gloriously naked and riding me hard, flashed through my head, reminding me why all was right in my world again. Now that I had her back in my life, I could count on football taking care of itself.

"What are you smiling about, Finnegan?" Callahan asked as he fell into step beside me on our way to the locker room. "From what I saw today, you were one step away from burpees till you puked up that fine breakfast burrito I spent all of last Sunday afternoon cooking up for you."

"Yeah, Ainsworth might have told Larkin I needed some motivation. Yesterday, he was right. Today, not so much." I stepped over to the bench in front of my locker and started stripping off my sweaty T-shirt and shorts.

The perplexed look on his face cracked me up. "What? Did you decide to move on?"

"Move on?" I knitted my eyebrows. "Move on from what?"

"Not what. Who. Are you over Chessly?" He grabbed a towel from the end of the bench.

Snagging a towel for myself, I followed him to the showers. "Not even a little bit. I doubt I'll ever be over her." I turned the water over to hot and stepped under the spray.

"What gives?"

"Your girl is a genius, you know that?" I ducked my head and let the hot water wash away an hour and a half of sweat and exertion.

"What does Jamaica have to do with your cheesy smiles?"

I detected a whiff of hostility in his tone, and I laughed. "Calm your ass down. Jamaica fixed it so Chessly couldn't ignore me." I lathered up and stepped back beneath the spray. "She's tricky, your girl. No wonder she runs your ass in circles."

"You and Chess are back together? Thank fuck." He turned off his shower and toweled off. "About fuckin' time." Grinning, he snapped his towel at my ass when I snagged mine from the hook on the wall outside the showers. "We were about to stage an intervention."

"What-the-fuck-ever." I wrapped my towel around my waist and returned to my locker to dress for the day.

"Now maybe you can remember you're a senior and a starter and start playing that way."

"Did Ainsworth put you up to that speech?" I didn't bother to hide my irritation.

"Nope. I want to win a national championship. With my best friend. But I can't do that if my best friend isn't giving everything he's got every time he steps on the field." He shrugged. "Just sayin'."

Bax stepped into the conversation. "What are you just sayin', 'Han?"

"The three of us came in together with one goal. We have one last chance to meet that goal, which means Finn needs to pull his head out and play like the pro prospect he is. That's all." 'Han pulled a hoodie over his head and sat on the bench beside me to lace up his shoes.

"Now that he's back with Chessly, he'll be all right," Bax said. "At least *he* only fucked up in practice rather than in a conference game." He coughed into his hand. "Just sayin'."

A grin lifted the corner of my mouth. "Good point, Bax."

"Fuck you." Apparently, Callahan had a sore spot when it came to us reminding him how he fucked up last fall when things with Jamaica went south.

"You catching a ride to campus with me?" Bax asked.

"Yeah. If you don't mind." I shoved my duffel bag into my locker, snagged my backpack off the floor in front of it, and followed Bax to his truck.

I had a full slate of classes and labs on Fridays. Not the best schedule. Certainly not a schedule someone with three years of college under his belt should have arranged. But I'd missed the window on setting up my chemistry labs in the two-hour Tuesday/Thursday slots, which meant I was stuck with them on Monday, Wednesday, and Friday. After reconnecting with Chess, all I wanted to do was meet up with her somewhere on campus, but our classes fell at successive times, so we couldn't find even ten minutes for a quick hello. Or a kiss or several.

The day had dragged on to at least double its length by the time practice started. She'd texted that she'd be there, but when I glanced up at the stands, only her friends were seated in their usual spot. My heart sank, but then I remembered she had a late lab. Though she'd said she'd get out of it, with her medical school goals, she couldn't afford to skip classes. I relaxed.

We ran a few drills, practicing our footwork and breaking down to tackle. Coach Ellis was a stickler for proper footwork and form tackling. Over time, the drills had become so repetitive, I probably could have done them in my sleep, except for the fact the coaching staff scrutinized every single one of us on every single repetition. The work was a kind of meditation, and during drills, I forgot everything except for the mechanics of what I was doing.

When we moved on to plays, true to his word, Ainsworth stuck me with the second string again. Bax shot me a sour look as he trotted off the field after running the series with the rest of the defensive starters. But I didn't panic. As Ainsworth chewed my ass—before I'd run even one play—I glanced up into the stands again and saw my lady sitting with her friends. She smiled and offered me a little wave, and my whole world lit up like the sun bursting through a cloud.

Four plays later, I'd "sacked" the backup QB twice and hurried him once. And I'd managed those impressive stats without jumping offsides. At. All.

"So you've decided you want to play football after all, huh, McCabe?" Ainsworth asked as he marked something on his clipboard.

"Yes, sir."

"Uh-huh. Just for today, or is this a permanent choice?" He didn't look up from his notes as he let loose with his sarcasm.

"I told you I'd pull my head out. Told Larkin the same thing this morning too."

"We'll see. Get back out there."

I joined the starters and ran four more plays. My late night had started catching up with me, but this wasn't the time to give in to fatigue. Sneaking a peek up into the stands, I caught Chess's eye and the grin on her face—the one that said she was thinking about last night. When Coach sent me out yet again with the second string, I blew up the tackle and guard double-teaming me and accidentally put the QB on his ass. Or. rather, I twisted mid-air and let the poor kid land on me.

"Fuck, McCabe." Ainsworth shook his head. "You've made your point. Go grab some water." Turning his attention to the rest of the defense standing on the edge of line of scrimmage, he yelled, "Jones! Get in there!"

"Well, well, well, looks like you're back," Bax said as I joined him on the sideline while the second string practiced the series.

"Look, I know I've been AWOL these past couple of weeks, but it's all good now." I shot back some water. "Tomorrow's scrimmage is going to be awesome."

He laughed and bumped my fist.

When my roommates and I arrived at Stromboli's after practice, we found our girls seated together in our usual booth with two pitchers of beer and enough glasses to go around. We rearranged the seating so each of us could sit beside our ladies. It was a tight squeeze, which I liked since it meant I was touching Chess from her shoulders to her knees along my right side.

With a playful wrinkling of her nose, she allowed me to squish her into the corner of the booth. For her ears only, I said, "Thanks for showing up today. It meant a lot." I enjoyed her little shiver when I ghosted a kiss over the shell of her ear.

Troubled eyes met mine. "Um, are you back in the starting lineup?"

"Yeah, I think so." I slipped my arm around her shoulders and gave her a squeeze. "I'll find out for sure during our scrimmage tomorrow."

"I'm truly sorry for my part in your demotion."

Setting my lips next to her ear, I whispered, "Not your fault," and followed up with another kiss because damn, she smelled so good, like flowers and spice, and she was next to me and everything was right in the world.

"Nice to have you back in the gang," Bax said to Chess. "We don't have a clue what to do with a quiet Finn."

Piper elbowed him in the ribs, and he squawked.

"What was that for? I was only stating facts."

She gifted him a massive eye roll.

"Agreed." This from Jamaica, who'd stopped exchanging googly eyes with Callahan long enough to toss in her two cents.

"I'm looking forward to burning you for a teeder, Bax," Callahan said with a grin.

"Be prepared to get your ass kicked," Bax said.

"You're not actually going to play each other like you play real opponents, are you?" Jamaica sounded aghast.

It seemed Callahan still had some football lessons to teach his girl.

"Oh, hell yes, we are," I said, grinning. "Except for the QB. He's safe. This guy?" I indicated 'Han. "Not so much." Bax and I fist-bumped over the top of the table.

"If you hurt Callahan, I'm going to—" Jamaica pursed her lips.

"Short-sheet his bed?" Chessly supplied.

"Yes. And probably worse." Her emphatic tone cracked me up. "I'll make sure it's on a night when you're on call, Chess."

"Even when I'm cheering hard for Finn and Bax to stop this guy?" Chess asked, her voice saccharine-sweet.

Jamaica leaned around me to stick her tongue out at my girl. "How are we friends, again?"

Callahan laughed. "That's it, Island Girl. You're already in the game, and we haven't even stepped onto the field yet." He kissed her temple and tugged her closer to his side.

"The whole lot of you are pathetic. If any more hormones start flying around this table, I may have to relocate." Saylor shook her head and took a long pull from her beer. "Personally, I'm going to cheer for sunshine and some frat boys to show up in the stands with beverages." Her eyes danced as she drank deeply again and licked the foam from her lip with a smack.

Pizzas arrived before anyone had a chance to call her out for her BS. The girls had ordered three extra-large pies and a basket of wings, with about half a gallon of ranch dressing for dipping. Saylor passed plates around, and conversation dropped right off as we dug into dinner. In only a few minutes, all that was left of the food was what we were licking from our fingers.

As if by magic two more pitchers of beer appeared, and we lingered over them for a bit before Callahan said, "Since we have to be at the field early in the morning, it's prolly a good idea we grab some shut-eye." He slid to the edge of the booth. On some silent signal, his girlfriend followed him.

Bax stretched and dropped his arm back over Piper's shoulders. "Yeah, we should head out. Rest up for kicking the offense's asses tomorrow." The devilish gleam in his eyes dared 'Han.

'Han returned his dare. "I'll remind you of that when I burn you for a touchdown—or two."

"Seriously, you guys aren't going to go after each other for real, are you?" Jamaica's concern manifested in her wrapping her arms around Callahan.

It was cute how she thought she could protect him.

"The point of the scrimmage, Jamaica, is for the defense to show up the offense," I said, fist-bumping Bax across the table.

Callahan gazed down at his girlfriend. "Trust me, babe, the point of the scrimmage is for the offense to make fools of the defense."

Saylor chimed in. "This is going to be so much more fun to watch than usual."

"Why is that?" Piper asked.

"Because you three"—she waved her half-full glass to indicate Piper, Jamaica, and Chessly—"will have to try to remain friends, while this bunch"—she pointed to my roommates and me—"will be actively trying to cream each other on the field." She slugged back her beer and thunked the glass on the table. "Highly entertaining."

"On that note it's time to go." Callahan fished some bills from his pocket to cover his part of the tip.

With my arm still draped over Chessly's shoulders, I tugged her with me as I scooted to the edge of the booth. "Ready, babe?"

She shot me a side-eye. Guess it wasn't lost on her that we were already on our way out.

Standing, I pulled my wallet from the back pocket of my jeans and added some bills to the pile 'Han had started.

"Saylor—" Piper began.

Saylor waved her hand. "Don't worry, Piper. I already texted an Uber."

Piper smiled and followed Bax out of the booth. At the door we split up to drive home in our respective outfits. I'd parked a short way down the street from the bar, so we didn't have to walk far.

"Your chariot, milady," I said as I unlocked the passenger side and held the door for her.

"Um, if you need to rest or whatever for the game tomorrow—"

I cut her off. "What I need is private time with you." Cupping her cheek, I leaned in close. "Do you know how long it's been since my mouth has been on yours?" Brushing my lips over hers, I whispered, "Way more hours than acceptable."

I meant for the kiss to be slow, gentle. Easy. But Chess fisted her hands in the front of my hoodie, opened her pretty mouth to me, and sent all my good intentions right out the cab of my truck. In the space of two heartbeats, the kiss raced from ten to molten. The only reason she wasn't in the middle of my lap, dry-humping me right there on the street in full view of anyone walking down the sidewalk, was because the gearshift was in the way.

At last we let each other up for air. Panting, I said, "We're going to my place." When she blinked at me, I clarified. "My bed is bigger." Pushing a strand of hair behind her ear, I added, "And in spite of our house being old with thin walls, it's still way more private than the dorm."

"Okay."

"Really? That easy?"

"Are you implying I'm easy?" Her tone matched the arch of her brow.

As I turned the key in the ignition, I cracked up. "There she is."

Chess sent me a narrow glare out of the corner of her eye as she buckled herself in.

"But we should probably stop at your place on the way." I put the truck in gear and eased out of the tight parking space some moron had created when he'd nosed his ride up to my back bumper.

"For . . .?"

"Your toothbrush unless you don't mind using mine in the morning." I shot her a grin. "I don't mind if you don't mind."

"You were serious about me spending the night? We haven't even had our second date."

Her observation unsettled me until I caught the grin teasing the corner of her mouth.

"We just triple-dated with an extra in Stromboli's. You don't think that counts?" I wheeled my old truck through the roundabout near her dorm. "And you can't forget all our study dates. I recall some serious flirting with you in Hillman."

A quiet chuckle escaped her, and then she sobered. "Spending the night is a big step for me, Finn."

I extended my hand palm-up in the middle of the bench seat. After a beat, she set her hand in mine, and I gave her a reassuring squeeze.

"It's a big step for me too, Chess. It's been more than three years since I last woke up with someone in my bed." Rubbing my thumb over the soft skin of her hand, I left myself wide-open. "But more than anything, I want to wake up with you beside me in the morning."

The hitch of her breath did more for my peace of mind than any words could ever do. Then she squeezed my hand back. In that moment, our entire relationship shifted. The number of official dates we'd been on didn't matter. Chess and I were a couple. We were together, and that was it.

Chapter Thirty

Chessly

THE HORSESHOE DRIVEWAY in front of Hanover was a fifteen-minute-only parking area—something I had to remind Finn about when he flattened me against the back of my dorm room door with his big, sexy body.

"I mean it, mister. The desk clerk will call a tow company to have your truck hauled away and laugh the whole time he's making the call."

Mischief danced in his whiskey eyes. "It's one kiss, Chess. I need it to tide me over."

I raspberried out a breath, which he covered with his mouth, promptly making me forget my point.

A long, long time later, I clocked my knee resting on his hip and the hard outline of his erection behind the fly of his jeans rubbing up and down my needy center. From the way were both moving, it was a wonder we hadn't set the fronts of our jeans on fire.

Swallowing hard, I slowly lowered my leg. "Toothbrush," I mumbled.

He blew out a breath and nodded, so I guess he heard me. It still took him an age to step away from me. I had to admit I liked that he didn't want to stop touching me. Lord knew I didn't want to stop touching him.

Wasting no time, I snagged my backpack from the floor beside my desk and stuffed in clean socks and panties, my toothbrush and toiletries bag, and a clean T-shirt for under my sweater and jacket while watching tomorrow's scrimmage.

"You did that impressively quick." He smirked.

"I hope we still have a ride to your place when we hit the lobby," I sassed back.

When we emerged into the lobby, I caught the desk clerk hanging up the phone. "Did you call the tow company just now?"

He shrugged. "Rules are rules. They apply to everyone—even RAs and Wildcats players."

"Better call 'em back so they don't charge the dorm for a false callout." I tugged on Finn's hand to hustle him to the door. The campus towing company was only about ten minutes from Hanover.

The guy was new and one of those people who followed every rule to the letter. I bet he'd never once even jaywalked on campus. "They charge for not having a tow when they arrive?"

"Sure do," I said over my shoulder. "You'll have to file a report with the dorm supervisor for the charge."

The phone clattered across the desk when he knocked it from its cradle in his haste to cancel the tow. I saved my giggles until Finn and I were in his truck.

"Seriously? The tow company charges for a false alarm?" he asked as he started his pickup and put it in gear.

"Have to, or else people would be calling in tows all the time as pranks. It's only a twenty-dollar charge, but there truly is paperwork so the tow company gets paid. Becky, our supervisor, hates paperwork." I wrinkled my nose in the direction of the lobby. "I probably shouldn't have told him after his snarky comment about the rules."

Finn's hand found its way to the top of my thigh. "Nah, you did him a solid. If he's any kind of guy, he'll remember that next time."

I kind of forgot what we were talking about when his fingertips moved back and forth along the inside seam of my jeans. Though the contact was short-lived due to his having to shift gears, the lingering sensation of his touch sent a flurry of tingles straight to my clit. My entire body tightened in anticipation of what we could get up to in the privacy of his bedroom, and I had to wonder at myself.

Never before had things with a guy moved this fast for me. Not sex. While my experience was limited to the digits on one hand, I hadn't been holding out until my wedding day. I'd had two semi-serious relationships that had fizzled out and a couple of good-time hookups that had lasted for a few months before each of us wanted to move on.

Then there was Finn.

Starting with that first night when he'd offered me a ride home from the Homecoming bonfire, I'd sensed something different about him, something special. I'd wasted too much time making excuses denying the chemistry between us since the moment we met. Yeah, we'd only had one formal—epic—date, but we'd been seeking each other for months.

When he pulled into the driveway of the Victorian, he let out a mild curse and parked behind a green Mustang.

"What's wrong?"

"Nothing. I thought Danny was spending the night at his girlfriend's is all." He killed the engine and hopped out, running around the front of the truck to open my door for me. "You'll have to be super quiet. Will that be possible?" His eyes twinkled as he snagged my backpack from my hand, slinging it over his shoulder with one hand while linking the fingers of his other hand through mine.

"I'm sure I can contain myself," I said, my tone far more nonchalant than I felt.

He gave my hand a squeeze. "Sounds like a dare." Waggling his eyebrows, he said, "I live for dares."

Hustling us up the steps and through the front door, he didn't give me a chance to respond before we were in the front foyer. He let me go long enough to unlace his boots. Straightening, he said, "It's my turn to clean the downstairs. Help me out, Chess." He gave a pointed stare at my still-booted feet.

After shucking off my hikers, I lined them up neatly on the mat. "Satisfied?"

"Not yet, but I have no doubt I'm about to be." The wicked intent in his eyes was its own dare, but before I could call his ass out on his terrible double entendre, he dropped a shoulder. In one quick move, I was ass-up, face-down over his shoulder, his laughter echoing up the stairs ahead of us as he carried me to his room.

"You're a beast, Finn McCabe!" I yelled.

"Shh, Chess," he chided me. "Inside voice."

Rich laughter followed his words, and even though I gave a valiant effort, I couldn't stop the smile that spread over my face at his antics.

Closing his bedroom door behind us, he walked through the dark to the side of his bed and flipped on the bedside lamp. A second later, my backpack hit the floor in front of the nightstand with a thump right before I landed in the middle of his glorious king-size bed.

"Remember, babe." He nodded toward the headboard. "The walls in this place are thin, and Danny's home." He put a finger to his lips. "Shh." Then he pounced on me.

"Finn!" I screeched as he started tickling me. "You're such a brat."

With a laugh he said, "Babe, we discussed this. Inside voice."

For a few breathy seconds, I tried to fight off his naughty hands before the lightbulb went off, and I changed the game. Reaching between his legs where he straddled me, I cupped his balls, massaging him through his jeans with the palm of my hand. His silliness stopped abruptly mid-tickle as he sucked in air.

"Underhanded, Chess. Extremely underhanded."

"You like it when I underhand you." I darted my gaze to where he was rubbing himself in my hand.

"That's it. Time to show you who's in charge around here."

He slid off the bed and tugged his hoodie off, sending it somewhere behind him. His T-shirt followed. The low light did incredible things to his firm torso, highlighting his glorious pecs and shadowing the ridges of his slightly defined abs. Unlike a lot of guys who played on the line, Finn didn't carry an ounce of fat, but he also didn't sport the washboard definition of some of the skill players.

I loved his body—something I was pretty sure he'd figured out.

In one go, he shucked his jeans, boxers, and socks to stand in front of me deliciously naked, a certain part of him standing proudly at attention. For a long minute, he let me look. When I sat all the way up with the intention of touching, he preempted me by taking my hands and pulling me up to stand in front of him.

"You are overdressed. Shall we take care of that?"

Answering his own question, he pushed my jacket off my shoulders and tossed it in the direction of his desk. Next, he gripped the hem of my sweater and tugged it up, giving me no choice but to lift my arms so he could pull it over my head. Cool air rushed over my skin, alerting me to the fact he'd divested me of my T-shirt too.

"Damn, Chess. You are so perfect."

With the pads of his forefingers, he toured the swells of my breasts above my bra. Goose bumps pebbled my skin, and he slipped his hands behind my back, flicking the clasp open. Reverently, he slid his fingers under the straps and slowly glided the scrap of satin off my body. His heated gaze on my exposed breasts threatened to light me on fire.

"So fucking perfect."

All the playfulness of the past thirty minutes evanesced in the raspy tone of his voice.

I was far from perfect, my top nowhere near in proportion to my bottom. I barely filled out the B cups of my bra, while my hips stretched every pair of jeans in my closet to their breaking point. Yet when Finn looked at me the way he was looking at me now, I believed I was perfect.

Tugging at the fly of my jeans, he said, "These have to come off. Now."

Obeying his command, I unzipped and pushed my jeans down my legs, stepping on them to step out of them.

A hint of a smile tugged at the corner of his sculpted lips. "These too." Slipping his fingers beneath the elastic of my plain white bikini panties, he pulled them down to my ankles.

His breath ghosting over my skin raised more goose bumps ahead of his hands feathering over the backs of my calves, the sensitive spots behind my knees, and the length of my hamstrings. Kisses joined the sensory party he'd started over my body, his mouth setting the tops of my thighs on fire. When he nibbled and licked the crease where my thighs met my hips, I worried about embarrassing myself with a gush of wetness between my legs.

"Finn." My voice was so breathy, I didn't think he'd heard me. Not that it mattered.

"Open for me, babe." I heard the low rumble of his voice just fine.

When I didn't move right away, he smoothed his fingertips along the insides of my thighs, turning my knees to jelly. I wobbled and grasped his powerful shoulders to remain upright, eliciting a dark laugh from him.

"So that's how it is." His eyes found mine. "I like that. I like it a lot."

In one smooth move, he stood before me, gathered me up in his arms, and gently deposited me back on the bed. Without warning, he palmed my knees, urging them apart. Then he kissed and nibbled his way along the sensitive skin of my thighs. By the time he'd reached his destination, he'd lit my body on fire. I wanted him so much, I was shaking, yet he took his time tasting me, his moans of pleasure going straight to my head.

If all the world came to an end with the movement of my hips, I still couldn't have stopped myself from writhing and bucking as he suckled and licked, kissed and played the hard nub of my clit and the depths of my pussy. Another dark laugh escaped him as he draped one heavy forearm across my hips, adding pressure to still me. I plowed my fingers into his hair, tugging at the thick strands as he enjoyed me.

The pressure building low in my belly crescendoed into an explosion of sensations the second he added his fingers to the ministrations of his mouth. Arching my back, I cried his name as waves of pleasure washed through me. He moaned against my clit, the vibrations exciting me even more, and I bucked against his restraining arm as the climax overwhelmed me.

A second later his hand was over my mouth as he chuckled against my belly. "Chess, remember? Inside voice."

"You do that to me and expect me to be quiet? Seriously?" I meant to sound stern, but the aftershocks rolling through me stole the command from my voice.

Reaching into the drawer in the nightstand, he fished out a condom, tore open the packet, and sheathed himself. His whiskey eyes glittered down at me as he said, "We'll work on it, yeah?"

For a few minutes he held himself in his hand, teasing me with the head of his cock against my sensitive flesh. Digging my nails into the tops of his thighs, I lifted my hips, silently demanding he follow up on the promise he was making.

"You're a greedy little thing, aren't you?" His smile was positively wicked. "You're also dripping wet. Do you have any idea how hot that is?" He centered himself at my entrance then set his hands on the pillow on either side of my head. "Fuck, I need this, Chess. Need you."

His mouth covered mine at the same time as he thrust inside me. He swallowed my gasp of delight as our lips and tongues mirrored our bodies' movements. My hands roamed the broad expanse of his muscled back, and I reveled in the tremors my touch sent over his skin. When he settled himself against me, flattening my breasts with his chest, I wrapped my arms and legs tight around him and held on for the ride.

Though he started out with a steady rhythm, the friction building between us overwhelmed his leisurely pace. Soon he pushed himself up, straightening his arms as his hips pistoned between my thighs. Then he changed the angle, hooking my ankles over his shoulders as he gripped the backs of my thighs and drove into me.

"Jesus, babe. Fuck. You feel so incredible." His words came out with a grunt. "Chessly. Baby. You need to come. Fuck. Please." Rubbing the pad of his thumb over my clit, he added another kind of pressure and friction that sent me over the edge.

With my hands fisting the sheets, my body bowed as my inner muscles clamped down hard on his thrusting cock. Behind my eyelids green stars danced a wild dance as the most powerful orgasm of my life ripped through me.

My eyes flew open as Finn clamped his hand over my mouth. In wonder, I watched the cords of his neck straining against his own shouts, his teeth gritted as he suddenly went rigid. A series of thrusts I didn't think he could control followed before he relaxed his hold on me.

After gently lowering my feet to the bed on either side of his thighs, he let himself rest on top of me, our labored breathing loud in the otherwise quiet room. I played my fingertips along the long muscles of his back as intense aftershocks like mini-orgasms rolled through me.

"Finn—" I swallowed over my raw throat and tried again. "I never saw you coming."

Chuckling into the side of my neck, he said, "That's because you had your eyes shut tight."

"Not what I meant."

"I know."

As the sweat began to cool on our bodies, he rolled off me and disposed of the condom in the trash beside the bed. Then he pulled me into his side so my head rested on his chest. We remained quiet as he drew lazy circles on my arm that I mirrored on his chest.

"Having you back means everything, Chess. Thank you for giving me another chance."

I wrapped my arm around him, hugging him tight. "Thank you for not giving up."

Chapter Thirty-One

Finn

"**G**OOD THING DANNY didn't come home last night. That's all I gotta say." Bax had just finished filling his to-go mug with steaming coffee and was returning the pot to the warmer when I met my roommates in the kitchen on Saturday morning. "We could hear your girl in my room with two walls and a hallway between us." He smirked as he grabbed a warm wrapped breakfast burrito from the pan Callahan pulled from the oven.

With a shake of my head, I said, "You're jealous of how well I can please my lady."

"My lady is not complaining." He shot me a look over his mug and sipped his coffee.

"You're both ridiculous. A word to the wise—keep some things to yourselves," Callahan chimed in.

"Okay, Dad." Bax snorted.

"Those women we left passed out in our beds are all friends with each other. That's all I'm sayin'." He stepped around Bax to fill his mug.

"He has a point," I said. "And it's not even on top of his head."

With his free hand, Callahan messed up my hair. "Surprise, surprise. You're not pointy-headed either." He laughed, bowing his body to avoid my fist.

"That in honor of the first scrimmage?" I asked Bax with a nod to his T-shirt, which read "That's a horrible idea. What time?"

Grinning down at his chest and back at me, he said, "Seemed appropriate."

I bumped my fist to his.

Spring scrimmages were an opportunity for the coaches to assess our skills, to figure out who of the underclassman would move up on the depth chart, and which of the starters was truly ready to lead. For the three of us, it was the start of the most important season of our lives. While none of us were taking it lightly, each of us was focused on having a good time playing the game we loved.

At the facility, the locker room had an air of game-day anticipation. Guys went through their game-day rituals, like the class clown Tarvarius Johnson doing some kind of electric slide as he listened to R&B through his earbuds. Dalton Sneed, no longer our rookie kicker, did something with touching his thumbs to his fingertips over and over in a pattern. Weirdest damn thing I'd ever seen, but I couldn't argue with nineteen of twenty field goals last season and no missed PATs. Dallas "Dally" Cousins, our center, gripped a football like he was trying to make it one with his hand.

I sat quietly in front of my locker and closed my eyes, visualizing jumping off the line of scrimmage at the exact second the opposing center hiked the ball. This season, I was determined not to penalize the team by jumping offsides in my eagerness to blow up the opposing teams' offensive plays.

Coach Ellis and the rest of the staff entered the locker room together. "All right, men. Huddle up." The guy never raised his voice, even over the din of fifty-four players moving around in pads and cleats, music playing, and other nonsense going on, yet by the third word, we were all quiet and ready to listen to him.

"Fans and media will be watching today's practice. They'll want to know if we're going to be a contender for the national title again this year." His steely ice-blue eyes roamed the circle of players. "We already know the answer to that."

The seasoned players nodded, while a couple of freshmen walk-ons let out some "Hell yeahs!" that Coach shut down with a narrowing of those intense eyes.

"What the coaching staff wants to know is who is in it for the long haul? Because making it to the title game starts today, and it doesn't stop until next January." He let that sink in for a minute. "Go out there today and play hard. Play smart. Show us you're in it for the title."

That was our cue to let loose with our victory cries. Bax and I fist-bumped each other from where we sat together on the bench. 'Han might have been my best friend, but Bax was my partner in the defensive trenches. Today it was defense versus offense, and Callahan and our other roommate Danny were fair game.

Donning our helmets, we rolled out of the locker room and jogged down the tunnel. Though we ran out onto Holland Field without all the fanfare of the band and cheerleaders and twenty thousand screaming fans, the small crowd on hand to watch the scrimmage shared their enthusiasm for Wildcats football with cheers and wolf whistles and applause loud enough to give us an adrenaline rush. I scanned the stands for Chessly, locating her with her friends Saylor, Piper, and Jamaica. Squinting my eyes against the spring sun, I noticed a fifth girl with them and recognized Danny's lady, Taryn. Guess the gang was all here, which put a warm glow dead center in my chest.

I loved showing off for the crowd, but showing off for Chess was a whole other thing. I wanted her to be proud of me.

Over the course of the sixty-minute practice, the offense ran the forty plays Coach had scripted, with the starters in for half of them. I managed not to jump offsides even once, which earned me a few attaboys from Coach Ainsworth and a nod of approval from Coach Larkin. By the time we'd finished, we were tired, sweaty, and amped up. Coach Ellis had even managed a grin or two at the success of our play.

The raucous noise of fifty-four excited players reverberated around the locker room as we showered and dressed. I was looking forward to spending the rest of the day with my girlfriend. The word had been rattling around in my head for weeks now and had settled in. We were in a committed relationship, and Chess was my girlfriend. The thought brought a smile to my face.

As I headed down the hallway to meet her in front of the facility, Coach Ellis stepped out of his office. "McCabe. A word, please."

The tone of his voice gave nothing away. But after the way I'd played in the scrimmage, I thought I might be in for some attaboys from Coach for once.

"Tell Chess I'll be out in a few," I said to Callahan, who nodded and kept walking.

"Hey, Coach. What's up?" I asked as I strolled through the door.

"Have a seat, son."

Only then did I register other people were in the office with him, a man I'd never seen before and a girl I vaguely recognized.

"We have a problem, Finn," Coach began. "My players play fair—with everyone, all the time." His steely-eyed stare said I'd broken that rule, but damned if I knew how.

"It's been brought to my attention that you've been ignoring your responsibilities to this young lady. Perhaps you'd like to explain?"

Only then did I pick up on the thunder on the strange man's

face as he directed his gaze from me to the girl. Looking back at her, my heart dropped to my knees. While I could harbor a wild hope, I was pretty sure she wasn't hiding a basketball under her shirt.

Fuck!

"Coach, I don't know what's going on here." For once I thought about my words. "But I barely know this girl. And I swear I'm not responsible for her situation." Staring directly into his eyes, I willed him to believe me: to take my side.

The man jumped up from his chair to loom over me. From the looks of him, he could have played my position at one time. "Are you calling my daughter a liar?" he yelled.

It was tough to hold my ground while I looked up into his mottled-red face, but I had to stand strong. Whatever this girl was up to, I wasn't going to take the fall for some other guy's mess.

"I'm saying I've only seen your daughter on a couple of occasions at the library last fall when she was with the other jersey"—I cleared my throat—"when she was with some other freshman and sophomore girls who like to study with the team." Wracking my brain, I worked to remember this girl's name.

"Penelope says you're her child's father, and she knows better than to lie to me." The man's angry eyes darted between his lying daughter and me.

Penelope. She was one of Tory Miller's buddies. She hung out on the edge of the crowd, and I think I'd heard her say three words once: "Good game, Finn." *Why the fuck would she pick me to pin her pregnancy on?*

"Mr. Walker, sit down." As usual, Coach didn't raise his voice.

After a beat "Walker" complied.

"In all my dealings with Mr. McCabe over the past four years, he's never lied to me either."

I let out some pent-up air.

"However, someone in this room is lying."

"I'll volunteer to take a paternity test. I'll even pay for it," I said.

Penelope's face turned ashen.

I had no idea what I was thinking when I turned to her and asked, "Out of curiosity, when did we do the deed?"

"McCabe," Coach interrupted. "Don't be crass."

"My future is on the line, here, Coach."

"Homecoming," she whispered.

Well, that made it easy. I had an entire group of witnesses to back me up. Still, I pressed her for more details—details I hoped would prove my innocence. "Where? Where did we hook up?"

She stared hard at the floor, her voice barely audible. "In the back seat of your pickup."

"I don't know what your game is here—Penelope, right?"

Her head snapped up.

"But I don't need to pay for a paternity test since I can't possibly be the father."

"Watch yourself, mister. You're calling my daughter a liar, and as we've already established, she doesn't lie to me." Walker flexed his fists between his knees.

I felt sorry for the girl, but not sorry enough to give up my life to save her from whatever she was lying to cover up.

"To be crystal clear, we hooked up in the back seat of my truck. You're sure it was my truck?" I asked.

She nodded. "It was your truck. You flirted with me during the bonfire and we went back to the parking lot where you'd parked. One thing led to another, and now here we are." She spoke as though she was on autopilot—or had memorized her story.

Coach's expression didn't change, except for a slight narrowing of his eyes, telling me he'd heard what I heard.

"It happens that my truck is parked in the lot right now. How 'bout we go out there and you can point it out."

"That's not necessary," Walker growled.

"No. I think it is," Coach said.

He stood from behind his desk—the cue for the rest of us to do the same. Being polite, I gestured for the Walkers to precede me out of Coach's office. As we neared the front of the facility, I saw my friends waiting near the doors. Their expressions of curiosity morphed to concern as they clocked the pregnant girl walking between her dad and Coach with me in the rear.

"Finn?" Chess said as I neared her.

I gave her a subtle shake of my head, and my insides twisted at the hurt I saw spring into her eyes.

Not many outfits were left in the lot, as most of the players had already left for the day, what with our "conversation" having taken a while. I recognized my roommates' rides, a couple of other players' trucks, and Piper's sweet Camaro parked a short distance from the front of the stadium. My truck waited between Callahan's pickup and Danny's Mustang.

My nerves threatened to make me throw up when Penelope headed in the direction of my truck. Then it was all I could do to hold in the smile when she walked right on by it without giving it a second look. She didn't hesitate in purposefully pointing out a sleek black Ford with a crew cab parked in the row reserved for the coaching staff.

Huh.

"That one's yours," she said, her eyes pleading with me to play along.

Sorry, sweetheart.

I fished my keys from my pocket and handed them to Coach. "You wanna try these to open that?"

Instead, Coach directed his stare at Penelope. "You want to explain yourself, young lady?"

"Excuse me?" Mr. Walker took a step in Coach's direction.

I noticed her dad liked to use his size to intimidate people, but Coach ignored him. "You're one hundred percent certain this is Finn's truck?"

"Y-yes." She faltered. Then, squaring her shoulders, she rallied. "Tell them, Finn."

"What's going on here?" Coach Larkin said as he joined the four of us. "Are you trying to sell my truck?" He shot Coach Ellis a smirk.

"No, but for argument's sake, you want to try opening it with this?" Coach Ellis held out my key fob.

Coach Larkin scrunched his forehead. "Why would I try to do that?"

"Humor me."

With a shrug, Coach Larkin took my keys and pushed the unlock button several times. Of course, nothing happened, so he handed my keys back to me.

"Now yours," Coach Ellis said.

His puzzled expression morphed into something a bit terrified when he clocked Penelope's protruding belly. But he fished his key fob from the pocket of his khakis and pushed the unlock button. The flash of the headlights accompanied the muffled clunk of the doors unlocking.

Coach Ellis turned from the truck to stare Penelope Walker in the eyes. "I don't know what is going on here, but I do know who hasn't been telling the truth. Whoever fathered your child, he wasn't one of my players."

"How dare you!" Walker bellowed. "It was dark and chaotic at the bonfire, and Penelope is used to refined cars, not redneck trucks."

"Hey—" Coach Larkin protested.

Coach Ellis cut him off. "I gave her multiple opportunities to change her mind, and she said she was one hundred percent certain this was Finn's pickup." Though he spoke calmly, steel girded his tone. "Finn was telling the truth, which is clearly why he volunteered for a paternity test and asked that she identify his vehicle."

"She has witnesses," Walker growled, his face turning the mottled shade of red again.

"So do I," I countered. "In fact, they're right over there." I pointed to my friends who were staring at the spectacle going on across the lot from them. "Callahan!" I called.

I watched as 'Han said something to the others before jogging over.

When he joined us, I asked, "Where was I and who was I with at the Homecoming bonfire?"

He pulled a face and said, "You were with us and mooning over Chessly until Jamaica and I fixed it so you had to give her a ride home." With a smirk, he added, "You're welcome."

"Not the time for jokes, O'Reilly," Coach Ellis said.

'Han straightened right up. "Sorry, Coach."

"Of course he'd back his teammate, but it changes nothing," Walker insisted.

"It changes everything. Finn is not the father of your daughter's child. She knows it, Finn knows it, and now you know it." Every player on the team knew better than to argue when Coach used his "you know it" tone.

Mr. Walker didn't play for Coach Ellis. "Buzz Miller is right. This program is run by people who don't understand how the game is played. I'll be meeting with the college president about pulling my support—then we'll see who you believe."

"Do what you have to do, but you're not ruining two young people's lives with your baseless accusations." Turning to Penelope, Coach added, "Good luck to you, young lady." In uncharacteristic Ellis fashion, he said, "You're going to need it."

He took two steps from us before he turned and nodded in our direction. "Gentlemen, a word, please."

"One sec, Coach." It was my turn to stare down Penelope

Walker. "I have a question. Why target me? We've probably only ever said two words to each other."

She sniffed, slid her eyes in the direction of her dad, and mumbled, "It was Tory's idea."

"Tory Miller put you up to this? Why?"

She shrugged.

"Why did you go along with it?" I didn't clock that I'd raised my voice until Callahan put a hand on my arm. Swallowing hard, I jacked down. "Why would you want to saddle yourself with someone you don't even know?"

"It was easier than facing my parents with the truth," she mumbled in the direction of her shoes. "They don't like my baby's father."

Out of the corner of my eye, I saw Mr. Walker's jaw flex.

The beep of Coach Larkin locking his pickup interrupted the conversation. Without another word Callahan and I fell into step behind Coach Ellis while Larkin took up the rear, leaving the Walkers alone on the pavement to deal with their own damn mess.

I sent Chess what I hoped was a reassuring smile when we passed our friends on the way back to Coach Ellis's office. I had no delusions about how this next part was going to go. Coach had stuck up for me, but his displeasure at being put in a position of having to stick up for me over a girl didn't sit well. Anyone with eyes could see it.

The door to his office had barely closed behind us when he started in. "What is it with you guys getting into entanglements with donors' daughters? The program needs those alumni dollars so you can have a state-of-the-art weight room, an indoor practice field, the big, comfy busses for road games . . . In case you missed it, those funds don't come from student fees." He stomped around his desk and sat down.

Behind us, Coach Larkin took a seat on the leather couch

pushed up against the wall. Having not been invited to sit, Callahan and I remained standing.

"All due respect, sir, I didn't start the mess that led to Buzz Miller pulling his funds." 'Han stood at ease with his hands folded in front of himself.

Mirroring my best friend, I said, "I saw that girl maybe two or three times at the library last fall when she was with Tory Miller and a bunch of other girls. I damn sure didn't knock her up."

"Language, McCabe. You will show respect."

"Yes, sir. Sorry, sir."

"That's what was going on out there?" Callahan asked. "Fuck, Finn. We warned you about hanging out with jersey chasers."

"O'Reilly." Coach's tone hauled my friend up short.

"Sorry, Coach," 'Han said.

"This is why we lecture you guys every year about paying attention and not putting yourselves into situations. Using protection. Knowing how old the women are before you engage in certain activities." Coach Ellis sighed. "You're a fourth-year junior with an impressive GPA in *biology*, McCabe. You of all people shouldn't have been the one accused."

All the talk about donors and Buzz Miller and Callahan and Bax's warnings about jersey chasers in general and Tory Miller specifically came flooding in, and I blurted, "That Penelope girl is friends with Tory Miller. When Tory was a freshman, she lived on my girlfriend's floor. All I know is some bad shit went down between them." I cleared my throat. "I didn't know either of them at the time, but on Homecoming last fall when I drove Chess back to the dorms, Tory saw us together. And she didn't like it."

Coach pinched the bridge of his nose. "It keeps coming back to the Millers."

Callahan and I exchanged a look.

"Ol' Buzz has a hard-on for football players and wants his girls to end up with guys who have a chance to play at the next level." I splayed my hands with a shrug. "Although how Penelope Walker factors into that doesn't make sense."

"At the risk of pissing you off, Coach, maybe that guy out there"—Callahan gestured in the direction of the parking lot—"shouldn't be the only one having a conversation with the college president."

Coach Ellis blew out a long-suffering sigh. "Yeah, I've figured that out, O'Reilly."

"What was the deal with my truck?" Coach Larkin asked.

Turning to him, I said, "Guess Penelope thought her story would be more believable if I drove a fancy pickup since that's where I supposedly knocked—" I cleared my throat. "Supposedly got her in a family way."

For the first time since he'd called me into his office an age ago, Coach Ellis cracked a grin. "You probably should have showed her what you actually drive, McCabe."

"Hey! There's nothing wrong with my truck," I protested. "I mean, other than it's twenty years old, isn't a crew cab, and has a stick shift, which makes doing certain activities in it dicey." I smirked.

"And the heat is temperamental and it could use some paint, and—"

I cut Callahan off with a fist to his bicep. He laughed even as he rubbed his arm. *Fucker.*

Coach Ellis shook his head. "All right, you two. Get out of here. And do not do anything stupid, at least for one day."

"Yes, Coach," my best friend and I said in unison.

Neither of us wasted a second in scrambling out of Coach's office. As we headed down the hall on our way back outside, Callahan asked, "Did you learn your lesson, Finnegan?"

"I haven't hung out with a single jersey chaser since all that shit went down with you and Tory last semester. You know that," I grumbled.

'Han relented. "Yeah, I guess you're right. But before we step outside, I need to warn you that your girl was not at all pleased with what she saw going down in that parking lot."

"Fuck," came out on a long exhale. Just once I could use a break from patching things up with Chessly.

Chapter Thirty-Two

Chessly

MAYBE THERE WAS something to Orch OR theory. Maybe Finn and I were connected on another universal plane.

Or maybe after being so physically and emotionally connected to him less than twenty-four hours ago, I was experiencing a kind of intuition.

Whatever it was, when Finn's roommates exited the stadium without him, a terrible sense of doom descended over me. If someone had asked me to explain it, I doubt I could have. I only knew Finn was facing serious trouble, something life-altering, and he was terrified. More than anything, I wanted to march into the stadium to stand right beside him as he confronted whatever danger was threatening him.

Then he'd walked out behind a massive man in a fancy gray suit whose thunderous expression could put the fear of God into the Devil. Beside him walked Penelope Walker. The reason I hadn't seen her around Hanover much protruded from the front of her long wool coat, which she couldn't button at the moment. Next came the head coach with Finn in the rear. The pleading expression on his face had dropped a ten-ton ball into my stomach. Whatever was going on with Penelope involved Finn?

Silently, Piper and Jamaica flanked me, one rubbing her hand across the tops of my shoulders, the other wrapping her arm around my waist and hugging me close. After Finn called out to Callahan to join them, Bax narrowed his eyes, his thoughts on the tableau in front of us a total mystery.

When a second coach joined them, things heated up with Finn shouting, forcing Callahan to lay a restraining hand on him. Then everything stopped. The coaches flanked Finn and Callahan, and the four of them disappeared back into the stadium. After a minute of the man—apparently her dad—flexing his hands while Penelope stared back at him with a jutted chin, he wrapped his hand around her upper arm and led her to a fancy Porsche SUV. As he pulled out of his parking space, he laid a patch of rubber, and I felt a little sorry for the girl whose father was super angry with her.

"Do you know who that girl is?" Piper asked Bax.

"Seen her around a few times last fall with Tory Miller and the band of jailbait she hangs out with," he answered, and my heart threatened to make a permanent move to my throat.

"Of course whatever is going on has something to do with that Miller witch," Jamaica said, her tone pure acid.

"Not helping, J," I managed to say over the lump in my throat.

"Finn's an idiot." Bax shot me a look. "Sorry, Chessly. I'm not dissing you in saying that. But he's always been too nice to people who don't always deserve it. Maybe he gave that girl a ride home or something last fall and now she's 'repaying' him," he explained with air quotes. "Wouldn't be the first time a jersey chaser has tried to trap a football player."

I couldn't tell from his tone who he was more disgusted with: Penelope or Finn. But something about how Bax didn't believe Finn had anything to do with her round belly let me breathe.

By the time Finn and Callahan finally walked out of the stadium again, more than hour had passed since the scrimmage ended. All my happiness at seeing Finn's return to the starting lineup had evanesced in the intervening sixty minutes as I'd prayed that what I'd seen was not what I thought I'd seen.

"Hey, Chess." Finn's voice was low, tentative. "Sorry for making you wait out here so long." He stepped in front of me but kept his hands to himself. Then he said the worst four words in the English language. "We need to talk."

With a nod, I fell into step beside him as we headed over to his ancient truck. As usual, he held my door open for me before jogging around the front to hop into the driver's side. For a long wordless minute, he stared out the windshield. As the silence closed in, weighing me down and making it hard to breathe, he whispered, "I'm not the father of that girl's baby."

"But she accused you?" I whispered back.

He blew out a breath. "Yeah."

"Could you be? The father, I mean."

With way his shoulders slumped, I hated to ask, but I had to know.

Tipping his head back against the back window, Finn stared up at the ceiling, and I worried he wasn't planning to answer my question. Then he turned his head to the side, his eyes on mine. "I barely knew her name before she made the accusation. I saw her around a few times with Tory Miller last fall. At the library. She seemed too quiet to be hanging out with the rest of the jersey chasers." He pulled in another long breath as though the entire situation had made breathing painful.

I could relate.

"Bax and 'Han have warned me for the past two years to stay away from those girls."

"I know. You told me."

"After they interrupted our first time alone together during finals week, I've stayed hell and gone away from jersey chasers. But I did hook up with a couple of them last fall."

Before we met, which meant it was none of my business, but I couldn't help the stab of betrayal I felt.

He sat up and turned in his seat, facing me. "I never went far enough with any of those girls to knock one up. While I'll admit I liked their attention, I also had no doubt my friends were looking out for me when they warned me to stay away. I played somewhere in the middle." Running a hand through his hair, he added, "Which was obviously the wrong move. I'm sorry, Chess."

Somewhere along the way, I'd crossed my arms over my chest, holding myself together. But Finn's pain and remorse worked their way into me. Consciously letting my hands drop into my lap, I said, "You don't need to apologize to me."

"Yeah, I do. I can't imagine what was going through your head when you saw us all come out to the parking lot, that girl and her dad and Coach." He clapped his hand over the back of his neck. "Honestly, I wouldn't have blamed you if you'd left the second you saw us." Dropping his hand to his knee, he added, "You should never have to wonder if the guy you're dating is honest and decent and not going around knocking other girls up."

"Finn." I covered his hand with mine. "You are honest and decent. Maybe that's why she chose to accuse you."

Squeezing my hand, his eyes narrowed. "No. She chose me because Tory Miller put her up to it."

I tugged my hand from his and crossed my arms over my chest as I stared unseeingly out the windshield. "What is it with that bitch? First she tried to have me fired from my RA job and kicked out of school last year. Then she went after Jamaica and Callahan. Now she's siccing her friends on you?"

"She tried to have you fired—and kicked out of school? Why?" The shock in his voice drew my gaze to his.

"Because I wouldn't look the other way when she broke every single dorm rule in one rowdy party. I called the dorm supervisor who called the campus police. Tory's dad's money kept her out of jail for drug possession and underage drinking, but she had to move out of the dorm." Mirroring Finn's earlier posture, I tipped my head back against the window and looked up at the ceiling. "Tory insisted I had her kicked out of the dorms, so she bribed some girls to say they saw me participating in the party, taking shrooms and breaking Tory's bed by dancing on it. During the investigation, I was barred from my RA duties, and there was some discussion about me having to move out of the dorms too.

"Tory had a safety net in her father's money and her mom's sorority legacy at Delta Chi, so when she moved out of Hanover, she had somewhere to go. If I'd been forced out of the dorm, I would have had to drop out of school."

"Fuck, Chess."

"Anyway, another girl Tory had delighted in torturing all year somehow found out about the bribes and tipped off the dorm supervisor to have the girls' bank accounts checked. Again, Tory's dad smoothed things over with a generous gift to College Services for dorm improvements, and it all went away."

His hand on my arm drew my eyes to his face. "I'm sorry, babe. I had no idea she and her friends could be so vicious."

Twining my fingers with his, I said, "That's because you're the guy who makes a life plan for easing little kids' suffering after seeing a TV commercial."

His brows came together in confusion.

"On the field you're a take-no-prisoners badass. But in real life, your soft heart only lets you see the best in people—even people who have no redeeming qualities—like Tory Miller."

"Um—"

I squeezed his hand. "Don't ever stop seeing the good in others. I love you exactly the way you are."

The silence in the cab thumped at my chest as it dawned on me what I'd revealed. It was too soon. We were barely a couple. I must be out of my mind.

Then memories of those miserable weeks without him crowded my brain, and I couldn't deny the truth of what I'd said.

Finn slid closer on the bench seat, his hand coming up to palm the side of my face. "You love me?"

Swallowing hard, I nodded. "It's okay if you don't feel the same—"

His lips on mine cut me off. The kiss started off as soft, sweet, a gentle acknowledgment of my words. Then his other hand, firm on my hip, pulled me closer to him as he explored the seam of my mouth with his tongue. With a tiny sigh of happiness, I wrapped my arms around his neck and opened for him, kissing him back with all the love I'd finally allowed myself to show him.

Soon, moans and whimpers filled the silence. The way the man kissed sizzled my blood. The molten heat in my core threatened to become a volcano of desire as his left hand roamed along my thigh and hip while his right hand held the back of my head as he devoured me with his lips and tongue. When I moved closer, something hard pushed against my ribs followed by a loud *thunk*.

"Finn?"

"Mmm?" He pressed his lips to mine.

"I think we're moving."

With a curse, he sat up so fast he bumped his head on the window. Scrambling back into the driver's seat, he slammed his feet on the clutch and the brake and jammed the truck back into gear from where we'd pushed it into neutral with our fooling around. Just in time too, or we would have made someone's compact car, parked directly in front of the truck, into a hood ornament.

Though I tried, I couldn't stop the giggles that erupted at watching this big, strong man desperately trying to keep his truck from rolling into another car.

"Put on your seat belt, Chess. And text our friends we won't be able to make it to Stromboli's with them after all."

"We won't?"

"No. We're finishing this conversation. In my bedroom."

Chapter Thirty-Three

Finn

BACK AT THE house, I locked the door behind us as I ushered Chessly into my room. This conversation required privacy.

"Now. Say it again."

From the way she blinked up at me, I could tell she was stalling, maybe trying to pretend she didn't know what I meant.

I tipped my hand to tuck a strand of her hair behind her ear, letting my fingertip linger on her soft skin in the way that triggered her. "Say it again, Chess."

"I love you, Finn. I don't know how or when it happened, but seeing you walk out of the stadium with that girl who could have ruined your life, I figured out I didn't want to lose you." She covered my hand with hers, tugging my palm to her lips where she nuzzled a kiss in the center that shot straight to my dick. "Actually, I figured it out that day in the Union. It's why I reacted the way I did."

Slipping my arms around her, I hauled her up flush to my body. "Want to know when I started to fall in love with you?"

The smile that stretched across her face warmed every corner of my heart.

"At the bonfire."

Her eyes rounded in shock.

"You were the hottest girl there, and you kept eye-fucking me. Even after our friends called you out for it—and you denied it—you kept doing it. If not for that shitty interruption from she-who-will-not-be-named, we would have started this relationship last fall." I stole a little kiss and continued. "Our time apart was the worst time of my life. I don't ever want to go through that again."

I felt her body tremble and knew without her words she didn't want to experience that again either.

"I love you, Chessly Clarke. I love you so much."

"I love you, Finn McCabe." Her grin turned wicked. "This is the part where we should show each other how much."

Laughing, I picked her up and tossed her onto the bed where I pounced on her, flattening her to the mattress as I kissed us both stupid. When I let us up for air, I said, "Great idea. Glad we thought of it."

A few minutes later, our clothes were scattered over the floor, and Chess was beneath me, gloriously naked as she scored her nails over my chest. Her eyes caught on my shoulder, and she ran a tentative touch over my skin. "Does it hurt?"

I glanced down at the bruise starting where Callahan had managed to get a step on me and blow past me on one play. No doubt he'd be rubbing that in at film tomorrow.

"It will feel all kinds of better if you kiss it." I aimed for sincere, maybe a bit innocent.

The teasing in her eyes said I hadn't pulled it off. Still, she leaned up and brushed a soft kiss over my owie.

Pointing at a spot on my chest, I said, "I think I have a bruise starting here too."

A smirk tugged at the corner of her mouth before she blessed me with another soft kiss.

"This too." I pointed at the side of my ribs.

She slid down and nibbled over my skin, sending blood rushing directly to my already rock-hard dick. Somehow, she leveraged herself so that she could put her weight behind pushing me over onto my back, and the next thing I knew, she was hovering over my thighs as she gave them careful inspection for bruises.

"Is this what I can expect during the regular season?" she asked as she planted more soft kisses along my quads while her hair tickled my dick, making me groan.

"The bruising?" I managed through clenched teeth. "Yeah, it's an endless thing. I think the last season's marks faded by the end of January."

"You're saying you're going to need weekly TLC?" Her soft lips left a trail of fire over my skin. My dick ached with wanting those lips kissing it. Instead, she kissed her way down to my knees.

"Daily." The word came out raspy, and I didn't give a shit how the sound exposed the knots she'd tied me in.

"Mm-hmm."

At last she reversed course, her fingers leading the way as her mouth inched closer to the place I most wanted it. When she touched her pillowy lips to my balls, I surged up off the sheets. Splaying her fingers over my belly, she pushed me back down while she tickled my shaft with the tip of her tongue. I plowed my fingers into her hair and worked my ass off to talk myself down from shoving my cock into her mouth.

She hummed along my length, the vibration driving me wild. But as bad as I needed her to keep going, I knew I had to say the thing I didn't want to say. "Chess. Babe, you don't have to—"

Wrapping her mouth around the head of my dick, she shut me right the fuck up. She swallowed me whole on one smooth downstroke then licked and sucked her way back up. Popping off me, she raised her eyes to mine. "I thought we established we were going to show each other how we feel."

"Uh-huh," was all I could manage.

"Then do not tell me I don't have to show you how much I love you."

Without giving me a chance to respond, she went to town on my cock, licking and sucking, kissing and palming me until I gave up.

"You are so hot and hard. Mmm. And delicious," she purred. "I've wanted to do this for so long."

"You like to talk during sex, don't you?"

"Only when the guy really turns me on."

My eyes rolled back in my head as a stupid smile spread over my face. Fisting my hands in the sheets, I held on while Chessly did exactly as she damn well pleased and gave me the most intense pleasure of my life. Afterward, she kissed her way up my belly, across my chest, and up the column of my neck before she settled herself on top of me, cuddling me as though I were her favorite pillow.

"That was a such a good time."

I played my fingertips along the length of her spine as we lay quiet for a few minutes. Once I'd caught my breath, I said, "For the record, we're in trouble if my package is ever bruised in practice or a game. But when you kissed my cock, I forgot all about the battering my body took in the scrimmage."

A chuckle puffed out of her. "Good to know."

"Something else can make me forget bruises."

"Yeah?"

Without giving her any warning, I flipped her onto her back. "Kissing you all over is my favorite distraction."

Starting with the hollow of her throat, I kissed my way over her collarbones, along the swells of her breasts to the delectable tight peaks of her nipples where I lingered until she was writhing and panting beneath me.

"Babe, I adore these beauties. Especially how they poke right up when I put my mouth on them."

Then I decided to give her a taste of her own medicine, pecking light kisses along her ribs, down to her hips, and over the tops of her pretty thighs. I tickled the backs of her knees with my fingertips, and she rewarded me by opening herself to me. In the daylight streaming through the window at the foot of the bed, I looked my fill at her pink pussy, my mouth watering at the thought of eating her. In a minute. After the torture she'd put me through, she needed a bit of turnabout.

"Like what you see?" She might have been trying for flirty, but her words came out breathy and needy.

I loved it.

Nibbling my way along the sensitive skin of her inner thighs, I delighted in the crescendoing moans and whimpers coming from her throat. When she lifted her hips off the bed, offering herself to me, I grinned against her skin and kept playing.

At last she growled, "Finn," her tone a warning, and I relented. Sealing my lips over her hard clit, I went to work licking and sucking, tickling and teasing until her head rolled from side to side on the pillow, and I had to hold her bucking hips down with my forearm. When she plowed her hands into my hair with a scream, her tight sheath convulsing around the two fingers I'd slid inside her, it was all I could do to keep from shouting my triumph to the world. Making Chessly Clarke come was number one on my list of favorite things to do.

As she came down from her climax, I climbed up her body, reached into the drawer of the nightstand, and extracted a condom. Before she'd caught her breath, I was suited up and positioning myself at her center. "Catch your breath quick, babe. The fourth quarter is about to start." Leaning in close, I whispered, "I'm going for the tie."

I heard the smile in her voice. "So we both win."

"Exactly."

In one smooth thrust, I sheathed myself all the way to my balls. Gripping my shoulders, she pulled me down for a long, wet kiss, giving me no other option but to start moving. Initially, her hips kept time with my thrusts, but after the first two rounds, we were both too keyed up for slow, easy lovemaking. In seconds, I'd pushed up on my knees, my hands wrapped around her hips as I pounded into her. Scoring her nails over my thighs, she urged me on.

"More, Finn. More. Please. Harder," she pleaded. Then a long "Yeesss!" ripped from her throat on a scream as her walls clamped down on me.

My own orgasm sizzled down my spine like lightning, my body going rigid with a release that went on and on and on. A couple of involuntary thrusts followed, and Chess's body went nuts around mine, pulsing and squeezing, and driving me straight out of my head.

It took more than minute for the two of us to come down from the most epic sex in the world. I'd thought the first time we were together was the best I'd ever had, but every time with her was better than the last. At the rate we were going, I was headed toward a massive explosion. I grinned against her skin. If that was a biological possibility, I'd die a happy man.

After I rolled off her to dispose of the condom, I snuggled her close, pillowing her head on my chest. "I like this game," I said as I kissed her hair.

"What game?" she asked, her voice sounding faraway, like she was on the edge of dropping off to sleep.

"The showing each other how much we love each other game."

She pressed a kiss to my pec. "Me too. I could keep playing it forever."

"That's a great idea."

Epilogue

Chessly

FOLLOWING THE SECOND scrimmage of spring football, Finn cemented his spot in the starting lineup. His enthusiasm for his senior year was more contagious than a virus, and I couldn't wait for fall to sit in the stands and cheer my lungs out for him. On the Friday before finals, he found me in Hillman and dragged me upstairs to an out-of-the-way study carrell on the third floor.

"Aren't you supposed to be in class?" I asked.

He answered by pulling me down onto his lap. "Had some news you needed to hear."

My brows came together. "It couldn't wait till tonight?"

His eyes sparkled. "I wanted to be the first to tell you." He tucked a wayward strand of hair behind my ear. The pad of his thumb ghosting over the shell of it drew a shiver, and he grinned. "I just came from Coach's office. Besides the fact I'll be a team captain in the fall—"

I squealed in delight. "That's awesome!

You deserve that so much." I planted a congratulatory kiss on his mouth that drew a groan from him.

"Mmm, hold that thought." He stared at my lips in a way that made me question who he was talking to—me or himself. "That's not the biggest news."

"What could be bigger news than that?"

"Coach met with the college president. Tory Miller has caused enough trouble at Mountain State. She's going to be strongly encouraged to transfer."

His wickedly delighted smirk threw me. I had no idea Finn had a vindictive streak.

"But what about her dad's money? Doesn't the team need it?"

He shrugged. "Someone else stepped in to take up the slack. But that doesn't matter." Tugging me closer, he said, "After this semester, none of us will have to look over our shoulder for whatever trouble that woman is in the mood to cause."

"Yeah?"

"Yeah."

"I can't think of anyone who will miss her, which is sad."

He pulled a face.

"But she brought that on herself." Smiling, I said, "I can't wait to watch Jamaica's happy dance when I tell her."

Finn chuckled. "You probably already missed it."

I hiked a brow.

"Callahan was with me when Coach gave us the good news."

I slumped against his chest then I rallied. "Maybe we'll do a happy dance together."

"Make sure I'm around to watch." He laughed. Settling deeper into the chair, he tightened his arms around me. "There's something else." He cleared his throat. For a beat he stared at my lips before finding my eyes again. "Your job requires you to be in the dorms, but your bed isn't going to hold up to the two of us much longer." A naughty gleam came into his eyes. "Plus, when

I have away games, I'll want to have sleepovers in my bed during the week, which doesn't work well for you." Blowing out a breath, he cut to the chase. "I want you to move in with me."

I opened my mouth, but before I could get a word out, he added more.

"I know it's soon, but I'm all in with you, Chess."

"You asked me to hold a thought, and I've been holding it for way too long." Wrapping my arms around his neck, I kissed him with all the love I had in my heart.

When at last we came up for air, I answered his unspoken question.

"Yes."

Thank you for reading *Offsides*. Watch for Danny's story in *Delay of Game*, coming in the fall of 2024. Turn the page for a first look at the unedited version.

Chapter One

Taryn

DANNY CHAMBERS WAS back in town.

The loud rumble of his vintage Mustang set my heart racing when it turned onto the street in front of my parents' house. Glancing down at the worn cut-offs and ratty Balefire T-shirt I'd thrown on before I came out on the front porch to read, I groaned. It had been seven months since we'd seen each other, longer since we'd spent any real time together, and this outfit would be his first impression of me after all that time? *Gah!*

Couldn't be helped.

As he pulled up to the house and cut the motor, I shook my head. What did it matter what I had on? He'd pay about as much attention to my clothes as he would to a new table cloth. I could be wearing a lace string bikini, and Danny wouldn't notice.

Five seconds after we'd met after he'd started his senior year at Central Valley High, he'd friend-zoned me and kept me in the friend zone for the past five years. I gritted my teeth at the ridiculous way my heart somersaulted in my chest when he stepped from his car and pushed his aviator sunglasses on top of his head.

"Hey, T! You're home!" The smile that broke over his face lit me up like sunshine.

Pathetic.

Even more pathetic? I'd made a visit home to see my parents for the weekend because Danny had mentioned in one of his recent emails that he'd be discharged at the end of June. I could have waited to come home until the Fourth of July, but that would have meant he would have been back for nearly ten days before I saw him. I couldn't wait that long.

God, I was beyond pitiful.

"Yeah. I needed a break from slinging lattes." Sliding a bookmark into the romance novel I'd barely started, I set it on the patio table beside a glass of iced tea and stood as he bounded up the stairs to the front porch.

"It's so good to see you, T." Wrapping me in a brotherly hug, he picked me up and swung me in a full circle before setting me down. With a laugh, I swatted at him even as I did my damnedest to sneak a noseful of his delicious scent. He smelled of the berry citrus body wash he always used, sunshine, and clean sweat. I wanted to bury my nose in his neck and stay there for a week.

Something flashed in his eyes, and for a weird second, I had the idea he didn't want to let me go either. Then he dropped his arms and stuffed his hands into the front pockets of his jeans, and I dismissed that absurd idea.

"You're home for good now, huh?" I slid my hands into the back pockets of my shorts and rocked back on my bare heels. "No more jetting off around the world to save it?"

He snorted. "You're hilarious, Taryn. But yeah, I passed my ETS physical with flying colors."

I shot him a look from beneath my brows. "Of course you did."

Grinning, he said, "My CO signed my honorable discharge papers, and at twenty-four hundred hours day before yesterday, I pointed that baby north"—he gestured with his thumb at his car—"and headed home."

Furrowing my brow, I asked, "So you've been home for a day and you're just now hitting my mom up for cookies?"

His tone took on a serious note. "Is that what you think? The only reason I come around here is for your mom's to-die-for chocolate chip cookies?"

"Yep. That and her dinners." I shot him a smug grin. "Since I'm only home for today, she's cooking *my* favorite meal tonight. You'll have to wait for yours."

His face fell. "You're leaving tomorrow?" Then he rallied. "Guess that means I can talk Mrs. H. into cooking pork chops tomorrow night."

As though he'd conjured her with her name, Mom stepped onto the porch with a glass of iced tea in her hand. "I thought I heard voices out here." She set the drink beside mine on the table. Beaming at Danny, she opened her arms. "Welcome home! It's permanent this time, isn't it?"

Stepping into her embrace, he laughed and said, "Yes and no."

Mom held him at arm's length. "Explain."

He slid a grin in my direction. "I'm not going back to the Air Force, but I am leaving town."

At his pronouncement, my stomach bottomed out. He'd only been back for a minute and already he had a foot out the door.

"I'm walking onto the Wildcats football team. Fall camp starts the Monday after the Fourth, so I'm headed to Mountain State then." He slid me a sly side-eye, and at his news it took everything in me not to choke or do a happy dance.

Clapping her hands, Mom turned her thousand-watt smile

on me. "That's wonderful. I had no idea. Did you know about this Sweet Pea?"

Though I tried to suppress it, I truly did, the eyeroll accompanying her use of my little-kid nickname couldn't help itself. Tilting my head at Danny, I answered, "No. First I've heard it. When did you decide on Mountain State?"

Gesturing to the deck chairs, he waited until Mom and I sat before joining us. "From everything you've said over the past three years, it's obvious you really like the school, *Sweet Pea*." He emphasized the hated nickname with a positively diabolical grin.

I bared my teeth at him and shot Mom a glare. She shrugged but I caught the slight uptick at the corner of her mouth.

Ignoring my attitude, he said, "I checked into their engineering program and discovered it's top ten nationally. From what I've seen from watching YouTube videos, the football team could use an ace receiver." Waggling his brows, he smirked. "All things considered, Mountain State is a good fit for me."

A swarm of bees buzzed in my belly, and I gulped down some iced tea to cool them off. "Wow. That's—wow." Sipping again from my glass, I gathered my thoughts. "Do you have to live in the dorms like regular freshmen? Might be kind of weird to be four years older than most of the guys on your floor."

"When I talked to the coach, he said most players except for freshmen live off-campus. Since I'm non-traditional, he thought I'd probably find some guys on the team who might need an extra roommate." He tipped back some tea. "After living in barracks off and on for the past four years, I could do with a break from that kind of communal living."

"You're playing football. And you already reached out to the coach. Wow. You move fast." Struggling to wrap my head around all of his news, especially the part where he was enrolling in the same college I attended, I latched onto to the easy questions.

A cloud passed over his features. "If the Captain had left the service sooner, settled in one place sooner, I might have had a chance at a football scholarship." He drank more tea and set the glass back on the table. "As it was, I couldn't accumulate stats or a rocking GPA with how much we moved when I was in high school." Running his hands down the tops of his jeans, his tell when he was embarrassed or nervous, he said, "I went into the Air Force so Uncle Sam could put me through college. You know that T."

I nodded.

"But I never gave up wanting to play football."

The quiet conviction of his words pulled memories to the surface, memories of Danny tearing it up on the Central Valley High field every Friday night, the announcer booming his name through the PA system. Other memories followed, memories of me on the sidelines in my cheerleader uniform cheering my heart out for a guy who would only ever see me as a friend.

"Well, I think that's just wonderful, Danny. Taryn can show you the ropes for getting along on campus."

For my own sanity, I had to put a stop to Mom gushing about Danny and me hanging out at Mountain State. "Danny will be on campus with the team for weeks before classes start. No doubt his teammates will have him all lined out by the first day of class."

"Oh, but the two of you will still be able to hang out, I suppose." Her eyes twinkled, and I wanted to shout at her for the bazillionth time that the two of us were *friends*. She'd been reading more into our relationship from the first time I brought Danny home to study together when I was a junior in high school.

Admittedly, I'd been hoping for more too, but he'd made it clear as glass he didn't see me as datable. We were buddies. End of story.

Yet Mom loved to feed him and fuss over him, especially after she found out his parents divorced when he was small, and he'd spent his life as a vagabond with his dad, moving every year or two following Captain Chambers' military assignments. Mom always said she was quite happy to parent my sisters and me, but the big deal she made about Danny implied she maybe had wished for a son in there somewhere with her three daughters.

"We're having chicken enchiladas for dinner. I made plenty, so I hope you planned on staying to eat."

"I'd never say no to an invitation to sit at your table. I've been dreaming about your food for months, Mrs. H." Danny flashed his million-watt grin, and exactly like every other female who ever came into contact with that smile, my mother swooned a little.

I couldn't blame her. The man could coax a woman into absolutely anything when he turned that smile loose.

My mother grinned back at him. "Well then, you should probably make plans to come over for dinner tomorrow night too. I believe pork chops are on the menu." With a wink, she stood and headed for the door. "I'll leave you two to catch up. Your dad should be back from his afternoon golf outing anytime now, Taryn. Dinner will be ready in twenty minutes."

"Pretty good timing there, Ace," I said with a smirk.

"As usual, the Captain's cupboards are pretty bare." Another cloud rolled over his features before he finished off his tea. "I've only been back in town for a few hours, long enough to drop my shit off at the house, take a little nap, and run my car through the car wash. While I was washing my car, I saw your sister who said you were home for the weekend." He waggled his brows. "I'm definitely up for dinner with your family but I'd also hoped to see you before you headed back to campus."

Author's Note

I love physics, but my abysmal math skills precluded my pursuit of studying it. So when Chessly showed up in my head as a physics major, I had to do some research. That's where I stumbled onto orchestrated objective reduction theory (Orch OR), which sent me down a fun rabbit hole.

In a nutshell: two scientists, Dr. Stuart Hameroff, an anesthesiologist, and Sir Roger Penrose developed the Penrose-Hameroff Orch OR theory of consciousness. Their theory suggests that consciousness "arises from the quantum vibrations 'orchestrated' in microtubules inside brain neurons, orchestrated vibrations which are proposed to interfere, 'collapse' and resonate across scale, control neuronal firings, and generate consciousness." (Stuart Hameroff, MD. *hameroff.arizona.edu*) In other words, deep in the neurotransmitters of our brains, we have the capacity to be conscious of everything everywhere all at once. How cool is that?

Of course, science has a long way to go figure out how it all works and if we can harness consciousness, but it does explain how sometimes we "know" things we think we couldn't possibly know, or we make connections with other people the way Chessly and Finn seem to be able to read each other.

If you want to learn more about Orch OR theory, read "The Emperor's New Mind" by Roger Penrose (1989), *Ultimate Computing* by Stuart Hameroff (1987), or watch the documentary *What the Bleep do We Know?*

Acknowledgments

When I first started writing books, I figured out how much joy writing them gave me. I told CruiserMan that even if no one else read them, I'd keep writing. Fortunately, people do read and enjoy them, and for that I am forever grateful. Thank you.

I'm indebted to my critique group for your comments and encouragement. LindaRae Sande, Sara Vinduska, JR Cobourn, and KJ Gillenwater, I'm so happy you enjoyed this book. It's better for your insights.

To my editor—at some point I'm going to figure out the difference between last and past, I promise. Until then, thanks for your patience, Bryony Leah. Thank you for taking me on and helping me to make this book the best it can be.

Coleene Torgerson and Erin Allen, thanks so much for letting me run things by you and for giving me your honest feedback.

Maria at Steamy Designs, your covers always rock.

Levi Meyer, thanks for making my website user-friendly and always up to date. Your tech skills save me.

Most importantly, thank you Reader for picking up this book and giving it a read. I hope you loved reading Finn and Chessly's story as much as I loved writing it. I appreciate your time, and if you have a few more minutes, I'd love it if you left a review wherever you like to rate books.

If you're interested in what else is going on in my world, subscribe to my newsletter at *https://www.tamderudderjackson.com*. Let's stay connected.

About the Author

Like the tagline of her first novel, Tam DeRudder Jackson's personal motto is "love is worth the risk." Readers and reviewers have praised her stories for their swoon-worthy characters, movie-quality world building, and strong writing. Though she's a voracious reader of all genres of romance, her favorite genres to write are paranormal and contemporary. When she's not writing or reading, she's traveling or skiing or dancing at a rock concert. Follow her on Instagram *https://instagram.com/tamstales32*.

www.ingramcontent.com/pod-product-compliance
Lightning Source LLC
LaVergne TN
LVHW091621070526
838199LV00044B/884